WHAT HAPPENS IN LONDON

KRISTINA ADAMS

Copyright © 2017 Kristina Adams

All rights reserved.

This book or any part of it must not be reproduced or used in anyway without written permission of the publisher, except for brief quotations used in a book review.

First published in 2017.

ISBN: 1537717855
ISBN-13: 978-1537717852

Cover design by Kristina Adams.

Book 2.

To those who inspire me to always keep going
no matter what obstacles life puts in the way.

FEBRUARY

One

'What the fuck is this?' snarled Patrick, slamming a glossy mag onto the kitchen island.

'Didn't peg you for a reader of gossip mags,' said Fayth. She turned off the tap and began to wash up. The pub was busy and they were running short on crockery; she didn't have time for Patrick's theatrics.

'It's my sister's,' he said, a little too quickly.

Of course it was. His ex-wife being in it had nothing to do with it. She'd been waiting for him to confront her about it since she and Hollie had returned from New York three weeks earlier. Several punters had already popped in to show Fayth her face all over the front cover *and* in a double-page spread. Holding hands and ice skating with film star Liam York. Walking around Central Park with film star Liam York. Being film star Liam York's 'new girlfriend'.

The Cock and Bull had received a sudden surge in popularity thanks to Fayth's new rank as a Z-lister. She hid in the kitchen as much as she could. Most punters respected the rule that only staff were allowed in the kitchen. Her ex-husband did not.

'Aren't you even going to look at it?' he asked as she continued to wash up.

Whatever she did, she wouldn't be able to get rid of him, so she reluctantly dried her hands, picked up the magazine, and flicked to the front cover. Liam's floppy hair and espresso-coloured eyes stared back at her from one half of a broken heart. Trinity was on the other side, Fayth Photoshopped between them. They'd given her demon eyes, just because. *LIAM YORK'S SHOCKING TWO-TIMING!* read the headline. Ugh. How much longer would they insist she was responsible for Liam and Trinity's breakup?

She skimmed the rest of the cover. Exclusive details of Trinity's 'heartbreak' from an 'insider' (that they'd made up – you needed to have a heart to be heartbroken), an interview with Camilla Persia, and something to do with the boyband HATT. And a date. 'It's two weeks out of date.'

'That's not the point!' he snapped, snatching the magazine from her and flicking back to the double-page spread. 'Look!' He pointed to a shot of her and Liam holding hands.

Fayth yawned. She still hadn't caught up on the sleep she'd missed out on in New York. Her body ached from all the extra hours she'd had to do thanks to the pub's newfound popularity. She rubbed her forehead. He was giving her a migraine. 'I was teaching him how to skate. I held your hand when I taught you how to skate, too.'

'Why should I believe you?'

Fayth clutched the bridge of her nose. 'I don't care if you do or not, but I never lied to you when we were together, and I have no reason to now.'

She grabbed some carrots from the fridge and began to peel and chop them. He wasn't going to take the hint, so she may as well get on with things. There was nobody else to pick up the slack if she fell behind – her dad was on the bar, her younger sister Brooke was at college, and it was Ross's day off. Conversations with Patrick only ever ended up going around in circles anyway.

'I get it. You wanted to get even after what happened in Magaluf. Well, you did.'

Fayth snorted. Getting even after he'd cheated on her had never occurred to her. She just wanted to get divorced. He still hadn't grasped that.

The knife slammed on to the chopping board as she hacked at a stubborn carrot.

Patrick tried to shove his face into her line of vision. She continued to attack the carrot. He refused to go away.

She looked up, her face expressionless.

'Does our relationship mean nothing to you?'

She sighed. 'We don't have a relationship any more.' She resumed chopping the carrots.

'You don't mean that. You're not supposed to make rash decisions after losing family members. You lost two. That means you shouldn't make rash decisions for twice as long.'

Fayth ground her teeth. Would he *ever* take the hint? 'That's not how it works.' Chop. 'And it wasn't a rash decision.' Chop. 'I'd wanted to do it for months.' Chop chop. 'Losing Mum and Mhairi made me realise life's too short to waste it doing things you don't want to do.' Chop chop chop.

He fell silent for a few glorious moments. Then he said, 'What happened to you?'

She stopped chopping the carrots and looked up at him. He looked like a sad, needy child who'd finally realised that his mum didn't want him any more. Guilt tugged at her heart. She'd once loved him. She'd once envisioned a future with him, happily married with kids and dogs and a picket fence. And then it'd all been torn away from her when her mum and sister were killed in a car accident, then Patrick had cheated on her less than a month later. What she wanted from life had changed. Who she wanted to be in life had changed.

She wiped her hands on her apron. 'I grew up.'

'No, it's not that. You seem…different. What happened to the woman I married?'

'She wasn't a woman: she was a naive little girl that thought she could get a fairytale from the first guy that came along. She was wrong. Relationships are about so much more than that.'

'You've changed.'

'Yeah,' she agreed, 'I have. And I hope that one day you realise it's for the better.'

He gave her one last look of longing then left, leaving his glossy magazine behind.

She waited until she heard his dirt bike spit and sputter past the window, then picked up the magazine and studied it further. They'd picked the most unflattering photographs they could find. There wasn't a single photo taken at a good angle. The content of the article was fairly tame compared to what had been said about her online though. They probably couldn't get away with such slander when they had advertisers to please. She'd almost got to the point where she found all the trolling funny instead of hurtful. Almost.

She took a photo of the magazine and sent it to Liam with the caption, *Look what the ex dropped off.* It took a few attempts to send – the phone signal was having another of its off days – but when it finally did, it wasn't long until she had a reply: *Tell him to get a better hobby.* She laughed. When she and Hollie had left New York, she'd expected that to be the end of their Hollywood adventure. She was under no illusion that Hollywood was a welcoming place, or that most of its inhabitants were genuine. But Liam was different. He texted again before she had chance to reply. It was a photo of a mound of brown sludge on a plate. Mushed chocolate cake?

Wtf is that?

Burned.

Oh my god. Is that supposed to be an omelette?

Maybe.

Did you set the fire alarm off?

No. But I did have the windows open.

Good. Maybe next time?

Maybe next time I'll just get My cook to make it for me. It is what I pay her for…

You'll get there with practise :)

Offering cooking advice to Liam York. If her mum and sister could see her now.

※

Against her will, Fayth worked the bar that evening. It was technically her turn. She'd also lost Rock, Paper, Scissors to her dad, meaning he was tucked away in the safety of the kitchen while Fayth was left to deal with people. She didn't mind it sometimes. When she wasn't featured in gossip magazines or hounded by people who were more interested in what Liam was like than being served. The trouble with villages was that there were no secrets. Everyone knew everyone, and everyone knew everything.

She was pulling a pint when one of the regulars, Monica, hopped on to the barstool in front of her. 'Long time no speak,' she said, flicking her shiny red hair. Fayth couldn't remember the last time her own hair had looked so healthy. How did Monica manage it when she worked twelve-hour days as a solicitor? She was also Fayth's divorce solicitor, but she hadn't had much chance to do anything given that Patrick wouldn't sign the papers and they were still waiting on a court date.

'How's life as a high-powered solicitor?' asked Fayth. She finished pulling the pint, handed it to the punter, and took his money.

'Wouldn't call it high-powered. I did have some pretty shocking news this afternoon though.' She fidgeted in her seat. 'You got a sec to talk in private?'

Fayth glanced around the pub. Nobody was at the bar, and those sat at tables were preoccupied with themselves. 'Sure.' She and Monica went into the kitchen where her dad was crouched over the oven, putting some chips in. All the bending and lifting at the pub was starting to give him back problems, but he still worked harder than anyone else, despite being close to retirement age. Even though he had two grown-up children, he insisted on doing most of the hard work himself. That, along with losing his wife and daughter, had taken its toll. His once dark hair had faded to salt and pepper; his once chubby cheeks were gaunt. Fayth had tried to talk to him about it many times, but he wasn't interested in looking after himself, only his daughters and the pub. He closed the oven door and turned to them. 'Monica, how's it going?'

'Good, good,' said Monica, standing just beside the door. 'You?'

'Can't complain,' he said, massaging his lower back. Even if he was in pain, he wouldn't complain. He wouldn't even take painkillers. Stubborn old git.

'Dad, could you give us a minute please?' said Fayth, gesturing to Monica.

He looked between his daughter and her solicitor. 'I'll go keep an eye on the bar,' he said, patting Fayth's shoulder as he went past. The door swung a few times after he'd gone through. Fayth waited until it had stopped, then leaned against the island. 'So.'

Monica paused. If it was for dramatic effect, Fayth didn't appreciate it. 'Patrick's solicitor got in touch just before I left. He wants to move forwards with the divorce. No court date necessary. It's going to be an easy and amicable—'

Fayth raised an eyebrow.

'—Ish – divorce.'

Fayth's legs turned to jelly. She clung on to the island for support.

Had it really only taken a stupid article in a gossip magazine to make Patrick change his mind?

'Sorry. Should've mentioned you'd need to sit down,' said Monica.

Fayth stared at her friend and solicitor. She grinned. It was a genuine *I'm-not-shitting-you* smile. Patrick really was ready to move forwards with the divorce. After all the fuss he'd kicked up for the past six months, he was finally, *finally* ready to let her go.

Two

Paper crumpled underneath Hollie's chair as she pushed it away from her desk. The blue carpet – along with her desk, TV cabinet, and parts of her bed – hadn't been visible for at least a week.

Her chest was so tight it felt like an invisible hand was trying to strangle her. She inhaled through her nose, then breathed out slowly through her mouth. Just like Mum had taught her. Having a nurse as a mum came in handy sometimes. It was even handier when she worked nights and was around during the day when Hollie needed her…except that Hollie's mum had recently switched to daytime shifts.

Pacing the length of her small room, she checked the clock above her TV. Five minutes. Breathe. Keep breathing. Keep—

Her polka dot socks slipped on a discarded sketch. She fell forwards, putting her hands out just in time.

A *thud* echoed through the Edwardian house.

A sharp pain shot through her wrists. She glanced back at the design she'd slipped on. A tight-fitting silver playsuit. And her least favourite. Typical. She squeezed her eyes shut as tears formed. She needed to calm down. She couldn't face Tate Gardener in the state she was in. She massaged her throbbing wrists.

'What are you doing up there?' shouted her nan from the bottom of the stairs.

Hollie scurried to get up – almost slipping over again – and poked her head around the top of the stairs. 'Sorry.' She sniffled a couple of times.

'You sound like Nelly the Elephant!'

'Sorry,' she repeated.

'What happened?'

'I slipped.'

'You should tidy your ruddy room then,' said her nan, her arms folded. George, their Golden Retriever, appeared beside her nan. He sat at the bottom of the stairs, looking from one to the other.

'Yeah,' said Hollie. She sighed. She had more important things to think about than how tidy her room was.

'You'll be fine. Stop worrying so much. You're making me nervous.'

'Sorry.'

'You don't know what's going to happen when you meet with this Tate person, so why worry?' said her nan.

'That's the problem, though. I don't know what's going to happen.'

'You can't control everything in life.'

'Which is another problem,' said Hollie.

Her nan shook her head. 'Sometimes you just have to accept things and move on.'

Hollie's nan had so many health problems Hollie couldn't keep up, yet she kept going like nothing was wrong. She used her wheelchair when she went out, and she didn't like going out at night as she couldn't see, but her mind was as strong as anyone's. Stronger, even. Hollie admired her tenacity. How did she do it? *How*?!

'I suppose,' said Hollie with a sigh. If only she'd inherited her nan's tenacity.

The stupid singing clock in the lounge broke out into *Für Elise*. One o'clock. A few seconds later, Hollie's laptop rang.

'Is that your phone?' said her nan.

'Close enough,' said Hollie. There was no point explaining Skype to her nan. She wasn't interested in technology beyond phones and TVs. 'See you in a bit.'

'Good luck. Not that you'll need it.'

Hollie closed her eyes. Deep breath.

She returned to her desk – careful not to slip on any more sketches – then sat down. Her hand trembling, she answered the call.

Tate's Disney Princess-like face appeared onscreen, her formerly long blonde hair cut into a bedhead bob. She only had a little bit of make-up on, but she didn't need it – she looked perfect whatever she did.

'Love the new hair,' said Hollie.

'Thanks,' said Tate, shaking her head so that the ends tickled her neck. 'It's fun. So, what've you got for me?'

Her hands still shaking, Hollie held up two designs. The first was a silver halter-neck jumpsuit with a neckline that fell just above the belly button. The second was a gold backless jumpsuit with a turtleneck and lace panel from the neck to the belly button. Her foot tapped against the desk as she talked Tate through the two designs.

Tate wrinkled her nose. 'I prefer the gold one. It would stand out more against the set.'

'What colour is the set?'

'Blue and grey.'

'I could do the silver one in gold fabric?' offered Hollie. Her wrists throbbed. She put the sketches down for a minute and massaged them.

'No, I like the gold one. It's very Kylie. Although…' She moved her lips around, an expression Hollie had come to realise was Tate's thinking face.

Although? There was an *although*?

She could hardly breathe. Was Tate about to go with another designer?

'Could we leave out the lace? Have it as a cut-out panel instead?'

Phew.

'Do you want it transparent or will you just use tape to hold it in place?' said Hollie.

Tate moved her mouth around a few times. She bit her lip. 'We'll just use tape, I think. I won't be doing that much dancing in it.'

Hollie turned the paper over and started sketching on the back. 'What about making it sleeveless too?'

'Yes!' said Tate. She clapped her hands together. 'Perfect!'

Hollie finished off the sketch and held it up. 'Picture this in a gold lamé fabric. It would catch the light perfectly.'

'I love it!' said Tate. 'If I send you the money now, could you put something together for the end of March? That's when I'm next in the UK.'

'Sure,' said Hollie. The end of March was five or six weeks away. Plenty of time. Especially given that her current status was 'unemployed'.

No.

It was '*self*-employed'. She'd made that decision while in New York. She just hadn't made any money from it yet.

'Awesome! I'll organise the transport. Maybe you and Fayth could come to the show, then we could hang out after? I'm going out with some friends after the second show. You're welcome to join us.'

'No!' said Hollie, a little too suddenly. The one celebrity party she and Fayth had been to in New York was enough to put her off for life.

Tate giggled. 'Netflix and soya ice cream it is. I'll be pretty wiped by the last show, but you're welcome to join then.'

'Works for me. I doubt Fayth will complain either. Except about the soya part.'

'Oh you can't tell the difference,' said Tate. She looked at something offscreen for a minute, then turned back to Hollie with a mischievous smile. 'I hear it's your birthday soon.'

'Yeah,' said Hollie. 'Three weeks.' She wasn't feeling very enthusiastic about it. It just marked that another year had passed and nothing had changed. Except she now had a handsome stunt performer for a boyfriend.

'Doing anything nice?'

Hollie scoffed. 'Around here? There's nothing *to* do.'

'I think you'll like Astin's present.'

'Present? What present?'

Tate grinned. 'You'll see. I've got to go, but if you have any questions, text me and I'll reply when I can, OK?'

'But what about—'

Tate blew her a kiss then hung up.

Three

Liam ran his hand over his hair. Three months in and he still hadn't got used to the copious amounts of hair gel needed onstage. He liked the character, though, and that was what was important. He'd taken to doing a Daniel Radcliffe after his breakup with Trinity, wearing the same outfit going into, and leaving, the theatre. That way the press had no idea when the photos were taken. They'd got bored pretty quickly after he'd started that tactic. Ha.

The play over, it was time to change into his signature outfit – jeans and a peacoat – then go home and play some *World of Warcraft*.

He rounded the corner towards his dressing room. He'd be home in less than half an hour and could—

Why was his dressing room door open? He'd definitely closed it behind him. He was pretty sure he'd locked it, actually.

He swallowed. How many people had a key? He pushed the door open. Carnage lay inside. The mirror was smashed. The chair lay on its back. His photographs were ripped from the walls. He ran to them to find his favourite photo – of him and his sister, the summer before she'd died – torn in half and lying on the floor.

He banged his fist against the wall, rage burning inside him. Why would someone do that?

His assistant ran in, her red face clashing with her blonde hair. 'What happened?' She went to pick up the chair.

He held out his hand to stop her. 'Don't, Ola. It wasn't me. Someone broke in.'

'But…how? You locked it, didn't you?' She crouched down and studied the lock on the door.

'Yeah.' He took a gold key from his pocket and showed it to her.

'Looks like someone's fiddled with it,' said Ola, a regular Nancy Drew. 'Is anything missing?'

'Doesn't look like it.' He stood up, still clutching the torn photo.

'Well, that's something.'

Liam held up the photo.

'I'm sorry,' she said. She hadn't been his assistant for long, but she knew what had happened. 'Do you still have the original?'

He ran his hand over his hair. When the play finished, he wouldn't miss the hair gel. 'Hard drive crashed. My parents might, but I can't tell them about this. They worry enough already.'

'I'll ask them. I'll say I'm making you a collage for your birthday.'

'My birthday's in October.'

Ola shrugged. 'It's my job to be organised. I'd better go let management know and call 911. Sit tight, yeah?'

'What else can I do?'

Looking down at the torn photograph, his eyes filled with tears. Who would do that? What had his dead sister done to anyone? Or was someone trying to get to him, knowing his dead sister was the way to do it? All of the photos on the wall were of his friends and family. There were more that included Saoirse, but that one was his favourite. It told a story of simpler times, between *Highwater* films and just before she'd got engaged.

He waited until Ola was out of sight, then punched the wall again. It probably echoed through the theatre, but he didn't care.

Still in his replica WWII uniform, he left the theatre and walked out into the New York winter. He didn't feel the cold. He was numb. There were no press outside waiting for him, and if there were any fans, he didn't notice. He was in a trance. He didn't know where he was going. It didn't matter. He just needed to get away. Away from work, memories of his shitty ex-girlfriend, the damaged photos of his loved ones, and his dressing room that had been broken into.

He stopped and looked around. He was a few blocks from Astin's apartment, so he carried on to there. When he pushed the buzzer, nothing happened. He pushed it again. A moment later, Astin's gruff Texan voice said, 'Hello?' It sounded like he'd just woken up.

'It's me.'

'Dude, shouldn't you be at work?'

'No.'

There was a pause. Liam stared at the intercom, as if doing so would magically open the door. It didn't. Finally Astin said, 'Door's open.'

Liam made his way through the front doors and up to Astin's floor. The door to his apartment was open when Liam reached it. He entered, collapsing onto the sofa. 'Man, I wish you had beer in.'

'Jack drinks enough without it lying around here, too,' said Astin. He went over to the coffee machine in the kitchenette and made a cappuccino. That would have to do. As Liam reached for the coffee with his right hand, he realised he still had the torn photo in his hand. He unravelled it and placed it on the coffee table, blinking back tears. 'Someone broke into my dressing room.'

Astin sat beside him and picked up the photo. 'Why would they rip up a photo of you and your sister?'

'How should I know?'

'Did you call the police?'

He took the crumpled photo from him and pocketed it. 'Ola did.'

'Did you speak to them?'

'I left before they got there.'

'You need to be there,' said Astin.

'All right, Mom.'

'I'm serious.'

'Don't start, all right?'

'I'm not, I'm just saying—'

'I'm an actor. Weird shit happens all the time.'

Astin's blue eyes bored into his friend. 'Not like this.'

Liam's phone broke out into the *Pokémon* theme tune. He put his coffee down, then took his phone from his pocket. Ola. 'I'm at Astin's,' he said.

'Why?'

'Needed some air.'

'So you walked miles to your best friend's house? I've been worried sick! The police are here. They need a statement. Do you want me to come get you?'

'No, it's all right, I'll get a cab.'

'Get a cab where?' Astin interjected.

Theatre, Liam mimed.

'I'll drive you,' said Astin.

Liam shook his head.

'I'll drive you,' Astin repeated.

Liam rolled his eyes. 'Astin will drive me.'

Astin smiled triumphantly.

Astin drove Liam to the theatre in his DeLorean and insisted on going inside to see the damage. He – like Ola – was making a big deal out of nothing.

By the time Astin and Liam entered, the whole of Liam's dressing room was sectioned off. It was surrounded by people: Ola, three theatre staff he didn't recognise, several uniformed police officers, and his bodyguard, Wade. He stood by the entrance to Liam's dressing room with his arms crossed and a death stare on his face. When he saw Liam, his expression warmed very little. 'Well if it isn't Houdini.'

'Good to see you too,' said Liam.

Wade shook his head. 'You should know better.'

'I went for a walk. Exercise is good, you know. You should try it some time.'

'Come on guys, this isn't the time for jokes,' said Ola. She stood between them, her arms also crossed.

'Would you prefer blind panic?' said Liam.

Ola frowned.

'There's no need to overreact,' said Astin. He peered over the police tape into Liam's dressing room. 'Fuck.'

A policewoman in her mid-thirties approached them, notebook in hand. 'I'm Detective James. I'd like to take your statement, if that's OK?'

'Of course,' said Liam. He wanted to say *no*, but he didn't have a choice. He had to cooperate. Not to mention he could never be too sure if someone would leak to the press that he'd been anything but polite. He had to maintain his 'good guy' reputation at all times. All. Freaking. Times.

'Thalia's stuck in traffic but said she'll wait for you then drive you home,' said Ola, her phone in hand.

'Do you have somewhere to stay tonight?' asked Detective James. 'It might be best if you stay somewhere else tonight, just in case this isn't random.'

Ripping up personal photos didn't feel random, but what else would it be? Why would someone target him?

'You can stay at mine if you want,' said Astin.

'Thanks,' said Liam.

'Is there somewhere we can go to talk?' asked Officer James.

'Over here,' said Ola, leading the way.

'After you,' said Liam, holding his hand out and following Ola and Detective James down the corridor to a seating area.

Giving his statement took longer than he thought it would. Wade waited for him anyway. Astin went to get some sleep and left a spare key with Wade. Ola left not long after.

It was almost three o'clock in the morning when he finally made it to Astin's. Astin lay on the sofa, spread out so that his feet hung over one end and his head hung over the other. It didn't look comfortable.

He crept past his friend, up the stairs, and into the spare bedroom. He wasn't tired, but he didn't want to wake Astin either. It would be morning in Scotland, though…

But Fayth wasn't listed as online when he checked Skype. He ran his hand over his hair. It still hadn't moved.

Would Fayth be awake yet? He didn't want to worry her by telling her what had happened, but he needed to talk to someone. They'd promised to be there for each other. And it was an emergency. He dialled her number. She answered right before it went to voicemail. Her voice was husky and quiet, like she'd just woken up. 'Hello?'

'Did I wake you up?'

'Mm-hm.'

'Sorry. I'll call back later,' he said.

'No, it's fine. I need to get up anyway.'

'Are you sure?'

'Yeah,' said Fayth. 'Has something happened?'

He relayed the story of what had happened. She remained silent throughout, only speaking when he'd finished.

'Shit. Do the police have any ideas who it is?'

'If they do, they haven't told me,' he said.

'Ugh,' said Fayth. 'It's not fair.'

'What isn't?'

'You signed up to show off your incredible talent, not to have people develop obsessions with your characters and break into your dressing rooms!'

'You think I have "incredible talent"?' he said, smiling.

'Er…I…yeah…kind of.'

'"Kind of"?'

'Yes! Fine, yes. I thought you were amazing in *Mortalis*. I cried,' said Fayth.

'Thanks,' said Liam. He couldn't stop grinning. 'I love it.

Theatre is so much more intimate than film.'

'Do you prefer it?'

'I don't know. I've done less of it. I still get to act but I get less attention. I don't really see a downside.'

'Could the lack of attention be for another reason?' said Fayth.

'Such as?'

'Trinity…'

'Oh. Yeah. The lack of an attention-seeking girlfriend who tips off the paparazzi probably helps too.'

Fayth was tidying the kitchen in preparation for the lunch shift when her phone rang. She grabbed it from her apron pocket. Liam. It was the second time he'd called her that day, and while she was happy to hear from him, she'd expected him to sleep for a little longer given his late night. 'What's up?' she said, clutching her phone between her face and shoulder as she unloaded the dishwasher. The line crackled. The dodgy phone signal was at it again.

'Sorry, are you at work? I shouldn't have called.' His voice was serious. It had a note of sadness to it she hadn't heard before, even when he'd broken up with Trinity. Even when his dressing room had been broken into.

'It's fine,' said Fayth. She stopped putting stuff away so that he couldn't hear the clinking of crockery through the phone. As she lifted the phone from her shoulder, the line went dead.

'Oh for fuck sake.' She called him back again. 'Sorry. Shitty phone signal.' The line was marginally clearer than it was before. 'You were saying?'

Liam sighed. 'They cancelled the play.'

'What? It wasn't because of the break-in, was it?'

She and Hollie had purchased tickets to see *Mortalis* their first night in New York. Had it not been for that play – which Hollie had missed thanks to a poorly-timed toilet trip – Hollie never would've met Astin, and Fayth never would've met Liam. Without that play, their holiday to New York would've been just like everyone else's.

'No, it's not that. It's just not making enough money.'

'But it was so full when we were there!'

'Yeah, well. It didn't last. You never know what will be a hit these days. The critics loved it, but that's not enough. No one bothers giving stuff a chance any more. If it's not an instant hit, they cancel it.' He sighed again. 'Now what do I do?'

While Fayth loved helping people, she'd never been very good at giving advice. Advising Liam York on his career choices when she could barely decide on her own seemed like even worse of an idea than advising him on what shirt to wear. 'I wish I could help,' she said.

'It's just nice having someone to talk to,' he said.

'When does it finish?' She leaned against the kitchen island.

'End of the month. It's not like I *need* to work, you know? But I enjoy it.'

'Could you audition for some more parts?' she suggested. 'What about that producer you met with a few weeks ago?'

'Wasn't really my thing. I've got a couple meetings lined up for tomorrow in LA. We'll see how they go.'

'Good idea,' said Fayth. She longed to be able to give him a hug, to promise him that it would all work out, but she knew that that would be a lie. She had no guarantee that everything would work out, and she wouldn't lie to him.

'Thanks for hearing me out,' he said.

'There's nothing to thank me for. We said we'd be there for each other, didn't we?'

'Yeah.' The line went silent for a minute. Then, 'Can you get on camera?'

'Why?' She'd invested in a smartphone since returning from New York, but their internet connection was almost as bad as their phone signal. It still felt like a waste of money, but on the rare occasion it did work she could see Hollie and Liam in person. She missed them a little less because of it.

'I need your opinion on something.'

She hesitated. Liam had seen her without make-up, but that didn't mean she wanted him to see her in her apron. She pulled off the apron and chucked it behind her, then tightened her ponytail. That'd have to do. 'You can try.'

They hung up, and a moment later, Liam video called her. The video was jumpy, but she could hear him all right. It was better than it had been the last time they'd video chatted, when it had crashed every ten seconds. Ah, country life.

'What do you think to this?' said Liam, holding up a black and white polka dot shirt.

Fayth frowned. 'Why are you asking me for fashion advice?'

'Because there's no one else around I can ask?'

'Send a photo to Hollie or Astin or Tate. Or anyone but me.

Fashion's not my thing.'

'I'm already talking to you,' he said. 'What do you think?' He held the shirt up a little higher.

'I think polka dots look good on Hollie.'

'Meaning?'

'Meaning I don't like patterned shirts,' said Fayth.

'What about plaid?'

Fayth scowled. 'I *hate* tartan. And plaid. And gingham. And whatever other checkered patterns exist.'

'Really? Why?'

She shrugged. 'Always have. Hollie loves them, and she always blames her love of them on me.'

'Why?'

'Wish I knew. What's the shirt for, anyway?'

'The meeting's tomorrow. I get on a plane to LA right after I finish tonight. I'm not too sure on any of the movies they've mentioned, but it can't hurt to see what they say. People aren't exactly knocking my door down any more.'

'How come?'

'I've been gone too long. Most people these days just ask me about Trinity.'

'Ugh.'

'Exactly,' said Liam. 'The sooner I can get their attention back on my work, the better.'

MARCH

One

In the post that morning was the paperwork Fayth had spent the last eight months waiting for: the decree nisi. The sign that their divorce was being processed. In just six weeks' time, she would finally be single. Not married. Not separated. But single.

It was bittersweet. She mourned a part of her life she'd never expected to end – the one part of her life she'd always planned for. In just a matter of days, that plan had been snatched from her. She had no idea when she'd have a new one. If she'd ever have a new one.

The snow crunched under her feet as she walked their three dogs down by the canal. The ice on the canal broke up as it defrosted. She took some photos on her phone, keeping one eye on Rio to make sure he didn't try to go for a swim. If he did, his sisters Paris and Vienna would follow suit. That dog was cute, but a bugger.

The dogs curled up by the pub's fireplace when they got back. She left them to it and headed upstairs to the flat she'd once shared with Patrick. It had been eight months since they'd separated, but he'd never fully accepted it. Until he saw photos of her with Liam. Why did people refuse to believe that they were just friends? Was she missing something?

While she did her best to keep the flat tidy, it was mostly used as a dumping ground for things they didn't know what to do with. It still had the faint aroma of Patrick's feet and his cheap deodorant as she walked through the living room and into the bedroom. The old, uncomfortable bed was still there. So was a piano-shaped jewellery box Mhairi had bought her for her sixteenth birthday. It sat on the windowsill, as pretty as it had been the day her sister had given it to her. Fayth had barely been able to look at it since Mhairi's death. That's why it was still at the flat. Almost everything else from her old life she'd thrown out or put into storage.

Her hand reached for the clasp. She hesitated.

The outside windowsill was covered by a thin layer of snow. So was the picnic area a few feet below. They'd had to close it off because the snow turned it into an ice rink and a health and safety nightmare. The last thing they needed was to be sued because someone fell on their arse.

Mhairi had loved the snow. They all had. It had been a family tradition to go ice skating. Not any more.

Her dad and sister didn't seem to mind that she'd gone ice skating in New York. Her dad had said that Mhairi would've been jealous, but proud of her. She'd always wanted to ice skate at the Rockefeller Center. Nobody had ever thought homebody Fayth would be the one to do it instead. They'd definitely never expected her to go with Liam York. Or for him to be such a crap student.

Fayth opened the jewellery box. Tucked inside the velvet lining were her wedding and engagement rings. She twirled them around her fingers, the gold cool against her skin. They weren't expensive rings, but that had never bothered her. They hadn't had much money: it was the sentiment that was important. The wedding band was a simple gold one, the engagement ring gold with a fake emerald in the centre. She'd never really liked gold, but Patrick had always insisted it was pretty so she'd worn it and liked it because of that.

He'd never really paid attention to her, but she'd always doted on him. It had always been about him and what he wanted. About pleasing him. Him, him, *him*! How had she not seen it? How had it not bothered her?

The Christmas before everything changed, Fayth had bought tickets for her and her mum to go and see *Mamma Mia!* The performance was the end of August. Her mum had died a month before.

She'd asked Patrick to go with her, but he'd refused. He hadn't had anything better to do, he just didn't want to go. The tickets had gone unused, £100 wasted because everyone else was too busy to go with her and she couldn't sell them or get a refund.

Not long after they'd argued about the tickets, Patrick had gone on holiday to Magaluf with his friends. He'd missed the funeral. A few hours later, Brooke had found a photo of him on Facebook with his hand on another woman's arse. She'd tried to brush it off, but she couldn't. When she confronted him about it, he admitted he'd slept with her but refused to accept he'd done anything wrong. So she moved out. The only things she'd left behind were the rings, the jewellery box, and a few tins of food.

Six weeks to go until the divorce was finalised.

She returned the rings to their spot inside the jewellery box. Was she supposed to give them back, since she'd been the one to file for divorce, or were the rules different when someone cheated? Not that they were worth anything anyway.

Ross was setting up in the kitchen when she went downstairs. She hadn't even heard him come in. After a quick hello, she grabbed the dogs and headed home. It was her day off, and she planned to spend it catching up on some sleep. She had so little energy lately. She felt like she was 23 going on 73 with how much sleep she needed.

Neither her dad nor Brooke looked up from the sofa when she walked in. Brooke sat glaring at her dad, her eyes bloodshot and filled with tears.

'What's wrong?' said Fayth.

The dogs tangled themselves up trying to get at her dad and younger sister. Fayth unclipped their leads, and they ran to Brooke and her dad. When they tried to jump on Brooke's lap, she told them to go away. Sulking, they went to their corner in the living room and lay quietly.

'Dad wants to sell the pub,' growled Brooke.

Fayth turned to her dad. 'What?'

He sighed. 'I didn't want you to find out like this, but your sister overheard me on the phone. I just wanted to see what we could get for it. Turns out, it's more than I thought. We've not paid off all the mortgage, but we've paid off enough that we'd get some money from it.'

'Dad—'

'No, Fayth. The pub is struggling, and I don't want to be the one that has to close it down. Things have improved a wee bit lately, but I don't know how long it will last. I want to get out while we can still make some money from it. I want you to get out while you still can. You've had a taste of what it's like to get out of here. Don't you want more of that?'

She did, but she wasn't going to admit that. Not when he was about to sell what he'd spent fifteen years of his life working on.

'The pub was your mum's dream, and god, I love her and I miss her, but I can't spend my life living *her* dream.'

'Then what's your dream, Dad?' said Brooke.

'It was to be with her, and to raise my threef beautiful girls. And now, it's for my two beautiful girls to go live their lives and do whatever it is that makes them happy. Can you do that for me?'

'Dad, are you sure about this?' asked Fayth.

'Aye, I am. It's the first thing I've been sure about for a long time.'

Her family had run the Cock and Bull since Brooke was a toddler. She and her sisters had grown up pulling pints and cooking in the pub kitchen. It hadn't been the same since her mum and sister had died, but she hadn't realised just how different – or difficult – it had been for her dad. Everywhere she went, at home and at the pub, something reminded her of them. Was the same true for her dad? For Brooke?

She squeezed in between them and pulled them into a hug. 'We're happy so long as you are, Dad.'

Brooke made a gagging noise. 'Speak for yourself.'

'Well what do you want to do then?' said Fayth, letting go of her. She kept her arm around her dad, and he kept his around her.

'I've not really thought about it,' said Brooke.

'College won't let you get away with that for long,' said Fayth.

Brooke turned her death stare on to Fayth.

'Just making sure you're prepared. It's my duty as your big sister.'

'Bite me,' said Brooke.

'There's something else,' interrupted her dad. 'I want each of you to take half of the money.'

'Dad, we can't,' said Fayth.

'Yes you can,' he said. 'I don't need it. You two can put it towards whatever you like, so long as it's productive.'

'Productive? What does that mean?' said Brooke.

'Uni, or something. Something you'll enjoy.'

What would she enjoy? Was it the perfect opportunity for her to go to uni? To finally see what student life was like? But what would she study? What *could* she study? She wasn't good at anything outside of cooking and suppressing her emotions.

'We haven't paid it all off, but there's enough in it that you'll get something from it,' said her dad.

'OK,' said Fayth. 'If that's what you want.'

'What!' screamed Brooke. 'How can you agree to this!' She stood up, waving her arms around like an air traffic controller. 'This is a joke!'

'It's Dad's decision,' said Fayth. 'If he wants to sell it, it's our job to stand by him.'

'Like hell it is!' protested Brooke.

'Brooke!' shouted her dad. 'Don't talk to your sister like that.'

'Then how about you talk to us before making any life-changing decisions!' Brooke stomped upstairs and slammed her bedroom door. The house shook.

'She'll snap out of it,' said Fayth.

'Is that how you feel too?'

'No,' said Fayth. 'It's up to you, not us.'

'No it isn't. Your sister's right. You're both old enough now that it should be a family decision.'

'Two out of three is enough for it to be agreed though, right?'

'Is it what you want, or what you think I want?'

Fayth sighed. 'Both.' She paused, picturing herself old and grey, still working in that damn kitchen. 'I don't want to spend the rest of my life cooking in a pub kitchen. Or cooking at all, really. I enjoy it, but I don't want to do it for a living.'

'What do you want to do?'

Fayth sat on her bed, Liam's face on her laptop screen. He sat at the desk in his parents' office, a cup of tea beside him.

'How do you feel?' he asked after she'd finished updating him on everything.

'I don't even know any more,' she said. 'I've grown up at the pub. It not being ours any more is scary. But kind of liberating.'

'So what are you going to do now?'

'That's what I've got to figure out. The pub may not go up for sale yet. Dad's still thinking about it. Brooke's pissed.'

'But it's your dad's pub, not hers,' he said, sipping his tea. He'd made it in a *Rescue Rover* mug. The image was faded, but it was still a ten-year-old Liam – and rescued Rover – that stared back at her. He'd likely done it in the mug to wind her up, knowing that it was one of her favourite films as a kid. She wasn't going to take the bait.

'She's a teenager, though,' said Fayth.

'She'll come around.'

'Will she?'

'Eventually,' said Liam. He sipped his tea again, his ten-year-old face still watching her. She bit her lip. She would *not* take the bait.

'Like my mug?' he said, an eyebrow raised.

'Vain, much?' she teased.

'I can't believe my parents still have it. It's embarrassing.'

'Then why are you using it?' she asked, shaking her head.

'Thought you'd find it funny. Anyway, what will you use the money for?'

'I don't know. What constitutes as "productive"?'

Liam shrugged. 'Productivity's not really my thing.'

'You never sit still,' she said.

'Sure I do. I sit still *a lot*. That's how I get in so much game time. Well, when I'm not in the theatre. Which I won't be soon.'

Fayth gave him a sympathetic smile. 'You'll find something.'

'I hope so. The press are loving it. Dressing room broken into, can't get any good film roles, now my play's finished too.' He sighed, sipping his tea again.

Fayth looked up at the photos around her bed. She'd added some since their return from New York. Hollie, Astin, and Liam's faces looked down at her. It was a strategically angled selfie she'd taken their last night there. Considering she'd used her camera and not a phone to take it, it was a damned good photo.

'Fayth? You still with me?' said Liam, waving the mug in front of the screen.

'Stop it, Rover,' she said.

'Calling me by the dog's name. Harsh. His name was River in real life, you know.'

'Really?'

'Yeah. He lived to like, twelve. Did a few movies, but *Rescue Rover* was his biggest. What were you staring at?'

'That photo we took in your apartment,' she said. She moved her laptop from her lap, pulled the photo from off the wall, and showed it to Liam.

'I like that photo,' he said.

'Me too.'

She'd got them all at their best angles. Even she looked good. She looked terrible usually. It helped that Astin and Liam were photogenic, but really, a great photo is as much about its photographer as its subject.

She was good at taking photos! She was *good* at taking photos!

'You look like you just had a eureka moment. Your eyes are bigger than your head.'

'Flattering,' said Fayth.

'It is if you're a cartoon character,' said Liam.

'I wasn't the last time I checked,' said Fayth. 'Not unless I'm missing something.'

'What was your eureka moment, anyway?'

'I want to be a photographer,' declared Fayth.

Liam raised his mug and nodded. 'River and I approve.'

'Well, there's no going back now,' said Fayth's dad, looking up at the *For Sale* sign on the side of the pub. It swung in the wind.

Brooke folded her arms and walked off in a huff.

'She'll be OK,' said Fayth. She put her arm around her dad.

'I know, but it's harder for her. She doesn't remember a life without it.'

'Exactly. But one day she'll realise it's for the best,' said Fayth. 'I think I've decided what I want to use the money for.' She hadn't told anyone other than Hollie and Liam yet. They'd both given it their approval. Hollie had gone off on one about how great Fayth's photos were and how she could take some for her fashion line. It would be great practice. But first, she needed to find a better camera. Some lessons wouldn't hurt, either.

'What've you decided?' asked her dad.

'Photography,' she replied.

He smiled. It was one of the few genuine smiles she'd seen from him since the accident. 'Do it.'

She squeezed her dad's shoulders. 'Thanks, Dad.'

'You don't need to thank me. I'm just doing my job.'

'I know, but Brooke and I don't thank you enough. You've done so much since—'

He held up his hand. 'I wouldn't have it any other way. Now, we've got to keep this place going until the sale, and prove that it's a worthwhile investment. Think you can help me with that in the meantime?'

'I'd love to.'

Two

Hollie sat cross-legged on her bedroom floor, surrounded by sketches, cash flow forecasts, business plans, website mock-ups, audience research, and other random pieces of paper. The only spot on her floor that wasn't covered in paper was where she sat.

She picked up a sketch and examined it. It was a cocktail dress with a cape attached. The one thing she hadn't decided on was just what type of clothes she wanted to make. Would she specialise in evening wear, or casual wear? What about accessories? Did she want to appeal to the masses, or a more specialist clientele? Just who *was* her target audience?

She'd drawn every idea she'd come up with since leaving New York, but there wasn't a significant theme or style.

She rested her head against her wardrobe and closed her eyes. There was so much to do. She was stressed out already, and she'd only been working a few weeks. What would she be like by the time Tate's video was released?

A knock echoed through the house. Hollie jumped up and peered out of the window. They weren't expecting anyone. A black cab pulled away from across the road. Why would someone get a taxi to theirs?

Hollie could be down the stairs before her nan had even found the control for her electric chair, so her nan only answered the door if she was on her own. Those that visited regularly knew they'd get a faster response at the window. She could tell from the sound of the knock that this person wasn't a regular.

She ran down the stairs. A figure was visible through the frosted glass panels, but she couldn't make out who it was. When she opened the door, her jaw fell. 'Astin!' She jumped up, wrapping her arms around him tightly. He smelled of patchouli and citrus, just how she remembered.

'Miss me?' he said, hugging her back.

'What're you doing here?' She pulled away just enough that she could see his face, but not enough that she'd completely let go of him. His light brown hair was short and simple, his stubble just long enough to give him that laid-back look. He hadn't changed a bit in the six weeks since she'd last seen him.

'I thought instead of sending you a card and present for your birthday, I'd send you me.' He grinned.

He was there. At her house. All six-foot-one of him. All leather jacket and blue jeans.

'Who is it?' called Hollie's nan from the living room.

Astin raised his eyebrows.

Hollie took a deep breath and stepped aside to let him in. He dumped his bags behind the front door then followed her into the living room. She had no idea how her nan would react – she'd never brought a boy home before. Well, aside from her ex-flatmate Cameron. But Cameron didn't count. He was more of an annoying little brother.

Hollie's nan's chair faced away from the door, so while she could tell Hollie was no longer alone, she couldn't tell who it was.

'Who is it?' she repeated.

'Hi, Mrs B,' said Astin.

'The American.'

Astin walked around so that her nan could see him. Hollie closed the living room door and sheepishly followed him. 'It's good to meet you,' he said. 'Hollie talks a lot about you.'

Hollie's nan studied him, looking him up and down with what little eyesight she had left. Hollie wrapped her arms around herself, resting her weight on her left leg.

'He's come all this way to see you, and you're looking like that. You could at least look happy to see him!' said her nan.

'Sorry Nan. I just…'

'Just what? You're 22, lass.' She turned to Astin: 'Do you want a drink or anything to eat?'

'I'm all right, thanks.'

'Are you sure?'

'She'll keep asking until you have something,' Hollie warned him.

He chuckled. 'My grandparents are like that, too. Do you have any coffee?'

Her nan turned to Hollie. 'I'll have some tea, please.'

Naturally she'd be enlisted to make it. She grabbed Astin's arm and dragged him into the kitchen. George stirred as they entered, looking up from his bed in the corner. When he noticed a new friend, he stood up and walked over. Astin bent down, rubbing behind George's ears. That was it. He had a friend for life.

Hollie flicked on the kettle and took three mugs from the nearby cupboard. A pair of arms snaked around her waist. Astin perched his head on top of hers. She leaned back into him.

'You are happy to see me, aren't you?' he said.

She turned around. 'Of course I am! I've just…I've never had a boy at home before.'

'What?'

She blushed. 'You know the story.' Hollie had spent her university years pining after her best friend only for him to go off with someone else. She'd then gone and lost her virginity to a bartender who'd just broken up with his girlfriend. Because misery loves company, after all.

'Did they ever meet whatshisface?'

'You mean Will?' She put a teabag in her nan's mug and filled a cafetière with ground coffee for her and Astin.

'Yeah, if that was his name.'

'Mum did, Nan didn't. We went for lunch together a few times. She thought he was great.' She rolled her eyes. 'How wrong she was.'

'And now you have me,' said Astin, ruffling her hair.

'Yep,' she said, flattening her hair where he'd messed it up.

'I get it. I surprise you with a romantic gesture and you don't even want me here. George is more excited to see me than you are.'

George nudged Astin's hand. Astin petted him a few times. When he stopped, George resumed nudging his hand.

'He'll never leave you alone now,' said Hollie.

The kettle boiled, and she continued to make the drinks. After putting some milk into her nan's tea, she took it in to her then returned to making coffee.

'I don't know where you're going to sleep,' she confessed.

'In your room?'

Hollie scoffed. 'Like they'll go for that. Plus, it's a single bed.'

He put his arm around her waist and leaned in to whisper in her ear: 'Even better.'

The stupid singing clock broke out into *The Farmer Wants a Wife*. Six o'clock. Hollie's mum would be home from work any minute. She hadn't told her much about Astin. They didn't really talk about boys. They didn't talk about anything, really.

Hollie twitched her foot as she sat beside Astin on the sofa. He glanced at her foot, then up at her, his eyes narrowed. She stopped twitching and pulled her sleeves over her hands.

'Right. I'd better go put yer mam's dinner on,' said her nan. She pushed the button on her electric chair and it tilted upwards to help her out of it. She, Hollie, and Astin had already eaten a couple of hours earlier. Astin had gone for chicken and rice due to his looming filming, while Hollie and her nan had had the far more appetising pie and mash.

The chair finally reached its standing position and her nan got up and made her way into the kitchen. George woke up from where he lay by the radiator and relocated to his second favourite spot by the door. He knew what time it was.

Headlights lit up the front window. A car door slammed shut. George's tail wagged as he stepped out of the way of the door. Hollie's mum walked in seconds later. She closed the door behind her and went to put her bags on the sofa. When she noticed Hollie and Astin, she stopped.

Astin jumped up. 'Hi. I'm Astin. Hollie's boyfriend.' He held out his hand. She dumped her bags by the door and shook it.

Boyfriend. The long distance hadn't put him off after all. Gulp.

'It's nice to meet you...' He trailed off. She'd never told him what to call her relatives! Shit!

'Bernie, you can call me Bernie,' said her mum. George nudged her leg. She scratched behind his ears. 'And you can call that one over there annoying.' She gestured to Hollie's nan, who was hobbling back into the living room.

Hollie sniggered.

'Oi! I heard that!'

'You were supposed to,' said Hollie's mum. 'I don't know where you're supposed to sleep; a bomb went off in Hollie's room.'

'I'm sure it's not that bad,' said Astin.

'I'm sure it is,' said her nan. She leaned back against her chair and pressed the button to lower it.

'It's just designs and stuff,' said Hollie.

'Wouldn't it be easier to find "designs and stuff" if it was tidy?' said her nan.

'It's organised,' said Hollie.

'No it's not,' said her nan.

'It's an organised mess,' said Hollie.

'No it's not,' said her nan.

Hollie glared. Astin patted Hollie's head. 'George won't mind me sharing, will you?'

George paid no attention: he was too busy pestering Hollie's mum.

'He may look cute, but he's not very good at sharing,' said Hollie's mum. 'All the papers on Hollie's floor will make for good padding if you slip over in the night.'

'More like cause you to slip over in the night,' said her nan.

'All right, all right. I can take a hint,' said Hollie, walking to the landing door.

'Good girl,' said her nan.

Sunlight streamed in through the gap in Hollie's bedroom curtains. Astin lay behind her on her single bed, his hard-on pressed into her back through his boxers. His arms were wrapped around her, her hands on top of his. His breath tickled her neck.

She'd dreamt of waking up beside him again everyday since she'd left New York, but she'd never expected it to happen again so soon. It was so unreal she still expected to wake up any moment.

'I missed you,' he whispered.

'I missed you too,' she whispered back.

He rolled her over so that she faced him. 'Just making sure you know.' He pressed his lips to hers. She kissed him back, his hand creeping inside her slip. She put her hand on top of his. 'Not here. It's weird.'

'Why is it?'

'Nan's two doors away.'

'Two doors is plenty,' he said. 'If you're quiet enough.'

'Not sure I could be quiet if I wanted to,' she said coquettishly.

He pulled her on top of him. 'Did you make this?' he asked, stroking the fabric of her nightdress. It was purple silk with a sweetheart neckline and princess seams to give the illusion of curves. She didn't wear it much, but Astin turning up unannounced seemed like the perfect occasion.

'Yeah.'

'Damn, you look hot in it.' He put his hand to her hips. 'And no underwear? Tease.'

'I always sleep without underwear!'

'I thought you didn't want your nan to hear us?' He smirked.

Hollie put her hands to her mouth. 'Was I really that loud?'

'More squeaky than loud. Now, where were we?' He snaked his hands inside the slip and on to her breasts. 'Much better.' He gave a satisfied smile.

'You all right there?'

'Yep,' he said, still smiling.

'You know there's nothing there, right?'

'Well my hands are touching something.' He moved one hand to her back and ran the other through her hair. They paused, breathing heavily. Being so close to him again was intoxicating. Her body cried out for him and refused to accept no as an answer. She leaned forwards and kissed him.

'That was naughty,' said Hollie, tracing the outline of the tattoo on Astin's arm with her finger. *05.16.06.* His little brother's birthday. The American way, of course.

'You loved it,' said Astin. 'And you were surprisingly quiet.' He pulled the covers up over them.

'Because you kept kissing me to shut me up!'

'It worked, didn't it? And we both got what we wanted.'

Hollie closed her eyes, her body relaxed. Yes, she had got what she wanted. Not just more amazing sex with him, but *him*. With her. He'd travelled from New York just to see her. If that wasn't a good sign, what was?

'So how'd you like to go to London for your birthday?'

She sat up. 'London?'

'I hear there's nothing to do around here.'

Hollie narrowed her eyes. She said that a lot, but she didn't recall saying it to him.

'What?'

'Who'd you hear that from?'

'Just…around.'

'Who's your mole?'

He smirked.

She nudged him. 'Tell me!'

He nudged her back. 'Nope.'

'Come ooooon,' she said.

'Does it matter?'

'Yes!'

'Then I'll tell you later.'

'Oi!'

He chuckled. 'All right, all right. It was Tate. I asked her to

find out if you had any plans.'
'The cheek!'
He grinned. 'If you don't want to go to London…'
'No! I want to go!'
'Prove it.'
She wriggled back down beneath the covers and kissed him.

Three

'Are you two awake?' called Hollie's nan from the bottom of the stairs.

Hollie lifted her head from Astin's chest. Thank god she hadn't shouted five minutes earlier. And her mum was at work. Her nan hadn't heard them, had she? They hadn't made *that much* noise. Had they?

'YES!' cried Hollie.

Astin rubbed his ear. 'Ow.'

'Sorry. If I don't shout she can't hear me.' She raised her voice again: 'WHAT TIME DO YOU WANT TO GO OUT?'

'Whenever you two are ready,' said her nan. 'But not before *Bargain Hunt*.'

Hollie checked the time on her clock. Half eleven. They had at least half an hour, then. 'OK!'

'There's no need to shout,' said Hollie's nan. The downstairs door closed.

Astin chuckled.

'She usually can't hear me if I speak normally.'

'You could've gone to the top of the stairs.'

'Yeah. I'm gonna do that in my birthday suit,' she said, flashing him a deadpan look. 'Wait a minute. She said "you two".'

'Are you planning to leave me here while y'all have all the fun?'

'No, but taking Nan for her pension and lunch isn't particularly interesting. I love spending time with Nan, but—'

'I don't mind. Especially if it means I get to spend more time with you.'

She smiled. How could he be so perfect?

Cobblestones. Cobblestones were evil. Pretty, but evil. They were uncomfortable to the person in the wheelchair, and even worse for the person pushing said wheelchair. Especially when the person in said wheelchair weighed more than double what the person pushing said wheelchair did.

Hollie persevered anyway. Her nan hated anyone else pushing her wheelchair, and neither of them were going to let a few cobblestones spoil their fun.

'Want me to push?' offered Astin as they headed up a steep hill.

'No, it's OK,' said Hollie in between huffs. She was practically at a 45 degree angle pushing it.

'Let him push,' said Hollie's nan.

Hollie stopped. 'Are you sure?'

'I'm sure.'

Astin took the wheelchair from her. Letting him push the wheelchair was her nan's way of saying she approved of him. It was a small gesture, but from her, it spoke louder than anything else.

Astin maintained a similar pace to Hollie's, allowing her nan to check out the sights despite her poor eyesight. If anything, he walked slower than she did. Hollie had to maintain a certain pace on the cobbled streets because if she lost too much momentum, she'd lose control.

'Where do you want to go for lunch, Nan?' said Hollie.

'I don't mind, it's up to you. What do you two fancy?'

'I'll eat anything,' said Astin.

'What happened to being healthy?' said Hollie.

He shrugged. 'All good things in moderation.'

'Exactly,' agreed Hollie's nan. 'Fish and chips?' she suggested, gesturing to a chip shop to their left.

'Works for me,' said Hollie.

'Let's go,' said Astin as he manoeuvred the wheelchair towards the doors.

They picked a table just inside the door and parked it at the end of the table. The seats were fixed so there was no chance of getting the wheelchair in the side. It was one of her nan's favourite places to eat, but it was *not* wheelchair friendly. It was even worse if a kid had been throwing chips on the floor beforehand – ketchup-covered chips *loved* to stick to the wheels of the chair. Luckily the white vinyl floor was clear.

'I'll have the usual,' said her nan. She put her hand in her handbag. 'Oh! I forgot to post this!' She took out a padded plastic envelope. Her talking newspaper. It was a cassette tape that arrived in the post each week, updating her on the local news without her having to squint at the tiny print in the paper. She sent it back after she'd listened to it.

'We'll post it once we've ordered,' said Hollie.

'All right,' said her nan. She held out her purse.

'I'll get it,' said Astin.

Her nan frowned. 'Are you sure?'

'Yes, for being such lovely hosts.' He flashed her his most charming smile.

'All right then.' She returned her purse to her bag.

Hollie and Astin joined the queue a few feet away. It was moderately busy, but not busy enough that they'd have to wait forever. 'So, what'll it be?'

'I don't know what half of this stuff is,' he confessed.

'There, there,' she said, scratching his arm affectionately. 'What about fish and chips?'

'That'll do.' He looked from the counter to Hollie and back again. 'Can you see over that thing?'

'Just about,' she said. It was about four and a half feet tall. Why it needed to be so tall she'd never worked out.

When they reached the front, Hollie ordered three portions of fish, chips, and mushy peas – making Astin's an extra large – some tea for her nan, and some water for her and Astin to drink. Astin kept his promise and paid – despite Hollie's protests – then they went down the road to the post box.

'I don't know why you hate this place so much. It seems nice,' said Astin.

'The cover may be all right, but the content isn't so great.'

'Well when you're a world-famous fashion designer, you can live anywhere in the world.'

'Where would you like to live?' she asked.

'Anywhere, so long as I'm with you.' He kissed her cheek. She wrapped her arms around him, resting her head on his shoulder. Why did he have to live so far away?

They reached the postbox and posted the talking newspaper, then headed back to the chippy. Hollie's nan was exactly where they'd left her, but she'd acquired a friend. An elderly man Hollie didn't recognise sat in the seat beside her.

'Who's that?' said Astin.

'Never seen him before,' said Hollie.

They approached the table. Hollie folded her arms.

'Ah, this must be your sister,' said the old man.

Hollie's eyes widened. He did *not* just say that.

Astin sniggered.

'Not likely,' said her nan. Her handbag sat in her lap, her hands over the top of it.

A tangible silence hung in the air. Was he going to take the hint, or did they need to ask him to leave?

'Well, I'd better leave you to it,' said the man, standing up. He gave her nan one last glance, then left.

Hollie and Astin sat back down. Hollie stared at her nan, her eyes still wide.

'What?' said her nan.

Astin was still laughing.

'I cannot believe that just happened,' said Hollie.

'What's so funny? An old gal like me can't get chatted up?'

'It's more the cheesy pick-up-line that went along with it,' said Hollie.

'It's not my fault he needs stronger glasses,' said her nan.

Four

The train was full. Hollie and Astin sat near the back of the carriage, their suitcases in the storage compartment behind them. Hollie was by the window, Astin the only barrier between her and the crowded train. He held on to her hand, squeezing it occasionally. It was a reassuring gesture, and for that, she was grateful.

The sun was high and bright in the sky. So high and bright that Hollie wore her sunglasses so that she didn't get blinded. It was a rare moment of March sunshine, and while she enjoyed it, she also liked being able to see. It wouldn't be long until the days were longer and the nights shorter. Until the sun was out for more than five minutes a day. Until she was 23.

Twelve hours, in fact.

Hollie looked away from the window and turned her attention to her boyfriend. 'So where are we staying?'

'You'll see.' He unclipped the lid from a protein shake bottle and took a few swigs. He offered some to Hollie. She wrinkled her nose. The smell of fake strawberries was bad enough.

'Why won't you tell me?'

'Because I want to surprise you. You'll like it, I promise.'

'How do you know?'

'I'm just that good,' he said, nonchalant.

'I'm not convinced.'

Astin leaned back in his seat. 'You'll see.'

'Tease.'

'Yes?'

Hollie nudged him. He kissed her. He tasted of fake strawberries. 'What do you want to do while we're there? Go shopping?'

'Is it weird if I say no? I'm so fed up of looking at clothes.'

'Culture it is.'

'Do you mind?'

'Why would I mind?'

'Museums and art galleries aren't everyone's kind of thing,' she said, looking out of the window. The sun had disappeared behind a cloud, so she propped her sunglasses on top of her head and looked out across the endless fields of green. It was beautiful.

He put his arm across her shoulder. 'Well they're mine, and if that's what you want to do, then that's what we'll do. You deserve a couple days off.'

'But I've got so much to do—'

'Make one of your lists, and you can get back to it after a few days away. Unless you want me to go to London on my own and leave you to work.'

'I can always do some stuff before bed,' she said.

He kissed her cheek. 'You won't get behind because of me, don't worry.'

Hollie and Astin got the Tube from King's Cross Station to Covent Garden. She hated underground transport even more than trains, but having Astin with her helped. It was the middle of the day, so it wasn't as busy as it could've been. Once she was outside in the fresh air again, she released her breath. Astin was more familiar with London than she was, so he led the way through Covent Garden and to the hotel.

'Whereabouts is this place?' asked Hollie as they walked past the Apple Store. The glass walls showcased its clean, modern design. And its size. Everything was so much bigger in London. Except the roads. They were about half the size with double the traffic.

'Just around the corner,' said Astin. 'Want me to carry anything?'

'I'm OK,' said Hollie. The exercise would do her good.

Astin's definition of 'around the corner' was very different to hers. She still refused to let him carry her suitcase, though. Having to tug something so heavy might teach her to pack light. Or not. She'd tried to, but her mum had taught her to always be prepared. And to be prepared, it was impossible to pack light.

Five or ten minutes later, they rounded a corner where a car drove on the wrong side of the road. There was only one hotel in the UK where that was allowed. 'No. Way!'

Astin grinned. 'You like?'

'I *love*.'

They were at the Savoy. The Savoy, the hotel she'd wanted to stay at since she was a child. She'd never mentioned that to

Astin, though. How had he found out?

She leaned over and kissed him. How long had he spent planning his surprise trip? How much had he spent? She didn't like him spending his money on her. It was *his* money.

Beautiful Edwardian architecture stood before her, more of it waiting just inside the revolving doors. 'We'll sort your bags, madam. Sir,' said a porter as they reached the doors.

'Thanks,' she said.

Astin handed the porter a tip, then put his arm around Hollie's waist and led her inside. The people around them wore outfits that cost more than her student loans, while the staff all wore tailored suits. Thankfully she'd dressed neutrally, unsure of where they were going. You could never go wrong with cigarette trousers, a well-fitted blouse and a leather jacket. Astin, meanwhile, had on jeans, a white t-shirt, and his usual leather jacket. So casual. Then again, when you looked like him, it didn't really matter what you wore.

Hollie's reflection glinted back at her in the polished checkerboard floor as she approached the wood-panelled walls. They were embossed with different designs that she just had to take photos of. It made her feel like a tourist, but she had to share them with Fayth.

Astin checked them in then they headed upstairs to their room. It was bigger than any hotel room Hollie had ever stayed in, and far more lavish. Art Deco paintings adorned the walls; geometric patterns were everywhere. It was incredible. And expensive. 'You didn't have to do this, you know. You don't have to impress me.'

'I wanted to,' he said, putting his arm around her shoulders. 'Am I not allowed to spoil my girlfriend?'

It had been almost three months, but being referred to as someone's 'girlfriend' still sounded strange to her. She'd always been just the friend, maybe the best friend if she was lucky. Girlfriend gave her a whole new level of importance. A whole new level of responsibility. A whole new level of pressure.

'I thought we could either go out for dinner tonight, or have a quiet night in,' said Astin, interrupting her paranoia.

Hollie went into the bathroom and admired the marble suite. The last time she'd had a bath had been in New York. With Astin. She ran her fingers across the edge of the bath. 'Let's stay in.'

Five

Hollie stretched out across the bed, expecting to find Astin beside her. He wasn't there. She rolled over and grabbed her phone from the bedside table. No text from Astin. There were texts from Cameron and Tate wishing her a happy birthday, though. As she sat up, she noticed a piece of paper on Astin's pillow. It said, *Gone to gym, back soon x*. Duh. He couldn't put his workout schedule on hold just because they'd gone away for a couple of days, not when he started filming soon.

She replied to the texts from Cameron and Tate, then climbed out of bed and put on a dressing gown. It was soft and silky. She pulled it tighter around her.

The chair at the other end of the room was full of presents. She knelt down to read the tags. Fayth. Liam. Tate. Mum and Nan. Astin. She didn't want to open them alone, though. She wanted to wait for Astin.

But opening the card from her mum and nan wouldn't hurt, would it? She crouched down and picked up the envelope. *Hollie* was scrawled on to it in her mum's handwriting. Inside was a card with a Golden Retriever puppy on it. It looked just like George when he was younger, but with golden fur instead of white and cream. She opened the card. £50 fell onto the plush carpet. Written inside the card were the words, *To Hollie, Have a wonderful birthday and enjoy your time in London. Lots of love Mum, Nan and George xxx*. Hollie smiled. £50 was a lot of money, but she knew they wouldn't take it back.

Astin entered wearing trackies and a vest top, a towel slung over his shoulder. And carrying two coffees. When their eyes met, they both smiled. Hollie approached him and kissed him. His forehead was shiny with sweat.

'Happy birthday,' he said.

'Thank you.' She took one of the coffees from him. A vanilla latte. Yum.

'When did you wake up?' he asked.

'Just now,' she said. 'How long were you at the gym?'

'An hour, maybe two?' He patted at his forehead with the towel.

'You don't know?'

'I knew it was too early for you to be up,' he said with a chuckle. She glared at him, but it was true.

Astin gestured to the chair with his coffee cup. 'They're from me, Fayth, Liam, Tate, and your mum and nan. The envelope is from them.'

'I saw,' she said.

'Been looking already, have we?'

'I wasn't going to open them yet! Although technically it is my birthday so I am allowed.'

Astin sat on the edge of the bed, looking from her to the chair and back again eagerly. 'Go on then.'

'You didn't want me to open them a minute ago,' she said. She folded her arms and stared at him.

'Do I have to pick you up and carry you over to them?'

'No, but if you want to I wouldn't say no.'

He put his coffee and towel on the floor then picked her up. She put her arms around his neck, snuggling into him. 'I'll just stay here.'

He spun her around.

She giggled. The one thing she'd always hated was being picked up. Being the smallest and the lightest, friends and family had always liked picking her up and spinning her around. She didn't trust any of them to not drop her.

But things were different with Astin. While she didn't know what weights he lifted, she knew it was more than what she weighed. For all she knew, he lifted the equivalent of Wade's bodyweight everyday.

There was a safety in his arms that she'd never felt before. Not just from his physical strength, but from what he said and did, too. He could pick her up and keep her going if the monsters in her head tried to drag her down. But he didn't need to. Being around him made her happy. Happier than anyone else could.

Her phone rang. They were snapped out of their game with a start. Astin put her down in front of it. It was Fayth, wanting to video call. Astin's phone started ringing too. When he picked it up from his bedside table and saw who it was, he laughed.

When Hollie answered, Fayth grinned, clearly waiting for

something. A minute later, Liam's face appeared on Astin's phone. They propped their phones beside one another on the bedside table.

'Ready?' said Fayth.

'Ready for what?' asked Hollie.

'Not you!' said Fayth.

'Ready,' said Liam.

'I'm so confused right now,' said Hollie.

Astin sat on the bed, watching with a look of amusement.

Fayth and Liam broke out into *Happy Birthday*. Astin joined in. His voice stood out the most – it was deep, with a Texan twang. It gave her goosebumps.

When they'd finished, they both beamed at the camera. 'Happy birthday, Bea!' said Fayth, using her shortened version of Hollie's middle name, Beatrice.

'Thanks,' said Hollie, giggling.

'Sorry about the singing,' said Liam. 'I was dubbed in *Rescue Rover*.'

'What? But what about that scene where you sung to Rover after he got hit by the car?' cried Fayth.

'Dubbed, sorry. Even aged ten I couldn't hold a tune,' said Liam.

'No!' cried Hollie.

Fayth wiped a fake tear from her eye. 'You just ruined my childhood.'

Hollie nodded, pouting.

'Why don't you open your presents? That'll make you feel better,' said Liam.

'I don't know. That's fifteen years of childhood illusion you just ruined. What else have you lied to us about?' said Hollie.

'It wasn't my lie. It was the producers',' said Liam.

'But you went along with it for all this time,' said Hollie. 'We're so disappointed in you.'

'That's Hollywood,' said Liam.

'Isn't it just?' mumbled Fayth.

'Why don't you open my presents first?' suggested Astin. He sat on the bed, his coffee in hand.

'Are you sure that's safe?' said Fayth, lowering an eyebrow.

'Is it something dirty?' asked Hollie. She glanced over her shoulder at him.

'No. I know better than to buy you clothes without you there, lingerie included,' said Astin. 'As for anything else…'

'La la la, not listening,' said Fayth, covering her ears.

Hollie giggled. 'OK, which is it?'

'The tartan gift bag,' he said.

She'd worn a tartan dress on their first date. It had clearly made an impression.

Inside were two things: a light blue box with a white ribbon tied around it, and an envelope.

'Box first,' said Astin.

She reached inside and picked up the box. Tiffany's. She gasped.

'Astin—'

'Open it.'

She opened it. Inside was a white gold necklace with a clock pendant.

'Because the time we spend together is special, and it won't be long until we see each other again,' said Astin.

'I think I just threw up a little in my mouth,' said Liam.

'Me too,' said Fayth.

Hollie ignored them. She gasped, diving on top of him and kissing him. His arms snaked around her waist and pulled her closer. She tasted macchiato as he parted her lips with his, his hands moving lower…

Fayth cleared her throat. 'Still here.'

'Me too,' said Liam.

'Sorry,' said Hollie, climbing from Astin. They couldn't see anything from the angle of their phones, but she was embarrassed all the same. She returned to her spot by the chair – Astin kneeling at her side – and opened the envelope. Two tickets to something called The Candlelight Club that night.

'What's The Candlelight Club?'

'A modern-day speakeasy,' he said proudly.

She gasped. 'Really?'

'Yep.'

She pecked his lips, conscious of both phones pointing in their direction.

'You can thank me properly later,' he said with a smirk.

'Open mine next!' said Fayth. 'It's the purple bag.'

Hollie turned back to her presents. Purple was Fayth's favourite colour, so it was no surprise to Hollie that her present was inside a purple bag. Nor that Fayth hadn't wrapped it – she didn't have the time or the patience.

She sliced the sellotape with her nail. Inside was a photo

album. With a picture of her and Fayth on the front. Astin leaned over her shoulder as she flicked through the pages. It was filled with photos from their trip to New York. 'Fayth, this is amazing.'

'Thanks,' she said, beaming.

Hollie closed the photo album and studied the outside. It was pink with purple calligraphic swirls embossed into it. 'Did you design this?'

Fayth blushed, looking away from the camera.

'It's gorgeous.'

Fayth's face lit up. 'Thanks.'

Hollie placed the photo album back inside the bag.

'Liam's is the *Highwater* bag,' said Fayth.

Why was she not surprised?

He smiled innocently. 'What? You're a fan.'

Highwater was a fantasy film franchise Liam had starred in with Trinity. He'd played the hero Eric, while Trinity had played his love interest Melitha.

Hollie wasn't so much of a fan since finding out the woman behind Melitha – one of her favourite characters – was a crazed sociopath with a vendetta against her best friend, but she appreciated the gesture all the same. It wasn't Liam's fault his costar was a lunatic.

The black and green tote bag was filled with *Highwater* goodies: a mug, a colouring book, a t-shirt, a hoody, and a photograph signed by the cast. 'Did everyone *actually* sign this?' Hollie asked, raising an eyebrow accusingly. After recent events, she was skeptical.

'Some of us did,' said Liam, looking away from the camera.

'What does that mean?' said Fayth.

'I may have faked one or two,' mumbled Liam.

'That's two lies in one conversation. There was me thinking you were a good guy,' said Hollie.

'I am!' said Liam. 'But I couldn't get hold of everyone.' And probably didn't want to get hold of Trinity. 'I've seen everyone's signatures enough times to know how to copy them.' He'd designed the *Back to the Future* tattoo on Astin's shoulder blade – so it was no surprise that he could fake signatures. Still. Shattered illusions, much?

One last present lay over the arm of the chair in a white garment bag. The one from Tate. Hollie unzipped the bag, unsure of what she'd find inside. Sequined geometric patterns glistened against black fabric as she held it up to the light. A flapper dress. Perfect for a modern-day speakeasy.

'That's so pretty!' said Fayth.

Hollie glanced at Astin.

'I may have mentioned where I planned to take you and asked what kind of outfit she'd recommend,' he said. 'She picked good, you've got to give her that.'

After a romantic afternoon walking around London they headed back to get ready for The Candlelight Club. Hollie changed into the dress Tate had given her, while Astin changed into a navy suit complete with waistcoat and bowtie. He spiked his hair up, while Hollie straightened hers and added a fascinator she'd found in a vintage shop on their walkabouts.

'Where is this club anyway?' asked Hollie as she applied her crimson lipstick.

'Somewhere in London,' he replied. 'It changes venue, just like a real speakeasy.'

'That's so cool!' said Hollie.

Astin smiled. 'Thought you'd like it. Ready to go?'

'Yep.' She put the lid on her lipstick and shoved it into her clutch.

They grabbed a taxi and it dropped them off somewhere in London. A bearded man in a suit stood outside the door, a clipboard in hand.

Astin gave him their names. The man flicked through the guest list then ticked them off. 'Welcome to The Candlelight Club,' he said, holding open the door for them.

Astin gestured to the bar. 'Drink?'

'Yeah,' she said, gazing around the room. Everyone around them was dressed in 1920s-inspired outfits. Even the bartenders and staff were dressed up to fit the theme. It was like they'd hopped into Astin's DeLorean and travelled back to the roaring '20s.

They got some drinks then found a seat and listened to the band. All around them people danced and talked and ate. Hollie tapped her foot to the music.

'Want to dance?' asked Astin, gesturing to the dance floor.

'Noooo thank you.'

Astin stood up, holding out his hand. 'Come on.'

'I'm really not a dancer,' said Hollie.

'Don't worry,' he said. 'Neither am I.'

He'd done dancing lessons as a kid, and he couldn't dance? Then again, so had she. She'd given up when she'd realised she had zero hand-eye coordination.

Astin grabbed her hand and spun her around. She spun into him then back out again.

'See? You can dance!'

'That's hardly dancing,' said Hollie.

'Sure it is.' He spun her around again.

She followed his lead as they danced, picking up the odd move. The last time she'd attempted dancing was when she was at university and Cameron had dragged her out. That had been at an alternative nightclub that was very, *very* different.

A few feet away, a woman in a lace dress danced with her friends. She checked Astin out every chance she got. Hollie tried to shrug it off, but it bugged her. He was an attractive ex-underwear model. It was inevitable that people recognised him. And checked him out. It seemed to happen so often Astin didn't even notice. He gave her his full attention, his eyes barely leaving her the whole time they danced.

They danced for a little while longer then sat down at their table, ready for food.

Hollie leaned back in her chair and watched the other dancers. Some were good, some were bad, but they were all having fun. No one cared. She liked that.

'Astin! Didn't expect to see you here!'

Hollie turned around. A weedy man with blond, curly hair that reminded her of a poodle stood in front of them. His beige tweed suit washed him out.

'Girlfriend's birthday,' said Astin. 'Hollie, this is Lawrence Roskowski, the director of the movie I'm working on while I'm over here.'

'Nice to meet you,' said Hollie.

'Likewise,' said Lawrence. 'How do you like it here?'

'Yeah, it's good. Our food should be here in a minute,' said Astin. He leaned away from Lawrence and towards Hollie, his expression vacant. Was he trying to give Lawrence the brush-off?

If he was, Lawrence was oblivious. 'Listen, I had an idea for the scene—'

'You should really take that up with Mike, the stunt coordinator, not me,' said Astin.

'Right, right, of course, I just wanted your thoughts. It'll only take a minute.'

If Lawrence noticed how unwelcome he was, he didn't react to it. He continued to talk. Hollie zoned out, watching the people around them. The woman in the lace dress was still checking out at Astin. Hollie wanted to say something, but what could she say? It wasn't like she was outright hitting on him.

Astin couldn't have looked more relieved when their artichoke soup arrived.

'Well,' said Lawrence. 'I'll leave you to your food and see you in a few days.'

'Bye,' said Astin, turning away from him.

Lawrence wandered off towards the bar. There was something about him that reminded her of Nick from *The Great Gatsby*, but she couldn't work out what.

'Ugh,' said Astin. 'That guy just can't take a hint.'

'What do you mean?'

'We're on a date, so he continued to talk to me about work. He just doesn't go away.'

'You could've told him to piss off,' said Hollie. She unfolded her napkin and placed it on her lap.

'As much as I wanted to, I can't say that to my boss. A director gets the final say on a movie set. He could easily replace me with someone else if he wanted to,' said Astin.

'He wouldn't do that,' said Hollie.

'I've seen it happen,' said Astin. 'It's not pretty.'

But it was petty.

'What kind of stunts are you doing anyway?' asked Hollie. They didn't talk about his work much; she was curious.

'A few fight scenes, some parkour, the usual,' said Astin. He dipped his spoon into his soup.

'Parkour?' echoed Hollie.

'Moving from one place to another anyway you can.'

'Now I'm just confused,' said Hollie.

He got out his phone and showed her a video. He started off in the middle floor of a car park. He ran to the edge and jumped off it to the next building. He rolled across the roof, then catapulted himself off the end and onto the next rooftop. None of the rooftops were the same height: some were higher, some lower. He finished the video by swinging from a monkey bar and landing on a patch of grass.

Hollie widened her eyes in horror. 'That looks dangerous.'

He reached over and squeezed her hand. 'Don't worry; I do it all the time.'

She squeezed his hand in return to try and show her support. There'd be safety precautions in place, but still. *Jumping from buildings?* He said it so casually, like he did it all the time. Then again, he was a stunt performer. He *did* do it all the time. And he got paid bloody well for it, too.

That didn't mean she didn't worry, though.

What if something went wrong?

What if something happened to him?

'Hollie? Are you all right? You look pale. Paler than usual,' said Astin.

Hollie shook her head to get her out of her anxiety-induced daze. 'Uh-huh. I'll be fine. I'm just going to powder my nose.'

She disappeared into the toilets to calm herself down. She was supposed to be having fun and enjoying her birthday. Not panicking because Astin was doing what he was paid to do. Most jobs weren't as dangerous as his, but health and safety was a big deal these days. Stunt performers made calculated risks that paid off and looked good on camera. A lot of it was done in studios with lots of padding and CGI anyway. He wouldn't be out doing anything dangerous.

Would he?

She clutched the edge of the sink. She *had* to calm down. What would she do, stop him from doing stunt work? Not likely. It'd be like him asking her to stop making clothes. She couldn't ask that of him. She wouldn't.

Leaving Astin in London the following morning was more painful than leaving him in New York was. She'd known him longer; she was more attached to him. She didn't want to be without him.

But she had to be.

Kind of.

They made plans to meet up in a couple of weeks, when Astin had a day off and Hollie was back in London for Tate's fitting. Knowing that it wouldn't be long before she saw him again helped, but she still ended up crying on the train within seconds of him disappearing out of sight.

It wasn't long before she had a text: *You'd better not be crying x*

She laughed, wiping a tear from her eye.

You know me too well x

Two weeks. It'll be here before
we know it x

Before *we* know it. *We*. Is that how he saw them? As a we? What did that mean? Did that mean they had a future together somehow, somewhere?

She wanted one, of course, but how?

She rested her head on the back of the chair and closed her eyes, twirling the necklace he'd bought her between her fingers. All she saw was Astin. His sparkling blue eyes. His soft, light brown hair. His perfectly toned body. Mmm. She wished she could spend every moment wrapped in his arms, inhaling his scent, caressing his skin. But if she did, she'd never get anything done. She had work to do.

She sat up, took her notebook from her handbag, and carried on writing her business plan.

Six

Liam's second trip to LA was an even bigger waste of time than the first. The films were all big-budget action films with no personality. All the explosions to bring in all the money. That, or cheesy romantic comedies where the heroine had no agency and the male character had no personality. He couldn't wait to get home and curl up in bed with the latest *Superman* comic.

Fayth had texted him to ask how the auditions had gone when he was on his way back. He couldn't be bothered to text back, so he called her instead.

'Hey,' she said, her Scottish accent bringing a smile to his face.

'Hey,' he said.

'How'd it go?'

'Ngh.' He reached his floor and took out his key. Rounding the corner, he realised he didn't need a key. The door was already open. 'What the hell?'

'What's wrong?' said Fayth.

'The door's unlocked.'

'What? Who else has a key?'

'My parents, the security guard, my assistant. That's it.'

'Go get the security guard.'

'No, it's fine,' said Liam, pushing the door open. It was probably nothing. Just someone doing maintenance.

'Liam, don't. Please,' begged Fayth.

'It's fine,' he repeated. 'Hello?' he called out.

No answer.

His skin prickled. If someone was hiding in his apartment, where would there be? They'd hide in a closet somewhere, or under the bed. He curled his hand into a fist. Someone had been in his home while he was away. His *home*. He placed his bags just outside the door. 'I've gotta go, I need to call the police.'

'Be careful, OK?'

'I will,' he said, hanging up and dialling the police. After calling them, he called Wade.

Then he left. He had to get away. It didn't matter where to. Anywhere that hadn't been broken into. Anywhere his stuff hadn't been damaged by someone he didn't even know. Was someone out to get him? Was he safe out on his own? Would someone try to hurt him in a crowded street?

Would they?

'I've been looking for you for a half-hour!' shouted Thalia.

Liam jumped. Where had she come from?

'Get in!' she instructed, pulling up beside him. He shoved his bags into the back seat and climbed in, then she drove back towards his building. He didn't want to go there. That's why he'd walked off. He shifted in his seat, running his hand through his hair, over his jeans, over his arms. She could take him anywhere. Anywhere but there. But he couldn't tell her he was scared to go back. He couldn't tell anyone.

Wade and the police were already inside when they got back.

Wade greeted them, his expression stern. 'Are you OK?'

'Uh-huh,' said Liam.

'Did you have a look around before you left?' Thalia asked.

He shook his head.

'Fine my ass,' she grumbled, marching off towards the kitchen. Liam and Wade followed. The kitchen looked the same. The sparse dining room hadn't been touched either. His comic book collection was missing from a display cabinet in the study. He doubled over, leaning on a chair for support. That collection was worth a fortune. It'd taken him years to put together.

He stormed into his bedroom. It was carnage. Furniture was scratched and broken. The bed sheets were all over the room. The lamp was smashed. More photos were ruined, some were missing. They were photos from when he was a child, at birthdays and Christmases. Photos of his family, of his closest friends. And they'd been ruined, like they meant nothing at all. He tensed his body, not wanting to show how distraught he was in front of so many people.

'Oh my god,' said Thalia, her hand over her mouth.

What the fuck had the security guard been doing? It was his job to watch the door and the security cameras.

Cameras! Of course! They'd have whomever was responsible on video.

But the damage was already done. They'd not only invaded his space, but his possessions. Some of the photos left behind were damaged beyond repair. And as for his comic book collection…

Nobody could deny this break-in was personal.

Wade took out his phone and left the room, muttering to himself. Thalia put her hand on Liam's shoulder. 'I don't know what to say.'

'There's nothing you can say.' He shook his head, blinking back tears. 'Who would do something like this?'

'A stalker?'

'Is that supposed to be helpful?' said Liam. He stuffed his hands into his pockets. A *stalker*? No. No way. Shit like that didn't happen in real life. Not to him. It happened to other, more famous celebrities.

He shuddered. Did that mean the other people in his life were in danger, too?

A police officer entered, his baby face covered in fine lines that showed he'd seen too much for a young age. 'Hello, my name is Detective Christie. Do you have any idea who would target you like this?'

'No,' said Liam. 'I've only just got in. I was in LA last night.'

'Was the door open when you got home?'

'Yes. There's only me, my parents, my assistant, and the security guard with a key.'

'I see. I'll check to see if the locks have been picked. Has anything been stolen?'

He listed the things he'd noticed missing so far. He hadn't even checked the guest bedrooms yet. What else would be missing?

His phone buzzed. He reached into his pocket. A text from Fayth: *I know I shouldn't worry, but I can't help it. Is everything OK?*

'Could you excuse me a minute please?' he said.

'Sure,' said Detective Christie.

Thalia gave Liam's arm a quick squeeze, then Liam went into the kitchen. Being somewhere that hadn't been touched – as far as he could tell – made him feel calmer. He called Fayth. He didn't speak right away. His whole body shook. He was afraid that if he spoke, his voice would, too.

'Liam?' said Fayth.

'Photos. Again,' he managed to say. 'And my comics. Gone.'

'I'm so sorry,' said Fayth.

He sighed. 'Part of the job, right?'

'It shouldn't be,' said Fayth, her voice filled with disapproval.

'Just because people know your name that doesn't mean they know you, and that definitely doesn't give them a reason to break into your apartment. Ugh. How are you so calm?'

'Shock?' Or fear. Or being a good actor.

'Have you called the police?'

'They're here now. Wade's talking to someone – god knows who – and Thalia is in more of a state than I am.'

'I'm worried about you,' said Fayth.

'I'm fine,' he said, although the more times he said it the less he believed it. 'I'll stay at a hotel tonight.'

'What about your parents?'

'What about them?' If he called his parents they'd only worry. They were neurotic enough already.

'Couldn't you stay with them? Have you spoken to them yet?'

He'd worried them so much over the last few years he wasn't sure he could put them through much more. His mum's hair was already greyer than it should've been at her age; she dyed it chestnut brown to hide it. He was fairly sure his dad did, too.

'You know you have to, right? The press find out everything. They need to hear it from you.'

Goddamnit.

He ran his hand through his hair. 'I'd better call them now, get it over with.'

He hung up, his fingers hovering over the number for his parents' landline. He needed to tell them. But the dressing room break-in had already made them want him to move back in with them. A break-in at his apartment would make them practically beg. But Fayth was right. He needed to be the one to tell them. His hand still shaking, he pressed call. Their housekeeper answered initially, saying that they were busy eating dinner. When he insisted it was an emergency, she sighed, taking the phone into the dining room where they ate, and placing it on speaker.

'Liam? You said it was an emergency?' came his mum's concerned voice down the receiver.

A lump formed in his throat. 'Someone's broken in,' was all he managed to say before he started to choke up. His parents had been through enough, damnit. They didn't need to worry about him any more than they already did.

'To your apartment?' finished his dad.

He nodded, then remembered they couldn't see him. 'Yeah.'

'Did they take anything?' asked his mum.

'Comics. And…they trashed photos.' He hated telling them. He hated hurting them all over again.

'Oh my god,' cried his mum.

'What the hell is wrong with people?' said his dad.

'We'll be right there,' said his mum.

'No, Mom, it's OK. You don't need to.'

'Of course we do. We're your parents.'

Liam's mum engulfed him in a bear hug as soon as she saw him. 'Oh, honey.'

His dad patted him on the back. 'How are you holding up?'

Liam didn't react. The shock and fear hadn't lessened any.

His mum pulled away, cradling his face in her hands. She was almost a foot shorter than him, but she somehow still managed it. 'You'll stay with us tonight. Wade can too, if he wants. Where is that bodyguard of yours?'

'On the verge of getting arrested by the NYPD if he's not careful,' said Liam. Since getting off the phone, Wade had been interrogating the NYPD as if they were the suspects. God help the security guard when he moved on to him.

'I'd better go distract him,' said his dad. 'The last thing we need is your bodyguard behind bars for obstruction.' He patted Liam on the back again, then followed the sound of Wade's booming voice into the dining room.

'How are you really holding up, honey?'

'They trashed my photos. They don't mean anything to anyone but us. Why do it? Why?' His eyes filled with tears. He blinked them away, looking up so that his mum wouldn't see. When they'd broken into his dressing room, he was angry. When they broke into his apartment, he was scared. Seeing his parents, he was wrought with guilt.

'Cry all you want,' she said.

Maybe he wasn't such a great actor after all.

'Come on,' she said, guiding him to the sofa. They sat down. 'We'll find you someplace else right away. I'm not having you stay here another night.'

'This is my home, Mom.'

He had so many memories attached to that place. He didn't want anyone to corrupt it for him. But then, they already had. Not to mention the security staff were useless.

'We'll find you a new home. A safer home. In the meantime,

you can stay with us.'

Moving back in with his parents. Could things get any worse?

Liam sat on his parents' cream sofa surrounded by people: his parents, Wade, Thalia, Ola, and Detective Christie. The walls of their apartment were covered in paintings and sketches, most of them done by his mum, some done by him or his sister. He used to find the paintings homely. Now they made the rooms feel smaller, like the walls were closing in on him.

Thalia had picked Ola up from the airport and filled her in, then taken her straight to his parents' place. She sat beside him; Wade and Thalia stood behind them like a second pair of overprotective parents. His actual parents hovered in the doorway a few feet away. Didn't any of them have better ways to spend their time?

'Have you received any threatening emails recently?' asked Detective Christie. He sat opposite Liam and Ola on an identical cream sofa.

'No,' said Liam.

'Yes,' Ola mumbled.

His mum gasped. His dad rubbed her shoulders. Wade tensed. Thalia remained stoic.

Liam turned his head. 'What?'

'I don't tell you, I just dismiss them. But I file them away just in case.' She stared at her hands in her lap. 'You never know.'

'We'll need to take a look at those, please,' said Detective Christie. He scribbled in his notebook.

'Of course,' said Ola. She took her phone from her pocket and made a note.

'What about phone calls? Have you received any threatening calls, silent calls, anything that's made you uncomfortable?'

'No,' said Liam. He looked to Ola for confirmation.

'No,' she agreed.

Thank fuck.

'What about any negative comments online?'

Liam scoffed. 'Are you kidding? I'm an actor. I get them all the time.' He took his phone out and showed him the lock screen. He had so many new notifications his phone had stopped bothering to display them.

'Are there any you've found that are cause for concern? Any you've had to report?'

'A few,' he said.

'What sort of threats?'

He glanced over at his parents. He didn't want to discuss it in front of them. They had no idea what people said about him online – he shielded them from it as much as he could. All his staff were under strict instructions to only tell them things that were 100% necessary. They didn't need the stress. 'Mom, do you mind—'

'No. I want to hear it,' she said. She folded her arms, tensing her body in preparation.

'Mom, please—'

'No.' She refused to move.

Liam stared into his lap as he spoke. 'Violence, rape, murder. Some of them are pretty graphic. I usually just block the person responsible.'

His mum went into the kitchen.

'Sorry,' said his dad. 'She's just concerned.'

'Understandable,' said Detective Christie. 'But we have to ask.'

'I know,' said his dad. He followed his wife out of the room. He'd talk to them later.

'Are you OK to continue?' asked Detective Christie.

'Yeah,' said Liam. 'Sorry about Mom.'

'Don't worry. Where were we?'

'What about the CCTV?' interrupted Wade.

Detective Christie shifted in his seat. 'I'm afraid it looks like the CCTV in your building is broken.'

'*What?*' chorused Liam, Wade, and Thalia.

The detective sighed. 'We're not sure yet if it was already broken and the burglar knew this, or they were the one to break it.'

Fuck. Fucking fuck. Liam sat on his hands, spending the rest of the interview talking through clenched teeth. Fucking broken. Fucking brilliant.

The theatre hadn't had any either. They couldn't afford it, apparently. There were a few dummy cameras dotted about, but whomever had trashed his dressing room must've known they were fake. Fuck.

When the detective had gone, Wade, Thalia, and Ola hovered around him.

'You know, I don't pay you to babysit me,' said Liam.

'No, you pay me to keep you alive,' said Wade.

'And me to keep you organised,' said Ola.

'And me because you're lazy,' said Thalia.

He laughed. It was good to know that they were on his side, even if they were overprotective.

'Wade is technically a grown-up version of a babysitter,' said Thalia.

Wade cracked his knuckles.

'Enjoy your arthritis when you're older,' said Thalia.

'You know that's a myth, right?' said Ola.

'Shh! He doesn't!' said Thalia.

Seven

After a two-hour train journey where she'd had to listen to screaming babies, the heavy bass booming through the headphones of the person beside her, and the stench of cheese and onion crisps, Hollie desperately needed coffee. If she had to visit London again on her own, she'd suck it up and drive.

She climbed off the train lugging her suitcase in one hand, her sewing machine in the other. Her handbag was draped across her, banging against her hips as she walked.

Tate had said a driver would pick her up at the station. She could not *wait* to sit somewhere quiet.

Right near the train timetable, a man stood with a sign saying *Hollie Baxter* on it. She approached him.

'Miss Baxter,' he said with a smile. He wore a suit – no hat, unfortunately – and had kind green eyes. 'Miss Gardener sent me to collect you and Miss Campbell. Miss Campbell is already in the car. May I take your things?'

'She is?' Hollie's face lit up. Her best friend was nearby. Everything else was already forgot. She handed him her suitcase and sewing machine without hesitation, then followed him back to the car – a Tesla Model S. Tate just couldn't do anything by halves, could she?

She dived on Fayth as soon as the door opened.

'Can't…breathe…' said Fayth.

'Sorry,' said Hollie, letting go.

Fayth handed her a cardboard coffee cup. 'Got you your usual.'

'Bless you,' said Hollie, taking the cup and holding it to her. The aromas of coffee and vanilla filled her nostrils. Her body instantly relaxed.

After placing her bags in the boot, the driver climbed into the front. 'Ready to go?'

'Where are we going?' said Hollie.

'Miss Gardener asked me not to spoil the surprise,' he said

with a smile.

'I really need to tell people how much I hate surprises,' grumbled Fayth.

'Sorry,' said the driver. 'But it's a good one, I promise. We all seat belted?'

Hollie and Fayth put their seat belts on and continued their conversation as the driver took them to their unknown location. Where would someone like Tate stay in London? What was her kind of hotel? The Savoy? The Dorchester? Some small, quiet hotel no one had ever heard of?

Fayth took a few photos along the way, but the weather wasn't great so she didn't bother too much.

'How's the pub?' Hollie asked as they drove past the British Library. It was so much bigger than Hollie could've imagined. Its red bricks and sharp lines contrasted with the ancient treasures hidden within. She'd have to go in if they had time. She and Astin hadn't had chance when they were there before.

'We've had a couple of viewings, but no offers yet. Not that Brooke's complaining,' said Fayth.

'You can't blame people for being cautious the rate pubs are closing,' said Hollie. She sipped her coffee. 'Brooke will understand one day.'

'We hope,' said Fayth.

'She's never known anything different. She's just scared.'

'I guess.' Fayth returned her phone to her bag as they pulled up outside a large, red-brick building. Above the entrance was a sign that said 'Claridge's'.

'Bloody hell,' said Fayth. She leaned over Hollie and stared up at the sign.

'She's got taste, that's for sure,' said Hollie.

'We already knew that from her liking your designs,' said Fayth.

Hollie nudged her.

The driver turned around. 'I'll get your bags taken up to your room. If you go up to reception and introduce yourselves, they'll take you up to Miss Gardener.'

'Thanks,' said Hollie as the passenger door opened.

'Good afternoon,' said one of the porters. He was a middle-aged man in a double-breasted coat and a top hat. 'Would you like me to dispose of your coffee cup?' he offered, gesturing to the cup Hollie had been clutching so tightly she'd forgot about it.

'Yes please,' said Hollie, handing it to him as she stepped out of the car and through the revolving doors. Beside a grand staircase was an ornate glass statute that twinkled in the light. The ceiling was so high it gave Hollie vertigo. Fayth wrapped her arms around herself. She had on boyfriend jeans and a unicorn t-shirt.

'You're fine,' said Hollie, grabbing her arm and leading her to reception. She had on jeans, too, but they were skinny ones teamed with a Guess jumper dress.

'This is like Liam's party all over again,' mumbled Fayth.

'Well if you're going to stay friends with him you'd better get used to being a sore thumb,' said Hollie as they reached reception. She gave their names then they waited as the receptionist rang up to Tate's suite. A few minutes later, a butler came down. He wore a suit, a kind smile on his narrow face. 'Good afternoon Miss Baxter and Miss Campbell. I'm Jamal. If you'd like to follow me, I'll take you up to Miss Gardener.' He guided them to the lift, continuing to talk as he did so. 'If you need anything at all during your stay, big or small, don't hesitate to get in touch.'

'Are you Tate's personal butler?' asked Hollie.

'For the duration of her stay at Claridge's, yes,' he replied. The lift arrived and they stepped inside. Just how much was Tate paying to stay there if she had her own personal butler?

Jamal led them out of the lift and down the corridor. 'Welcome to the Brook Penthouse,' he said, opening the door. They stepped into the most exquisite suite Hollie had ever seen. It was decorated in an art deco style with modern accents: her idea of heaven.

'Hollie! Fayth!' squealed Tate, running to them from the terrace. She placed an arm around each of them, pulling them into a group hug. 'It's so good to see you both!' Her hair had changed again. It was down to her back, with purple tips.

A dog yapped in the corner.

'Moxie! Shush!' said Tate. She pulled away and picked up the tiniest dog Hollie had ever seen. It was black and brown with a button nose and floppy ears.

'She's gorgeous!' said Hollie, reaching out to fuss her.

'Isn't she?' said Tate. 'She's half Yorkshire Terrier, half Maltese.'

'I've seen bigger guinea pigs,' said Fayth. She fussed Moxie too. She couldn't say no to a cute dog.

'I hope your journeys were OK?' said Tate as they continued

to fuss Moxie. The little dog let them, licking their hands to show her approval.

'It could've been worse,' said Hollie. 'I survived the train. We'll say that much.'

'Stop being such a drama queen,' said Fayth.

'Me? Never,' said Hollie.

'You two are so much fun! Come on, Cami and I are just having drinks on the terrace,' said Tate.

'In this weather?' said Hollie. The sun was just about out. It wasn't exactly warm.

'Cami?' said Fayth.

'Camilla Persia. She's my support act on the European leg of the tour.'

Camilla Persia was a former Disney starlet that was trying to shed her innocent Disney starlet image. Her approach included dying her hair every colour of the rainbow and getting her breasts out on camera a lot.

'Cami, this is Hollie and Fayth,' said Tate as they stepped out on to the terrace. Camilla sat on one of the cream cushioned chairs, her elbows resting on the glass table as she flicked through things on her phone.

Tate put Moxie on the floor. The tiny dog curled up on a blanket in the corner. 'Hollie's the one designing my outfit for *Comet*, and Fayth is her best friend. Her family own a pub in Scotland.'

'Good to meet you,' said Camilla in a deep, husky voice that sounded like she'd been a chain smoker since she was two. Her current hairstyle was a bleach blonde pixie crop that contrasted with her olive skin.

'How are you finding the tour so far?' asked Hollie, sitting beside her. Fayth took the chair to Hollie's right, and Tate took the one one the other side of Fayth.

'It's incredible,' said Camilla, pulling the blanket she was wrapped in over her shoulders. 'I've never experienced anything like it. Tate's fans are crazy!'

'They're not nearly as crazy as your fans!' said Tate. 'I haven't had dirty underwear thrown onstage!'

Hollie wrinkled her nose. Fayth frowned.

'Yeah. That was gross,' said Camilla with a shudder. 'Can we get some more wine please Jamal?'

Hollie looked around. Jamal had appeared on the terrace without making a sound. He stood by the door, his hands behind his back, staring into nothingness.

'Certainly. Can I get anyone anything else?'

The other three declined, so Jamal left to get some more wine.

'That's pretty creepy,' said Hollie.

'What is?' said Camilla, taking a strawberry from the fruit bowl on the table and examining it.

'Him just standing there. Don't you worry about him eavesdropping?' said Hollie.

'We don't talk about anything private when he's around. It's nice after a long day to come back and know that there's a bath and a glass of champagne waiting for you,' said Tate.

Deciding the strawberry was up to her standards, Camilla popped it into her mouth.

'He does what?' said Fayth.

'Fayth's ex never even turned the shower on for her,' said Hollie with a snigger.

'He did too,' said Fayth. 'He tried to run me a bath once, but we'd ran out of bubble bath. He ended up using tea tree and peppermint shower gel. The smell was enough to make your eyes water.'

'Sounds like heaven to me,' said Hollie.

'Me too,' said Camilla.

Tate shook her head. 'I don't get the obsession with peppermint. It's way too strong.'

'I don't get *your* obsession with jasmine. It's so *boring*,' said Camilla.

There was something about Camilla that reminded Hollie of Trinity. She couldn't quite put her finger on what.

'Speaking of boring,' said Tate, 'how's things with whatshisface?'

Camilla rolled her eyes. 'He's not *that* boring.'

'Who?' said Hollie.

'Ethan Howard,' said Tate.

'From HATT?' said Hollie.

'That's the one,' said Tate. 'He and Camilla have been hanging out for months.'

HATT were a boyband that had been manufactured by a TV talent show Hollie couldn't remember the name of. The band had originally consisted of five members: Ethan Howard, Luke Andrews, Sebastian Taylor, Kai Turay, and Greg Hauer. To the dismay of fans, Greg had left a couple of years earlier. To the delight of their record label, the band had sold even more records since he'd left. Greg's solo outing hadn't been so successful.

'What's wrong with that?' said Fayth.

'Nothing, he's just so different to her usual type!' said Tate.

'I like how quiet he is,' said Camilla. 'It's refreshing.' She popped another strawberry into her mouth. 'How are things with you and Jack, anyway?'

Tate looked over at Jamal. He stood as he had before. There were no indicators that he was listening, but his face was so devoid of expressions it was impossible to tell. 'Jamal, could you get us some more fruit please?'

He nodded, then disappeared.

'He's gone off the deep end again. Astin and I don't know what to do. He's on his own in New York right now. I dread to think what state the apartment will be in when Astin gets home in a few weeks.'

Hollie smiled at the mention of her boyfriend. She'd get to see him in just over 24 hours. She couldn't wait. In the meantime, she got to hang out with Fayth, and talk fashion with Tate and Camilla. Things were *good*.

'I don't get why you keep going back to him,' said Camilla. 'He's so bad for you.'

Tate sighed. 'I ask myself that everyday.'

Eight

Tate checked the time on her phone. 'The car will be here for Cami and me in an hour. We should get the fitting done now.'

Her final show at the O2 was in a few hours' time, so if they wanted to get the fitting done beforehand, their window was growing ever-shorter. Hollie had hoped they could put off the fitting until the following morning, or maybe even the twelfth of never.

Apparently not.

Hollie tensed. Tate liked the design on paper. Seeing it in real life was very, *very* different.

'I'll stay here, take advantage of the weather while it's nice,' said Fayth.

'You call *this* nice?' said Camilla. Surely if she was cold she could go inside, instead of sitting on the terrace in a blanket?

Some of the clouds had subsided, but it was far from a summer's day. It was barely even a spring day, despite it being the end of March.

'I'm from Scotland. If it's in double figures and the sun comes out, people start walking around in shorts and flip flops.'

Camilla wrinkled her nose. 'Scots are weird.'

'You should check out the English,' said Fayth, flashing Hollie a wry smile.

'I'm just going to ignore that,' said Hollie, standing up. 'See you in a bit.'

'Laters,' said Camilla.

Moxie followed Hollie and Tate back into the living area. Hollie's suitcase and sewing machine sat near the door.

'Where's Fayth's bags?'

'In your suite just down the corridor. They brought your things in to make the fitting easier,' said Tate. 'They'll move them across when we're done.'

'Oh. OK.' Hollie opened her suitcase and took out the garment bag containing Tate's outfit and handbag. Her chest tightened as Tate led her into the bedroom and she hung the bag up, ready to start the fitting.

'I can't wait to see it!' said Tate.

Hollie's shaking hand hovered over the zip. She was excited for Tate to see it, but also terrified. She knew Tate would like the bag – she'd asked her to make it after seeing Hollie's black version in New York – but what about the jumpsuit? That was what really mattered.

She passed Tate the handbag. It was black with plaid lining, just how Tate had requested it. She was also making one for Tate's assistant Maddy, but she hadn't finished it yet.

Tate unzipped the bag, studying each of the pockets. She grinned. 'It's the perfect size!' She hugged it.

Barely able to breathe, Hollie lifted out the jumpsuit.

Tate put her hands together and beamed. 'I love it!' She put the bag down then took the jumpsuit from Hollie and held it up. 'I adore the colour.' She moved it around so that the fabric shimmered in the light.

'Thanks,' said Hollie, her eyes on the pink carpet.

'I'll go put it on,' said Tate. She disappeared into the bathroom. Hollie sunk on to the edge of the bed. Her chest was tight. Tate was helping her achieve her dream, but that didn't make it any less terrifying. She was just as afraid of achieving her dreams as she was of failing at them.

Tate emerged from the bathroom looking every bit the goddess. The jumpsuit fitted her almost perfectly, but there were a couple of places where it needed to be taken in.

'What do you think?' Hollie asked, her voice shaking.

Tate approached a mirror in the corner of the room and twirled. 'It catches the light so well!'

'It just needs taking in in a couple of places,' said Hollie, fishing in her handbag for a box of pins.

'Yeah, it could do with being a bit tighter on the waist,' agreed Tate, pinching the fabric at the back so that it clung to her more tightly. 'But it's not much.'

'No, but it'll make all the difference,' said Hollie.

Tate pulled the jumpsuit off and began to turn it inside out. Tate had no bra on and a skimpy pair of knickers. Hollie averted her gaze. Oh, to be that comfortable with your body.

'So how are things with Astin?' asked Tate as she pulled the inside-out jumpsuit back on.

Hollie smiled. It wouldn't be long until she saw him again.

The outfit would hopefully be done by then and she could relax for a few hours.

'I know that look,' said Tate. 'The Honeymoon Period.'

'Is that what this is?' said Hollie, sticking a pin into the side seam.

'The cutesy looks, not being able to stop thinking about each other, your heart doing that flippy thing when you see them… yep. The Honeymoon Period.'

'How long does it last?'

'It varies. Jack and I lasted about a week.' Tate and Jack had dated on and off for years. They'd always seemed good together, but then, so had Liam and Trinity, and Trinity had turned out to be completely unhinged.

'Really?'

'Jack's different, though. He's more high maintenance than me.'

'You're not high maintenance,' said Hollie, sticking another pin in.

Tate giggled. 'Thanks, but we both know I am. There's nothing low maintenance about the kind of lifestyle I lead. I wake up in one continent and fall asleep in another. It's not an easy life for anyone.'

'Then how do you manage relationships?' asked Hollie. There was every chance she and Astin would end up in that kind of relationship. As a stunt performer, he regularly travelled all over the world. He was based in New York, but he didn't spend that much time there.

Tate shifted her weight from her right foot to her left. 'It's different for everyone. Jack and I have way more baggage than you and Astin. Things'll be different for you two.'

Would they?

It was a late night. Not because they'd gone out, but because after Tate's concert they'd stayed up late watching *Gilmore Girls*. Camilla drank a lot of wine. The rest of them stuck to camomile tea. Hollie was reluctant to try it, but she didn't want to seem rude. It turned out to she didn't mind it so much.

She wasn't sure what time they went to bed. She and Fayth had crept down the corridor to their suite then crashed out a few minutes later. The moon was still out when Hollie woke up. There was work to be done. She could sleep when it was finished.

Lugging her sewing machine on the train hadn't been easy,

but it was worth it. It meant she could finalise Tate's outfit while she was with Tate, then move on to her next project. She could've finished it by hand, but her hands were too shaky and she wanted a clean finish. She settled in just after sunrise.

Hollie finished tightening the waist on Tate's outfit and smiled. Her masterpiece was – wait. The thread wasn't supposed have loops in. She cut the thread off. Somewhere, something had gone wrong. Instead of neat, flat lines, the lines were messy and tangled. The machine must've been knocked at some point on the train and thrown the thread tension off. Ugh. She needed to unpick it all and risk damaging the fabric. Bloody brilliant. But she couldn't give it to Tate in the state it was in. So she put her headphones in, turned up No Doubt, and began the arduous task of unpicking the waist. It took her nearly half an hour, but when she was done, the fabric wasn't as damaged as she'd feared. So long as the thread played nicely second time around, the outfit would be fine.

She rethreaded the needle and adjusted the thread tension, then began to resew the waistline again. When she'd finished, it looked even worse than before.

'No!' cried Hollie. 'Shit!' She slumped back in her chair.

Fayth ran in, her hair sticking up at odd angles and her Wonder Woman pyjamas crinkled. 'What's wrong? What happened?'

Hollie held up Tate's outfit and pointed to the ruined waistline.

'Can you unpick it?' asked Fayth.

'I already have once. Bastard thing.' She slammed the lid of the machine and switched it off. 'It's going to ruin the fabric if I'm not careful.'

'So what are you going to do?'

'Sew it by hand, I guess.' She reached for the unpicker and began to undo the mess the sewing machine had created. Again. 'You should go back to bed; it's still early. Sorry I woke you.'

Fayth yawned. 'It's fine. I usually get woken up by barking dogs or cockerels.'

There was a knock at the door. Yawning again, Fayth answered. Tate burst into the room, her face red and blotchy. Hollie dropped her sewing things and ran over to her. Tate curled into her arms and sobbed. 'What's happened? What's wrong?' asked Hollie, exchanging a worried look with Fayth.

Tate looked up from Hollie's shoulder. Her pyjama top was

soaked with tears. Hollie pulled the wet cotton away from her skin.

'It's Astin.' Tate took a few deep breaths. What about Astin? What had happened? 'There w-was an accident on the film set. He's in the hospital.'

Hollie's legs buckled. She clutched the back of the sofa for support.

No. He couldn't be. She was supposed to see him in a few hours' time. He had the day off! 'What happened?'

Tate began walking in circles around the room. 'One of his stunts went wrong and he fell into a camera crane. They've taken him in for surgery. Something to do with his spine.'

'What? Right now?' Hollie's eyes welled with tears. What if he didn't make it through the surgery? She'd never see him again! She'd never see that cheeky smile, or feel his warm skin against hers, or taste his peppermint breath…

She couldn't breathe.

Spinal surgery meant all sorts of crazy damage to his back. He could lose his ability to walk. Or talk. Or function at all. What did that mean for him? For *them*?

Tate stopped pacing and leaned against the back of the sofa beside Hollie. Her voice broke as she spoke. 'Mike said he – he kept drifting in and out of consciousness as they waited for the ambulance. Apparently all he managed to say was your name and Cooper's. Mike promised him he'd contact you both.'

A lump formed in Hollie's throat. He'd been thinking about her, even as he was practically unconscious. Had his life flashed before his eyes? What had he thought about?

Fayth gave Hollie's shoulder a reassuring squeeze. 'He'll be OK, Bea. No one's as tough as he is.'

Tate broke down into sobs again. Hollie hugged her.

They had to get to the hospital.

What had she taken with her when Nan was admitted?

Phone.

She saw Astin being lifted into an ambulance.

Purse.

Astin lying on a hospital bed.

Tissues.

Astin being sedated.

Keycard.

A nurse handing the surgeon a scalpel.

Drink.

The surgeon slicing Astin open.
Snacks.
His eyeballs moving underneath his eyelids.
Book.
An ECG monitor flatlining.

Nine

Hollie, Fayth, and Tate arrived at the hospital as Astin came out of surgery. There'd been a delay between the accident and them being told. Lawrence had wanted to wait to pass on the message, apparently. No one knew why. Mike, the head stunt-coordinator, had gone behind his back and contacted Tate's dad, who was a producer on the film but in New York at the time. Nobody had any contact details for Hollie, so contacting Tate was the only way they could think of to get hold of her.

They couldn't see him while he was in recovery, so the three of them headed to the cafeteria. Fayth guzzled her food, but Hollie and Tate mostly played with theirs.

'How long do you think it'll take him to come round from the anaesthesia?' asked Tate, stirring her fruit salad with a spork.

Hollie drew a heart in her scrambled eggs on toast, then cut through it with her knife. 'A couple of hours. They'll want to keep an eye on him once he starts to come round. Just in case.' Just in case something went wrong. Just in case he reacted badly to the anaesthesia. There were too many *just in cases* to comprehend. He was in the safest place, and that was all she had to cling to. Unfortunately, she had little faith in the medical profession. It was as much guesswork as it was science. At the end of the day, Astin's recovery would be down to him as much as the doctors and nurses.

They finished their food, grabbed some supplies from the shop, then headed to the ward where Astin would be staying. The nurses allowed them to wait in the communal area for him after they'd quizzed Tate about her tour and various other things. Every so often Fayth would put her arm around Hollie and try to reassure her, but it did little to make her feel better. The only thing that would was seeing Astin. But what kind of state would he be in?

The rooms off the main reception were filled with people hooked up to monitors that flashed and beeped to say that they were still alive. How many would Astin be hooked up to? Was the damage permanent? They had no idea how bad his injuries were. It being a short surgery didn't mean it wasn't serious. Short surgeries could be just as risky as longer ones.

Hollie excused herself and went to the toilet, locking herself in as she began to cry. How could he have been so stupid? He was supposed to be the responsible one! Responsible people didn't get into accidents. Their risks didn't backfire, they were based on logic and reason. They weren't meant to make them need surgery.

Tears streamed down her cheeks. It felt like someone had wrapped a rope around her windpipe. She squeezed her eyes shut as the invisible rope tightened. Her breathing was rapid and heavy and the room spun when she opened her eyes. She lowered herself onto the floor and hugged her knees. He'd come out of surgery. That was good. But what if the surgery had gone wrong? What if they missed something? What if there were side effects?

She opened her mouth, gulping in the stale, urine-scented air. God, she hated hospital toilets.

She curled her hands into fists and buried her head into her knees. Her nails indented her palms. She needed to stay positive. How could she expect Astin to stay positive if she couldn't? He needed her. That was all that mattered. She had to stay strong. For Astin.

'Hollie?' Fayth knocked on the toilet door. 'He's back.'

'Thanks. I'll be out in a minute,' said Hollie. She wasn't sure if it was obvious in her voice that she'd been crying. If it wasn't from her voice, it would be from the redness in her eyes. She washed her face, then held a couple of cold coins to her eyes to try and disguise their puffiness. After a top-up of mascara and eyeliner, she straightened herself up. She couldn't hog the bathroom much longer. Patients might actually need it.

She opened the door.

Astin's room was just around the corner. Fayth and Tate were already inside. Hollie hovered just outside the doorway, still shaking. She couldn't go in like that. It wouldn't help Astin. She dug into her handbag and took out a Dairy Milk. Just what she needed. She hurried to unwrap it and bite into it. The sweet, sugary chocolate melted on her tongue and offered her some instant comfort.

Fayth came out. When she noticed Hollie, she frowned. 'Why are you out here?'

'Just having some chocolate,' she said, holding up the bar. She'd almost finished it. 'How is he?'

'See for yourself,' said Fayth, jerking her head in the direction of the door. Tate walked out from Astin's room and gave Hollie a small smile. She gave her a quick hug, then she and Fayth sat down. Fayth took out her Kindle, while Tate picked out a Tess Gerritsen book from the handbag Hollie had made her. They were giving them some space. What did that mean?

She inhaled the smell of disinfectant. She'd seen bad before – her nan after a heart attack, and after a stroke – but with Astin it was different. Her nan was an octogenarian whose body was slowly turning against her. Astin was a perfectly healthy twenty-three-year-old who'd been in a preventable accident.

She stepped into the room. An ECG monitor stood near the bed, beeping. A walking frame was in the far corner, near the ensuite. Astin lay flat on the bed with his eyes closed and the blanket around his waist. The his upper body was attached to some sort of medieval torture device so that he couldn't move. A black strap was fastened around his forehead, which was attached to a plastic collar supporting his chin. An n-shaped piece of plastic disappeared underneath his hospital gown. His right arm and hand were wrapped in a cast. His face was covered in cuts and bruises.

At the sound of her boots clicking against the lino, he opened his eyes. 'Hollie?' He picked up a hand mirror from beside him on the bed and pointed it at her.

He looked so fragile. He wasn't meant to look fragile. He was meant to be the strong one, physically and mentally.

'How did you know it was me?'

'Recognised the sound of your walking. This wasn't how I planned our lunch date to turn out.'

She gave a small laugh, her eyes filling with tears.

She needed to stay calm, make him believe that seeing him like that didn't bother her. Acting never had been her strong point. Her hands curled into fists inside her skirt pockets, she stepped forwards.

'Hey, come on,' he said. He held out his left hand. Wires jiggled as he moved. A pulse oximeter was attached to his finger, a drip attached to the back of his hand. Hollie shuddered. Needles. She walked around the side of the bed and held his hand, keeping her eyes far, far away from the needle. His skin was raw, especially on his fingers, as if he'd played guitar nonstop for a year.

'Don't worry about me.' He rubbed her hand with his thumb.

'You're in hospital!'

'I'll be fine.'

'Astin!'

He jerked his hand away. Every exposed part of skin she could see was battered or bruised. If he could've turned his head away from her, he probably would've. As it was, he couldn't move his head *at all*.

'I brought you something,' she said, opening her handbag and taking out the bear she'd bought downstairs. It was a mottled brown with a yellow Mohican, somewhere between cute and ugly. And one of the few teddies they'd had in the stupid shop. 'The gifts were crap,' she added, holding it out for him.

He smiled, taking it from her and hugging it. 'I like it. I think I'll call it Hollie, and I'll call you Bear.'

'You're calling a bear with a Mohican Hollie?'

'You don't mind being called Bear?'

'Doesn't bother me.'

'Bear it is.'

'I'd rather you didn't call the teddy Hollie, though,' she said.

'What would you prefer?'

'Adrian?'

'*Adrian?*'

'As in Adrian from No Doubt. He always has crazy hair,' she said.

'Adrian it is,' he said. He held out his arm and gestured for her to come closer. She curled into him. He smelled of blood and disinfectant and body odour.

'I'm sorry,' he said.

'For what?' said Hollie. She put her hand on his shoulder.

'For you having to see me like this.'

'Like what?' She took her hand from his shoulder and held his hand.

He gestured to the head brace with his plaster-covered hand. '*This.*'

'It's better than seeing you in a coffin,' she said. Something flickered in his eyes, as if he disagreed with her. Did he?

'Don't worry about me,' said Astin. 'You should go finish Tate's outfit.'

'Are you kidding me?' she said.

'I don't want y'all making a big deal out of this.'

'It *is* a big deal, Astin! We want to be here for you.'

'Y'all don't need to be.'

Hollie sighed. 'Like it or not, I'm here, and I'm here for you. We all are.' She rubbed the chapped and bruised skin of his hand. 'Do I like seeing you like this? No. But I'm not going to run in the opposite direction because of a few cuts and bruises.'

Astin squeezed his eyes shut. 'This isn't "a few cuts and bruises", Hollie. I can't go to the bathroom on my own. I can't walk. I can't even sit up.'

'I don't care. I'm not going anywhere.' She folded her arms.

'What, you're just going to stay and look after me?'

'Why is that so crazy? I'm your girlfriend. It's my job!'

'No it's not! Your job is your fashion line!'

'And I can still do that while looking after you,' said Hollie.

'No.'

'Fine. Get a carer. But what will you do when they're not there?'

'I'll get a live-in carer!'

Stubborn git.

'What if I dumped you?' he said.

What?

What?

Her body shook as she started crying. What the actual fuck did he think he was doing?

'Don't do that,' pleaded Astin. He held out Adrian and waved it around a few times. 'I'm sorry. I shouldn't have said that.'

'Damn right you shouldn't have,' she said with another sniffle. She took Adrian from him and hugged it. 'I'm here for you, whatever you need. The line can wait.'

'Hollie—'

'No, Astin. You come first.'

He closed his eyes and sighed.

How many drugs was he on if he thought she'd just up and leave him because he was in a wheelchair? She'd grown up with someone in a wheelchair. She'd cared for someone in a wheelchair. So what if he was in a wheelchair for the rest of his life? It was his heart and mind that mattered, not his body. If stunt work had done this to him, it was a good thing if he couldn't do it any more. At least then he'd be safe.

'Thank you,' he finally said.

She nodded, although she wasn't sure if he could see her. Hopefully he couldn't. That way, he wouldn't be able to see how hard she was crying.

Fayth clutched her Kindle. She was glad Hollie had suggested she take it with her. What else was she supposed to do? Tate kept running off to make phone calls, and she wanted to give Hollie and Astin some privacy, so she was on her own. In a hospital. She hated hospitals. They reminded her too much of…things.

Where was Liam when she needed him?

She chanced a look away from her Kindle. The entrance to the main men's ward was directly in front of her. Most of the patients looked significantly older than Astin. Was that why he had his own room, or was it because someone had requested it? Who knew when Hollywood was involved?

There were so many people within those walls in wheelchairs, on gurneys, who didn't get special treatment but were unable to move for themselves too. Some unable to think for themselves. Like Mhairi might've been had she survived the car crash. The doctors had said that her brain injuries were so bad that it was highly likely she would've needed round-the-clock care if she'd survived. They would've had to sell the pub so that they could afford to care for her, and so that they had the time to do it.

But she hadn't even made it to a ward. She'd been declared dead on arrival. Her mum was declared dead at the scene.

She huffed. Astin was different. Not every hospital trip ended in death. She had to remember that. If not for her, then for Hollie and Astin. The last thing they needed was for her to fall apart because they were in hospital.

'It's such a shame, a kid so young having his career end like that,' said a nurse sat at the reception desk a few feet away. She looked to be in her mid-fifties, with salt-and-pepper hair and bushy eyebrows.

'He's the same age as me,' said her colleague.

'And you're a baby,' said the nurse.

Fayth stifled a laugh.

The younger one rolled her eyes.

'At least it's only a C3 fracture. He may not be able to do stunt work again, but at least he'll be able to walk again,' said the older one.

'But he can't even sit up! Can you imagine how frustrating

that must be for a stunt performer that used to be a model? He needs his body to work.'

Shit. He hated being recognised for his modelling work.

'He's a model?' said the older one.

'Yeah. He did some Calvin Klein ad with Tate Gardener.'

'Who's Tate Gardener?'

'The blonde that won't sit still.'

'She his girlfriend?'

'I think that's the redhead – she's the one that won't leave his bedside. Tate's more worked up though.'

'These Hollywood types. They just can't handle the stresses of real life,' sighed the older one.

Heels clicked against the lino. The nurses turned to see who was responsible for the noise. When they realised it was Tate – on her way back from her latest phone call – they continued to watch. Typical.

Tate's lips were pouted, her nostrils flared. She looked like an angry child.

'What's wrong?' asked Fayth, her grip still tight on her Kindle.

'I can't get hold of Jack.' She sank into the chair beside Fayth.

'He could be asleep?' offered Fayth.

Tate snorted. 'I doubt it. Something's wrong, I know it. He's been harder and harder to get a hold of lately.'

Fayth didn't know what to say. Jack was an alcoholic and drug addict. There was every chance that something *was* wrong given his history.

'Astin's in the hospital and he won't even answer the fucking phone!'

The two nurses exchanged glances.

'Shh,' said Fayth. She flashed the nurses a smile. They returned to their work. Fayth had no doubt they were eavesdropping.

'Sorry. You're right.' Tate sat up. 'I'll go try him again.' She walked off without waiting to hear Fayth's opinion.

Hollie wanted to ask Astin about what had happened, but she didn't want to upset him. She just had to be there for him and do whatever she could. She grabbed one of the plastic chairs from beside the door and plonked it beside his bed. That way she could hold his hand and he could see her more easily. They talked about nothing in particular. It was almost like when they'd first met. Except with a hospital room as the setting.

To stop herself from asking something that would upset him, she took out Tate's outfit – which she'd carefully folded into a carrier bag – and a needle and thread, and began to fix the waistline by hand.

'What're you doing?' Astin asked, pointing the mirror at her.

'Bastard sewing machine ate the fabric,' she grumbled.

'What's wrong with it?'

'If I knew that I wouldn't be bringing in the waist by hand,' she sighed. It was only a few inches so it wouldn't take long. But she had to do it neatly. The bright, incriminating hospital lighting made it easy. She could see the holes left in the fabric from unpicking, so she passed the thread through them again so as not to create any more holes.

'That'll take forever,' said Astin.

'Not that long, and I don't have a choice so I may as well get on with it.'

He left the mirror pointed in her direction, but didn't say any more. She hated people watching her as she sewed – it put her off. But she couldn't say no to him. Not after what he'd been through. And it wasn't like he had any other way to entertain himself. She focused on putting the needle through the fabric, not his gaze on her. And finally, she was done. She lay back in her chair and smiled.

'Done?' said Astin.

'Done,' said Hollie. She tied off the thread then folded the outfit back up and put it into her bag. 'I'll have to take my machine to be serviced. It's bloody brilliant timing.' Stupid piece of shit. 'Coffee. I need coffee. You want anything?'

'Usual,' he mumbled before closing his eyes.

She left him to sleep and went outside to where Fayth sat, still reading on her Kindle.

'I'm going to go get some drinks, you want anything?' said Hollie.

'I'll go,' said Fayth. She stood up and stretched. 'I can't sit any longer. What do you want?'

'Astin wants a macchiato and I need a vanilla latte. Where's Tate?'

'Communal area, I think. She's been up and down like a yoyo since we got here. Keeps going off to make phone calls.'

They found her talking on the phone in the communal area,

walking in circles around the sofas and chairs and tables.

'Just get here, Liam. It's bad. It's really bad,' said Tate. She dabbed at the edges of her eyes with her fist.

Fayth smiled.

How much longer would she keep denying she liked Liam?

'All right. I'll see you later.' She hung up. 'Ladies!' Tate jumped, wiping at her eyes again. 'I didn't see you there.'

'Going on a coffee run,' said Fayth. 'You want anything?'

'Can I get a half caf extra hot hazelnut latte with coconut milk please?' said Tate. She shoved her phone back into her handbag.

Fayth stared at her. 'Pardon?'

Hollie giggled.

'A half caf extra hot hazelnut latte with coconut milk,' Tate repeated.

Fayth shook her head. 'Why am I surrounded by obnoxious coffee drinkers?'

'You drink tea. Everything seems obnoxious to you,' said Hollie.

'Do they even sell that downstairs?'

'It's a Costa,' said Hollie. It was also right by the entrance, meaning that she could pick Astin something up on her way to visit him each day.

'Of course it is,' said Fayth. 'I'll be back in about a decade. Should take me most of that time to relay Tate's order.'

Tate beamed at her.

Fayth flashed her a deadpan stare then left.

'Is Liam on his way?' asked Hollie.

'Uh-huh.' Her eyes were red from crying. She sank on to one of the sofas by the window.

'Are you all right?' asked Hollie. She joined her on the sofa.

Tate sniffled a few times. She turned to look at Hollie, her head cocked to the side. There was an intense scrutiny to her gaze that made Hollie shuffled away a few inches. 'Why are you so calm?' Tate asked after what felt like an age.

'What do you mean?'

'Your boyfriend is lying in a hospital bed and may never walk again, and you're not even crying!' She took a tissue from her pocket and dabbed at her eyes.

'Why does that mean I have to cry? Not everyone handles things in the same way,' said Hollie.

'But you're so…*calm*!'

'"Calm"? Do you call having a panic attack in the toilets "calm"?'

Tate looked away, her cheeks flushed. Exactly.

'Astin needs me. And with my sewing machine broken, I've had to adjust your outfit by hand. Getting worked up doesn't fix anything. If you want to cry and snap and whatever then knock yourself out, but leave me out of it.' Hollie stormed out of the communal area before Tate could respond. How dare she tell her how to react to Astin's accident?

Hollie brushed herself off, took a few calming breaths, then went into back into Astin's hospital room. He wasn't there.

'He's gone for some more tests,' said one of the nurses on the reception desk.

'Oh. Thanks,' said Hollie. She went into his room anyway, picked up his clipboard, and sent a photo of it to her mum. She'd be able to translate it and let her know what was really going on, no hospital speak required.

Tate appeared in the doorway as Hollie settled into the armchair. 'Have you got a second?'

Yes, she had a second. But she didn't really want to talk to Tate after her accusations. Given that Tate was not only buying her clothes and accessories but also wanted to invest in her company, though, she couldn't ignore her.

Tate closed the door to the little room and sat on one of the plastic chairs. 'I'm sorry. I can't get hold of Jack, and I have to leave tomorrow, and I took it out on you. I've tried calling and calling but his phone has been off all afternoon. What if something's happened to him too?' She took out the tissue from her pocket and dabbed at her eyes. Her make-up was still perfect. 'I don't know how you do it. I envy you.'

Hollie scoffed. 'Don't. I know what I'm doing because I've been here before. Three times. And I don't wish to be here ever again.'

'I'm sorry,' repeated Tate. She held her arms out. 'Do you forgive me?'

Hollie leaned forwards and hugged her. How could she not? Tate was upset that Astin was hurt. Being snappy was acceptable. Kind of.

Ten

When the media found out about Astin's injury, they covered it, but barely. He was a has-been, as far as they were concerned: no longer in the public eye, therefore no longer a person of interest. *However*, they did know that he was still friends with the likes of Liam and Tate. So they camped outside the hospital.

Thankfully for Hollie, nobody knew who she was, so she had little problem making her way through the makeshift camp outside the front of the hospital.

She hurried inside then texted Fayth and Tate to warn them. She may not have been a person of interest, but they most definitely were. After picking up a couple of coffees and a newspaper, she snuck upstairs to see Astin. It was too early for visiting time, but she was desperate to see him. If she was careful, she could sneak past the nurses and into his room. Once the blinds and door were closed, they'd never know.

But stealth was not one of her skills. The Sister on duty caught her. Thankfully, she greeted her with a warm smile and waved her through. Phew.

Hollie had slept so little that night she looked and felt like a zombie, but she didn't care. She needed to see Astin.

He was awake when she walked in, Adrian beside him and the mirror propped up in the teddy bear's arms.

'Morning,' she said, unable to stop herself from smiling at his presence. She kissed his cheek. His skin was rough, his stubble dotted with scabs.

'It's not visiting time yet, is it?'

'No,' said Hollie, not the slightest bit fazed, 'Sister let me through. Got you a coffee and a newspaper. Thought the puzzles would help pass some time.'

'Thanks.'

She put the newspaper on the side then helped him take a few sips of his coffee.

'Is this decaf?'

'Yeah.' She put his macchiato down and picked up her vanilla latte. 'Mine is too. Mum thinks cutting down will help my anxiety.'

'Do you think it will?'

'I hope so,' she said. Her anxiety had been bad enough before Astin's accident. Him being in hospital wasn't doing her already terrified brain any favours.

Her mum had replied to her photo of his notes explaining that he'd fractured a vertebrae in his spine so had to stay on his back and gradually increase his movement. He'd had to go straight into surgery to prevent it from doing serious damage that could've left him paralysed. It had worked. But there was skill a risk of permanent damage if he did too much too soon. Hollie tried not to think about it. If he had to take it easy, surely that meant he couldn't fly back to New York? What would he do instead? Stay and be treated in London, alone? That wasn't fair. The whole situation was so many levels of unfair.

A tall man wearing a black suit and yellow shirt walked into the room as Hollie sat down. His tie had music notes on. 'Good morning,' he said. 'I am Doctor Bengali, but you can call me Ben.' He shook both their hands as the three of them exchanged greetings.

'I'd like to ask you some questions.' He stood to the side of the bed, next to Hollie. Astin angled his mirror so that he could see.

'Sure,' said Astin.

Ben hesitated. His eyes gravitated to Hollie.

Astin held out his hand. She took hold of it and gave it a squeeze. 'She's my girlfriend. She'll be my next of kin while I'm over here,' said Astin.

He was making her his next of kin? What about his parents? What did that *mean*?

'I'll make a note of it on your file,' said Ben. 'How are you feeling this morning?'

'Sore. Lightheaded. Stupid.'

'I see,' said Ben. He didn't react to Astin's bad joke. Instead, he took the clipboard from the end of Astin's bed and scribbling some notes. 'Where are you sore?'

'Everywhere,' said Astin.

Hollie rubbed his hand.

'Is anywhere worse?'

'My back, where I had the surgery.'

'On a scale of one to ten, how would you rate the pain?'

'Seven.'

Hollie cringed. Seven. That was almost as bad as her nan rated her arthritis pain. She regularly rated it at an eight, but refused to go on stronger painkillers. She hoped Astin wouldn't be that strong-willed.

'We'll keep you on the morphine a little longer and see if that helps,' said Ben, scribbling on the clipboard.

'No, it's OK,' said Astin, 'I can handle the pain.'

'Astin,' said Hollie sternly.

He sighed. 'Fine. I'll take it.'

'We'll slowly increase the levels until they help with the pain and go from there,' said Ben. 'Can you just clench and unclench your fists for me please?'

Astin held out his hands and did as instructed. All looked good. Ben scribbled some more notes. He lifted the blanket from Astin's feet. 'Can you wiggle your toes for me please?'

Astin wiggled his toes.

'Good, that's good,' said Ben. He made some more notes, then said, 'I'd like you to do this regularly. We don't know the full extent of your injury yet, so we'll start you off small and build you back up gradually.'

'When will I be able to sit up?' asked Astin.

'We'll see how things go,' said Ben.

Hospital speak for *we don't know*.

He made a few more notes on his clipboard, then said, 'I'd like to arrange for a counsellor to visit.'

Astin scoffed. 'Why?'

'What you've been through is quite traumatic. It will require a lot of adjustments. I think—'

'I don't need a counsellor,' said Astin.

'Hear him out,' said Hollie.

'I'll adapt on my own,' said Astin.

'Very well,' said Ben, his tone neutral. 'If you change your mind let me know.'

'I won't,' said Astin. Idiot.

Ben spent less than ten minutes talking to them. Hollie knew he was busy, but she wished she could dissect his brain somehow, get answers to all her questions. But it was hard. She couldn't verbalise most of the questions running through her head. She was too scared to. Too worried she'd seem paranoid, overprotective. She'd nodded along with everything he'd said, only asking questions when she thought they'd be something that her mum would ask. She'd get her to translate anything that didn't make sense later on.

Once he'd gone, Hollie dumped her things into the cupboard then settled into the armchair.

'What are you doing?' said Astin as she sat down.

She opened her handbag and took out her sketchbook and pencil case. 'Sketching.'

'Shouldn't you be doing that at home?'

'I want to be here for you.' She took out a HB pencil and began to sketch.

'You don't need to be,' he said sternly.

'Yes I do,' she said.

'Why? Why are you so bothered about looking after me?' He angled the mirror towards her.

'Does it matter?'

'Yes!'

She slammed the pencil on to the sketchbook. 'Because I love you!' She clapped her hand to her mouth. Shit. Shit shit shit. Shit. Shit.

'What did you just say?'

She looked anywhere but at him. 'You heard me,' she mumbled. She tucked her legs underneath her, curling into herself.

Astin put the mirror down and held his plastered hand out to her. She took it.

'I couldn't imagine my life without you,' she confessed.

'Neither can I.'

'Then stop trying to push me out. It's not going to work. I know there isn't much I can do, but I want to do what I can. I want to be here for you.'

He stroked her hand with his thumb. 'I love you too. I just don't want to burden you.'

'You're not a burden. Don't you ever think that!' She blinked back tears. She would *not* have him think that about himself.

'God, you're amazing,' he said. 'I love you so much.'

'Do you? Because it doesn't feel like it right now.'

'I'm sorry.' He kissed her hand. His lips were rough and chapped, but the affectionate gesture still sent shivers through her. 'I shouldn't have said what I did yesterday.'

'Damn right you shouldn't have. You scared me.' She looked up at the ceiling in an effort to stop the tears. The last thing he needed was her crying. 'I don't want to live without you.'

'I hate feeling so helpless,' he said.

'Don't you see how lucky you are?' She perched on the edge of the bed, glancing out of the window to make sure no hospital staff were watching. Officially, guests weren't allowed to sit on beds. Health and safety, and all that. But she didn't care. She needed to be closer to him.

'I don't feel it.'

'That accident could've killed you. You could've ended up paralysed. The wheelchair and head brace are only temporary. You'll be out of them in no time.'

He gave a small laugh.

'What?'

'You being the optimist.'

'I don't like it either. You'll just have to rest plenty so that we can get back to normal,' she said.

'But things will never be the same again, will they?'

'You don't know that. You're fit and healthy. There's no reason you can't go back to how things were.'

He sighed, a defeatist look in his eyes that suggested he'd already made his mind up. 'We'll see.'

She squeezed his hand again. She would *not* let him give up.

A short, fuzzy-haired figure walked past the window. Seconds later, Lawrence Roskowski entered the room. His shoulders were slumped, his head bowed. Astin used his spare hand to angle his mirror so that he could see who'd entered. When he saw who it was, his face turned red. His grip on her hand tightened. She placed her other hand on top of his, hoping it offered him a small amount of comfort. Unable to think of anything nice to say, Hollie remained silent. Greeting Lawrence with disdain wouldn't do anyone any favours, much as she wanted to punch him in the face.

Lawrence stepped farther into the room, avoiding eye contact with them both.

'Get out,' said Astin.

'Astin, I—'

'GET OUT!'

Astin cringed, the volume of his voice seeming to have caused him pain. He pulled away from Hollie, his jaw clenched.

A tangible silence hung in the air. She'd never heard him shout like that before. It hurt knowing that he was in so much emotional and physical pain and there was nothing she could do about it.

A nurse appeared just outside the window, eyeing them all. *It's OK* Hollie mimed. The nurse nodded and continued past.

'I think you should go,' she said to Lawrence. She led him out of the room. The nurse that had peered into the window looked up from the desk. Hollie flashed her a downturned smile. It was the best she could do to try and reassure the nurse that everything was fine. Especially since it wasn't.

'He's never going to forgive me, is he?' said Lawrence.

'I don't know,' said Hollie, her voice flat.

Fayth and Tate rounded the corner. A muscular man in jeans and a white t-shirt followed them. Hollie didn't recognise him, but from his size and the way he tagged along, his eyes darting around the room, he looked like a bodyguard. A far less friendly one than Wade.

On sight of Lawrence, Tate stiffened like a meerkat on guard. Her bodyguard stopped too. Fayth kept walking, talking to herself until she realised Tate had stopped. Tate's eyes were filled with more rage and hatred than Hollie had ever thought possible for someone so chirpy.

Her hands curled into fists, Tate approached them, the carrier bag in her hand swinging like a mace. Fayth followed, a look of confusion on her face.

'You should leave,' said Tate monotonously. There was no recognition or emotion in her voice; it was impossible to tell if they'd met before.

'Tate,' said Lawrence. His voice conveyed that did know each other after all.

'Excuse me,' said Tate. She pushed past them and into Astin's room. The bodyguard picked a spot outside Astin's room, folded his arms, and looked straight ahead.

Lawrence sank into one of the chairs outside Astin's room and buried his head in his hands. 'It's all my fault.'

Hollie remained silent. *If you can't say anything nice…*

'I shouldn't have insisted on doing all the stunts outside, or having the camera at that angle, or all the fake rain, or—' He cut himself off, shaking as he sobbed.

Tate had got hold of the dailies through her dad, so she and Hollie had made the bad decision to watch them. The fake rain had made the surfaces so slippery it was impossible for Astin to grip on to anything, and for whatever stupid reason, he hadn't had a harness on. The fear in Astin's face as he realised what was about to happen would always haunt her.

She towered over Lawrence as he stared into his lap.

Fayth stood beside her, her arms crossed.

His hazel eyes, when they finally looked up, were filled with guilt and fear. 'Do you hate me?'

She tensed her jaw.

'Let me have it,' said Lawrence. 'I deserve it.'

Hollie widened her eyes. 'Are you taking the piss? What, you want me to berate you and tell you what an irresponsible, inconsiderate and selfish twat you are to make you feel better? To justify your self-hatred somehow? I've got bigger things to worry about than your pity party. Go find someone who gives a shit.'

Eleven

Lawrence didn't stick around. It was one of the few good things to happen in the last few days. Hollie drifted off to sleep in the armchair. When she woke up, she could hear American accents echoing down the corridor. Tate and her entourage had left that morning for Barcelona, so it wasn't anyone to do with her.

Hollie sat up as a man walked in wearing a Yankees baseball cap, blond bits of hair sticking out the ends. His face was covered by sunglasses.

Hollie studied him. His dress sense – designer shirt and well-fitted jeans – was familiar. And so was the gigantic guy in a suit behind him. Liam took off his baseball cap and sunglasses, and handed them to Wade.

'Sup,' said Wade, shoving Liam's disguise into his pockets.

Hollie got up and hugged Liam, burying herself in his Tommy Hilfiger shirt. 'Are the press still outside?'

Liam rubbed her back. 'Could be worse.'

'Word got out that Tate was here,' said Wade. 'They must've missed the part where she left for Spain.'

'Don't they have anything better to do?' grumbled Hollie.

'Nothing that pays as well,' said Wade cynically.

Hollie let go of Liam and returned to her chair.

'How long's he got to wear that contraption for?' asked Liam. He stepped forwards and studied the contraption around his friend's torso.

'Three months,' mumbled Astin, angling the mirror so that he could see the new arrivals. He squinted, as if he'd just woken up and his eyes hadn't adjusted to the light yet.

'Good to see you, man,' said Liam.

'You look rough,' said Wade.

'You don't look great either,' said Astin. 'Girlfriend been keeping you up?' He glanced to Liam.

Liam rolled his eyes. 'He's in overprotective mode.'

'As he should be,' said Fayth, returning from a coffee run.

She put the drinks on the bedside table and ran over to Liam. She hugged him, her arms tight around him.

When would they get together already? Could they not *see* it?

Hollie put Astin's macchiato on to the table and took the lid off so that it could cool. When it was cool enough, she'd put a straw into it. She took her camomile tea from the holder and sat down beside him.

'It's been weeks. Nothing's happened. You're all overreacting,' said Liam, his arm still around Fayth. *Still.* He reached into his pocket and handed a chocolate bar to Astin. 'Brought you some Hershey's. It might've melted a bit.'

'You brought me Hershey's from the States?'

Astin put down the mirror and held the chocolate bar in his plastered hand, trying to open the wrapper with the other.

'Nah. They sell them in the shop downstairs. Twice the price, though,' said Liam.

The chocolate bar slipped from his hand. Everyone stepped forwards to help, but he brushed them off. Stubborn as ever, he bit into the wrapper and pulled it open with his teeth. He spat out some foil.

'Gee I wonder why,' said Hollie, rolling her eyes. Dairy Milks were better anyway.

'You never know what kind of weirdos are out there,' said Fayth, returning to the previous subject. 'They went after your photos. That's personal.'

Liam cut in before anyone else could respond. 'We're here for Astin right now, not me.'

A nurse came in, her face stern. 'Excuse me, but there are only two guests allowed at the bedside at a – oh my god, are you Liam York?'

Hollie's eyes stung from lack of sleep. Everything around her was blurry or doubled, like she had a terrible hangover. Her head pounded. She yawned.

Astin lay in bed, doing the Metro crossword. Fayth, Liam, and Wade had gone back to the hotel once they'd finally shaken off what seemed to be every staff member in the hospital wanting Liam's autograph. Astin had tried to get her to go with them, but she'd refused. She wasn't ready to leave him yet.

'Hey, what's a synonym for talkative? Nine letters.'

'Loquacious,' said Hollie.

'Thanks.'

'Astin?' said a nurse, poking his head through the door. 'You ready to go?'

'Go? Go where?' said Hollie.

'X-ray. Nothing to worry about, just routine,' replied the nurse.

'Bit late for that, isn't it?' said Hollie.

The nurse shrugged. 'I just do what I'm told.'

He gestured for a porter to help him, and they took the brakes of the bed and began to push him out of the room.

'If my phone rings, can you get it please?' asked Astin as they lowered the bed ready to move it. 'I promised Cooper I'd talk to him when he gets home from school.'

'Will do,' said Hollie. She kissed his hand as he was wheeled away.

And then she was alone.

Hollie leaned back in the armchair and closed her eyes. They didn't like staying open, but her mind didn't want her to sleep, either. It took great pleasure in replaying the clip of a terrified Astin falling on to the camera crane and bouncing off it to the ground.

A phone buzzed from inside the cupboard. She opened it and took out his phone, but didn't recognise the number. It was definitely from the States, but surely if it was Cooper he'd already be in his contacts? But who else could it be? A journalist?

'Hello?' she said.

'Who's this? Where's Astin?' It was Jack.

'It's Hollie.'

'Hollie?'

'His girlfriend,' she said. Idiot.

'Oh. Where's Astin?'

'In hospital. Tate left you a message. Didn't you get it?'

There was a pause. She pictured Jack pacing, trying to remember what was going on.

'Um...I lost my phone. You couldn't pass a message on to someone, could you?'

Hollie sighed. 'To whom?'

'Astin. Or Tate. Or Maddy. Or anyone, really. Not my parents – they're dead, so they can't help – but I'm in jail—'

'*Jail?* What've you done?'

'Nothing. It's fine. Doesn't matter. I've got the bail money, but, you know, can't post it myself. Could you let someone know so that I can get outta here? Usually Astin helps me out.'

'Usually'. So it was a regular occurrence. Why was she not surprised? Could Jack be any more irresponsible? She had the urge not to tell anyone, to teach him a lesson about relying on people and being so bloody irresponsible. But that would be wrong. Not to mention it'd upset Astin. 'Who?'

'Tate. No, Maddy. Tate will go mad. Maddy likes me.'

'Tate and Maddy are in Madrid. They left this morning.'

'But they'll know someone that can help me. They know everyone.' There was a pause. '*Please?*'

Hollie sighed. As if she didn't have enough to do already. 'Fine.'

'Thanks.'

She hung up, then called Maddy using her own phone. She didn't offer any greetings when Maddy picked up, she simply said, 'Jack's in jail.'

'*Again?*' said Maddy.

'Again.'

Maddy exhaled loudly. 'Leave it with me.'

'Thanks. He wasn't keen on telling Tate. He said she'd go mad.'

'Damn right she will. Do you have any idea how many times she's had phone calls from him in the middle of the night about stuff like this?'

She didn't want to. The less she knew about the consequences of Jack's alcoholism and drug taking, the better. How Tate was attracted to someone who was as irresponsible as she was responsible she'd never understand.

'I'll sort it,' said Maddy. 'How's Astin?'

'Stubborn. Stubborn. More stubborn.'

'And his injuries?' said Maddy, laughing.

'Less stubborn, but it's still going to take a while.'

'Tell him we say hi,' said Maddy.

'Will do.'

'Thanks.'

Well, that was that sorted. The rest was up to Maddy.

Astin returned from X-ray not long after Jack had called. He wanted to call him back, but with no way to do so, he had to accept that Jack would be in touch when he was ready.

Hollie had been at the hospital all day. She refused to leave his bedside. He almost expected her to fall asleep there. A part of him wanted her to, but he knew it wouldn't do her any good. She needed her rest – she had a business to set up. That was time-consuming in itself. There was no way she'd have time for him too.

He did his best to hide his fears of losing her when she kissed him goodnight and left for her hotel. The vanilla and blackcurrant from her perfume overshadowed the scent of hospital for just a few minutes. It reminded him of when they'd met in New York. She was already a better, stronger person since then. Would she outgrow him? Would he hold her back?

He closed his eyes and pictured the life they'd had planned: a nice house, a couple of dogs, lots of clothes and gadgets… could they still have that life? It was still too early to tell how much damage had been done to his back. He could spend the rest of his life in a wheelchair. Having to lie on his back without moving for a few weeks was one thing, but being in a wheelchair for the rest of his life? That wasn't what she'd signed up for.

He wiped a tear from his eye with his cast. Cooper was due to video call any minute. He couldn't let his little brother see him like that. He'd hoped to keep it from his family at least until he was out of hospital, but someone – probably Mike, trying to do the right thing – had contacted them. Since finding out, Cooper texted him hourly. If he didn't reply within thirty minutes, Cooper panicked. The time difference made replying within that space of time difficult.

To try and pacify his little brother, Astin got Hollie to charge his tablet and take it in. The wifi signal wasn't great – he was surprised they even had wifi – but if it offered Cooper some solace – and got him to stop texting every hour – he'd do it.

Their mum had already phoned to lecture him on how stupid and irresponsible he was. She wasn't going to visit him, and neither was his dad, meaning that Cooper couldn't either. He spent most of his time with their grandparents anyway – as Astin had – but there was no way their octogenarian grandparents were up to a nine-hour plane ride.

It was late and almost bedtime, but Astin had begged the nurses to let him speak to his brother before bed. He could only speak after a certain time because of school.

'You look horrible!' cried Cooper when they finally connected. Homesickness swept over him at the sound of his brother's voice and thick Texan accent. He didn't miss Texas often, but when he couldn't move or do *anything*, he wanted nothing more than to have his oldest friends and family around him. But they couldn't be.

'I'm fine Coop. Really,' said Astin.

'You don't *look* fine,' said Cooper.

Astin tried to change the angle of the tablet, but the only angle where he could see Cooper was if he held it above his head. He'd have to keep the conversation short. 'Don't worry about me. How's school?'

'School's school. You're in the *hospital*.'

'I'm in good hands,' said Astin.

'But it's the *hospital*.'

'You already said that.'

'I miss you,' said Cooper.

'I'll be fine,' said Astin. He needed to get a t-shirt with *I'm fine* printed on it with the amount he'd said it recently. It could be his new catchphrase.

'I don't like it,' said Cooper, pouting. 'I want to come see you.'

'I'll come visit as soon as I can, all right?' So long as he could avoid his parents in the process.

Cooper perked up a little. 'Promise?'

'I don't know when it'll be.'

'Maybe I could come visit you in the summer,' said Cooper.

'Maybe,' said Astin. He hoped he wouldn't. That was a bad idea. Cooper couldn't see him like that. Cooper needed to see him out on the field playing football or on the court playing basketball or in the gym doing weights. Not in the hospital where the only exercise he was allowed to do was wiggle his toes.

'Hey Astin?' said Cooper.

'Yeah?'

'I'm scared.'

'Why?'

'When Mom told me you'd been in an accident, I thought – I thought—' His eyes filled with tears. Astin wished he could reach through the tablet and hug him. There was nothing worse than seeing his little brother upset.

'I'll be fine,' said Astin. 'Doctor said so himself.' Kind of.

Cooper brightened. 'He did?'

'Yeah. Just a few months relaxing, that's all.'

Cooper smiled.

If only he could convince himself it was that simple.

APRIL

One

'Excuse me, I'm really sorry to interrupt, but I have to ask. You really look like...I mean, are you Ben Barnes?'

Liam stared up at the shaggy-haired man standing before him. Ben Barnes? *Ben freaking Barnes*?

Guy sniggered. The twins, Aly and Ava, looked at each other with *oh no he didn't* expressions. Liam hadn't seen his London friends in over a year so had agreed to go out with them while he was in London, but as he looked at the scruffy man before them asking if he was Ben Barnes, he regretted it.

Was he really that insignificant?

Wade sat at the bar, waiting for Liam to run both hanvds through his hair – the signal he wanted Wade to intervene. Liam gave a small shake of his head. The guy was annoying, but harmless. Wade continued to watch.

Just in case he was recognised by his voice, Liam put on a Scottish accent and replied, 'No, sorry.'

He may not have liked being confused with an English actor, but he didn't want to be recognised for *Highwater* either – he just wanted to enjoy his drinks with his friends in peace.

'Oh. I'm really sorry, I just had to ask. You look so much like him!' He paused awkwardly for a moment, his long, shaggy hair swaying as he rocked on his heels. 'Well I'll leave you to your drinks. Have a good night.'

Once the man had returned to his table just a few feet from Wade, Guy and the twins burst out laughing. Ben Barnes? Was he really irrelevant enough that people didn't even recognise him for being the guy from *Highwater* any more?

'Oh come on, you've got to laugh,' said Guy.

'*Ben Barnes*?' said Liam.

'You do look a little like him,' said Aly.

'It's the hair,' said Ava.

'He doesn't even have hair like me any more!' said Liam.

'No, but he does in *Caspian*,' said Ava.

'He's *so* dreamy in *Caspian*,' said Aly.

Liam glared at them.

'What?' said Aly. 'He is!'

Liam took a large gulp of his Guinness. There was no way out of this one.

'So anyway,' said Ava. 'What's the deal with you and the Scottish chick?'

He nearly choked on his Guinness. He hadn't mentioned Fayth to them, but he figured they'd have heard about her from somewhere – everyone had.

'Fayth? We're just friends,' he said.

'Uh-huh,' said Aly, nodding. 'Looks like it.'

Liam frowned. 'What's that supposed to mean?'

'You look very…*close* in some of the photos of you two together,' said Ava.

He looked to Guy. He shrugged, as if to say *don't look at me, mate*. Some back up he was.

'We're just friends,' Liam repeated.

'Say that one more time and you might just start believing it,' said Ava.

'What have you been smoking?' said Liam.

'Nothing,' said Ava. She glanced at her sister, who giggled. 'Well, maybe the odd joint, but that's besides the point. You're getting very defensive.'

'Because you're annoying me,' said Liam.

'Did you really break up with Trinity because of her?' asked Aly.

'No!' He stood up, leaning over the table. 'Fayth and I are just friends. She had nothing to do with why I dumped Trinity.' Except that Fayth was the one to see Trinity snort coke in his club, which had led to their breakup. But that wasn't why they were asking about her. 'How can you believe that shit?'

He stomped off outside to get some fresh air. The twins were models, and Guy was a photographer. They knew the kind of shit that got printed in the press! They were supposed to know better! How dare they invite him out for drinks then quiz him about his relationships ten minutes in? Fayth was just a friend. Trinity was someone he'd rather forget. She'd caused enough trouble already. No doubt she'd find a way to cause more trouble soon enough. She'd been unusually quiet.

He didn't talk about Trinity much, but their breakup was still a sore subject. How had he not realised how much of an attention-seeker she was? Or how she'd lied to him for most of their relationship about her drug-taking? How was he so naive?

He leaned against the concrete wall and took a few deep breaths. A couple of smokers nearby did a double take, but neither of them approached him. A taxi driver leaned against his vehicle, staring up at the sparkling sky. It was a clear night – or as clear as it could be in London. A handful of stars circled the glowing full moon. The moon. Now there was somewhere he could escape his problems.

He shook his hair. It fell into his eyes like curtains over a window. Fucking thing. He tucked it behind his ear.

'What happened?'

Liam jumped. Wade had appeared beside him and he hadn't even noticed. He leaned against the windowsill beside him, eyeing the taxi driver.

'How long have you been there?'

'Long enough,' said Wade.

Liam stared up at the stars for a few seconds before responding. 'They asked about Fayth. And Trinity.'

'Oh,' said Wade, propping a foot up against the wall.

'I may have overreacted.' He shoved his hands into his pockets, staring at the tarmac.

'"May have"?'

'I lost my temper. But it's none of their business. They actually think I dumped Trinity for Fayth!'

'You make it sound like that would've been a dumb thing to do,' said Wade.

'What?'

'Well, Fayth's a way better person than Trinity will ever be. Nobody that knows you or her would blame you if you had,' said Wade.

'But I didn't!'

'I know, I know. I'm just saying.'

A limo pulled up and a hen party jumped out, screaming and dancing and ready to party. They knew it was meant to be a quiet bar, right?

Liam turned his head away so that his hair covered his face. A screaming hen party was the last group of people he wanted to recognise him.

They carried on inside, oblivious.

Phew.

'Do you want me to make something up and get you out of here?' offered Wade.

'No, it's fine. I need to go apologise.'

The twins hadn't meant any harm, they were just curious. And a little dumb, sometimes. They weren't very good at taking hints. And they *loved* gossip.

'All right. Send me the signal if you change your mind,' said Wade.

After spending a few more minutes inhaling the smoggy air, Liam returned to the table and apologised, while Wade returned to his perch at the bar. Liam didn't explain the full reason he'd overreacted, he just said that his break up with Trinity was still a sore subject. That seemed to be enough to pacify them without feeding their curiosity any further.

'So,' said Liam. 'Who wants shots?'

Liam rubbed his eyes. He hadn't planned to stay out that late. Or to wake up with a hangover. He rolled over in bed and pulled a pillow over his head. The curtains did little to block out the bright, blinding sun.

Wade barged in a few minutes later. He had the spare room key in case anything happened. Bad decision. It wasn't meant to be used for interrupting sleep.

'Go away,' Liam mumbled into the pillow.

'Don't you want breakfast?' said Wade.

'Hell no,' said Liam.

'I'll go tell Hollie and Fayth, then,' said Wade. At the mention of Fayth's name, Liam tensed. What had he told Guy and the twins about Fayth once he'd had some shots – and more Guinness – in him? Had he admitted how he felt about her? He hadn't, had he?

Fuck, he couldn't remember.

Which possibly meant the others didn't either.

Hopefully.

His stomach rumbled.

Something greasy. He needed something greasy.

'McDonald's,' mumbled Liam.

'What was that?' said Wade.
Liam scrunched his eyes and pulled the pillow from his head. 'McDonald's breakfast thing.'
'I'll see what I can do,' said Wade.
Liam pulled the pillow over his head and fell back to sleep.

Two

There were no new updates on Astin's condition, but Tate called to check in daily anyway. Hollie only left his bedside when instructed to by the Sister on duty. Fayth and Liam felt like they were imposing whenever they went to see him, so they stuck to normal visiting times and spent the rest of their time exploring London. A part of Fayth felt like she should go home since she was totally useless in London, but the pub was managing fine without her, and the longer she spent away from it, the less she wanted to be there. She'd also never been to London, and Liam hadn't had much chance to do the tourist thing, so they took advantage of the opportunity.

Wade followed them, as did the odd paparazzo or fan. Liam greeted the fans with warmth and compassion while Fayth slunk into the background beside Wade, wishing she were invisible. He wasn't recognised every time they went out, but it happened most days. Some recognised Fayth as his 'girlfriend', others didn't. She preferred it when they didn't.

Having already visited the most of the art galleries and museums, the Tower of London, and Buckingham Palace, their next stop was the London Eye. Fayth wasn't a huge fan of heights, but her desire to get some shots of London from a height outweighed her fear. What concerned her more was Liam being cornered by a group of fans and not being able to escape. Liam insisted it would be fine and that he had Wade to protect him. And that Wade was good at his job. But the other people on the pod would outnumber them. She'd suggested getting one to themselves, just to be on the safe side, but Liam had refused. He said it was unfair given the amount of people waiting. Fayth gave up arguing, and they were put on a pod with twenty or so others. Everyone's eyes were on the River Thames as the doors closed. Nobody noticed Liam at first. They'd been in the swinging pod for about five minutes when Fayth heard someone say, 'Hey, does that look like Liam York and his girlfriend to you?'

The hairs on the back of her neck pricked up. He'd been spotted. Again. Even with sunglasses on. Then again, his hair was distinct, and so was his voice. She nudged him. Liam nodded. He must've heard too. Wade was a few feet away, half-facing the view and half-facing the crowds.

'ERIC!' cried a little girl. She ran up to Liam and wrapped her arms around him.

Wade ran over, glaring at the mother, who was a few feet away.

'Katy!' called her mum. Katy cowered, letting go and backing up. 'I'm so, *so* sorry.'

Liam flashed her his most charming smile, lifting his sunglasses so that they could see his eyes. 'Don't worry about it.'

'She hasn't learned to differentiate between fiction and reality yet,' said her mum.

Katy tugged on her mum's blouse. 'Mum, it's Eric! He's alive!'

Liam put his finger to his lips and crouched down. 'You can't tell anyone. We don't know how many of Melitha's gang are still out there.'

Katy pretended to zip her mouth shut.

Liam ruffled her hair. Katy giggled.

Fayth stepped forwards. 'Do you want me to take a photo?'

'But what about Melitha's gang?' said Katy.

'We can keep it just between us,' said Liam with a wink.

'OK,' grinned Katy.

The mother took out her camera and handed it to Fayth. It was a simple point-and-click. In bright red. Ugh.

'Liam, if you stand just there,' said Fayth, taking his sunglasses from him and handed them to Wade, then positioning him side-on to the camera. He shook his floppy hair out then pushed it away from his espresso-coloured eyes. Goddamn, he was hot.

Focus. She needed to focus.

'Now you stand like this,' she said to the mum, getting her to stand similar to Liam, 'and you stand in front.' She got the little girl to stand front and centre. The mum put her hand on the girl's shoulder.

'Perfect,' said Fayth. 'Hold it…' She pressed the shutter. Liam twitched. 'One more.' She scowled at him. He gave her an innocent smile. She took another. It seemed to turn out better, but it was hard to tell on the small screen. 'There you go,' she said, returning the camera.

'Thank you!' said Katy, beaming.

Fayth gave a small nod.

'Sorry for disturbing you,' said the mum.

'Don't worry about it,' said Liam. He flashed her a smile again.

Katy ran over to the other side of the pod to look out across London as they reached the top. The pod swung in the breeze.

'That was really sweet of you, Campbell,' said Liam. They found a quiet spot away from the rest of the group. Wade joined them, returning Liam's sunglasses to him. He put them back on.

'That was sweet of *you*,' said Fayth.

Liam clutched the railings. He looked a little…green.

'How's your hangover?' she asked.

'Room's spinning,' said Liam.

'That's hangovers for you,' said Wade.

'Why don't you take something?' suggested Fayth.

'Oh yeah. The press would *love* that. *Ex-Heroin Addict Gets High on London Eye in Front of Child Fan*,' said Liam.

'I was only going to suggest paracetamol,' said Fayth.

'They wouldn't know that. They wouldn't care,' said Liam.

Wade opened his bag and handed Liam a bottle of water. He chugged half of it without stopping.

'Better?' said Wade after Liam had returned the bottle to him.

'A little,' said Liam. He walked into the middle of the pod and sat down on one of the chairs.

'Should we be worried?' asked Fayth. 'I mean, he is…'

'I know,' said Wade. 'Don't worry. I won't let him fall into that trap again. He just got carried away last night, that's all. Don't worry so much, Scot.'

'You still haven't come up with a better nickname for me than "Scot"?'

'Still working on it,' said Wade.

A couple of others asked Liam for photos or autographs on the London Eye, but most people didn't bother with him. Visiting time wasn't long after they got off, so they ordered a taxi ahead of time to take them to the hospital. As they reached the bottom, it was clear to all three of them that a crowd had gathered below. It looked a lot like said crowd had cameras, too. Professional ones.

'How did they find out we were here?' said Fayth.

Wade gave the other London Eye-goers the evil eye. 'It has to be one of them.'

'Could be someone we bought the tickets from,' suggested Fayth.

'It doesn't matter,' said Liam.

'But what do we *do*?' asked Fayth.

'Deal with it,' said Liam.

Fayth snorted. 'You may be used to this, but I'm not. They want my blood just as much as yours. And you can't get away with breaking the camera this time.' The first time the two of them had been assailed by a paparazzo, Liam had broken his camera and Wade had stolen the memory card. He'd said he'd return it once he'd checked it didn't have any photos of Fayth and Liam on it, but Fayth had never asked him if he really had. That had been one paparazzo in a quiet spot of Central Park, though. This was a group of them in a busy part of London.

She unfastened her hair and shook it out. Her hair would offer her a little bit of protection, if not much. Hopefully it would cover Jupiter's great red spot, too, which was in the process of migrating on to her cheek.

Liam ran his hand through his hair. 'I'm sorry. I don't know what to say. We just have to make our way through the crowds to the taxi.'

What a joke. A nice afternoon out had been ruined by someone with a big mouth. And she was stuck. 'How are you so nice to people all the time?'

Liam gave a small laugh. 'It's called acting. Surely you have to be nice to people you don't like all the time at the pub?'

'Sometimes, yeah.'

There *was* the odd regular that she hated and had to pretend to be nice to. Like Patrick's brother, who liked to make jokes about Patrick cheating on her. She still hadn't worked out how she hadn't punched him yet. If she could be nice to him, a bunch of strangers would be easy. Wouldn't it?

'Here.' He took his sunglasses off and handed them to her. 'To protect your eyes from the flash.'

'Thanks.'

Like it or not, through the crowd was the only way to get out of there. When the pod reached the bottom, Wade got off first, then Liam. Fayth curled her hands into fists, then followed.

As soon as they left the safety of the gates, they were blinded by flashing lights. Liam put on his broadest smile, shaking hands and posing for the odd photo. Paparazzi threw questions at him, but he ignored them, focusing on the fans.

Fayth kept her arms folded and her head down. His sunglasses may have protected her from the flashes, but they didn't protect her from self-consciousness.

Someone barged into her as she made her way through the crowds. 'Watch it, bitch,' growled a female voice.

Fayth frowned. There was no need for that.

The woman barged into her again. Fayth turned around. A woman about her height with mousy brown hair was sizing her up. Wade, who'd been herding Liam away from the crowds, stepped in while Liam posed for a selfie. 'Problem?'

The woman looked him up and down. 'No. No problem.' She backed away, then hurried off.

'Thanks,' said Fayth.

Wade leaned in to her and whispered, 'You always get idiots like that. They'd never actually do anything. Come on.' He guided her over to where Liam was then put his hand on Liam's back. 'We'll be late if we don't get going soon.'

'Sorry everyone!' said Liam. He ran his hand through the crowd as they walked off. A few people grabbed it and wouldn't let go, so Wade had to unhinge them. Fayth shuddered.

Some of the crowd of fans and photographers followed them to the waiting taxi. As Fayth, Liam, and Wade climbed in, the crowd swarmed around the black cab. Wade got out and tried to shoo them. The taxi crawled. Wade got back in, but the taxi was still surrounded. Liam continued to smile. Fayth bowed her head, covering her face with her hair and the sunglasses.

Eventually they made it through the crowds and headed towards the hospital. A few paparazzi followed them, joining the dwindling camp outside, but the hospital's security wouldn't let them in.

As they entered the hospital, it was the first time she'd felt calmer and safer inside one than outside of one in months. It was calmer and quieter than the furore outside or at the London Eye. It almost comforted her.

Was that what life was always like for Liam? Was it worse because his apartment had been broken into recently? Were they after the latest piece of gossip, searching for a sign he wasn't handling things so well after all?

'I overheard Astin talking to the doctors yesterday,' said

Liam, snapping her out of her ponderings. Wade walked in front, his back stiff and head jerking about in search of threats.

'What about?' asked Fayth.

'Him leaving. They said he can leave soon, if he has somewhere to go.'

'You mean he can't go back to New York?'

'Doctors said if he does it's at his own risk,' said Liam. There was a sad note to his voice. Fayth understood – it was one thing to have life-changing injuries like that, but to go through it in a different country, away from your friends and family? It was unthinkable.

'So what's he going to do?' asked Fayth.

'I was thinking of organising a hotel for him.'

'When you say "organising"…'

'I mean paying for it until he can go home.'

She stopped walking and placed her hand on his arm. 'You're already paying for Hollie and me to stay here. We should move to a Premier Inn. Save you some money.'

Liam scoffed. 'Money's really not the issue here. Paying for Astin's hotel is the only way I can think of to help.'

'But won't insurance cover it?'

Liam shrugged. 'Something basic, probably. No way am I letting him stay in some dump just because it's all they'll pay out for.'

She doubted Astin would accept his offer without an argument, but something tugged at her heart all the same. Even in the worst circumstances, even when he was unable to look after himself half the time, Liam still put his friends first. She put her arms around him, pulling him into a hug that surprised even her. She was so worried about losing Astin – and losing Hollie if something happened to him – she needed to feel close to someone; to be around someone that understood and cared as deeply as she did. And he did. He understood her more than anyone else ever would.

Liam kissed the top of her head, his arms as tight around her as hers were around him. 'Astin will be OK. Hollie will too.'

'I wish I shared your optimism,' she sighed, her head resting on his shoulder.

'Not every story has an unhappy ending, you know.'

Fayth lifted her head so that she could look at him, but neither of them let go. 'Most of mine do.'

'You're forgetting something,' said Liam.

'I am?'

'This isn't our story. It's Hollie and Astin's. And no matter how bad things get, they're both too stubborn to give up.'

Fayth forced a laugh. She wasn't convinced. She'd seen Hollie give up. A series of little things had led to irreparable damage to her mental health. What damage could Astin's accident do to her?

'They'll be OK, I promise,' said Liam. His arms were still around her. It was as comforting as holding her favourite teddy bear. Oh, how life had been easier when she'd only had her family and a bunch of teddy bears to care for.

'And if they're not?' she asked.

'Then you can blame me. For jinxing it. Feel free to never speak to me again.'

Fayth laughed. That was one thing she'd never be able to do.

Three

Fayth returned to the solitude of her hotel room after visiting Astin. After what had happened at the London Eye, she needed some alone time. She slept for a few hours, then called to check in with things at the pub. Brooke answered almost immediately. 'I get it. Now that you've got your celebrity friends you don't need us any more.'

Fayth stopped pacing and fell back on to the bed. She'd called to check in, not for a lecture. It had only been a couple of weeks. It wasn't *that* long. 'Say the word and I'll come back, you know I will.' She sat on the edge of her bed, conscious of the fact that Liam was the other side of the wall.

'I know you will,' said Brooke, 'but we're fine. Some of my friends from college have been helping out when Ross can't. They love the extra money and free booze.'

'Are you sure? I can come back if you need me to.'

'Sounds more like you *want* to come back,' said Brooke.

Fayth didn't answer. She felt like a spare part in London, but she also felt like if she left, she'd be abandoning Hollie. But then, hadn't she already abandoned her family?

'Hollie needs me,' said Fayth. 'She's got no one else to lean on right now.'

'Your family need you too,' said Brooke.

What did Brooke want her to say? What did she want her to do?

'If you want me to come back, just say so,' said Fayth. She wasn't in the mood for her sister's mind games. 'How did the viewing go this morning?'

'They've not put an offer in, if that's what you're wondering. They did ask where you and Liam were, though.'

'Really?'

'Yep. Ah, the lifestyles of the rich and famous,' said Brooke.

'Tell me about it.'

'I don't need to: you're already living it.'

'No I'm not.'

'Then why were you on the London Eye when you could be helping out here? Astin obviously doesn't need you if you and Liam are gallivanting around London like tourists.'

It hadn't taken the paparazzi long to sell the photos. She was impressed. It wouldn't be long until they were accompanied by comments berating her and Liam for enjoying themselves while Astin was in hospital. One thing she'd begun to learn was that no matter what she did, people were unimpressed.

'I can't spend all day at Astin's bedside, but Hollie needs someone to lean on right now,' said Fayth.

'Uh-huh,' said Brooke. 'Why don't you just admit it? You'd rather spend time with Liam than help your family try and sell the pub.'

'It's not like that!'

'Isn't it?' said Brooke. 'Then what is it like?'

'Don't start, sis,' said Fayth, lying back on the bed.

'Don't start what? Being honest? I'm just saying how it looks.'

'To whom?'

'Everyone! You're picking your pseudo-boyfriend over your family! Who does that!'

Fayth rubbed her face. 'What do you want? For me to drop everything to help with a pub that has caused us nothing but pain for the last year?'

'How do you think the rest of us feel? You're not the only one who thinks of Mum and Mhairi whenever we walk into that place. That doesn't mean you get to run away while the rest of us don't.'

'I'm not running away. I spend more time in that place than you do. Ross needs the money to help with a deposit for his house. He's not complaining.'

'Whatever,' said Brooke.

'I'll talk to you later.' Fayth hung up and covered her face with her arm. She hated ending the conversation that way, but she was done being berated. The locals were more than willing to help out if they needed it. The pub could last a few more days without her. It'd managed when their flight home from New York was cancelled. Wasn't Astin's accident more important?

She grabbed her pyjamas from the end of the bed, put them on the bathroom radiator, and turned on the shower. She needed a long, hot shower, then to curl up in bed with her Kindle.

After removing her clothes, she stepped into the shower and felt the water run over her hair, her face, down her shoulders, across her back and chest, and into the bath. The water was scalding against her skin, but she didn't care. She poured some shampoo into her hands, then rubbed it into her hair. Strands of hair came out as she ran her fingers through it. When she combed through the conditioner, it came out in clumps. She'd had hair come out before in the shower, but never that badly. It was almost as much as she got from the dogs during shedding season.

When she got out, she was reluctant to comb her hair again, but she needed to. It'd end up a frizzy, tangled mess otherwise. It was more likely to behave itself if she combed it when wet. She combed it slowly, afraid more hair would fall out. It did. Her hair was thick, and she had a lot of it, so a few strands falling out wasn't a big deal, but it falling out as much as it had worried her. Was something wrong with her?

'I think I should go home for a few days,' said Fayth over breakfast the following morning. She poured herself some tea from the pot, then poured some into Liam's cup, too. They sat in the foyer and reading room, awaiting breakfast. Fayth had ordered eggs Benedict, while Liam had gone for pancakes. Hollie still hadn't emerged.

'Is everything all right?' said Liam.

Fayth sighed. She leaned back in her chair, staring up at the ornate lighting feature above their heads. It looked like a cross between a Christmas tree and Medusa's hair. 'Brooke gave me an earful last night.'

'About what?'

'About how I'm here being useless when I could be there being helpful.'

'Is that how you feel?'

She unfastened the bobble from around her hair and toyed with it. Her hair fell over her face, probably with a kink in it from where the bobble had sat. She didn't care. She'd hardly slept after Brooke's lecture. 'I feel helpless here. I want to be here for Hollie and Astin, but what good am I doing? She barely leaves his bedside, and when she does she's working.'

'Does that worry you?'

'Yeah, but what can I do? She's a good listener until you start talking to her about herself.'

'Aren't we all?' said Liam.

Hollie stomped down the stairs and into the foyer. Her hair was lank and she had no make-up on. The bags under her eyes were bigger than usual, and the scowl on her face made her look as if she wanted to stab someone. She had on jeans and a hoody, her I-cannot-be-bothered-with-today outfit. She slammed her phone on to the table. The table cloth crumpled under the force. Fayth straightened it.

'What's up?' said Fayth.

'I've got to take Nan for her diabetic check. Mum's at work and can't take her.' She leaned back in the leather chair, her elbows resting on the arms.

'Can't any of your relatives take her?' suggested Liam. He sipped his tea.

Hollie scoffed as she flicked through the menu.

'At least you can take your sewing machine to your usual place to be serviced,' said Fayth, trying to find a bright side.

'I suppose,' said Hollie with a sigh.

'Is that why you're in a bad mood? Shitty relatives?' asked Fayth.

'No. I texted Astin to tell him and he barely reacted at all.'

'What did you want him to say?' said Liam.

She opened the text conversation and showed them the text. '"OK". That was his response. "OK"! What kind of response is that?'

'An acknowledgement?' offered Fayth.

'You're reading too much into it,' said Liam. 'There's nothing he can do about your nan needing you, so why get worked up about it?'

Hollie sighed. 'You're right.' She looked to Fayth.

Fayth nodded reassuringly. She patted Hollie's arm. 'He knows you love your nan. He's not going to stop you from looking after her when there's bugger all you can do here.'

A waiter appeared and took Hollie's order. She went for orange juice and a Danish pastry.

'Will you keep an eye on him for me?' said Hollie.

'Actually, I might be heading home for a few days too,' said Fayth.

'Is everything all right?'

'Yeah, it's just with the sale on the way and Brooke's exams looming, I'm of more use there than I am here,' said Fayth.

'True,' said Hollie. She sighed. 'I feel so helpless.'

'We all do,' said Liam. He reached over and rubbed Hollie's arm. 'I'll make sure he behaves.'

'That'll be a first,' said Hollie.

Fayth sniggered.

'The hospital staff won't let him get too out of line,' said Liam.

'I dunno, he's pretty good at laying on the charm,' said Fayth.

'And he knows it,' said Hollie.

Four

Having spent nearly two weeks in London, Fayth's hometown felt alien to her. Not as alien as travelling in a private jet, mind. Nothing would make her as uncomfortable as that. Especially when its owner was still in London. She'd tried to tell Liam the train was fine, but he'd won when he reminded her that it would mean she could a) get home faster, and b) return to London faster. Stupid logic winning out.

The worst thing about aeroplanes was how greasy they made her hair. No amount of dry shampoo counteracted the limpness, so there was only one thing for it: risk washing her hair again. More strands of hair fell out as she unfastened her hair from the bobble. It must've been too tight. Except that more strands fell out as she washed it too. What had she done to upset her hair so much? It'd fallen out in the past, but never like it had the last few weeks. Was she going bald?

She needed a distraction. She couldn't spend the whole of her last night off thinking about her bloody hair falling out. A few months ago, she would've been happy to spend her downtime watching a TV or film. Since returning from New York, she couldn't sit still – she always had to be doing something. Except there really wasn't much to do in the middle of nowhere.

An explosion echoed through the house. Brooke's TV. She'd decided to deafen herself, as usual. Teenagers.

The door to Brooke's room was ajar, so Fayth pushed it open and headed instead. But she wasn't just watching any film. She was watching the original *Highwater*.

'Seriously?' said Fayth, raising an eyebrow.

'What?' said Brooke. She lay on her bed, her phone in hand. 'It's good.'

Fayth grumbled. *Highwater* would never be the same to her again. She couldn't stand to look at Trinity on or offscreen.

The explosion was one Liam's character, Eric, had caused, to try and stop a pursuer. He flicked his hair from his face with a jerk of his head. She laughed.

'What?' said Brooke. 'He does that all the time.'

'Not in real life,' said Fayth. She'd spent enough time with him to notice. 'He runs his hands through it.'

'So why does he do the head flick thing on camera?'

'Cause his hairdresser will crucify him if he runs his hands through it and ruins the style. She also says it makes it go greasy quicker.'

'It does,' said Brooke. 'Upside of having hair so curly and thick you couldn't do that if you tried.'

'You straighten yours.'

'Shush!' Brooke pointed to the TV.

Eric pulled his damp t-shirt over his head and threw it to the side. Trinity's character, Melitha, appeared next to him, stepping closer and placing her hands on his torso. Fayth cringed. How many times had they done that in person? How many times had she seen him with more than just his top off?

Melitha kissed Eric, her hand still pressed against his chest. He pulled her closer, kissing her passionately.

Fayth left the room. Seeing Liam with his top off made her uncomfortable. It made her even more uncomfortable knowing that he'd got naked with Trinity onscreen *and* offscreen.

But he wasn't with Trinity any more. He wasn't interested in her.

Who *was* he interested in?

What was she thinking? It was none of her business.

She'd spent years in love with Eric from *Highwater*. He'd been her teenage fantasy, and she'd settled for just the opposite, thinking nothing better would come along. And now she knew the man behind Eric. And he was even better than Eric.

Shite.

She closed her bedroom door and rested her head against it.

The last thing she needed was to go from crushing on Liam York the actor to Liam York the person.

Being back in her own house, in her own bed, after everything that had happened, just didn't feel right to Hollie. Astin still lay in hospital, hundreds of miles away. She needed to be there for him. She was a traitor; a bad girlfriend. Good girlfriends didn't abandon their partners in times of need. But what could she do? He was in hospital. He was in one of the best bloody hospitals. That didn't make her feel any better, though. Every time she closed her eyes she pictured Astin slipping down the wall and crashing into the camera crane. If he'd fallen just slightly differently, would it have killed him? Would she have been preparing for his funeral? She sat up. She couldn't to think that way. He was alive. He'd get better. He had to.

The thing was, her nan needed her to. How was she supposed to split her time between them? She could hardly ask Astin to move to a town with a shitty hospital and half the tech and budget compared to the one that was treating him.

And as for her nan moving closer to London?

That would *never* happen.

She got out of bed and went downstairs. Her nan sat in her chair by the window, channel hopping.

'How was the nap?' said her nan.

'Pointless,' Hollie sighed, sitting on the floor by the edge of the chair. She rested her head on her nan's lap.

'Why?'

'I didn't sleep.'

'What's on your mind?'

'I don't know what to do, Nan,' said Hollie.

'About what?'

'Astin needs me, but so do you.'

Her nan lifted her head to look at her. 'I don't know how old and frail you think I am, but I can manage without you, you know.'

Hollie laughed.

'I'm serious! I've got yer mam, and the neighbours, and we managed just fine when you were in London and New York, didn't we?'

Yes, they had. That didn't stop the guilt.

'Astin's going through a lot more than I am right now. It'd do him good to know you're there for him.'

Hollie sat cross-legged in front of her nan. She looked up at her. 'But what if something does happen?'

Her nan frowned. 'You saying I'm past it?'

'No! I just worry, that's all.'

'You can waste your whole life worrying about things that'll never happen, gal. Eventually you have to go out and live your life. That or be stuck indoors until you're six feet under.'

Hollie stood up and hugged her nan. She'd always been the wisest person she knew. 'Promise me you'll look after yourself?'

'Don't I always?'

Hollie scoffed. 'No.'
'Well then I promise yer mam will look after me. Better?'
'A little.'

Five

'Bear? I thought you weren't due back until tomorrow,' said Astin as she entered the hospital room. The mirror was in his hand, pointed in the direction of the door.

'Shh,' she said, smiling at his use of her new pet name. She wasn't supposed to be there. She'd snuck in while the nurses did their rounds. It wouldn't be long until they realised she was there. She pulled the blinds of his private room shut. 'I missed you.'

After spending hours staring at her bedroom ceiling she'd decided to drive back and see Astin. She'd said goodbye to her mum, nan, and George, then got in her car and headed down the M1. There were few cars on the road in the middle of the night; most of the vehicles she drove past were lorries several times the size of her Toyota. With the exception of one or two that pipped their horns as she drove past, they left her alone. She'd ignored the sleazy drivers, putting her foot on the accelerator to get away from them.

She grabbed a crappy plastic chair from by the door and placed it beside his bed, resting her head by his side. He stroked her hair. 'I wondered why you hadn't replied.'

'Sorry. I prefer driving at night. The roads are so much quieter.'

'And filled with trucks like, three times the size of your car.'

Hollie shrugged. 'They either have added respect for me as a female driver in a small car, or less respect for me because I'm a female driver in a small car. Either way, it's their problem. If it causes an accident, they're the ones that get in trouble, not me.'

He pointed the mirror at her. 'That's not funny.'

'Sorry.'

Given the circumstances, it really wasn't. She should've known better.

'How did your nan's appointment go?'

'Same as usual,' she replied. 'Nan's fine, they'll see her in a few months.' She stood up and kissed him. The cuts and bruises on his face had begun to heal, but he refused to shave in case he exacerbated them. His beard scratched against her skin, but she didn't care. His chapped lips were rough against hers, but that didn't bother her, either. He still tasted of peppermint. Just like he had when they'd first kissed. Never could she have predicted how much – or how quickly – everything would change after that night. But she had no regrets. In or out of a wheelchair and a head brace, she needed him. And she knew that no matter how much he pushed her away, he needed her, too.

Hollie's neck was stiff. She'd fallen asleep in the chair, her head resting on Astin's bed. His hand was still tangled in her hair. She couldn't shake the feeling that something else would go wrong and that she'd lose him. There were few things that scared her more.

A nurse entered carrying a tray of food. When she saw Hollie, she scowled. 'What are you doing here?'

By some miracle, the nurses hadn't noticed her in the night – or if they had, they'd left her – but this nurse didn't look so impressed. Her lips were pursed, her eyes hard.

'Sorry,' said Hollie with a yawn. She wasn't, though. That night was the closest she'd felt to Astin since the accident. They'd talked, and they'd kissed, and they'd slept.

The nurse continued to glare at her. Hollie looked at her blankly.

'I asked her to come,' lied Astin. 'I had a nightmare.'

'Uh-huh,' said the nurse, clearly unconvinced. 'If that's the case, *you* can feed him.' She shoved the food on the table over his bed. 'He gets his stitches out at 11.' She stormed out, leaving the door open behind her.

'Someone's not a big fan of romance,' said Hollie. She reached for the controls of his bed and helped him to sit up. He couldn't sit up for long, but he could at least manage it to eat.

Astin gave a small laugh. 'You should get some rest after all that driving.'

'I want to be here for you,' she said, tilting her neck to the right. The tense muscles protested. She flinched.

'You are, I just don't want you to hurt yourself at the same time,' he said. The bed reached the right angle. He lifted his arms up and wiggled his fingers.

'I'll be fine,' she said, stretching her neck in the other direction. More muscles tugged.

She took a spoonful of porridge and held it up.

'I can feed myself now you know,' he said.

She put the spoon down. 'I was trying to be romantic.' She picked it up again. 'Would you prefer the choo-choo train? Here comes the choo-choo train! Open wide!'

Astin laughed, a flicker of amusement in his eyes. Somewhere deep down, he was still in there. All she had to do was keep him going.

'Choo choooooo!'

Six

Hollie's battered Toyota Aygo stood out like a cheap dress at a celebrity party as they pulled up outside Claridge's. Astin sat in the passenger seat, waiting for someone to help him into his new wheelchair. It didn't fit in her car, so a porter and nurse had used a hospital wheelchair to get him from the ward to her car. Fayth had returned from the pub again to help out – despite Hollie insisting it wasn't necessary – and had stayed behind to help Liam, Wade, and Jamal get everything ready. The four of them were waiting just inside the hotel doors as Hollie turned the engine off.

A nurse stood under the shelter away from the rain, Astin's custom-made wheelchair by his side. Its high back made it look more like an electric chair, but if it helped him, Hollie wouldn't comment. Such orders would usually take longer, but in Hollywood…

Two porters stepped forwards with the nurse. One held an umbrella as the other two helped Astin from the car and into the wheelchair. Hollie pulled the hood of her raincoat over her head and got out, then hovered beside them, utterly useless. Was that how Fayth and Liam had felt the last few weeks?

Hollie handed the car keys to the valet, and her scruffy car was driven away.

'I'm Declan,' said the nurse. He was a tall, skinny guy with a thick Yorkshire accent. Fayth and Liam had worked with an agency to find a suitable carer. They'd chosen him because he was bright, friendly, and optimistic. Just what Astin needed. Provided he could understand his accent.

'Astin.' He paused. He moved his torso a fraction, as if searching for something. 'Hollie?'

Hollie stepped forwards and put her hand on his shoulder. 'I'm here.'

'This is Hollie, my girlfriend.'

'Good to meet you,' said Declan. He shook Hollie's hand.

'You too,' said Hollie.

Astin felt around the controls on his wheelchair.

'Shall we check those out away from the rain?' suggested Declan. He pushed Astin's wheelchair inside before he could protest.

Hollie hugged Fayth as soon as they were through the doors. Fayth hugged her back, patting her back supportively.

After exchanging greetings and introductions, Jamal led them up to the suite that was to become Hollie and Astin's new home. Hollie had moved from her old room the day before, but she'd spent most of the night in Fayth's room. She didn't sleep well on the best of nights, but when she was about to move in with her boyfriend of four months and become his primary carer, her anxiety went into overdrive. Would she be able to cope? Would they get sick of each other? Did he even want her there? He'd threatened to break up with her right after it had happened. Was that an omen?

Was it?

They had their own bedrooms so that Hollie didn't accidentally kick Astin in the night and break him further. While Hollie understood this, it felt like even more of an omen, even with Fayth, Liam, and Wade just down the corridor.

With the exception of Declan, everyone left Hollie and Astin to explore their new home and disappeared into their own rooms, or, in Jamal's case, back downstairs.

Their suite consisted of a bright living area with modern decor that looked out across the city. Two sofas were arranged around a coffee table with a fireplace beside them and a dining table behind. A sewing machine was set up in the far corner, the rest of Hollie's sewing things around it.

'Where'd this come from?' said Hollie, running her hands over it. It was top-of-the-line with a built in overlocker. It probably weighed as much as she did.

'I thought you could use this while yours is being repaired,' said Astin. He appeared beside her, having already figured out the controls on his chair. 'Do you like it?'

'I love it. Thank you.'

He gave her a weak smile.

Declan hovered by the door, a vacant smile on his face as he rocked on his heels. He was an interesting one, that was for sure.

'Shall we go see the rest of the suite?' she suggested. She was eager to play on her new sewing machine, but also wanted to check out where they'd be living for the foreseeable future. Insurance had offered to pay for a hotel for Astin to stay in, but it wasn't Claridge's. Astin was using some of his savings to pay for his stay, but stunt work didn't pay nearly as well as acting, so Liam and Tate had chipped in too. Somehow, they'd got him to go along with it.

An adjustable seat was fitted to the bath/shower to help Astin get in and out, and to allow him to have a shower without having to stand. A walking frame was beside the toilet to help him pee when the catheter was removed.

The beds were high, which made it interesting for Hollie's short legs but easier for Astin.

'If you need anything else let me know,' said Declan.

'I can manage,' said Astin. 'I just need help standing up and sitting down, that's all.'

Hollie shot him a warning look. He didn't react. The least he could do was be courteous.

'Thank you,' said Hollie.

Astin's expression was neutral.

They returned to the living room and hovered awkwardly. Now what?

'Could you give us a minute please?' Hollie asked Declan.

'Sure.'

Hollie waited until the suite door closed behind him. 'You couldn't sound any less enthusiastic if you tried.'

'What do you want me to say? All this stuff is great, but it doesn't change anything. I'm still a prisoner in my own body.'

Hollie pointed her finger at him. 'You are *not* a prisoner. It's only for a few months. And in the meantime, you get to stay in *this*! I mean, look around you.'

The fancy sewing machine was probably the cheapest thing in there.

'I'm sorry,' said Astin. 'I'm just tired.'

Hollie slept even less than usual that night. Sleeping in separate rooms felt like more than just a physical barrier. A chasm was forming between them, and she didn't know how to stop it. He insisted he was fine whenever she asked. She couldn't tell if he was lying or telling the truth. She couldn't tell if he was sleeping OK, or if he was in pain and needed some stronger painkillers, or if something had happened and he'd—

No. He'd survived the worst of it. The greatest punishment

for him now was his own pride, and how he didn't like accepting help from people.

Astin groaned. Hollie jumped from bed and burst into his room. He sat up, trying to force a tartan shirt over his naked torso.

'What are you doing?' she said, running to him and helping him lift the shirt as far over his shoulder as it would go. He cringed.

'Getting dressed. I hate sitting around in my pyjamas all day.'

'It's only eight. Won't Declan be here soon?'

'Not for another hour,' he said. He pulled up his other shirt sleeve, swatting her hands away when she tried to help. 'Man, I feel like Liam. I hate wearing shirts.'

'I like that shirt. You look sexy.'

'You think I look sexy?'

'Yeah, as in really attractive and I'd like to do bad things to you.'

'Hate to break it to you but I think that's off the table for a while.'

Hollie's stomach fell. 'Does that mean flirting is too?'

'Sorry,' he said. He looked down at his stripy pyjama bottoms.

'Let me,' said Hollie, reaching for the waistband.

'NO!'

'Astin, come on. It's *me*.'

'Just let me do it myself, please.'

'The doctor said you need to rest. This isn't resting. This is unnecessary strain.'

'It's getting fucking dressed.'

'Give yourself a break, would you? There's nothing wrong with needing help once in a while.'

'I. Don't. Need. Help!'

'Fine. Be like that. Take longer to heal. Do more permanent damage. See if I care!' She stormed out of his room, slamming his door for dramatic effect. Why was it so hard for him to accept that he needed help? At least he'd be able to walk again one day. Her nan was slowly getting worse. And she'd abandoned her to put up with a stroppy boyfriend who didn't even want her help. Why was she even bothering?

She slammed drawers and doors in her own room as she decided what to wear. There was nothing like slamming around when in a bad mood.

She picked out a pink pinafore she'd made when she was at university. How would she feel if she couldn't design clothes any more? She'd be grumpy too. Not to mention if she had to spend the next few months sitting still. Sitting still wasn't her strong point.

Or Astin's.

Her phone vibrated on her bedside table. Astin.

She went to his room and hovered in the doorway.

'Hey,' he said, his voice weak. He still had on his pyjama bottoms.

'I'm sorry,' he said.

So he should be.

'I shouldn't have snapped at you like that.'

'Nope.' She sat beside him on the bed.

He put his hand on hers. 'I forget that I'm not the only one suffering here.'

'That's the problem, Astin,' she said, moving his hand from hers. 'You're playing the victim. There are people out there that are in wheelchairs for the rest of their lives. And those people don't go on about it. They get on with it. Because they don't have a choice.'

'And I do?'

'You can choose not to play the victim,' she said.

'I'm not!'

'Like hell you're not. Having someone or something to help you maintain some semblance of a normal life isn't a weakness, it's a strength, and the sooner you realise that, the easier your life will be. You're going to get better, but you'll get better a hell of a lot faster if you stop whinging and trying to do things yourself. Why is that so difficult for you to accept?'

'Because I don't need anyone's fucking help! Y'all are suffering because of me!'

'Shouldn't that be for us to decide?'

His eyes darted around the room, picking an abstract painting on the wall to stare at.

'Exactly. You're the only one that describes this as suffering, or that thinks you're a burden. We're all still living our lives.'

'And yours would be a hell of a lot better without me in it,' he mumbled.

'Would I be here if I believed that?' She waved her arms in exasperation. 'I'm here because I love you, but right now, I want to slap you.'

'How do you want me to act?'

'I want you to be honest with me, and if you're struggling that much, to get some counselling. There's only so much emotional support I can give you when I'm barely clinging on myself.'

'See? You *are* better off without me!'

'What? Because I have depression and it's only because of you and my fashion label that I'm finding a way out of it? Yeah. Great thinking.'

'Hollie, I—'

She put her hand up. 'I have work to do.'

The black cloud that had followed her around for so long threatened to burst, and arguing with Astin only made things worse. It wasn't like they were getting anywhere anyway. And she really did have work to do – she needed to finish off her website before Tate's video was released the following week. If she didn't, anyone interested in her clothes would end up redirected to her Instagram.

He was in a difficult situation. They all were. But that was no reason for him to take it out on her. She didn't have the emotional strength to carry him. Maybe she shouldn't have suggested she'd look after him after all. But then, if she hadn't, she would've spent all her time worrying about him and unable to concentrate. At least if he was nearby she knew exactly how he was. And he had Declan, so it wasn't like she was doing it *all* on her own. There was no way she'd be able to focus on her business if she was. She wouldn't have had time.

She didn't resent Fayth, or Liam, or Tate for not helping out as much. Fayth had her family and the pub to think about – and had already done too much – Liam needed to find a new apartment and job, and Tate was still on tour. But Jack? What was his excuse? Where the hell was he?

And as for Astin's family…she was glad she'd never met them. Cooper sounded cute, but she couldn't help but wonder what damage his parents' messed-up relationship had done. There was nothing healthy about being in a household where parents argued all the time, and there was only so much repair work his grandparents could do. But was it enough?

Seven

'How was your first night in your new home for the next few months?' asked Fayth as she sat with Hollie and Liam at breakfast.

Hollie grumbled, playing with her porridge.

'Is the bed not comfy enough?' said Liam, slicing into his scrambled eggs and caviar.

If the bed wasn't comfy enough in a place like that, it wouldn't be anywhere. Knowing Hollie, it had more to do with Astin and clothes than the bed. Fayth stirred the tea in the pot, then poured a cup for her and one for Liam.

'We argued again this morning,' said Hollie with a sigh.

'What about?' asked Fayth.

'He sees being in the wheelchair and brace as some sort of punishment. He doesn't get that they're fixing him and it's only short-term.'

'He's never been much of a long-term kind of guy,' said Liam.

'Reassuring,' mumbled Hollie.

'You're the only person I've ever heard him talk about long-term,' said Liam.

'Nice save,' said Hollie.

'He's just trying to process it all,' said Fayth.

'I know, that's why I'm trying to give him the benefit of the doubt, but it's hard when he's just so negative all the time. It sucks all the energy out of the room when I have so much to do already.'

Fayth reached over and patted Hollie's arm. 'If he's still being a dick in a few days, your nan and I will go after him. She with her walking stick and me with my martial arts skills.'

Hollie laughed. It was good to see her laugh again. She hadn't done it much in recent weeks. 'Thanks.'

Liam checked his Rolex. 'Is he not coming down for breakfast?'

'Doesn't look like it,' said Hollie. She shoved a spoonful of porridge into her mouth. She wrinkled her nose. 'Cold porridge isn't nice.'

'Serves you right for playing with it instead of eating it,' said Fayth.

Hollie glared at her.

'What? Food is important.'

'Excuse me.'

The three of them looked up. Jamal stood beside them, his hands behind his back.

'Mr Mack said to inform you that he won't be down for breakfast – he's eating it in his room instead.'

'Thanks for letting us know,' said Liam.

Jamal nodded then disappeared upstairs.

'You don't think he's going to turn into a recluse, do you?' said Hollie.

'It's his first day out of hospital, give him chance,' said Fayth.

'Yeah, you're right,' said Hollie. 'But, I mean, he barely left his room at the hospital.'

'That's because there was nowhere to go,' said Liam. He jerked his head, flicking his hair from his face. 'I need to go get ready. I'm surprising fans at 11 then I've got an audition this afternoon.'

'You never said anything,' said Fayth.

'It was a last-minute thing. My agent called me about it yesterday. Figured while I was here I might as well.' He stood up. 'See you later.'

'Good luck,' said Fayth.

'Don't break a leg,' said Hollie. 'Not after the last couple of weeks.'

He gave a small laugh then hopped up the stairs and disappeared out of sight.

'I should get on with some work,' said Hollie. 'I need to take some photos for the site.'

'Want some help?' offered Fayth.

'Sure.'

There was no sign of Astin when they got up to the suite, but they could hear him shouting at the TV from his room off to the right.

They left him to it and went into Hollie's room. A mannequin stood in the corner, a 1930s-style polka dot dress pinned on to it.

'You brought your mannequin with you?' said Fayth.
'No. Jamal found it for me,' said Hollie. She took out a steamer and began to steam the dress.
'Where are you going to do the photos?' asked Fayth.
'Haven't worked that out yet,' said Hollie.
'What about here?' suggested Fayth, standing by a spot of white wall. 'The natural light is good but not too bright. We can always edit it if we need to.'
Hollie put the steamer down and moved the mannequin to where Fayth stood. The two of them adjusted it then stepped back.
'Well?' said Hollie.
'Where's your camera? Let's try it and see.'
Hollie took her camera from her bedside drawer and handed it to Fayth. It wasn't the best camera in the world, but it had to do. Fayth held it up. The dress caught the light just right. She took a few shots, some crouching down, others standing on the bed or a chair. Angles made all the difference. Fayth showed Hollie the photos.
'Why can't you take all my photos?' asked Hollie.
'Because usually you live too far away,' said Fayth. 'But you know I'll help while I'm here.'
'Thanks,' said Hollie. She put her arms around Fayth's waist and rested her head on her shoulder.
'Got any more that need photographing?'
'Loads.'
'In that case,' said Fayth, 'we're going to need cookies.'

'Hey,' said Liam, poking his head through the oak door into the pub meeting room. A dozen faces turned to look at him, their mouths agape and eyes wide. 'Is this the Hard Water meet-up?'
Danni, the organiser, smiled. 'Do you want a drink?' she asked as he and Wade stepped inside.
'I'm good,' said Liam, giving her a hug. Her frizzy hair tickled his nose. Danni was the creator of Hard Water, the biggest *Highwater* fan site. Liam had met her at the very first HighCon five years earlier, and they'd stayed in touch. When he'd found out she was organising a meet up in London, he offered to stop by.
'He's not going to bite, you know,' said Danni, turning back to the others. They stood in a circle in the middle of the room. None of them had moved or spoken since he'd walked in. He

approached them, his face painted with his signature charming smile. 'So who's who?' he asked. 'I'm Liam.'

They laughed. Once they got over being starstruck, they'd be all right. Fayth had been the same when they'd first met; four months later she spoke to him like he was just another person. It was people like her that he wanted in his life because they kept him grounded. The more time he spent with his Hollywood friends, the more tempting it was to fall into old, bad habits.

One by one, they went round and introduced themselves.

'Can I get a photo?' asked Nadia after she'd introduced herself. Out of everyone, she seemed to have recovered from being starstruck the fastest.

'Of course!' said Liam, gesturing her over. She handed her phone to Sally, who wore a lot of eyeliner and a huge beanie hat, then Liam pulled her into his arms. Nadia adjusted her hijab then beamed at the camera. Once she'd had her photo taken with him, everyone else wanted one, too.

Danni lurked in the background, talking at Wade. He didn't respond much.

'What's happening with the *Relics*?' asked Des when it was his turn. He was a middle-aged man wearing a too-small *Highwater* t-shirt. Seeing his and Trinity's faces staring back at him made Liam want to vomit. It was the first time he'd seen a photo of them together since the break up. Given how people quoted *Highwater* to him on a daily basis, he was impressed he'd managed it for so long.

'I don't know,' said Liam. 'I'm not involved in it.' He and Fayth had played *Relics*, the multiplayer online battle arena game based on *Highwater*, for a few minutes at HighCon, and neither of them had been impressed.

'Not even doing Eric's voice?' asked Usain, who had the body of a fifteen-year-old and the voice of a fifty-year-old.

'No,' said Liam.

'Well that's dumb,' said Usain as he posed for his photo with Liam.

The indie studio responsible couldn't afford to pay him, so they'd gone with someone else. He didn't blame them. He also didn't want anything to do with a game that was that bad.

Individual photos taken, Danni ushered everyone in for a group shot then posted it on Hard Water, inviting any fans nearby to join them.

Within an hour the small upstairs meeting room was full and

the staff downstairs had to turn people away. Their little gathering had turned into something much bigger than Danni had anticipated. 'Maybe I should've waited until you'd gone to post about it,' said Danni in between him posing for more photos. She had to talk to be heard over the people around them, most of whom were trying to get Liam's attention.

'Don't worry about it,' he said. At least he wasn't claustrophobic. There were so many people they could only move a few inches in either direction. If any more people arrived, they'd have to relocate to Hyde Park.

A mousy-haired woman in a green cardigan stepped forwards. 'Hi. Can I get a photo?' she asked in a monotonous Scottish accent.

'Sure. What's your name?'

'Tawny.'

She didn't smile. Not once. Even when the camera flashed. It unnerved him. Why ask for a photo if she wasn't bothered?

Wade – who'd been hovering nearby – barged in before Tawny could speak again or another fan could ask for a photo. 'The pub want to call the police. It's getting pretty busy downstairs and they can't control it.'

'Is there anything you can do?' asked Liam. Involving the police would mean the end of the event; that didn't seem fair.

'This sucks!' said Danni, pouting.

Liam put his hand on her shoulder. 'It's fine. We'll sort it.'

She shook her head. 'I shouldn't have put out an invite like that! I should've known better!'

'How?' said Liam. 'You're not psychic.'

'I wish I had Melitha's crystal ball right now.'

Liam tensed.

'Sorry,' said Danni. She didn't know what had happened between him and Trinity, but she did know they'd broken up. She'd also met Trinity in the past and didn't like her.

The doors flung open and three police offers entered. 'All right folks, time to wrap things up,' shouted one of them.

The crowd booed. A guy in his late teens reached out and grabbed Liam's arm. 'No!' he shrieked. 'He's not going anywhere!'

His accent was from New York. It couldn't be, could it?

He pulled Liam closer, his grip like a vice. Liam's pulse raced. He tried to untangle himself but it was no use. Other fans looked on, their eyes wide. Liam could hardly breathe. Was this weedy guy the one responsible for the break-ins? Had he followed him all the way to London?

Using hardly any strength at all, Wade yanked Liam from the teenager's clutches and dragged him away. He yelped, but nobody went to him. They backed away, watching as Wade dragged Liam from the room.

'Sorry!' called Liam as Wade manhandled him through the door. He continued to apologise as they continued down the stairs and through the cramped pub.

'You can stop overreacting now, Mom,' said Liam, tugging his arm away when they got outside.

'You pay me to protect you,' said Wade.

'And you do. But you also overreact. I'm used to the crowds.'

'It wasn't safe. The pub was over occupancy. And don't even get me started on that kid.'

Liam shuddered. That kid. Could he really be the one that trashed his photos and stole his comics?

'You can tweet them later to apologise,' said Wade.

Liam rolled his eyes.

'Roll your eyes all you want. At least now you have more time to prep for your audition.'

Annoying as Wade was, he was also right. Not that auditions had got him very far the last few weeks. He'd just about had enough of them. Most of the attention he'd had recently was either about Trinity or the break-in at his apartment. Maybe fading away for a few months or years was just what his career needed.

Astin wasn't due to start physiotherapy at the hospital until the end of May, but he'd organised for a physiotherapist to visit him a couple of times a week at the hotel. Hollie had questioned it at the time, but asking a guy who'd spent his whole life being active to sit still was like asking a writer not to form words.

She and Fayth had worked on photos for her website while Astin spent some time with his physiotherapist. They heard the occasional grunt, but otherwise, all was quiet. When they heard the physiotherapist leave, Fayth went to find Liam so that Hollie could check on Astin. He was sat up in bed, watching TV.

'I'm sorry about earlier,' he said. 'I was insensitive.'

'Yup,' agreed Hollie, climbing on to the bed and resting her head in his lap.

'I can always trust you to be honest with me, can't I?'

'Yup,' she said. 'How was physio?'

'Painful.' He stretched his legs out and wiggled his toes. 'If I get much better at this I'll be competing in the Olympics.'

'Well at least you've got your new career sorted for when you're better,' said Hollie.

'Mmm.' He pushed a rogue strand of hair away from her face and tucked it behind her ear. Hollie closed her eyes. His touch still gave her shivers. They'd barely even hugged since the accident, and while Hollie understood Astin's reasons why, she missed being close to him. It wasn't just about sex, it was about the little things – a kiss here, a hug there. It all made a difference.

She sat up and straddled him, careful not to put her weight on him. He tilted his head, regarding her curiously. She smirked. They were so close she could feel his breath on her lips and smell the chocolate bar he'd just eaten. He smiled as their lips touched. She kissed him hungrily, desperate to go back to a time when things were simpler. When it was just the two of them and nothing else. No business, no head brace, no complications. Just them.

He ran his fingers through her hair, resting his plastered arm on her arse. She wrapped her arms around him – as much as she could with his head brace in the way – and kissed his cheek, his chin, his neck…

'Stop,' said Astin.

Hollie froze. Stop?!

He looked away from her. 'We can't.'

'What? Kiss?'

'You know it won't just be that,' said Astin.

'So?'

'So I don't like you seeing me like this. I don't feel…I can't do it. I'm sorry.'

'You were fine a minute ago. I don't get it.'

'Remember when we first kissed in New York? You told me to stop and I did? No questions?'

Yes, she remembered. She'd asked him to stop because she was so self-conscious about her body she couldn't comprehend how someone like him could ever find her attractive. Her anxiety had won out. Astin had helped her to get over it.

Was he now the self-conscious one?

Hollie removed her legs from around him and swung them to the edge of the bed. 'I'm sorry. I should've thought.'

He reached out and put his hand on hers. 'It's not you. I

just…I don't feel like me any more.'

Being self-conscious of her own body, she understood where he was coming from. What she didn't understand was why he refused to talk about anything. Every time she tried to get him to open up he slammed, bolted, and padlocked the door between them. And when she suggested he talk to a counsellor, she may as well have been telling George not to chase his tail. Despite her, Liam, Tate, and Jack all having gone for counselling at some point, he was still against the idea. He refused to say why, though.

She turned around and kissed his cheek. 'It's OK. I understand.'

'Thank you,' said Astin, looking downwards.

'How'd it go today?' Fayth asked as Liam walked into her room.

She sat on the bed, leaning back on her hands. He lay beside her, his legs inches from hers. He was so close she could smell the cinnamon and sandalwood in his cologne. She curled into herself. 'That good?'

He sighed, rolling on to his side and propping his head up with his hand. 'I had to leave the Hard Water meet up early because it got so busy the police showed up.'

'What?' She stretched her legs out in front of her.

'Yeah. The pub got overcrowded so they had to call in reinforcements. Had some great insults online about it. Oh, and some guy got real handsy right before I left.'

'What do you mean?'

'Grabbed me and said I wasn't allowed to leave. Wade had to get him off me.'

'Bloody hell,' said Fayth. No matter how she sat, she couldn't get comfortable. Her muscles were so tense she felt like she'd spent all day at the gym. She hadn't. She stood up and stretched.

'You get used to it,' said Liam. He said it so casually it unnerved her even more. Was he really used to things like that? How was he OK with it? How were other people OK with treating a total stranger like that?

'You shouldn't have to,' said Fayth, leaning against the windowsill. 'Have you spoken to the police about it? Or told them about any of the dodgy comments?'

'No,' said Liam, sitting up and crossing his legs. 'Why would I?'

'The person who broke into your apartment could've easily followed you to London. Danni shouldn't have posted that you were there. Not when you're in danger.'

He walked over to her and put his hand on her shoulder. Her skin tingled. She tensed her body, urging it not to react to his touch. It ignored her. She moved his hand and put it by his side.

'I'm not in danger, Campbell,' said Liam. 'And Danni doesn't know everything. I didn't want to worry her. Or for word to get out and freak out the whole community. I like Danni, but anything I tell her ends up on Hard Water.'

'You still need to report things like that to the police, though. Especially if someone got touchy-feely,' said Fayth.

'I guess.' A strand of hair fell into his eye. He shook his head, and a few more strands joined it. He ran his hands over it and pushed it away from his face, as he often did away from the cameras.

'How bad were the comments?'

'You sure you want to know?'

Did she? She'd seen how bad they could get. Very few comments could surprise her any more, but that didn't mean she wanted to hear them.

He took his phone from his pocket. '"Scum",' he read, '"You should get hit by a Boris bike". What's a Boris bike?'

'They're bikes that you can hire to get about London,' said Fayth.

'Huh. Killed by a bicycle. Now that's an embarrassing way to go.'

Fayth glared at him.

'What? Would you rather I get cancer? That's another one of them: "I hope you get cancer and die, traitor". Traitor? How am I a traitor?'

'Please stop,' said Fayth. She'd heard more than enough.

Liam tucked his phone into his pocket and put his hand on her arm. 'I'll talk to the police about it, but just don't tell Hollie and Astin. They've got enough to worry about already.'

Fayth hated not telling Hollie things. She told Hollie everything. Almost. But what difference would it make if Hollie knew about some nasty comments Liam had received online? Like he'd said, it was 'part of his job'.

'All right,' said Fayth, still not convinced he was taking the whole thing seriously.

Eight

With Astin and Liam still out cold, Hollie and Fayth ate breakfast without them the following morning. Fayth didn't mind so much – it gave her and Hollie chance to talk before she headed off later in the day. 'Are you sure you'll be all right if I head home? With Brooke about to start her exams Dad really needs the help right now.'

'We'll be fine. There's nothing you can do around here anyway. Are you and Liam heading off for the airport at the same time?'

'Yeah, about three o'clock.'

'What time's your flight?'

'About half five,' said Fayth.

'What time's Liam's?'

'He's taking his private jet, so whenever he wants, I guess.'

Hollie chewed on a slice of toast for a few seconds, a pensive look passing over her face. 'What's the deal with you two?'

'What do you mean?' Fayth dipped a slice of bacon into her tomatoes.

'You two have been *very* pally lately,' said Hollie.

'So? You know we're just friends.'

Hollie pursed her lips.

'Don't give me that look, Bea.'

'What look? You're already being punished for the crime!'

'What crime?'

'Dating Liam, duh. And may I add that there are far worse crimes out there than—'

'Morning,' said Liam. He sat down beside Fayth. She tensed. Having him so close after what Hollie had said unnerved her. Had she been giving off the wrong signals?

Hollie's gaze flitted from Fayth, to Liam, to Fayth, then back to Liam. Suspicious, much?

'Am I missing something?' said Liam.

'Yeah. Breakfast,' said Hollie. She gestured to hers and

Fayth's plates, which were almost empty.

Liam yawned. 'Sorry. Was up late arguing with Wade. He thinks I'm better off finding somewhere to lie low instead of returning to New York.'

'Why?' said Fayth.

'He's worried about what happened at the Hard Water meet-up. So there were a lot of people there and one guy got handsy. It's no big deal.'

'Maybe he's right,' said Fayth. 'It is his job to look after you. If he's worried, maybe you should be too.'

Liam gestured to a waiter. 'Can I get some tea, please?'

When it came time to leave, Fayth couldn't bring herself to go. Her bags were packed and inside the taxi but she refused to join them.

Hollie wrapped her arms around herself. She didn't have a jacket on, just a shift dress. Everyone else had a coat on, with the exception of the porters and valets, who were in their uniforms and probably roasting from how busy they were.

'Are you sure you'll be all right without us?' said Fayth.

'We'll be fine,' promised Hollie.

'But we're going to be late if we don't hurry up,' said Liam. He hovered behind Fayth, his hands in his pockets. Wade sat in the front of the taxi talking to the driver.

'Go,' urged Astin from his wheelchair beside Hollie. 'You can't all put your lives on hold for me.'

Hollie's jaw tightened.

Fayth wanted to give him a chance, but that sounded a lot like a dig at Hollie. He'd been snippy since the accident; she wouldn't put it past him. Hollie could still work on her business while she was with him. But the pub couldn't run itself. Fayth either returned to help while Brooke did her exams, or her dad hired someone else without being able to offer them any job security, which wasn't really fair.

She also had her divorce to think about. She could do most of it over the phone or via email, but she needed to meet with Monica to sign paperwork. And have a celebratory drink.

A woman a few feet away put up a bright red umbrella. Droplets of rain landed on Fayth's head. She wiped them away. 'We'd better go.'

'I said that five minutes ago,' grumbled Liam.

'Shh!' said Fayth. She gave Hollie one last, lingering hug,

then scurried off into the taxi. Liam slid in beside her.

'Go!' said Liam to the taxi driver. 'Before she changes her mind!'

The taxi pulled away, Hollie and Astin fading into the distance. Whatever happened next was on them.

Fayth and Liam spoke little on the way to the airport. She was so drained from everything that had happened she didn't know what to say. It wasn't an awkward silence, though; it was a comfortable, knowing silence. They were happy to just be in one another's company. She'd only ever had that with her parents and sisters before. Patrick had always insisted on filling the silence, taking her quietness as a sign that something was wrong. He didn't understand that sometimes silence said more than words.

They took their bags from the taxi, paid the driver, then headed inside. After saying a quick goodbye, Fayth checked in her bags then met back up with Liam in the departure lounge. Since he was travelling by private jet, he didn't need to check in his bags. Wade got to carry them around instead.

They had two hours to kill before Fayth had to board her flight, so there was no point saying goodbye when there was still time.

Until there wasn't.

The two hours went too fast. They spent most of it eating – McDonald's, as it was Liam's last chance to eat badly – then playing games in the arcade. When Fayth's flight was called, she flung her hand luggage over her shoulder.

Liam shoved his hands into his pockets. 'Look after—'

'Myself, yeah. You keep saying that,' said Fayth.

'It's important,' he said, running his fingers through his hair. 'After everything.'

'I'm not the one whose apartment was broken into,' she reminded him. 'Listen to Wade, yeah? You hired him for a reason.'

Wade hovered a few feet away, shooting evil looks to anyone if they stared at Liam for a second too long.

'I didn't hire him. My manager did.'

'And your manager hired him for a reason, and he cares about you. He only does what he thinks is best for you.'

'Like another dad?'

'If that's how you want to see it. Just be careful.' She stuffed her hands in her pockets, staring at the floor. What if someone noticed them? It didn't take a genius to recognise who she was talking to, and they *were* in London. They'd already been recognised enough times there.

Liam gave a small nod. 'You too, Campbell.'

Fuck it. She took her hands from her pockets and hugged him. After the emotionally draining few weeks since Astin's accident, she needed to spend just a few more moments with someone who understood. He kissed the top of her head. She squeezed him tighter. His arms tightened around her too, and for a few precious moments, nothing else mattered.

Wade cleared his throat. When had he got so close?

She pulled away, her cheeks burning. She daren't look around in case she noticed people watching them. 'Be careful, and text me when you land.'

'You too,' said Liam.

'You'll still be in the air.'

'WhatsApp, then. I'll still have internet.'

She nodded. He put his hand on her shoulder. She closed her eyes and everything else faded away again. The only thing left was her and Liam: his hand on her shoulder, his breathing as it moved her hair and tickled the top of her head. He was so close she could almost feel his chest moving as he inhaled and exhaled. It was just them.

The tannoy announced her flight again. They jumped apart.

It would never be just them.

Nine

Thalia picked Liam and Wade up from the airport. From the minute the plan landed, Liam couldn't sit still. He loved New York, but the police still had no leads on who'd broken into his apartment. Even though they'd said that he could return to it, he didn't feel comfortable doing so, meaning that his options of where to stay were limited. Ola hadn't found anywhere suitable for him to move into yet, so he could either go back to his apartment that had been broken into – which wasn't an option – or move back in with his parents.

He'd succumbed to their wishes and stayed with him before he'd gone to London, but the idea of returning to his parents' place again was almost as bad as all of his other options.

There were two spare rooms at Astin and Jack's with Astin in London, but he didn't want to live with Jack. He was too much of a bad influence. Not to mention no one knew where he was or what he was up to. He could stumble in at any moment, drunk off his ass. Or worse.

Tate was still on tour, and they weren't so close any more, so he couldn't ask her either.

There was a line between employee and employer that he wasn't ready to cross, so he couldn't ask any of his team.

Living in a hotel was OK, but it just wasn't the same. No matter what hotel he stayed in, they always began to feel cold when he'd been there a while. He'd never be able to call one home.

Which only left his parents' place. Sigh.

'What's up with you? Missing Fayth already?' teased Wade.

'Did they get together?' asked Thalia excitedly.

'As if,' said Wade.

Thalia slumped. 'Damnit, I bet Ola they would.'

'You bet on my love life?' said Liam.

Thalia's cheeks turned crimson. 'You two are so good together!'

He glared at her through the rear-view mirror. How often did his staff bet on his personal life?

He turned away from them and looked out at the city he'd once thought of as home. Had they driven past the person that'd broken into his apartment or his dressing room? Or someone that knew who was responsible? What if it was a guy Wade's size, someone he'd never be able to take on his own? No matter how much Wade wanted to, he couldn't be there 24/7. Wade would likely move into his parents' place too until the person responsible was caught, though. There was no way Wade would go twelve hours without babysitting him. And no way his parents would let him. Wade would need a serious pay rise.

Should he invest in more security? Would that help? Would it make him seem egotistical, as if he expected something to happen?

But then, he did.

'Ola said to tell you Jim wants to meet with you tomorrow, by the way,' said Thalia.

Liam jumped. He was so wrapped up in his thoughts he'd almost forgot Wade and Thalia's presence. A meeting with his agent. Just what he needed. Not.

'She's added it to your calendar.'

'Thanks,' said Liam. He'd had enough of arguing with his agent. He'd had enough of arguing with everyone. He'd been back in New York less than an hour and the walls were already closing in. He could never get any alone time. Wade hovered like a gnat. How could he ditch him? But then, if he *did* ditch him, would he feel safe?

Liam's mum woke him at eight o'clock the next morning. She opened the door without knocking. Good job he knew she would and hadn't slept naked.

'I brought you coffee,' she said, putting it on the side.

'Thanks.' He remained curled up in bed, hoping she'd go away.

'Don't you have a meeting later today?'

'Lunchtime.'

'Oh. OK.'

She continued to hover.

'Is there something else?' he said.

'You are being safe, aren't you?'

'With what?' He was too old for the sex talk.

'With…everything. I don't want anything to happen to you.'

'I'm fine, Mom. Wade's got my back.'

She nodded. 'Yes, he's a very nice man, that bodyguard of yours. Is he coming with you later?'

'Yeah. Thalia's picking us up at 12.'

'Good. OK then. I'll leave you to sleep a little longer.' She left the room but didn't close the door behind her.

He pulled the duvet over his head and fell back to sleep.

When Liam arrived at the restaurant, Jim was already sat at a table in the far corner. Wade remained by the door, eyeing up everyone who came and went. Liam reluctantly approached his agent and shook his hand.

'Hi,' said Liam.

'Good to see you again,' said Jim, clasping Liam's hand in his sweaty ones.

Liam sat down and the two of them engaged in small talk, then, after the starters, Jim finally got down to business. 'I had a phone call a few days ago about a role you're going to love. It's a great opportunity.'

Liam remained silent. He'd decide if he loved the role and if it was a good opportunity once he knew what it was.

The suited waiter arrived with their main courses. Too hungry to elaborate on his claims, Jim began to eat his steak. Liam did too. Jim liked to pause for dramatic effect. He also liked to eat. He'd continue with his story when he was ready.

A woman with long, dark hair walked past. She stumbled in her heels, grabbing on to their table to steady herself. 'Sorry,' she said in an Italian accent before stumbling across to the bathroom. From the back – and how she couldn't walk in heels – she'd looked like Trinity. But it wasn't her. Phew.

'So,' said Jim, finally ready to continue, 'It's a new science fiction franchise, based on some popular book series. Can't remember what it's called. They're renaming it for the movies anyway. It's about a young space cowboy and his future wife.'

He wasn't selling it so far. It sounded like a cross between *Firefly* and *The Time Traveller's Wife*.

'Trinity's already been cast as—'

'Trinity?' echoed Liam. '*Trinity?*'

'I really think you should consider this, Liam. A role like this could cement your Hollywood career. You could be the new Harrison Ford!'

'I don't want to be Harrison Ford! I don't want to do another franchise! Have you listened to anything I've said in the last year?' He slammed his cutlery on to his plate. Lunch meetings were the worst. He was stuck until they'd paid the bill.

'I really think you're overreacting,' said Jim. They'd worked together for years, but the longer they did so the more Liam felt it was time to move on. Jim completely ignored anything he said. It was all about the money. Then again, it was to most people in Hollywood.

Liam's nostrils flared. 'Overreacting? You just suggested I work with my ex-girlfriend. Have you forgot what Trinity is like? *Have you?*'

'Of course not. Please, Liam. Calm down. You're causing a scene.' He clasped his chubby hands and placed them on the table.

A few people around them did a poor job of pretending they weren't eavesdropping. When they met eyes with Liam, they turned away. Ugh.

Wade stood by the door, his eyes narrowed in their direction. Liam sighed. Time to reign in his temper. Even though Jim *deserved* his temper. He'd done the lead in a genre movie thing. He wanted to branch out, not make his pigeonhole smaller.

'The two of you worked so well together on *Highwater*. Your chemistry is off the scale!'

Liam folded his arms. 'I was a different person then.'

'A *bankable* person. Right now, frankly, you're not bankable.' He leaned back in his chair and stretched. His pot belly stuck out.

Liam leaned forwards, speaking through clenched teeth. 'What's *that* supposed to mean?'

'It means that the kinds of movies you want to work on just aren't interested in you. If you don't want to be forgot, you need to suck it up.'

Liam threw some money on to the table. 'We're done here.' He walked out, ignoring Jim's cries for him to return.

Wade caught up with him seconds later. 'That was short.'

'That was a waste of time,' said Liam. He stomped down the street. 'In what universe would I ever work with Trinity again? Did he think the role through at all before he suggested it?'

'Financially, yes, personally, no,' said Wade.

A man walked towards Liam, his head bowed and covered by a hood. Wade pulled Liam from his path, and the man barged into him instead.

'Watch where you're—' The man looked up and saw Wade. 'Sorry,' he squeaked before running off.

Was he not looking where he was going? Had he tried to barge into Liam intentionally? Liam hugged himself, his eyes darting around his surroundings. His stalker could be inches away from him. How would he even know? They didn't have any leads. It could be anyone.

Oh, for fuck's sake.

Not everyone was a potential stalker. But someone potentially *was* his stalker.

GAH.

'Do you always have that effect on people?' asked Liam, trying to distract himself.

Wade shrugged as they carried on walking. 'It varies. I'm not André the Giant.'

'No way. He was nicer than you.'

'If that's how you feel, you can hire him as your bodyguard.'

'Did you find a way to turn Astin's DeLorean into a time machine then?'

'If I have it means I don't have to look at you any more.'

'It also means you're unemployed,' said Liam.

'A smart, strong, handsome man like me? I'll find something else in no time,' said Wade, turning up his shirt collar and tugging on it. It didn't look as cool as he thought it did.

'Doubt it,' said Liam, 'most people wouldn't tolerate your sarcasm.'

'Pfft. We both know anyone would be lucky to have my wit bestowed upon them,' said Wade, flattening his collar.

'You mean unfortunate?'

'You know, I could tell your nutritionist how much crap you ate in London,' said Wade.

'You could, but you signed an NDA.'

'Damnit.'

Ten

Hollie couldn't remember the last time she'd had a decent night's sleep. If she wasn't worrying about Astin, she was worrying about Tate's outfit, or her nan, or her mum, or Fayth, or Cameron, or George, or whatever else her paranoid brain could think of. She'd lost count of how many panic attacks she'd had in the month or so since the accident. She was in an almost constant state of fight or flight. Sewing was *not* easy when your hands shook constantly. Cutting out fabric was even harder. She had to keep making things, though. If people liked Tate's outfit, they'd want to order things from her. The more things she had to sell to people, the better. She made a few tote bags and keyrings to go along with the clothes she'd made as they were quick, easy, and cheap.

She finished off another tote bag and added it to the pile of pink, teal, and red fabric in her little corner of the room. It was late, but she wasn't sure how late. Astin had gone to bed hours ago, she knew that much.

Someone grunted. Hollie jumped. The suite had been silent except for the sound of her sewing machine and her breathing.

'Bear?' called Astin.

Hollie exhaled. She ran into Astin's room. 'What's wrong?'

'It's 2am,' he said. He lay flat on the bed, his phone beside him.

'So?' She tightened the fastening on her dressing gown.

'So there's this thing called sleep—'

Her shoulders were tight. She'd been hunched over her sewing machine longer than she thought. She stretched. 'You don't sleep much either.'

'No, but I try to sleep when other people do. What's wrong?'

'Nothing,' she lied.

'I heard your sewing machine and when I saw the time I got worried.'

Staring at her shoes, she whispered, 'I'm scared.'

Astin held out his hand. She sat on the bed beside him and took it.

'It'll be OK. And if it's not, it's just one outfit. They're allowed to not like one.'

'But it's *the* one,' she said.

'No. It's *a* one.'

'That's not even a phrase.'

'I just made it one. It's one of thousands of things you'll make in your life. You can't put all your stock in one outfit. Tate loves it. Even if the rest of the world doesn't, she'll keep wearing your designs, and eventually, the fashion world will listen. Not to mention you always say how subjective fashion is. Some people may love it, others may hate it. Isn't that what great art is? Divisive?'

A smile crept over Hollie's lips. He was right. Fashion was art, and art was divisive. So long as it got people talking, wasn't that all that mattered?

'What?'

'Damn, you're good,' she said.

He grinned. 'Did you doubt my awesomeness?'

'Never,' she said, kissing his cheek.

'Would *Mario Kart* help?'

Despite doctors telling him to rest his hand, Astin had begun to acquire a collection of games and consoles for the TV in his room. When he wasn't doing crosswords or watching *Jeremy Kyle*, there was a good chance he was playing a game.

'What about your hand?' she asked. She wasn't keen on him gaming when he was supposed to be resting, but he seemed adamant to ignore doctors' advice.

'*Mario Kart* will only break me if you win.' He gave her a cheeky smile. She melted. It was his choice to make.

'Guilting me into throwing the game, are we?'

He put his hand to his chest. 'Me? Never.'

Hollie scowled. 'Really? 'Cause it sounds a lot like you are.'

'You're just reading into things too much.'

'Is that right?' she said.

'Yep,' he confirmed. 'So. *Mario Kart*?'

'Go on then,' she said, 'but I'm not going easy on you.'

'I wouldn't want you to.'

❉

After a couple of games of *Mario Kart*, they put *The Force Awakens* on. Hollie fell asleep somewhere near the start, her head resting on Astin's lap. She woke up just as the credits began to roll. She yawned.

'You should go to bed,' he said.

She yawned again. 'I'm fine.'

'Don't make me carry you,' he said. He yawned.

'You wouldn't dare.'

'Try me.' He picked his phone up from where it lay beside him. 'It's five o'clock. The video should be out by now.'

Hollie gulped. 'I'm not sure I'm ready yet.'

He tucked her hair behind her ear. 'You don't ever have to watch it if you don't want to.'

'Sure I do. I like the song.' She yawned. 'But not yet. I want to be awake for it. And I want you with me.'

'Always,' said Astin.

She smiled. It was reassuring to know that she wasn't alone, and even if things with Tate didn't go as planned, he'd still love her. She fluffed the pillows beside him and curled up into the foetal position.

'What're you doing?' he said.

'It's easier to sleep with some background noise.'

'You'll end up in a head brace yourself with all the weird sleeping positions you have.'

'At least we'll match,' she said before closing her eyes and falling back to sleep.

Hollie woke up in Astin's bed, still curled up beside him. Her neck was tense. Astin was right. If she continued sleeping like that, she would need a neck brace. Slowly, she sat up. But she couldn't straighten her neck. It was frozen to the right. She yelped. Every time she tried to move it, a sharp twinge echoed through her neck and down her shoulder. Sitting upright, she massaged her shoulder as best she could. The tenseness began to release, but fuck, it hurt.

'Told you not to sleep that way,' said Astin. He was sat upright, a sly smile on his face.

Hollie stuck her tongue out at him. 'How'd you sleep?'

'Better than you,' he said, that smile still playing over his lips.

'I'll be fine,' she insisted, still massaging her neck and

shoulder. It had almost stopped spasming, but it was still tense, like a someone had started to wring it out when she was asleep and hadn't finished the job.

'Want me to have a look?' he offered. He reached over, his hands outstretched.

'It's nothing.' Not compared to his injuries. 'How's your back?'

'You get used to it,' he replied.

He shouldn't have to get used to it. But then, that was better than him feeling sorry for himself, wasn't it? She kissed his cheek then returned to her own room, still massaging her shoulder. Was it a good thing that he was getting used to the pain? Did it mean it was going away? Did it mean he wouldn't want as many painkillers, or was he secretly taking too many? No. He wouldn't do that. Not when two of his closest friends had gone to rehab for drug addictions.

But then…we're a product of the five people we spend the most time with.

No! He wouldn't do that.

She grabbed her phone, needing a distraction. There were so many notifications she gave up scrolling through them. She didn't read any of them. She couldn't. She was inundated with texts, tweets, Instagram likes and more. If her phone was like that, what would Tate's be like? Then again, she was Tate Gardener. She had Maddy to organise her social media. Hollie had to do it all herself. She could ask Astin if she was really desperate, although he didn't use it much himself. Doing something useful might make him feel better. Less like he'd lost everything and he was a waste of space purely because he couldn't do stunt work any more.

That was probably why he'd been offering advice on the business aspects of her fashion line. His dad had run a mechanics since before he was born. Nearly thirty years later, it was still going. Astin had spent his summer holidays helping out there until he moved to New York.

The suite door opened. Usually she would've peered out to see who it was, but she didn't want anyone to see how worked up she was. She threw her phone across the bed and lay back on it. She sat up. No matter what position she was in, nausea overwhelmed her. She hadn't eaten in over twelve hours, but her body didn't care. It wanted to purge. It *needed* to purge. She started for the bathroom.

Astin sat in the doorway. 'Dude. Knock!'
He chuckled.
At the sight of Astin, the nausea began to settle.
'How did you get out of bed?'
'Didn't you hear the door? Declan just came in. I asked him to help me out so that I could come see you before I go shower,' said Astin.
'Why? Do they hate the outfit?'
He chuckled again. 'Have you read any of the comments yet?'
She shook her head.
'Where's your phone?'
She got it from end of the bed where it had landed and gave it to him. After a few taps, he read aloud: '"Your outfit is gorgeous," heart-eyed emoji. "Wow, that outfit is epic!", "I need that jumpsuit in my life!"'
'It does not say that,' said Hollie.
'It does,' said Astin. He turned the phone to her. 'There's loads of them. You've gained 1,000 new Twitter followers alone since the video went out.'
'How do you know how many Twitter followers I had before the video went out?' Even she didn't know that.
He blushed. *Actually* blushed. 'I had a look when you were asleep.'
Hollie pinched his cheek. He swatted her away. 'Aww. Aren't you cute!'
'I'm proud of you,' he said. He kissed her cheek.
'Thanks,' she said, resting her head on his shoulder.
'Ready to watch the video?'
'No,' she said.
'Anyone would think you were in the video,' said Astin.
'A part of me is,' she said. 'I put everything into that outfit.'
'And it's paid off,' he said. 'Now we just need to keep up the momentum.'
'"We"?' echoed Hollie, unable to hide her smile.
'Of course "we". We're a team, aren't we?'
'Always,' she said, cupping his cheeks and kissing him.

Eleven

Hollie was still processing what had happened when Fayth rang. 'Have you seen it?'

'I've seen the photos, not the video,' said Hollie. She paced around her bedroom as she talked to her best friend. If she'd been at home, there would've been bits of paper and all sorts covering the carpet. But she wasn't at home. People actually cleaned up after her. She wasn't keen on other people touching her organised mess, but it meant Astin could move around more freely, so she let it go. 'I can't bring myself to.'

'Why? The comments are amazing.'

'I'll find things I don't like. I'll want to change things.' Reaching a wall, she spun on her heels and continued to pace.

'You can't change any of it now, Bea.'

'I know. And it's a horrible feeling.'

'You always had to introduce your clothes to the world one day.'

'I know, but when I've made it for me I can change and fix things I don't like. When I've made it for Tate Gardener…'

'You get a massive ego and career boost?' suggested Fayth.

'I wouldn't call it an ego boost.'

'That's because an ant has a bigger ego than you. You need lessons from Liam.'

Hollie let out a forced laugh. 'If only it were that simple.'

'Hey, I'm proud of you. I know you're scared of what will happen next, but we're all here for you, and even if you fail, we'll still love you.'

A tear formed in the corner of her eye. She wiped it away with the sleeve of her polka dot dressing gown. 'Thanks.'

'Any time. Is it stupid to ask if you've checked your website yet?'

Hollie scoffed. 'Yes. Like Tate wearing my outfit would make any difference.'

'It's *Tate Gardener*. If she doesn't have any clout, no one does.'

Hollie wasn't sure what was more terrifying – opening her website to find an influx of sales, or to find that Tate's video hadn't made any difference.

'Why don't we go for lunch and celebrate?' suggested Astin.

Hollie opened one eye. Astin sat in front of her, dressed and actually shaven. Adrian the teddy bear sat on his lap. It was the first time she'd seen him make an effort in weeks. She'd fallen back to sleep after talking to Fayth, assuming he wouldn't want to do anything.

'Um, sure,' she said, sitting up. She wanted to question where his change of attitude had come from, but she didn't want to push him and risk him shutting down. 'Where do you want to go?'

'Anywhere,' he said, waving Adrian about. 'You choose.'

'I don't really know anywhere. You know London better than I do.'

'I'll ask Declan before he leaves, see if he knows somewhere.'

Hollie pulled the duvet from her and swung her legs around to reveal her Pikachu pyjamas.

Astin smiled. 'Cute.'

'They're super soft,' she said, standing up and holding out the edge of her t-shirt so that he could feel the fabric. He pulled her on to his lap. She giggled. Then, realising she might break him, she tried to stand. His arms were like iron around her waist.

'It's fine,' he said. '*I'm* fine. No pain. I want to go out and do something. I don't want to be stuck in a hotel room.'

She kissed him. 'Good. Give me half an hour?'

'All right,' he said. He slapped her arse as she stood up.

'Cheeky,' she said. The old Astin was back. Fingers crossed he was there to stay.

'Why don't we go for a picnic?' said Hollie as they left the hotel.

'You hate the outdoors,' said Astin.

'But you like it,' said Hollie, her circle skirt swishing in the breeze. He was out of the hotel, which was a miracle in itself. Anything she could do to remind him of how much he liked being outside of the hotel, she'd do.

'All right then. Where do you want to get food from?'

'Pret?' said Hollie, pointing to it as they went past.

'Works for me,' said Astin. 'I'll wait out here.'

'Why?'

'Less effort,' he said, but he didn't sound annoyed. He manoeuvred himself so that his back was to the window and he could watch as people went by. It was something Hollie's nan liked to do, too. She openly admitted it was because she liked to be nosy. 'There's not much room inside. I'll have porridge and coffee.'

'Coming up,' said Hollie, pushing the door open and stepping inside.

Hollie picked out a ham and cheese croissant and a vanilla latte for herself. As she stood in line, she kept glancing back at Astin, half expecting him to disappear. He didn't. Where would he go, anyway? It wasn't like he could hop on a plane back to New York.

She paid and shoved everything into a takeaway bag, then hooked it on to the back of his chair as they made their way to Hyde Park. The sun was bright, almost blinding, so Hollie took out her sunglasses and put them on. She'd packed Astin's just in case, but he didn't want them – he was used to the sun.

They found a bench that overlooked The Serpentine. Astin parked up beside it, then Hollie grabbed the takeaway bag and sat beside him. The water sparkled in the bright sunlight. People went past in pedal boats, chatting animatedly as they peddled. Life was so much easier for them.

Astin held the porridge pot in his left hand and used the spoon with his right. The plaster made it awkward, but he still managed to grip. Occasionally he'd miss his mouth and it would land on his green shirt or on his jeans, but he still didn't let Hollie clean it up. He did it himself, using the empty takeaway bag to put his used napkins in. It was a good job Hollie had taken plenty.

They ate in silence, listening to the sounds of people talking about nothing in particular and the buzz of park activity. It was the calmest Hollie had felt in a long time.

Her croissant devoured, she leaned back on the bench and felt the breeze on her cheeks. If she stayed out in the sun too long she'd end up with a Rudolph nose thanks to her stupidly pale skin, but she could enjoy it for a few minutes. She didn't want to ruin it for Astin.

'Feels good, doesn't it?' said Astin.

'Yeah,' agreed Hollie. It was the most serene she'd seen him since the accident. If only she could've bottled up that calmness in case of emergencies.

As much as Hollie wanted to stay there all day, she couldn't. There was work to be done. She picked up the rubbish-filled takeaway bag and walked to the nearest bin. A bunch of teenagers nearby laughed.

'Do you think he can get it up?' said one in a beanie hat. A beanie hat. In April. Honestly.

His friends laughed again.

'Who'd want to?' said a greasy-haired one. 'He looks like he belongs in a horror film.'

Hollie's back stiffened. Were they talking about Astin? She threw the things into the bin.

'You think that's his carer?' said beanie hat.

Hollie had heard enough. She didn't care how much bigger than her said teenagers were, or that she was outnumbered four to one. They were being rude. She turned to them. 'No, I'm his girlfriend. How would you feel if someone spoke about your sex life like that? Do any of you even have sex lives?'

They blushed, all looking anywhere but at Hollie or each other.

'Yeah, you won't with attitudes like that. Just because he's in a wheelchair and has to wear a head brace for a few months that doesn't make him any less of a person than you or me. But the respect he has towards other people makes him far more of a man than any of you. Next time you start to make a joke at someone else's expense, how about you ask yourself how you'd handle being on the receiving end of it first?' She walked off before they could respond. Fucking teenagers.

In Hollie's absence, a plump middle-aged woman had appeared and put her face inches from Astin's. Shit.

'You so are that guy from the Calvin Klein ads. I remember reading that you got into an accident on some film set. It's such a shame. I had your photo on my wall!' said the woman.

A shame? A shame? He wasn't someone to be pitied!

Hollie ran back to him and put her hand on Astin's shoulder. She gave the woman her most powerful death stare. It had little impact. Damnit.

'What happened?' probed the woman.

Astin's gaze was vacant.

'Do you have brain damage?' she continued.

What the fuck?

'That's really none of your business,' said Hollie.

The woman shot her an evil look. It was the first time she'd acknowledged Hollie's presence. It didn't faze her.

'Can I get a photo?' asked the woman, taking her phone from her pocket before either of them could answer.

'I really don't think that's appropriate,' said Hollie.

'I didn't ask you,' said the woman, her phone still in her hand.

Astin had recoiled into himself. He didn't speak. His expression was blank.

'He's been through a lot lately, the last thing he needs is a camera in his face,' said Hollie.

'That's up to him, not you,' said the woman, her eyes hard.

Hollie closed her eyes. Arguing with that woman was getting her nowhere. She needed to get Astin out of there, but the wheelchair was too heavy for her to push. If he wanted to leave, he'd have to do it on his own. She reached over and guided his hand to the controls. It seemed to jolt him from his daze. He pushed the joystick on his wheelchair and began to move away. Hollie followed. It sounded a lot like the woman shouted *'Bitch!'* behind them.

Astin was quiet for most of the rest of the day. He spoke only when he needed something. She tried to spark up conversations, but neither of them were really in the mood. Hollie couldn't let go of what the teenagers had said, and Astin's expression hadn't changed since the woman had accosted him. His eyes were emptier than she'd ever seen them.

After Declan had tucked Astin up in bed, Hollie went to see him. He wasn't asleep yet. He lay on his back, his eyes on the ceiling.

'Do you want me to read you something?' she offered.

'No.'

'Can I get you anything?'

'No.'

She couldn't help but feel like what had happened was her fault. He'd wanted to go out and celebrate her success, and he'd just been reminded of his failures. Instead of going to bed and leaving him to sleep, she slid into bed beside him and put her arm around him. He put his arm around her half-heartedly. She shifted up in bed so that he could see her. 'I'm sorry about today.'

He didn't respond.

'Don't you want to talk about it?'

'Nope.'

'All right then,' she said, climbing off the bed. 'Night.' If he didn't talk to someone about how he was feeling soon, she was fairly sure he'd explode. But what more could she do?

Twelve

Astin was quiet for the next few days. Hollie tried to get him to talk, but it seldom worked. They watched the odd film together and that brightened him up for a while, but it never lasted.

But, as the end of April rolled around, Astin had to leave the hotel whether he liked it or not. He was due to get his cast off, and Hollie was adamant he wouldn't miss his appointment. If only she could find him. He wasn't in his room, nor the living area. The bathroom door was locked. She knocked. 'What're you doing? We've got to leave soon!'

'What time is it?'

'Almost time to leave.'

'Just…give me a minute.'

'Are you sure you're all right?'

'Yes!' he snapped. He said it so suddenly, so sharply, Hollie knew something was wrong.

'I'm coming in,' she said.

'No!' he said, his voice cracking. 'Don't—'

She fiddled with the lock and found her way inside. He sat on the toilet, his walking frame just to the side. He didn't look at her.

'Do you want some help?' she offered.

'No,' he said. 'I just need a minute.'

'We don't have a minute. We need to leave.'

'Oh.' He stared into his lap as much as his head brace would allow.

'What happened?'

'I didn't take any painkillers yesterday or this morning but then as I went to *you know*, something jammed. I can't move my arm properly. It hurts too much.' Tears fell from his eyes and into his lap. She rubbed his arm.

'Do you need some help?'

'Yes,' he whispered.

She handed him some toilet paper to wipe his eyes, then

wrapped some around her hand and cleaned him up. She hated seeing him so fragile, but what else could she do? He couldn't sit there until Declan arrived that evening to tuck him into bed. They had to be practical. She finished wiping his arse then moved his walking frame in front of him and eased him on to it. He leaned forwards, his body convulsing from crying. She helped him to pull his trousers up, then flushed the toilet and washed her hands. He hobbled the short distance across the bathroom. She'd looked after her nan plenty of times, but she'd never had to wipe her arse after a toilet trip. Her nan was still capable of doing that on her own. Astin was sixty years her junior and more fragile than her. No wonder he was so snippy.

He reached the bathroom door and stopped. 'Can I borrow some BB cream please?'

'Sure. What for?' She helped him into his wheelchair.

'I don't like looking so ill.'

'But you *are* ill.'

'Please?'

'I'll see what I've got,' said Hollie. 'Most of my stuff might be too pale for you.'

'You should get out more, then.' He didn't say it in his usual jovial tone. It almost sounded like an insult.

'I like my paleness,' she replied defensively, going into his room to get some painkillers from the bedside drawer. The hospital had only prescribed him paracetamol and ibuprofen, so that's what she gave him. He swallowed the tablets then followed her into her room, where they rooted over the make-up covered surface of her dressing table.

She glimpsed at him through the mirror. He had on a light blue Jack Wills shirt that complemented his eyes. His hair was longer, but the unruliness suited him. 'I like that shirt,' she said.

'I'm not sure on it.'

You try to pay someone a compliment…

She found the BB cream and handed it to him with a brush. 'Do you want me to apply it?'

He tried to take it from her, but his arm wouldn't move more than a few inches.

'We should get that looked at,' said Hollie.

'I'll be fine once the painkillers kick in.'

Hollie squirted some BB cream on to the back of her hand and began to apply it, careful of getting it in his beard. It didn't look as pale on him as she'd expected it to. Then again, he didn't spend nearly as much time outdoors as he used to.

What she couldn't work out was why he wanted to wear make-up all of a sudden. It wasn't the make-up wearing that bothered her – he had to wear it on set sometimes – it was that he'd asked her less than a week after a stranger had been up in his face. Was he worried about being recognised again?

'Is this about what happened at Hyde Park?' Hollie asked as she blended the cream into his cheeks.

'I just don't like looking ill, that's all,' he said curtly. She didn't believe him.

Astin stretched his arm in front of him. After weeks of it being wrapped in plaster, it felt like something was missing. He moved his wrist around in circles, admiring how well it moved.

Hollie reached over to put his seatbelt on. 'You practising The Robot or something?'

He wiggled his fingers. Not having anything restricting their movement felt *good*. 'Do you have any idea how good it is to not have that thing on your arm any longer?'

'Nope. Never broken a bone,' she replied, putting on her own seatbelt.

'*Ever?*'

'Nope.'

'You never broke your arm climbing a tree or doing handstands at school?'

'Never.' She switched on the engine and they headed out of the hospital car park.

'Lucky,' he said.

'How many have you broken?'

'Three or four? No. Five including this one.'

'Five? What did you do as a kid?'

'Climbing, gymnastics, dance, martial arts…sometimes the only way to learn what to do is by learning what not to do.'

'Sounds dangerous.'

'It was for me,' he said. If only he'd known it back then.

'How's your other arm?' she asked.

'A little better now I've had some painkillers.'

'Good,' said Hollie. 'Fancy going for a coffee since we're already out?'

He tensed. As much as the head brace would allow, anyway. 'We don't have time. Tate will be here soon.' And her arrival was the perfect excuse for not going out. What if someone recognised him again? What would he say? Or worse, what if someone talked about him behind his back? He'd heard people mutter on the rare occasion they had breakfast downstairs. Did they talk about how hideous he looked? How pathetic he was? How needy? He didn't need to hear other people talking about him to know all those things were true.

Tate arrived a couple of hours later. It was the first time she'd seen him since the week of the accident. Astin grunted at her a few times. That was his greeting to one of his closest friends. Git. Hollie guided her away from Astin's room. 'Sorry. He's getting worse for that.'

'What's happened to him?'

'Shall we go for a coffee?' said Hollie. She didn't want to discuss it with him so close.

Tate agreed, and they went to a coffee shop nearby. The same bodyguard Tate had used when Astin was in hospital joined them, but he didn't speak and had the worst resting bitch face Hollie had ever seen.

'So what's wrong with him?' Tate asked as they sat down.

Her bodyguard sat at a table beside them and glared around the room.

'I don't know,' said Hollie, hugging her drink to her. She wished she did.

'How are things with you two?'

Hollie watched the baristas make the coffee. For some reason, it relaxed her. Hollie shrugged. Some days she saw the old Astin back. Other days he spoke to her so little she felt invisible.

Tate gave her arm a squeeze. 'Want me to talk to him?'

'No! God, no. That'd only make him worse.'

'Why don't you take a break, then? Go for a spa day?'

'I don't have time,' said Hollie.

'Do you have time to make me another outfit?'

Hollie stared at Tate. The reception for her *Comet* outfit had been great, but she'd assumed that would be it. Turned out, Astin was right.

'What for?' asked Hollie. She was short on time, but she could hardly say no to the woman that had launched her career.

'I'm hosting a gala at Nobu in August for orphaned children.'

'Cool.'

'You and Astin are invited, of course. So are Fayth and Liam. It has a theme, too.'

'Which is?'

'Modern fairytales.'

'I can do fairytales.' She'd made Cinderella-inspired outfits for her final project at university, and it had been a fairytale-themed exhibit at the Fashion Institute of Technology that had inspired her to start her business.

'My favourite fairytale is Cinderella, but going as a princess is so *obvious*.'

'Who were you thinking of instead?' asked Hollie.

Tate smiled. She picked up a coffee stirrer and pointed it at Hollie like a wand. 'The fairy godmother.'

Hollie grinned. Yes, that fitted Tate perfectly.

'Why don't we watch a movie later?' Astin asked as they ate dinner.

Tate had gone out with some of her London friends, no doubt put off by the negative energy that surrounded Astin like bees swarming their queen. Hollie didn't blame her.

She swallowed a mouthful of potato. 'I'd love to, but I'm inundated with orders, and now I have Tate's gala outfit to make too. If I don't stay on top of things I'll fall behind and my reviews will go to shit.'

'It's only a couple hours.'

'You can achieve a lot in the space of time it takes to watch a film. Especially these days.'

'What's that supposed to mean?' He stabbed a piece of fish.

'Nothing. If you work in the film industry, I get it, but I don't. I work in fashion. And I have clothes to make and sell. I'm lucky Jamal can help me post stuff, otherwise I'd spend half my time queueing at the bloody Post Office.'

He let his cutlery fall on to his plate. 'Why don't you get a PA?'

Hollie scoffed. 'With what money? I can barely afford to pay myself.'

'We hardly spend any time together lately.'

Hollie clenched her teeth. That wasn't her doing. It'd taken long enough to convince him to sit at the table and eat dinner with her. 'Forgive me for not wanting to spend all day lying in bed.'

'I can't do anything else!'

'Not this again,' grumbled Hollie.

'Not what again? That I'm stuck in a wheelchair?'

'You're not *stuck* in a wheelchair. You'd be stuck if you didn't have a wheelchair. A wheelchair gives you freedom.' She put her cutlery together on her plate. 'I've lost my appetite.' She went into her room and closed the door. When would he realise what an idiot he was being? How much longer would she have to put up with his self-pity? How much longer *could* she put up with it?

She reached for her phone and called Fayth. She didn't pick up. Sighing, she rolled over and curled into a ball. She'd go out back out into the living area – where her laptop and sewing machine were – once Astin had returned to his room. That way she'd have some peace.

Her phone rang. Fayth.

Hollie exhaled, sitting up and dangling her legs off the end of the bed. 'Hey.'

'How's things?' said Fayth.

'Nggggh.'

'That good, huh?'

'He genuinely sees his wheelchair and head brace as some sort of torture devices. I can't snap him out of it.'

'Well the head brace does kind of look like one,' said Fayth.

'Not the point. It doesn't mean he can't go out. Ever since that woman was in his face, he'll only go out for hospital appointments. He won't even go downstairs to eat.'

'Shit.'

'Yeah. See my point? I don't know what to do. We just keep getting into the same argument all the time.' She stared at one of the paintings on the wall. She still hadn't worked out what it was supposed to be of.

'He'll snap out of it once he gets his head brace off,' said Fayth. Her tone wasn't convincing.

'Yeah,' said Hollie. 'I wish I believed you.'

MAY

One

A pile of letters thudded on to the welcome mat. Fayth climbed out of bed and plodded down the stairs. Bills. More bills. And an A4 envelope addressed to her. It couldn't be, could it?

She took it, along with the other letters, into the kitchen. Brooke was at college and her dad had gone shopping, so there was nobody to share the moment with. She was all right with that. A part of her wanted to be alone, just for a minute. After dumping the other letters on to the dining table, she opened the A4 envelope. It was the decree absolute. The piece of paper signalling that she was finally divorced.

It was actually over.

It was actually, *finally* over.

There were no more cliffhangers. No more waiting on other people to get what she wanted. For the first time in her life, her future was entirely up to her. And it felt amazing. And nauseating.

Her stomach swirled, as if she'd eaten a dodgy curry. Bile rose in her throat. She ran upstairs into the bathroom. Seconds after she closed the door, her body purged. What seemed like a never-ending stream of vomit spewed from her stomach and into the toilet. The last time she'd chucked up like that had been when she'd had a virus as a teenager. She *never* threw up, not even when drunk. Ugh. She went dizzy. What was wrong with her? She sat on the green tiles for a few minutes to allow her head to stop spinning and stomach to settle. There was something very wrong with her digestive system.

She forced herself to stand up. The room still spun, but not as badly. Somehow, she managed to make a cup of tea and get some gingernuts from the cupboard. The tea would calm her. It always did.

Except it didn't.

The ginger didn't help settle the nausea, either.

She managed to keep the biscuits down, but she felt like any second they'd come back up. Was she coming down with something?

Fayth texted Hollie, Liam, and Ross, informing them of her freedom, then left the paperwork out on the dining table for her dad and Brooke to find. They'd never liked Patrick, but they'd never stopped her from doing what she wanted to do. That wasn't their style.

Hollie replied with a grinning emoji and suggested they go for a celebratory night out the next time they saw one another, but after everything that had happened, Fayth just wanted to curl up in a ball and sleep for about a decade. Maybe two. Her body felt like it was made of lead, and the nausea hadn't subsided much. Unable to eat, she headed to work and pulled on her apron. If only she had a blocked nose to go with her nausea. At least then she wouldn't have had to face the smell of food.

It was still early in New York, but, surprisingly, Liam texted her: *How's your first day of freedom? L x*

And he'd signed it with a kiss. He'd never done that before. What did that mean?

And when had she turned into Hollie?

Nauseating, she wrote. *Haven't been able to shake it since the letter came through.*

:(Rest up x

Wish I could. Work calls.

Reality. What a bitch x

Isn't it?

Skype later? x

Sure. Not working tonight.

What time? x

5ish? My time?

See you then x

Jim had tried to organise a meeting with Liam several times since their argument in the restaurant. Liam had no interest in meeting with him. He still hadn't forgiven him for suggesting that he work with Trinity again. If that's what his film career had come to, he was done with movies. He'd instructed Ola that under no circumstances would he meet with Jim, and that she was to tell him nothing other than that he was too busy. He almost felt bad for Ola having to do it for him, but, well, it *was* what he paid her for.

Unemployed and unsure of what to do, he spent his days playing *World of Warcraft*. The great thing about *WoW* was that it allowed him to escape from the real world into a virtual one. He could spend hours, days, even weeks in Azeroth if he wanted to. Nobody in Azeroth knew who he was. Nobody cared. The only thing they judged him on was his ability to play the game, and, luckily for him, he was damn good at it.

His parents weren't happy that he spent his days hiding in his room on his PC – and they were vocal about their disapproval – but what could they do? He was 25, and he had plenty of money. He still earned money from *Highwater* just by sitting on his ass playing *WoW*. He'd earned some time off. The only time he'd taken off had been after Saoirse had died and he'd ended up in rehab. All things considered, that didn't really count. Alone time was precious.

He stretched his arms in front of him and checked the clock. Midday. Almost time to Skype with Fayth. Woo. He closed the game and got up to get a drink before their video chat.

While the kettle boiled, he pulled his phone from his pocket. He had a voicemail from a number he didn't recognise. He wasn't expecting a phone call, but he checked his messages just in case it was important.

It wasn't work-related. It was a recorded message of some of

Trinity's song lyrics. He threw the phone across the room. It landed with a thud against the porcelain tiles. And continued to play.

'You burn me once, shame on you/you burn me twice, shame on me/you burn me three times, I'll get my sweet revenge'.

Fayth was curled up in bed, her laptop on her lap as she prepared to Skype with Liam. She'd put some Vaseline on her dry lips and used some mousse to try and tame her curls. It hadn't worked as well as she'd planned. She gave up in the end. He'd seen her with Jupiter's red spot on her face and not said anything. A bad hair day was nothing in comparison to that.

While she waited for him to come online, she opened Twitter. Since returning from New York, her guilty pleasure was to search for herself to see what people were saying. She still didn't have any social media accounts, but that didn't stop people from talking about her. Or creating spoof accounts that shared the most unflattering images they could find. Some comments were mild playground bitchiness about how unruly her hair was or how her nose looked like it'd been broken three times. Others threatened violence just because she was 'dating' Liam. And some made her feel sick. There was even an image where they'd Photoshopped her head on to someone else's naked body. Why would someone do that? What the hell kind of weirdo were they?

Liam's name appeared onscreen. She closed the dodgy tabs on her browser, as if he'd be able to see what she was looking at from a a video call. He called her immediately and her stomach swirled. Whatever was wrong with her needed to go away, and fast.

'Hey, Campbell,' he said.

'Are you all right? You look flustered.'

He ran his hand through his hair. Parts of it stayed sticking up, creating a unicorn horn. She didn't say anything. Her hair still looked worse. 'It's nothing.' He shifted in his seat. 'How's things your end?'

'OK. Feeling a bit rough.'

'Why?'

'Just nauseous, that's all,' she said. She yawned.

'You eaten something funny?' He ran his hand over his hair and flatted his unicorn horn.

'Maybe,' said Fayth, although she didn't remember doing so.

'If it's not that, I don't know what else it could be.'

'Stress?' offered Liam.

Fayth snorted. 'I'm not stressed.'

'After everything you've been through? As if.'

Fayth glowered.

'Give me that look all you like, Campbell. It's plausible.'

'Why would that make me nauseous?'

'Because stress can cause nausea. It can also cause indigestion and acid reflux. And make your hair fall out.'

Oh god. Was that why Fayth's hair fell out in clumps every time she washed it?

'What? You've gone even paler. I didn't think that was possible.'

'Ha ha,' said Fayth. 'Do you really think it could be stress?'

'I'd be more surprised if it wasn't,' he replied.

Fayth rested her head against the headboard. Could stress really do that much damage? She squeezed her eyes shut. She needed to change the subject. She couldn't think about how much her body hated her any longer.

'How's things in New York?' What she really meant was, *have you had any more signs of your stalker?*

'It's like Wade has superglued himself to me. He stays over almost every night. I'm sick of looking at him. If it's not him, it's Ola or Thalia. My parents call at least three times a day, even though I'm already *living* with them. I thought I lived in a bubble when *Highwater* was filmed, but fuck, that was nothing compared to this.'

'They're just worried about you,' she said. She didn't blame them. They all wanted to keep him in one piece.

'It might not even been a stalker. Just a coincidence.'

Fayth frowned. Did he really believe that?

'What? It could've been. Coincidences do happen, you know. It's the human brain that strives to create patterns in everything.'

'I know,' said Fayth, 'but that still doesn't mean that you don't have a stalker.'

'Yeah, well. Don't be surprised if I end up in Scotland.'

Goosebumps formed on her arms. Would she really get to see him again so soon, or did he just want to visit his grandparents in Fife? The way he spoke made it sound like he wanted to visit her, not his grandparents, but she suffocated the hope as quickly as it had appeared. He had more interesting people to spend his time with than her.

'Why would you end up in Scotland?' she asked, trying her best to pretend she didn't care.

'Cause I'm sick of being suffocated in New York.'

He wouldn't really end up in Scotland, would he?

Two

Hollie hated maths. She'd hated it ever since her GCSEs, when her teacher had been more interested in doodling on the whiteboard than teaching algebra. It wasn't that she couldn't do it, it was that she was out of practice and had too much else to do to relearn what she'd long forgot.

But it had to be done.

So she went down to a cafe and set up shop there. It was kitschy, with gingham curtains and the permanent smell of grease in the air. It reminded her of one of her nan's favourite cafes, where she often insisted on going after they'd been to get her pension. She may have hated her job then, but life had been so much easier. It was just her, her nan, her mum, and George. The things you miss…

She added some formulae to her spreadsheet. Formulae she could do. But it felt a lot like cheating.

"Scuse me, if you don't mind me commenting, you look a bit lonely.'

A middle-aged man who desperately needed to comb his hair stood in front of her. Apparently being on her own optionally wasn't allowed.

'Would you like some company?' said the man.

'I'm good, thanks.'

He pulled up a chair anyway. She shuddered. He reeked of cigarettes. 'Why are you here all alone?'

'I'm busy, actually.'

'Oh? What're you doing? Playing one of those games you young 'uns like?'

'No.' The cafe didn't even have wifi.

Her natural reaction was to talk, but there was something about him that made her uncomfortable. The more she spoke, the more he'd think she was open to conversation.

She focused on her laptop screen, hoping he'd take the hint. He watched her as she typed away, and after a few painful moments where she felt like a zoo animal, she slammed her laptop shut and packed up.

'Where're you going?' he asked.

'I'm leaving.'

'Oh. Where to?'

She shoved her laptop into her bag then power walked back to the hotel. He didn't follow her. Phew.

Astin was in his room watching *Jeremy Kyle* when she got back.

'Seriously?' said Hollie, her gaze flitting from him to the TV and back again.

'Shh, they're just about to announce the results of the lie detector test,' said Astin.

'You know those things aren't scientifically accurate, right?'

'Go ahead, spoil my fun,' said Astin as the show went to commercial break.

'You're watching *Jeremy Kyle*. I'm not sure you realise how bad this is.'

'What's wrong with *Jeremy Kyle*?'

What was *right* with it? She didn't say that. She perched on the end of the bed and tucked her knees underneath her.

'Did you have fun at the cafe?' asked Astin.

'Not really. Some weirdo wouldn't leave me alone.'

'I know the feeling.'

'Very funny.'

'How are you feeling?'

'Not great,' he said. 'Why?'

'Because I worry about you?'

'Why? There's nothing you can do.'

'Do you want to go out in a bit, get some fresh air?'

'No thanks.' The show came back on and his attention returned to the TV. She sighed. How much longer could he hold himself hostage for? She returned to her room. He was being ridiculous, as usual. She'd wanted to ask him to help her with her accounts, but if he didn't feel well, she didn't want to bother him. Instead, she called her ex-flatmate Cameron. They'd lived together at university, and he was always the one she called when she needed a brutally honest perspective. Or help with maths.

'He's watching *Jeremy Kyle*,' said Hollie when he picked up.

'What's wrong with *Jeremy Kyle*?' said Cameron.

'You're not serious?'

'I watch it every morning. When I'm not at work, of course.'

Hollie shook her head. 'I suggested going out for a bit. He turned me down for *Jeremy Kyle*.'

'OK, that is bad. But he's got a lot going on. Just give him some time.'

Time. That's what everyone kept saying. But how much time? Was she just expected to keep going until he was himself again?

'Hollie? You're not usually quiet for this long,' said Cameron.

'Oh. Yeah.'

'Do I need to come visit?'

'I wouldn't say no,' but she didn't have the gumption to say yes. She felt too guilty taking him away from his own life. 'I could use some help with the accounts.'

'Given I failed my degree I'm not sure how great I'll be, but I've got a few days off at the weekend. I could come down then?'

'Please,' said Hollie, already feeling better at the option of company. 'And you'll be better at it than me. I just make the clothes.'

'And market them like a boss,' added Cameron.

'That wasn't me: that was Tate.'

'Because she liked what you wore on your hot date with Astin,' he added.

'She didn't see that outfit. Well, she has now, but it was the black playsuit and white blazer that caught her attention.'

'That is one of your best,' said Cameron.

'Thanks. Hopefully I didn't hit my peak with it.'

'Why? Are things going badly?'

'No, it's not that. I just wonder if I'm in over my head sometimes.'

'You'll be fine,' Cameron reassured her. 'You'll feel even better once you've seen me.'

'Think a lot of yourself, don't you?'

'Yep.'

'You invited him to stay? Without asking me?' snapped Astin. He sat in bed with a console controller in hand, his current game of choice – *Diablo* – paused.

'What's the big deal? It's just Cameron,' said Hollie from the doorway. 'I need to get out of this place, and it's not like you'll come out with me, and he said he'd help me with my accounts.'

'So that means you have to invite him to stay? I don't even

know him! What's so wrong with going out on your own?'

'He's my best friend! I'm almost as close to him as I am Fayth. And I hate going out on my own. It's boring.'

'That doesn't give you the right to invite him over without talking to me!'

'Forgive me for thinking you wouldn't mind me having a friend over for a couple of days.'

'What? My company not good enough for you any more?'

She waved her arms as she spoke. He was overreacting. 'It's got nothing to do with that! I just want to get out of the hotel, go for a coffee, talk nonsense. I want to do the things we used to do!'

'I can't do that kind of stuff any more! You know that!'

'Says whom? The doctor said to rest your back. You have a wheelchair so that you're not stuck in or bed bound.'

'I don't want to be seen in that fucking thing!'

'Why? It's nothing to be embarrassed about.'

'Isn't it?' snapped Astin. 'You're not the one who gets stared at for going around in a wheelchair. People don't understand when they see a guy like me in one. They associate wheelchairs with old people. They see me and they look at me like I'm some kind of circus freak.'

'You think I don't know? You think I haven't noticed the kinds of looks you get? That Nan gets? I've had to watch my nan's body fail her over the last decade, getting weaker and weaker as I grew stronger. I've seen the looks she gets for being in a wheelchair. I've heard the mutterings. So don't you ever fucking tell me I don't know what you're going through.' She stormed into her room, slamming the door behind her.

Dick.

The tension between Hollie and Astin didn't lessen over the following days. They grunted at each other when they ran into each other, but they ate at different times, showered at different times, and movie night was no longer a thing. He stopped asking for her help if he wanted something, either waiting for Declan or summoning Jamal instead.

If he wanted to be like that, that was just fine by Hollie. She had plenty of work she could do instead of babysitting him.

He spent most of his time in his room playing games. That meant Hollie could use the lounge to sew and work on other things. The only time she saw or spoke to anyone was when Jamal or Declan walked through to see Astin. Once they'd gone into his room, she disappeared into her room so that she didn't have to face him.

The phone in their room rang. Knowing Astin wouldn't pick up, she went over to it. 'I have a Mr Woodruff to see you, Miss Baxter,' said Jamal.

Hollie switched her sewing machine off, tucking the dress she was making inside it and out of the way. Cameron had arrived!

'Thanks Jamal. Can you bring him up please?'

'Of course.'

She took the few extra minutes to tidy up around the suite. It was mostly tidy thanks to Jamal, but he didn't touch her sewing corner just in case. She made sure there were no rogue pins, went for a quick pee, then returned from the bathroom to find Cameron stood in the lounge, grinning.

'Nice digs.'

'Hey Cam,' said Hollie. She dived on him, wrapping her arms around his stomach. He was a big guy, and even on tiptoes she struggled to reach his neck.

He put his arms around her and patted her back. 'Someone missed my good looks.' She squeezed tighter, not realising how much she'd missed him, Fayth, her nan, her mum, George…

'It can't be that bad, can it?'

She nodded, still clutching him.

'Hmm. This may call for alcohol.'

She gave him a playful shove.

'Ice cream at least.'

'That's better,' she said.

'Do I at least get to see the rest of the suite before we go out?'

Hollie showed him her room, the bathroom, then hovered by the door to Astin's room.

She knocked.

Astin grunted.

She took that as an opening.

Astin sat in bed, staring at the TV and playing *Diablo*.

'Hey,' said Cameron. He hovered by the doorway, just behind Hollie. 'Nice room.'

Given the argument she'd had with Astin about his visit, she doubted Astin's greeting would be warm. She wasn't surprised when his greeting was a curt nod, nothing more.

Hollie closed the door to his room and left him to it. 'See

what I'm dealing with?'

'Typical man,' said Cameron. 'He's being disturbed when playing a game. You can hardly blame him.'

'Stereotype, much?'

Cameron shrugged. He sat on one of the sofas, stretching his arms across the back of it. 'So which do you want to do first? Coffee or finances?'

'Coffee. I can't deal with numbers without coffee.'

They left with barely an acknowledgement from Astin and headed to the nearest coffee shop. Once they'd settled down with their drinks Hollie burst into a full-on rant. 'Do I sound like a bitch?' she asked once she'd finished, ten minutes later.

Cameron sipped his caramel cappuccino, the picture of calm. 'Nah. You sound like a typical nagging girlfriend.'

She kicked him under the table.

He chuckled. 'I jest, I jest. Every couple goes through hating each other for a while. It's perfectly normal.'

'And?'

'And what? Either you'll grow out of it and learn to compromise, live in a permanent state of limbo, or eventually one of you will walk out.'

'And how long until we realise which is the path for us?'

Cameron took a few more sips of his cappuccino before replying. 'It varies.'

Hollie slumped in her chair. 'I hate this. I feel so isolated. I've got so much to do, and I just…' She stared into her decaf vanilla latte, her eyes filling with tears.

'Hey, come on now,' said Cameron, shifting his chair around so that he could hug her. She leaned into him, sniffling.

'You best not get the jumper wet. It's cashmere, you know.'

She lifted her head. 'Aren't we middle-class?' She flashed him a teasing smile.

'I wish. It was a birthday present from the 'rents, since they couldn't be arsed to come see me.'

'Ah yes, how are the Woodruffs?'

'Far happier in Wales than I was.'

Cameron was originally from Wales, but moved to Nottingham as a teenager. When his parents had moved back during his university years, he'd decided to stick around.

'Not tempted to go back, then?'

'Hell no,' said Cameron. 'Now back to you. You two will get

through this.'

'How do you know?'

'Because the chances are you've ended up with a guy who's just as stubborn as you are.'

Hollie wrinkled her nose at him.

'What? Are you denying that you're stubborn?'

'I prefer "tenacious".'

'Same thing. Point is, he still cares, he's just got a lot going on right now.'

'How do you know he still cares? He barely acknowledged us.'

'Because if he didn't care, you wouldn't keep getting into arguments. Arguments in relationships are a good thing.'

'Pardon?'

'It helps clear the air. Rainbow after the storm, and all that,' said Cameron sagely.

'Right.'

'Trust me on that one. My parents have been married thirty years. And they still get into blazing arguments. And afterwards —'

'Please don't finish that sentence. I've met your parents. I don't need that image.'

'What're you saying about my parents?'

'That I don't want to picture them naked,' she said.

'Why? Do you think they're unattractive?'

'Oh my god, are you serious?'

'Nah, just teasing,' he said, nudging her.

'I hate you,' said Hollie, nudging him back.

'No you don't.'

Hollie only returned to the hotel that evening because, technically, she lived there, and all her things were there. She still wasn't in the mood to deal with Astin and his bad mood, but she couldn't avoid him forever. He was in the living area eating and listening to something through EarPods when Hollie returned.

'Hey,' she said as she walked through the door.

Astin raised his hand in greeting, his mouth full of food. He paused whatever he was listening to and took out his EarPods. He was open to conversation. That was a good sign.

'What've you got?' asked Hollie. She hovered by the door, not taking her coat off. Just in case she needed to make a quick exit.

'Dunno. Something with fish in.' He had another mouthful. 'You gonna stand there all night?'

She took a few steps away from the door.

'Where's Cameron?'

'Downstairs, having a drink.'

'I see,' said Astin.

Hollie pushed her cuticles back. She hadn't had chance to paint her nails in weeks. It made her feel naked. 'I shouldn't have invited him without asking you first.'

Astin remained silent.

'I want to be here for you but I can't sit sewing all the time. I'm going mad.'

He manoeuvred his wheelchair so that he could face her. 'I'm not stopping you from going out.'

'No, but it's no fun on your own. Especially not when you don't like crowds.'

'I thought you were over that?'

'I'm not going to have a fully fledged panic attack from being outside any more, but that doesn't mean I enjoy being surrounded by people either. Plus, it's boring. I like spending time with you. We had so much fun when we came to London for my birthday. I hate the thought of you hiding in here all the time.'

'I'm not hiding! If you want go out, I'm not stopping you. But I'm not going with you either.' He pushed the gearstick on his wheelchair and went into his room. So much for resolving things.

Three

Fayth was doing her hair ready for work when the front door opened. 'It's me,' called her dad up the stairs.

'What're you doing home?' asked Fayth, leaving the bathroom and heading downstairs as she fastened her hair into a ponytail.

'Just came to grab some paracetamol,' he replied.

'Why?' said Fayth, following him into the kitchen. He never took painkillers. He was very anti-painkiller.

'Just feeling a bit off, nothing to worry about.'

'Your face is red.' She sat down at the dining table, watching as he raided the medicine cabinet and got himself a glass of water.

He coughed. 'It's windy out and I just walked here from the pub. Don't worry so much lass – I'm fine.' He popped one of the tablets from the blister packet. 'Just got a frog in my throat. All this talking doesn't help.'

'Sorry,' said Fayth. 'You sure you're up to working?'

'Yes.' He swallowed one of the tablets, then popped out a second and took that, too.

He didn't look up to working, and if he was coming down with something, he risked passing it on by going to work. It was May, though, so it could easily be hay fever. She didn't suffer from it, but she knew her dad did if the pollen count was high enough. Tree pollen was his worst enemy, and the house was surrounded by trees of various sizes.

'Have you taken an antihistamine?'

'Haven't got any,' he said. 'I'll pop to the chemist and get some after lunch.'

'Why don't you go now? I can open up. It won't take you long to grab some.'

'Nah, it's fine. I can manage.'

And it was that kind of attitude that worried her.

※

The following morning, Fayth's fears were confirmed: her dad was ill. Not just a sniffle here or a weak cough there, either. Full-on, raging flu.

Fayth watched from the dining table as he made his usual toast and marmalade for breakfast. He looked even paler than he had the day before. If it hadn't been so worrying, it would've been impressive considering he hardly got any sun anyway.

Brooke walked in, stopping the minute she saw him. 'You look like you haven't slept in a year.'

'Thanks. That's what having kids does to you.' He sneezed.

Fayth passed him a piece of kitchen roll. 'There's no way you can work like this. You're a walking germ incubator.'

'I'm all right,' he repeated before blowing his nose.

'You're not, Dad,' said Brooke. 'You look like shit.'

'Language, Brooke.'

'Germs, Dad.'

He started coughing uncontrollably. It was a hacking, chesty cough that only those who were really run-down did. His daughters ran to his side, but he held his hands up to keep them away. Fayth got him a glass of water and handed it to him.

He took a few sips in between coughs. 'Maybe you're right.'

'Of course we're right,' said Brooke. 'I'm always right.'

'I cannot wait for you to grow out of the teenage know-it-all-phase,' said Fayth.

'Enough,' said her dad. He coughed again. 'I'll stay at home. If Ross can do the extra hours.'

'Course he can,' said Fayth. 'He and his girlfriend are saving for a house. He'll be grateful for the extra money, same as he was when I was in London.'

'If you're that sure, I'm heading back to bed.' He coughed again, then took his glass of water and disappeared upstairs.

Brooke sneezed.

Fayth glared at her.

'Relax, it's just hay fever,' said Brooke.

They hoped.

Still unable to face the smell of food, Fayth asked Ross to work in the kitchen. She'd avoided it as much as possible since the divorce was finalised. Liam's suggestion that her nausea was stress haunted her, but she refused to believe it. The nausea and dodgy stomach had gone on for a while, though. Too long for a stomach bug. And too unpredictably. If it wasn't stress, what else could it be?

The lunch shift was quiet and uneventful, just how Fayth liked it. Ross had so little to do that he sat at the bar and talked to a couple of the lunchtime regulars. At the end of the shift, he returned to the kitchen to tidy up, leaving Fayth to clean up the bar area.

Even though it had been a quiet lunchtime, Fayth was still knackered. No matter how much sleep she got, she was *always* tired. Her body hated her, that was for sure.

She rubbed her face and stared out through the window at the front of the pub. A motorbike zoomed past. It looked like it indicated into the pub car park, but she couldn't be sure.

'Hey, do we know anyone who rides a Ducati?' asked Ross, poking his head out of the kitchen.

Fayth turned from the window. She *did* know someone with a Ducati, but he lived in New York. 'No, why?'

'One just pulled into the car park.'

It couldn't be, could it?

Don't be surprised if I end up in Scotland.

She dumped the cleaning stuff on the bar, then walked to the pub door and looked out. A figure in a brown leather jacket climbed from the Ducati Diavel. The bike and jacket were identical to the ones Liam had. The figure removed his helmet and shook out his floppy, dark brown hair.

Ross stood beside her, his mouth hanging open. 'Is that who I think it is?'

'Uh-huh.'

'Did you invite him?'

'Why would I do that?' said Fayth, shooting him an accusatory look.

'No reason.'

Liam noticed them watching and waved. 'Hey,' he said as he approached the door. He was so casual, like he'd been there a million times, rather than, you know, never.

'Hi,' said Fayth. It was all she could bring herself to say. Liam was right there. Not in New York. But right in front of her. In her hometown. At her pub!

'What're you doing here?' said Fayth.

He smiled at Ross and held out his hand. 'Hi, I'm Liam.'

'R-Ross.'

It was nice to know she wasn't the only one that got starstruck when first meeting him. She decided not to pass on Hollie's advice about picturing him on the loo.

'Good to meet you, Ross. Fayth's told me a lot about you,' said Liam.

'S-she has?'

'All good, don't worry. Are we going to go inside or stand in the doorway all day?'

Fayth and Ross returned to the inside of the pub. Liam followed.

'It's not much,' said Fayth.

'I like it,' said Liam. 'It's got character.'

That was the nice way of explaining the cheap paint and 1980's decor.

'Can we get you any food or a drink?' offered Ross.

'I wouldn't want to put you out. You're not even open yet, are you?' said Liam.

'We just finished lunch,' said Ross. 'But I can rustle something up for you if you're hungry. It's no big deal.'

'What've you got?' asked Liam.

Fayth reached on to a table and handed him a dog-eared menu. He was right there. And about to be served lunch. But why?

He had the same milky skin; the same espresso-coloured eyes and matching hair; the same cinnamon and sandalwood cologne. Nothing about him had changed. Her stomach swirled again. Oh god. She looked away.

'I wouldn't say no to a steak,' said Liam.

'How would you like it done?' asked Ross.

'Medium, please. With onion rings and those fat chip things.' He put the menu down on the wrong table.

'Someone's feeling unhealthy,' said Fayth, taking the menu and putting it back on the right table.

'I'm so over salad and spiralised vegetables. It's all I've eaten since I got back to New York. My nutritionist seems to think I won't eat healthily unless I'm force fed.'

Fayth snorted. He *wouldn't* eat healthily unless he was force fed.

'What?' said Liam.

'Nothing,' she said. She turned to Ross: 'Can you do me one as well please?'

'No, you can cook your own,' said Ross.

Fayth sneezed.

'On second thoughts, you're better off out of the kitchen.'

She sneezed again.

Ross took a serviette from a nearby table and handed it to her. She wiped her nose. 'Thanks. I really hope I'm not getting Dad's germs.'

Liam took a few steps back. 'Keep them to yourself please.'

'Sure you don't want them? I'm sure there are plenty of people you don't like you could pass them on to.'

'I'm good thanks.'

Ross stood beside them, gawking. He really was starstruck.

'Steak,' Fayth reminded him.

'Right. Yes. Kitchen.' He turned and disappeared through the swinging door.

Fayth walked over to the bar. Liam followed and perched on a stool.

'Are people always like that when you first meet them?' she asked.

'Most of the time, yeah.' He ran his hand through his hair, a coy smile on his cheeks that showed off his dimples. Damn, he was cute. 'I'm pretty sure you were the same when we first met.'

Fayth's cheeks burned. She'd hoped he wouldn't remember that. 'Yeah. Well. Back then I was in love with *Highwater*.'

'You're not any more?' He almost sounded disappointed.

She leaned against the bar. 'It's not the same any more.'

'Disappointed I'm not as ripped as in the films?'

'No, disappointed the real-life Melitha was as crazy as her character,' said Fayth.

Meeting the film's stars had ruined the illusion for her. It was why she hadn't wanted to go to the meet and greets at HighCon. Little did she realise when she booked the HighCon tickets she'd get a better version for free.

His face fell.

'Sorry. That was unfair.'

'No, no, it's OK. I know what you mean.'

'What do you want to drink?' Fayth asked, desperate for a change of subject.

'Anything non-alcoholic please.'

She poured him some Irn Bru and placed it in front of him. Without paying attention to the bright orange concoction in front of him, he sipped. Then he squirmed.

'What the hell is that!'

She giggled. 'Irn Bru.'
'It's…'
'Amazing?'
He pushed the glass towards her. 'No.'
She picked it up and took a few sips. 'Some people have no taste.'
'Says the woman who drinks something that tastes like metal.'
'Don't know what you're talking about,' said Fayth. 'Sure you don't want to give it another chance?'
'Positive.'
Fayth took another glass from underneath the bar and filled it from the tap with water.
'Much better,' he said, taking a sip.
She leaned against the back bar. Of all the people he could've travelled thousands of miles to see, he picked her. Of all the places he could've chosen to hide from his stalker, he picked her village. Why?
'You look confused,' said Liam. He sipped his water.
'Just trying to figure out how this place appeals to a city dweller like you.' He'd once told her he had to have ambient noise on to help him sleep. Had he brought one of those stupid contraptions with him? He'd never sleep otherwise. Not unless he liked the noise of crickets.
He smiled. 'I can't come visit my favourite bartender?'
'Don't you have auditions to go to?'
'I'm thinking of doing a film where the protag is a bartender. Thought I'd come get in some first-hand experience.'
Fayth raised an eyebrow. 'You want to work behind the bar?'
'If you'll have me. I mean, it wouldn't be bad for business, would it?' He flashed her a teasing smile.
No, it definitely wouldn't be bad for business.
'Figured since you're ill, your dad's ill, and Brooke needs to study for her exams, an extra pair of hands couldn't hurt.'
How much had she told him about her life? And how much attention had he paid? Didn't he have bigger things to worry about than a pub tucked away in the middle of nowhere?
'I'm *not* ill,' insisted Fayth. She shouldn't have told him about the nausea and the hair falling out. She wasn't stressed!
Much.
'You still look confused.'
She wasn't sure she believed him. Was that really the only

reason he was there? Was there more to it than that? But what more could there be?

'How did you even get here so fast?'

He grinned. 'British passport.'

Of course. His mother was half Irish, half Scottish. She'd grown up in Ireland then moved to the States.

A tickle formed in the back of her nose. She sniffed a couple of times. She sneezed.

She tried to sneeze into her elbow – hands were so unhygienic – but that didn't stop her face from being covered in snot. She scrambled to get a tissue from her pocket, unable to look at him. There was a mirror at the back of the bar, but she hoped there was enough booze on there to disguise her reflection as she grabbed the tissues and wiped at her face. She'd better not have her dad's germs too.

Shaking her head, she turned back to Liam. His eyes were glued to her. 'You sure you're all right to work?'

'Nobody else is here to help, are they?'

'I am,' he said.

'And how much bar experience do you have?'

'Er…'

'None, then.'

He smiled. 'I'm a fast learner.'

'Ice skating,' she reminded him. He'd given up on that when it hadn't been as easy as he'd hoped. There may have been photographic evidence of it happening, but he hadn't stayed on the ice long.

'That's different,' he said.

She wasn't convinced.

The pub phone rang. She went to the side of the bar and picked it up. 'Cock and Bull, how may I help you?'

'Fayth? Is that you? It's Wade. Have you heard from Liam? He's gone AWOL.'

She looked back at Liam. He was watching her. Slowly, she shook her head. What an idiot. He sunk down his barstool.

'Yep. He's here,' said Fayth.

'He's WHAT?' Wade took a deep breath. 'Can you put him on please?'

'Sure.' She held out the phone for him. He'd messed up. He had to accept the consequences.

Liam hesitated.

She put the phone in front of him. The cord was just about

long enough to reach where he sat.

Wade shouted down the phone before Liam had even picked it up. 'WHAT WERE YOU THINKING? DO YOU NOT UNDERSTAND THAT YOU COULD HAVE A STALKER? THAT IT'S NOT SAFE FOR YOU TO BE OUT ON YOUR OWN? DO YOU NOT GET THAT WE'RE TRYING TO PROTECT YOU? WHAT KIND OF FUCKING IDIOT ARE YOU? YOUR MOTHER HAS BEEN CATATONIC. IF SHE'D BEEN TEN YEARS OLDER YOU COULD'VE GIVEN HER A HEART ATTACK.'

Fayth pretended to busy herself reorganising glasses underneath the bar, but it was difficult not to hear Wade's shouting.

Liam York, her teenage crush, was in her pub. And wanted to stay with her. The guy was worth more than the house, pub, and her car put together. Worth more than them ten times over.

And he was being shouted at by his bodyguard for turning up unannounced. And she'd thought what happened in New York was surreal.

'I'm sorry,' said Liam.

'You need to stop this. Walking around the block is one thing, but getting on a plane to the other side of the world? Are you INSANE?' chastised Wade.

'Look, whoever it is is obviously based in New York,' said Liam, matter-of-factly. 'If I keep a low profile for a while whoever it is will get bored and move on. You'll see.'

Naive, much?

'Did it not occur to you that you're not the only one that can get on a plane?' said Wade. 'Have you forgot about what happened in London?'

'But how will they know where this place is? It's so out of—'

'I got the phone number, didn't I? It's not hard.'

'But it's just a phone number. Travelling all the way here is a lot of effort. Why bother if they can just harass someone else?'

Fayth slammed a glass on to the shelf. Did he actually believe that?

'I'll be there as soon as I can.'

'You don't need to do that. Take a holiday. You've earned one,' said Liam.

'This is serious, Liam. Put Fayth back on.'

Fayth placed her hands on the shelf. If she stood up before being prompted, it would be obvious that she'd eavesdropped.

Then again, it was hard not to with how loud Wade had shouted.

'Fayth?' said Liam.

'Yeah?' she said, standing up.

He handed her the phone.

'Hello?' she said as she picked it up.

'Promise me you'll look after him until I get there?' said Wade.

She looked over at Liam. He'd got his best guilty puppy face on. God, he looked cute. She turned her back on him. 'Of course.'

'He's an idiot sometimes, but he's our idiot. I can't have anything happen to him.'

'I know,' said Fayth. She couldn't either.

Four

The one person capable of making Liam feel guilty was his mum. She was a master manipulator; the queen of guilt. Hanging up after speaking to her, he knew that her spell had worked on him yet again. No matter how old he got, or how aware of her skills he became, he always fell for them.

He went back inside the pub, his head hung. 'Sorry. I shouldn't have shown up like that,' he said, putting his phone back into his pocket. A pint of Guinness waited for him on the bar. 'Thanks.'

Fayth turned from the back of the bar where she'd been cleaning. 'How was your mum? She talk some sense into you?' She twirled the cloth between her fingers.

He sighed. 'She made me feel bad, if that's what you mean.'

'So what are you going to do?'

'Stay put. If you'll have me.'

'Are you sure that's a good idea?'

'Saying you don't want me?'

'It's not that. You've got no one here to protect you if something happens. I couldn't handle the guilt if something did.'

'But don't you get it? I'm safer here. Nobody knows where here is. I don't even know where here is. I just followed the satnav. No one could ever find me here.'

Fayth frowned. 'So what? It's up to me to protect you until Wade arrives?'

'What is it with people wanting to protect me? I'm 25! I can look after myself.' Or at least, he hoped he could. He was too embarrassed to tell her the real reason why he'd ran away from New York.

'We're just looking out for you, that's all,' said Fayth. 'We don't want anything to happen to you.'

'Because of who I am or what I'm worth?'

'That's not fair,' said Fayth. Did he really think that was all that mattered to her?

'I'm sorry,' said Liam, running his hand through his hair. 'I just can't stay in New York any longer. With my parents and Wade and Thalia and Ola watching me all the time, I'm going mad.' He knew they wanted to protect him, but that didn't mean they had to watch him 24/7. His parents were one step away from putting a baby monitor in his room. New York no longer felt like home, and until the person who'd stolen his things was caught, he wouldn't feel happy or safe there. 'Please? The minute you get bored of me I'll leave and go see Astin, I swear.'

'What, and spend all day in bed playing console games with him?' said Fayth.

'See? We both know I'm better off here.'

Fayth sighed.

'Tell me you want me gone, and I'm gone.'

'You know I won't say that.'

'Why? If it's the truth, say it.'

She sighed. 'That's the problem. It's not the truth. I like having my friends around here. It makes the whole place feel less empty.'

'Well then. It's settled.'

After their perfectly cooked steak and chips, Fayth and Liam got into her ten-year-old Volkswagen Golf and headed to the shop. Compared to the Jag Thalia drove him around in, her car was practically ready for the tip. She hadn't realised just how scruffy it was until Liam had walked towards it. He hadn't said anything about the state of her car, but then he wouldn't – he was too polite. That didn't stop her from feeling self-conscious, though. How could she not when there was a plank of wood holding the passenger door together?

The car was filled with the sound of Radio 1, but she didn't pay attention to Scott Mills. She listened to Liam's breathing, conscious of just how close he was to her. He'd occasionally shift, causing his leg to brush against her hand as she changed gear. Each time, she flinched, jerking her hand away.

'You don't believe me, do you?' he said as they drove.

'About what?'

'Why I came.'

She glanced at him over her shoulder. No, she didn't.

He ran his hand through his hair and turned to look out of the window. Whatever it was, he really didn't want to talk about it. Given how he seemed to want to talk about everything, it had to be bad.

'I've been getting weird phone calls. Someone keeps calling me and quoting Trinity lyrics to me.'

Fayth almost did an emergency stop in shock. 'What?'

'That's why I changed my phone number. I panicked. I ran to the farthest place I could think of.'

'Without telling anyone?'

'I called the police and told them. So far they haven't got any leads. I don't feel safe in New York any more.'

She reached across and patted his shoulder. It wasn't fair. Liam's privacy got invaded enough already. What was wrong with people?

They stopped at some traffic lights. His sunglasses covered his eyes, propping his hair away from them. Stubble had formed on his face. She'd never seen him with stubble – in person or onscreen – before. It suited him.

The light turned green and Fayth pulled away. 'This is a small village. As soon as one person with a big mouth finds out you're here, everyone will go mad.'

'I can handle it.'

Fayth wasn't convinced, but then, wasn't Hollywood basically a village in itself? Didn't everyone know everyone and everything? Wasn't it filled with open secrets?

A car horn blared from behind them. She checked her mirror. They were being tailgated, despite driving at the speed limit. She put her hand back on the steering wheel and tensed.

'Arsehole,' she grumbled as the driver behind blared her horn again, getting right up the arse of the car.

Liam turned around. 'What's her problem?'

'Dunno,' said Fayth. 'It's a narrow country lane. What does she want me to do?'

The woman pushed the horn again. It took all of Fayth's strength not to make a rude hand gesture. That's when she realised where they were. She'd been so busy talking to Liam – and being tailgated – that she hadn't realised. They were at the site of the accident. Still clutching the steering wheel, she stared ahead. The horn blared again.

'For fuck's sake!' cried Fayth. She pulled into a meeting place. The black Clio overtook them and drove off, the passenger sticking her finger up as they drove past. Fayth clutched the steering wheel, breathing heavily.

'Are you all right?' asked Liam.

'It was here. The accident.' And they'd very nearly got into one there themselves.

Liam reached over and put a comforting hand on her arm.

'That idiot nearly caused another one,' she said.

'But she didn't. You did the right thing.'

She took a deep breath.

Liam opened the door.

'What're you doing?'

He ignored her, continuing to get out of the car. She followed him. He leaned against the car, looking across at the hill and forest that her mum's car had fallen into. The car wreck was long gone, but the memory was permanently seared into Fayth's mind. Their blue Ford Fiesta was unrecognisable after the accident. It had been written off, as had her mum and Mhairi. She was forever without them because of that stupid, stupid country lane.

'It's pretty out here,' said Liam.

'Yeah,' said Fayth, folding her arms. 'Pretty dangerous.'

They stood in silence for a few moments, staring out across the woodland. A red squirrel jumped between the trees, and Fayth wished her camera wasn't at home or her phone in the car. It would've made a great photo.

'What do you think your mom and Mhairi would think about all this?' asked Liam as the squirrel jumped out of sight.

'Which part?'

'Me being here.'

Fayth turned to look at him. His hair fell over his sunglasses. He tucked it behind his ear. 'Mum would treat you with the same scepticism she gave everyone. Mhairi probably would've made a sex joke or two.'

He laughed. 'Why?'

'We had lists. You were on mine, Thomas Griffiths was on hers.'

Thomas Griffith's was Liam's *Highwater* costar. She hadn't met him when they were in New York, but he'd hosted the *Highwater* panel where Trinity had revealed that she and Liam had broken up. Because Trinity had to make everything into a scene.

'I was on your list, was I?' He grinned.

She blushed. Why had she told him that?

'Don't worry. I don't blame you. I'd put me on my list if I were you, too.'

'Someone thinks a lot of himself,' said Fayth.
'Maybe I just know how highly you think of me,' he said.
She snorted. 'Yeah. Right.'
He put his hand on his heart. 'I'm wounded. You don't think I'm good enough?'
No. He was too good. That was the problem. Everyone loved Liam York, and whether she was friends or more than friends with him, she'd never feel like she could live up to everyone's expectations.
'I'll take your silence as a yes,' he said.
'Come on. We still need to get supplies for dinner.'

Five

After Cameron left, Hollie was forced to confront the elephant in the hotel suite.

Her arms wrapped around herself, she went into Astin's room. He was playing *BioShock Infinite*. Hollie watched him play for a bit. For a first-person shooter, it had a pretty good story. He hid his character somewhere quiet, then turned – as much as he could – to look at her.

'What?' said Hollie.

'What do you want?' he said.

'I was watching the game.'

'That's not why you came in here.' He put the controller beside him.

She stared at her cuticles. 'We can't carry on like this. It's a horrible atmosphere right now.'

Astin patted the bed beside him. She crawled up it, resting her head on his shoulder. He put his arm around her.

'When did we turn into passing ships? We live together, I work from home, and you're resting. How do we never spend any real time together?' she asked.

'I don't know,' he said.

'We should reinstate movie night.'

'All right,' he said, closing the game and opening Netflix. 'What do you want to watch?'

They watched a few episodes of *How to Get Away with Murder* before Declan arrived to tuck Astin into bed. Before she left for her own bed, Hollie kissed Astin for the first time in weeks. His lips were raw against hers and his ever-growing beard scratched against her chin, but she didn't care. It was a long, lingering kiss that left her with goosebumps. She'd missed those kinds of kisses.

❋

They ate breakfast together for the first time in almost a week the following morning. They had a connection again; things were almost back to normal. As normal as they could be, anyway.

One thing that was different was Astin's appetite. He'd always eaten a lot, but at breakfast that morning he hardly touched his food at all. He pushed it around the plate, toying with it and studying it instead of eating it.

'Is your food all right?' asked Hollie.

'I'm not hungry, that's all,' said Astin, continuing to play with his food.

'That's a first for you.'

He didn't react.

'Is something wrong?'

'Besides this?' he said, gesturing to his head brace.

'That hasn't stopped you from eating until now.'

'My stomach hurts, that's all.'

'Is there anything I can do? Something I can get you to help? Do you need to go—'

'No! No. I must've just eaten something bad.'

Hollie scoffed. 'Around here? I doubt it.'

'Just because the food is good doesn't mean my body can't disagree. I could've developed lactose intolerance or stomach ulcers from all the stress.'

She frowned. 'In two months? Conditions like that take years to manifest. I don't think so.'

'When did you become a doctor?'

'When the doctor diagnosed me with stress and warned me of the consequences if I didn't do something about it.' She slammed her cutlery onto her plate. If he was going to be like that, he could finish his breakfast alone.

She went into her room and lay back on the bed. She hadn't realised how tired she was until the mattress hugged her. There was still work to be done, but a catnap wouldn't hurt, would it?

Hollie usually had vivid, overpowering dreams when she was on her period. In recent weeks, she'd had no dreams, and her most recent period was so painful she'd opted to double up on her pill so that she didn't have to go through it again. That meant no vivid dreams, and a better night's sleep. That worked just fine for her.

Her cerebral cortex disagreed.

She fell asleep as soon as her head hit the pillow, something she hadn't done in years. After a few minutes of blissful sleep, she found herself in a dance studio with Astin. The same one she'd dreamed about in New York. She wore a black sparkly dress, while Astin wore a suit. Tango music played in the background. He took her hands and they tangoed.

Then, the music changed. They stopped dancing. Astin spun her out, then let go. She fell to the floor. When she stood up, he was gone.

Astin coughed. It jolted Hollie from her Tango-infused dream. He sat to the side of the bed, watching her.

'All right there, Cullen?' said Hollie.

'Team Jacob all the way,' said Astin.

'Agreed,' said Hollie.

Astin twirled something between his fingers. It looked like a cardboard packet of some sort. He tossed it onto the bed. It was a packet of pills. Imodium. The perfect pills to bung him up so that he didn't need to go to the loo.

'I started taking these after…you know. When Cameron came I took them even more.'

Something tugged at her heart. Did it really bother him that much that she'd had to help him in the toilet? She'd never thought about how embarrassed Astin would be if he needed to ask for help when someone else was there. He was bad enough at asking for help in the first place. Cameron's presence would've made him worse. Why hadn't she thought of that? Why had she put her own needs before his? But then, why didn't he just hire a full-time carer?

'Is that…*safe*?' said Hollie.

'Doubt it. Declan found them this morning and lectured me. Said he'd take them off me if he found any more missing from the packet.' He avoided eye contact as he spoke and rubbed his tracksuit bottoms.

'I'm sorry. I should've thought about you before I invited Cameron.'

'I thought you didn't want my help any more.'

She sat on the edge of the bed and reached out to touch his hand. 'I was worried helping out was doing you more harm than good. I didn't want that.'

'It helps me. It makes me feel less useless. That's why I keep doing crosswords. I'm thinking of giving sudoku a try too. It keeps my mind sharp even if my body isn't.'

She hugged him. He hugged her back, his breath warm against her neck.

'I do appreciate your help,' she said.

He rubbed her back. 'I appreciate yours too, even if I don't show it.'

She kissed the top of his head. It was the first time he'd admitted that he appreciated her help. She resisted the urge to cry.

Six

'Thanks for picking up the stuff,' said Fayth's dad as they entered the house. He sat on the sofa in the living room, surrounded by tissues. The three dogs sat in front of the TV, their ears pricking up as a cat appeared onscreen.

'Any time,' said Fayth.

'No problem,' said Liam, offering Fayth's dad his hand.

He sneezed into a tissue he'd been holding. His eyes were almost as red as his nose. 'I'm Darren, Fayth's dad. Best not to touch unless you want to catch this.'

Liam lowered his hand. Poor guy.

'How are you feeling?' asked Fayth.

'Been better.' He sneezed again. 'Sorry.' He wiped his nose with a fresh tissue, then sneezed again. 'Argh!'

Suddenly having turned up out of nowhere didn't seem like such a good idea. If Darren was anything like his daughter, he'd want to be a good host, but in that state, the only thing he needed to do was rest.

'You're welcome to stay here, Liam, if you're not afraid of catching these germs. Otherwise, there's room at the flat above the pub.'

'If we rearrange the boxes,' mumbled Fayth.

'Here's fine,' said Liam. 'I've got a good immune system.'

'In that case, Fayth can show you up to the spare bed, while I go have a sneezing fit back in my own.' He sneezed again. Huffing, he disappeared upstairs.

'Your dad seems nice,' said Liam.

'He's usually more upbeat than that. The germs are driving him mad. He doesn't usually get ill, but after everything that's happened…' She trailed off, her eyes growing distant. She'd been through a lot herself – some could argue more than her dad and sister – yet she was still going. Her trip to New York was supposed to be a fun and relaxing vacation, but it had been ruined by meeting him. She'd been hounded by paparazzi claiming she was his new girlfriend before he'd even officially broken up with Trinity. Trinity's accusations that they were together didn't help any.

They got along well, that was it. It had to be.

'Come on, let's get your stuff upstairs,' said Fayth.

They got his bag from the car and carried it upstairs. He was pleased with how lightly he'd managed to pack. He didn't want to drive around Scotland, so he'd had to pack light. Carrying extra luggage on a motorcycle wasn't easy. He had no idea how long he'd be there, but he could always buy anything he really needed. That or Ola would send it over for him. When Wade had told her where he was, she'd texted him chastising him for running off, but then said she was impressed he'd organised it himself. She hadn't thought he had it in him. It was a good job he had a rapport with his staff.

Fayth's bedroom was painted bright blue. The smell of fresh paint hung in the air. 'I only repainted it a couple of days ago,' she said. 'It used to be lavender.'

'I like it,' he said.

'Your bed's the one on the left.'

He figured that had belonged to Mhairi, but he didn't ask – he didn't want to risk prying open a wound that had only just begun to heal.

Liam joined Fayth at the Cock and Bull that evening, but she refused to let him serve customers. He offered repeatedly, but she ignored him. He had no experience and they weren't *that* desperate. Yet.

He sat at the bar, doodling on a napkin and barely touching the pint of Guinness in front of him. She spoke to him when she could, and he joined in with a few conversations with the regulars. Most of them were too old to recognise him, so they just spoke to him like they would anyone else. Having grown up in the spotlight, it had to be weird for him to be around a bunch of pensioners that didn't know who he was.

That is, until Brooke and her two best friends, Joanna and Leanne, burst in.

'Is it true?' cried Brooke as they bounced into the bar. They looked around, but they couldn't see Liam. He'd gone to the toilet. Fayth hoped he'd stay in there long enough for her to get rid of her sister and her friends.

'Is what true?' asked Fayth. Like she didn't know. 'Shouldn't you be studying?'

'Is he here? Is it really him?' asked Brooke's blonde-haired friend Joanna.

'Ohmygoditis!' cried Leanne, pointing to just behind Fayth.

Liam had emerged from the toilets. Damnit. The squealing trio of teenagers ran towards him.

'Ohmygoditsyou!' squealed Joanna.

He flicked his hair from his face, that smile Fayth found so alluring playing over his lips. She clutched the lever tighter as she pulled a pint for one of the punters.

The three teenagers fawned over him, as if they wanted to take a piece of his flesh to prove they'd really met him. Brooke and her friends were big *Highwater* fans, as Fayth had once been. Their fascination seemed to have grown worse at the knowledge that Fayth had met him. They'd all begged Fayth to introduce them to him. And now she had. Unintentionally, but still. She should've made him stay in the flat upstairs.

'Hi,' said Liam.

The trio squealed again. His voice was nice, but it wasn't *that* nice. Bloody hell.

'Leave him alone, would you?' said Fayth. The head began to disappear on the pint. She stopped pulling and let it drip for a moment.

'It's OK,' said Liam.

'No it's not. I won't have them ambushing you in my pub,' said Fayth.

'We're not ambushing him,' said Brooke, 'and it's *our* pub.'

'Still doesn't make it acceptable. There's this thing called personal space, you know.' She waved her hand to get them to step back a little.

'All right, grouch,' said Brooke.

They stepped back a few inches, but remained so close they looked like vultures about to descend on their prey.

'How would you feel if a total stranger got in your face like that?' asked Fayth.

'It's fine, really,' said Liam.

'He's used to it. It's his job,' said Joanna matter-of-factly.

Leanne remained silent. She always had been the quiet one.

'No, acting is his job,' said Fayth.

'Can we at least get a picture? Pleeeease,' pleaded Joanna.

'Sure,' said Liam. He glanced over at Fayth as Brooke and her friends rifled for their phones. *It's OK* he mouthed. Fayth shook her head, but she let it drop. It was his privacy that was being invaded, and it was up to him.

She put the dripping pint on to the bar in front of Abe. He'd been a regular at the Cock on Bull since long before her family had owned it. He frowned. 'It's all body and no head.'

Fayth stifled a laugh. There was a dirty joke in there somewhere.

Brooke and her friends eventually calmed down – as much as excitable teenage girls meeting their idol could – and the four of them fell into conversations about *Highwater* and general celebrity life. Fayth left them to it, uninterested in discussing it after the small taste of it she'd had in New York. She'd only just got over the bitter taste it left in her mouth.

They talked for a few hours, then Leanne's parents called, summoning her home. They were pretty strict, so they weren't going to care that she was talking to Liam York. She was out late on a college night, and they didn't like it. The three of them said goodbye, and Brooke said she'd be back later to help Fayth lock up. Fayth brushed her off, telling her to get an early night. She'd worked that night so that her sister could study. So much for that.

Custom started to slow down around half past ten. Fayth was glad of a break, no matter how brief it was. She leaned against the bar, glugging down a glass of cola to keep her going while Liam doodled on a napkin. He seemed perfectly content, and, to her own surprise, so was she. Having Liam there made bar work so much more entertaining and less arduous. They had a nice rhythm going. Or at least they had, until the door flung open and in stumbled Patrick, utterly bladdered.

'So this is the guy you divorced me for, is it?' snarled Patrick, waving his arms in the air.

'Go home Patrick, you're drunk,' said Fayth.

He didn't go home. He walked closer towards Liam. Fayth ran around the bar, blocking his way. Liam stood from the barstool he'd been sat on for the last two hours.

Even the punters that had ignored Liam all evening stopped their conversations to see what happened next. Bloody eavesdroppers. It wasn't a film set.

'You look a lot bigger in the photos,' said Patrick.

'Oh yeah? I could still take you,' said Liam. He was so close she could feel his breath on her neck. It gave her goosebumps.

'Don't,' said Fayth.

'Yeah Liam. *Don't*,' mimicked Patrick. She could smell the alcohol on his breath. Stella, as usual. Mixed with garlic. As if she hadn't felt nauseous enough lately.

'For god's sake Patrick, pack it in,' said Fayth. She crossed her arms. They would *not* get into a fight in her pub.

'You want to start something? Come on then. I dare you,' said Liam, rounding his shoulders and clenching his fists.

'All right then,' said Patrick, trying to push past Fayth. She shoved him back.

'Don't even go there.' Fayth had done karate for a decade. If she had to, she could take him, and he knew it. His fighting skills ended at being able to break his foot kicking the kitchen cabinet.

'What's the matter? Worried about me hurting your new boyfriend?' He didn't look at Fayth as he spoke; his eyes were fixed on Liam.

She sidestepped, blocking his view of Liam. 'He's not my boyfriend. And no, I'm not worried about him: he could take you as well.' She sneezed.

'Photos can tell you a lot, you know. Like how your wife cheated on you with the guy she used to have a poster of on her wall,' said Patrick.

Fayth's cheeks burned. Bastard.

'You had a poster of me on your wall?' said Liam, his voice ripe with amusement.

She ignored him. 'I don't know how many times I have to tell you this Patrick, but I didn't cheat on you. *You* cheated on *me*. Right after Mum and Mhairi died. And I will never, *ever* be able to forgive you for that. Now I'll ask you one more time. Leave my pub, and don't come back while Liam is here, or you're barred until the new owners take over.'

'You wouldn't dare.'

She nodded. 'Yeah, I would, 'cause just looking at you makes me want to throw up. Now get out.'

'How am I supposed to know when to come back?'

'However you found out Liam was here in the first place.' She jerked her head in the direction of the door.

Patrick jabbed his finger at Liam. 'This isn't over.'

Liam pushed past Fayth and shoved her ex-husband. 'Come on then. Show me what you've got.'

'Oooh, the puppy hasn't had his balls cut off after all,' said Patrick.

Fayth forced them apart. 'For fuck's sake put your dicks

away. I am *not* in the mood.' She pointed to Patrick. 'You, get out.' She pointed to Liam. 'You, bugger off somewhere else.'

Liam opened his mouth in protest.

'Don't even argue. You're playing right into his fucking hands.' There was a pause, where neither of them moved. Were they deaf? 'GO!'

Liam disappeared into the flat upstairs. Patrick stomped out. It wasn't until she turned around that she realised the whole pub was staring at her. Oops. A busy pub probably wasn't the best place for a showdown between Liam and Patrick, but what was she supposed to do? At least most of the punters were too old to be able to use a 3310, let alone a smartphone.

Ross stood in the kitchen doorway, watching her. Where had he been when it all kicked off? She went back to the bar and busied herself reorganising the wine glasses. He approached her. 'You OK?'

She grumbled.

'That was pretty impressive, I have to say.'

'Why didn't you intervene!'

'You handled it pretty well on your own,' said Ross. 'I would've jumped in if I'd needed to. We both know neither of them would've actually got into a fight there and then, though.'

'Wouldn't they?' said Fayth. She wasn't so sure.

'Not in front of you, anyway.'

'Thanks, that's really reassuring.' She rested her elbows on the bar.

Ross gave her a cheeky smile. He looked down at the floor, as if he wanted to say something else but wasn't sure if he should.

'What?'

'I'm just surprised you spoke to Liam like that.'

'Why?'

'Well, I mean, you two…'

'Us two *what*?'

'Nothing.'

Seven

Liam stayed upstairs out of the way for the rest of the night. Fayth eventually calmed down, and she felt bad for snapping at him. He didn't know what Patrick was like. It wasn't his fault he'd reacted exactly how Patrick had wanted him to.

Once the last customer had left and the doors were locked, Fayth went upstairs to apologise. He lay on the sofa, flicking through his phone, his shoes still on. Slob.

'Hey,' said Fayth as she walked through the door.

'Hey,' said Liam, his eyes glued to his phone.

'Sorry about before. Patrick just has this way of winding people up.'

'Huh,' said Liam, 'sounds familiar.'

Fayth laughed. It *did* sound familiar. 'He and Trinity are a lot alike.'

'Yeah,' he said, swinging his legs round and sitting properly.

Fayth joined him on the sofa and sat beside him.

'I shouldn't have let him get to me like that.'

'And I should've known better,' said Fayth. She sneezed into her elbow. Taking a tissue from her pocket, she wiped her nose. She was starting to think more and more that she was getting her dad's bloody germs. If she woke up in the morning with a runny nose, she'd know for certain. Her body really was against her.

'At least you're divorced now,' said Liam, putting his phone on the coffee table.

'Yeah, I just wish he'd acknowledge what he's done wrong. I don't get why he openly admitted to having slept with another woman, but seems to think that's perfectly OK, whereas you and I being friends isn't.'

Liam shrugged. 'I don't know, but if I were him, seeing you with someone else would make me realise what I'd lost.'

'He signed the papers!' said Fayth, waving her arms about.

'Because it's what you wanted.'

'So he's giving me what I want in the hopes that I'll go back to him?' She snorted. 'Not likely.'

'It's not a massive stretch given what you've said about him.'

Fayth ran her hand through her hair. It got stuck on a knot halfway through. She tugged at it, forcing it to loosen. When it finally did, a chunk fell out. Shit. She shook it away, hoping Liam hadn't noticed.

'So about this poster,' said Liam, a wry smile playing on his lips.

Fayth rested her head in her hands and twisted her head towards him, an exasperated expression on her face.

'What? I have to ask. What was it a poster for?'

'I don't remember,' she lied.

'It was on your wall and you don't remember? As if.'

'Doesn't mean I'm going to tell you,' she said. 'You're enjoying this too much.'

'What can I say? I love talking to my fans.'

'Not a fan any more, sorry.'

His face fell. He looked genuinely hurt. 'Why not?'

'You're too bloody annoying in real life.'

He grinned. 'What happened to said poster, anyway?'

'It's in the loft somewhere, I think. Patrick made me take it down.'

'Why?'

'He was jealous of it,' she said with a laugh.

'Now it makes sense,' said Liam.

Fayth stood up. She needed tea. 'What makes sense?' She flicked on the kettle. 'Tea?'

'Please,' said Liam. 'He was jealous of a *poster* of me. The fantasy, if you will. Then you go and meet the real me, right after he's screwed up. He knows he can't compete with my awesomeness.'

'You can be really cocky sometimes, you know that?'

He flashed her a smile.

Fayth's head throbbed. It had been a long day. And night. She closed her eyes and massaged the spot between her eyes.

'Why don't you go lie down for a bit?'

'There's too much to do with Dad and Brooke out of action.'

'I'll go help Ross. You get some rest.'

'Are you sure?' said Fayth.

'Yeah, I'm sure,' he said as the kettle boiled. 'You need to look after yourself too.'

❋

Liam left Fayth with a mug of tea, wrapped up on the sofa watching *The Hunger Games*, then went downstairs. The pub was empty except for Ross, who was cleaning tables.

'Where's Fayth?' he asked when he saw Liam was alone.

'Resting.'

'Good,' said Ross. 'She's never been good at looking after herself.'

'She's too busy putting other people first,' said Liam.

Ross nodded. 'She gets it from her mum,' he said, tossing Liam a cloth and gesturing to the table beside him. 'Make yourself useful.'

Liam stared at the cloth.

'You've cleaned a table before, right?'

'Er…'

Ross shook his head. 'Bloody rich kids with silver spoons in their mouths.' He showed Liam how to wipe down a table, and gave him a bowl to put any washing up in.

'I don't have a silver spoon,' said Liam.

'What do your parents do?'

'My dad's a computer programmer and my mom's an artist,' said Liam, attempting to clean his first table.

'Silver spoon,' confirmed Ross. 'Especially if they're still together.'

'What about Fayth's parents?'

'They were a rare exception,' said Ross. 'Most of the people here are from single parent families, or their parents have long moved on to other relationships.'

'Wow,' said Liam. He put all his strength into scrubbing a spot on one of the tables that didn't want to come off.

'Yeah, but it's not all bad,' said Ross. 'I think that table's clean enough. You don't need to spend all night on it.'

'This mark won't come off!' said Liam.

Ross stood beside him and stared at the mark. He chuckled. 'That's a knot in the wood.'

'Oh,' said Liam. Of course it was.

'Other than that, it looks pretty good. You're not bad for a guy with a silver spoon in his mouth.'

Liam started to protest again, but stopped himself. Was Ross right? He'd come from a happy family and never had to worry about money. What kind of life had Ross had growing up?

'Thanks. I think.'

They continued cleaning and talking. He'd never cleaned so much in his life. Whenever he made a mess at home his cleaner sorted it. Bizarrely, he found cleaning almost as relaxing as drawing. It was a welcome distraction from the constant craziness in his life, just like being around Fayth was. She was so grounded and distanced from the life he'd grown up with. He couldn't help but be drawn to that.

'I think we're done,' said Ross, standing in the middle of the restaurant area and looking around.

'We did a good job,' said Liam.

'Yeah. For a guy who's never cleaned before, you're not bad.'

'What can I say? I pick things up quickly.'

Ice skating not included.

'I can finish up here if you want to take Fayth home,' said Ross.

'You sure?'

'Yeah, she needs her own bed. The mattress up there sucks.'

'Slept on it, have you?' said Liam, cocking an eyebrow.

'Crashed out after the World Cup, more like. That's the one time we're busy. Until Fayth met you, I mean.'

'Has it really made that much of a difference?'

'Yeah,' said Ross, spinning a cloth around. 'It was dead in here most days before that. Now new customers come in hoping to get a glimpse of you and Fayth.'

'And I gave them exactly what they wanted, didn't I?'

'Yeah. We're not complaining – it means the pub'll sell for more money.'

'But what will you do when it does?'

Ross shrugged. He stopped playing with the cloth and tossed it on to a table. 'Hoping the new owners'll keep me on. If not, I'll just have to find something else. Que sera, sera.'

'That's a good attitude,' said Liam.

'Yeah, well. Sometimes you don't have a choice.'

And didn't Liam know it. It was his inability to roll with what life had thrown at him that had nearly landed him in prison, and caused him to end up in rehab.

Footsteps echoed from upstairs and a moment later, Fayth came down, rubbing at her eyes. 'What time is it? I fell asleep.'

Her usually tied-up hair was down and falling into her eyes. She had that bedhead thing going on that was more sexy than she realised.

'About one. Come on, I'll take you home.'

Fayth stretched, letting out a cute squeak as she did so. 'My back hurts. I'd forgot how uncomfortable that bed is.'

'Then it's time for you to get to your real one,' said Ross.

'Thanks,' said Fayth as she and Liam put helmets and leathers on and climbed on to his rented Ducati. Fayth wrapped her arms around him as he switched on the engine. Did she know how much of a hold she had on him? She was so guarded it was impossible to tell. Even if she did have feelings for him, there was little chance she'd let him see them. How had someone so cautious ended up with someone like Patrick? Or was he the reason she was like that?

Fayth knocked on the side of his helmet. 'Are we going to move, or are we going to sit here all night?'

'Sorry. Ready to go?'

'Yep.'

The lights were off when they pulled up outside the house, so they tiptoed upstairs. Fayth got ready for bed in the bathroom, emerging in green flannel pyjamas. Flannel. In May. Then again, it was Scotland.

He pulled off his jeans and shirt and climbed into the bed opposite hers. Being shirtless around people didn't bother him. Most of the world had already seen him shirtless thanks to *Highwater*.

'You're going to freeze,' said Fayth, climbing into her bed.

'It's May,' he said.

'And we're in Scotland. We don't really have warm weather around here.'

'I'm sure I can manage,' said Liam. He suppressed a shudder. It *was* cold. Not as cold as it had been in some locations where they'd filmed *Highwater*, but it wasn't really sleeping-in-boxers warm. Still, he hoped Fayth had enjoyed the view. She had had a poster of him on her wall, after all.

Wait. Had he just missed a prime opportunity to flirt with her? To suggest getting into bed with her? Damnit.

'Sleep well,' said Fayth.

'You too.' He closed his eyes, conscious of the silence around him. He didn't sleep well in silence. He usually fell asleep with his TV on, or the radio playing. He needed some sort of noise to focus on to help him drift off. He listened for the sound of her breathing. It slowed as she fell asleep, and not long after, he did, too.

Eight

Fayth's bed was empty when Liam woke up the following morning. It was neatly made, her flannel pyjamas folded on her pillow. She'd looked so cute in those pyjamas. He really should've flirted with her after she made the comment about him being cold. But he'd been tired. Too tired to be able to think fast enough to flirt. He'd needed that sleep. He hadn't slept that well in months.

The bedroom door opened and Fayth entered carrying a tray. It had on it two mugs of tea and a plate filled with slices of toast. She was already fully dressed in jeans and a *Bomberman* t-shirt. 'Didn't know what you'd want, so I bought jam, chocolate spread, butter, and pâté.' The mugs were Batman and Superman. Could she be any more awesome?

'Look at you bringing me breakfast in bed like we're an old married couple on Valentine's Day,' he said, unable to hide his grin.

She blushed. 'You looked like you needed the rest. I thought I'd let you sleep a bit longer before I woke you. How'd you sleep?'

'Pretty good, actually,' he said, pulling the covers back and studying the selection on the tray, which she'd balanced on the bedside table. He hadn't been cold while he slept, but sitting up in bed only wearing a pair of boxers, he was pretty cold. His nipples had serious hard-ons. He managed to hide the other hard-on he'd woken up with. That could've been…awkward.

He settled for Brussels pâté on toast. Fayth went for blackcurrant jelly – *jam* – then sat silently on the end of her bed opposite him. Every so often, he'd catch her staring at him, and she'd look away like a child caught with their hand in the cookie jar. It looked a lot like she was checking him out. But she couldn't be, could she? She'd barely reacted to his advances. But then, being physically attracted to someone wasn't the same as being attracted to them as a person. He didn't want to be with someone that was only with him for how he looked or what his job was. He wanted to be with someone who knew and understood him. And he was pretty sure he had that with Fayth, if only she'd let him in.

They left for the Cock and Bull not long after breakfast. They stopped off along they way to pick up some groceries then unlocked and headed inside. There was still an hour until they opened for lunch. Fayth liked being early. She said it was just in case anything went wrong. He didn't fully understand the logic, but he went along with it anyway and helped her unpack the car. When they'd finished he sat down at the bar as Fayth checked the stock levels.

A motorbike growled past the windows and into the car park.

'God, I hope that's not Patrick again,' said Fayth.

'I thought you said he had a dirt bike,' said Liam.

'Yeah. He bought it with our savings. Who knows? Maybe he's upgraded.'

'He used your money to pay for it?'

'Our savings for a house, yeah. Most of which came from my wages. He came home one day with it. Never did understand why I was pissed off.'

'Jackass.'

The figure that stepped off the bike was too big to be Patrick. They were easily the size of The Rock. But The Rock had no reason to turn up at the Cock and Bull. There was only one person it could be.

Wade stormed towards Liam. 'I don't know whether to punch you or kiss you.'

'Um…neither?' said Liam. He shrunk in his seat.

'I'll be in the basement if you need me,' said Fayth. He didn't want her to go. If she went, he had no protection from the lecture he was about to receive.

Wade waited until Fayth was in the basement to start his lecture. 'I thought your mom was gonna have an aneurysm.'

'She's just being melodramatic,' said Liam.

'And you running off to Scotland isn't!' cried Wade. 'Don't you ever do that to us again!'

Liam shrunk further into his seat.

'Well?' demanded Wade.

'What?' said Liam.

'Why are you *really* here?' said Wade. He walked the length of the bar, never taking his eyes off Liam.

Liam swung his feet on the barstool and stared at them.

'It's her, isn't it?' said Wade.

Liam looked up. 'What?'

'Stop saying "what"! You sound like a child. Act like an adult for once, would you? Maybe then people will treat you like one!'

Liam widened his eyes. Ouch. He'd known Wade would be pissed, but to call him a child? That was low. That was really low.

'Sorry. That was too much.' He sat on the stool beside Liam. His legs barely fitted in the gap between them. 'I'm just worried. Can't you see that? We're all worried.'

'But don't you think I'll be better off here? You said I should lie low somewhere quiet. This is perfect!'

'What can the police do to protect you out here? It'll take them on average nine minutes to get here. By that time, we could all be dead,' said Wade.

'Where did you get nine minutes from?'

'The internet. Where was I? Oh yeah. Be honest with me. Do you like her?'

Liam stared into his lap, still swinging his feet. Yes, yes he did. He more than liked her. But he could never say that aloud. Saying that aloud validated his feelings and would make it even harder to get over her should she decide he wasn't what she wanted. In the meantime, he still held out hope. And still felt he was safer there than in New York.

Liam turned his head to look at him. 'It's not that simple. Not with her. It's different. I can't push her.'

'And you think turning up here is going to help?'

'No! It's not just about that. I don't feel safe in New York any more. The police don't have any leads and I can't stand to live with my parents any longer. Everyone in New York wants something from me. They have expectations. But here? No one cares who I am; no one expects anything from me. I can just be me, no pressure. I've never had that before.'

Wade sighed. 'All right then. We'll stay as long as you want. On one condition.'

'What?'

'You stop your walkabouts. They're dangerous, man.'

He hung his head. 'I know.'

Nine

'What are you doing?' said Hollie. 'We need to leave soon.' She pushed open the door to Astin's bedroom. He sat on the bed, trying to pull a t-shirt over his head. A pile of clothes surrounded him.

'Come here,' said Hollie. She walked over to him.

He held out his hand. 'No. Let me do it.'

'We need to go.'

He grumbled. He tossed the t-shirt on to the floor and picked up a navy shirt. Hollie helped guide it over his shoulders. The scar from his surgery had begun to heal, but it was still a deep, angry pink that contrasted against his tanned skin and the white of his head brace.

'Ready to go?' she asked as Astin fastened the buttons on his shirt.

'I guess.'

She helped him out of bed and into the wheelchair. His private physio appointments had gone well, but they had more equipment at the hospital so they wanted him to do some exercises there, too. He hadn't been out of the hotel in almost a month, so when his physiotherapist had suggested he go to the hospital for more treatment, she was secretly glad.

When they arrived at the hospital, Hollie parked up, grabbed a wheelchair from reception, then went back to pick up her boyfriend. The physiotherapy department was through a maze of corridors, but somehow they found their way there in plenty of time.

'I'll be all right if you want to go get a drink,' said Astin once they'd checked in.

'Trying to get rid of me, are we?' said Hollie. Her tone was teasing, but deep down she suspected that he was. She tugged on the sleeves of her cardigan.

'No, just don't want you to get bored sitting around, that's all.'

Hollie dug into her handbag and fished out a paperback. She waved it about. 'This isn't my first hospital appointment.'

'I know.'

She settled in with her book while Astin did *The Guardian's* cryptic crossword. The physiotherapist called him right on time. Hollie put her book away and pushed him towards the door. 'I'll see you in a bit.'

'You not coming in?' he said.

'I didn't think you'd want me to,' she said.

'I do.'

It was a small gesture, but it meant a lot to her. Having her there was a sign that the trust and intimacy she thought they were losing was still there. She pushed the wheelchair into the physiotherapy room.

'How are you doing?' asked the physiotherapist once the door was closed behind them. He was a slim Indian man in jeans and a green t-shirt. So casual. So laid back. If only Hollie felt the same.

'Same old,' said Astin.

'It's been two months, yes?'

'Yeah.'

He scribbled some notes on to a clipboard. 'We're going to start off with some weights today to see how you get on.'

'OK,' said Astin.

He picked up some 1kg dumbbells from the corner of the room and handed them to Astin. Hollie sat in a chair by the door, forcing herself not to laugh. Just a few weeks ago, he'd been lifting more than twice her bodyweight. Now he was lifting less than she did. She was frustrated for him. When would he be able to walk properly again? *Would* he ever be able to walk properly again?

'Want to watch *Deadpool* or something?' asked Astin later that afternoon. He was in a good mood after physio, having made more progress than they'd thought he would. He sat beside Hollie in his wheelchair, a book resting in his lap.

She looked up from her laptop. The wooden coffee table was covered in her most recent orders. 'Maybe in a bit? I need to go through some invoices.'

'Do you ever stop working?'

'I can't, you know that.'

'Then why are you here?' He closed his book, turned his

wheelchair, and went into his bedroom before she could answer.

She sighed. What did he want her to do? She couldn't risk falling behind on her business. He knew that, didn't he?

She closed her laptop and went into his room. He was staring out of the window.

'Anything interesting?' she asked, joining him.

'Not really.' He wheeled away from her.

'Oh for god's sake,' she mumbled. 'What do you *want* from me? My undivided attention? My undying love? *What?*'

His hand hovered over the gearstick of his wheelchair. After a few seconds, he turned back to face her. 'I want to spend time with you! Is that such a bad thing? I speak to Declan more than I do to you!'

Hollie leaned against the window frame. She *had* been working a lot, but she'd thought he understood why. She'd stopped asking him for his help because every response was a 'later' or a 'maybe'.

'What do you want me to do? Give up on my dream, just as it's within my grasp?'

'No!'

'Then *what*? What the fuck do you want me to do?'

'I want you to slow down! You're working too hard!'

'Shouldn't I be the judge of that? If I let things slip, who's going to pick up the slack?' She pushed herself away from the window. 'I have work to do.'

Argument unresolved, she packed up her laptop, grabbed her bag, and left the hotel. The wind pounded at her chest as she walked past the tall, elaborate buildings of Brook Street, but she didn't care. The more time she spent in that suite, the less work she got done.

Hollie didn't return until the sun started to set that evening. She'd caught up on all her invoices, completed her social media schedule to the end of the month, and worked on her website's SEO. It was the most productive she'd been in weeks.

Could Astin really be the reason she didn't get much done?

It wasn't his fault he needed her attention.

Was it?

She went into her room and carried on working, eventually falling asleep with her laptop in front of her and her head lolled to the side.

'That can't be comfortable,' said Astin.

Hollie opened her eyes. Light shone through the bottom of the curtains. How long had she been asleep for?

She closed her laptop and straightened her neck. It tugged. 'Not really,' she said, massaging her shoulder. 'What time is it?'

'Ten. What time did you get in?'

'Dunno. You were already asleep.'

'Yeah, physio really took it out of me.'

'How do you feel now?'

He wiggled his fingers in front of him. 'Do you have any idea how frustrating it is to go from lifting weights to wiggling your fingers for exercise?'

'I wish there was more I could do to help.'

'But you do help. Just being around you helps. Why do you think I flipped out yesterday?'

She crawled across the bed and reached out to him. He held her hands. 'I'm sorry, I just can't risk falling behind. I've got so much to do.'

'I know, but you do need to take a break sometimes.'

'Not this again.'

'Everyone needs a break sometimes.'

She really didn't want another argument, let alone one first thing in the morning. 'How about we watch a film later? We could go to the cinema—'

'No. No cinema. We'll find something online.'

Ten

24. 24 and divorced. 24 and motherless. 24 and minus one sister. 24 and…what?

Fayth sat up in bed. She'd finally reached 24, but what did she have to show for it? She had no marriage, no children, no university degree, and the pub she'd spent her life working in was up for sale. What was she supposed to do next?

She looked over at Mhairi's old bed. Liam had slept in it his first night there, but with Wade around too there just wasn't enough room at the house for all of them. He and Wade had relocated to the flat above the pub to give them all some space. The boxes that had taken up most of the flat had been stacked neatly in the corner of the living room, covering most of the outside wall and almost blocking the window. They'd make it to the tip one day. Probably.

Him staying at the flat also meant she didn't have to wake up and risk him seeing her with bedhead or morning breath again. She missed waking up with someone next to her though. She'd never woken up on the morning of her birthday alone before.

She closed her eyes again. If she got emotional, her dad and Brooke would too. No matter how she felt, she couldn't show it in front of them.

She hopped out of bed and opened her door to head to the bathroom. And walked head-first into Liam.

She jumped. 'Liam! How'd you get in?' She clung to the bedroom door. So much for him not seeing her with morning breath and bedhead.

'There's this thing called a door.'

'It's like half seven.' She ran her hands over her hair, trying to look casual.

'And?' He was already fully dressed and perfect-looking as ever. How did he do it?

'Happy birthday,' he said, giving her a hug. He was warm, and he smelled of his signature cologne. She pulled away. 'Don't worry. I'm not going to sing to you.'

'Technically you haven't proven to me that you can't sing yet,' she said, letting go. 'I know you mimed to a recording on Hollie's birthday.'

He gave her a cheeky smile. 'What can I say? I'm not willing to embarrass myself around you just yet.'

'Why? Think I won't want to be friends with you any more?'

'Something like that,' he said. 'So, what do you want to do on your birthday?'

'I have to work.'

'But it's your *birthday*,' he said. 'You're supposed to celebrate!'

'I'm celebrating on the inside.'

Except she wasn't. She didn't want to celebrate it. She didn't even want to acknowledge it. She wanted Liam to forget all about it. That was unlikely to happen, though: his face looked like that of an excited puppy. Would he understand if she told him what was wrong?

'What? You look pensive,' he said, tilting his head.

'It's…' She rubbed her face with her hands.

'Oh. It's the first one without them, isn't it?'

She started crying. Hearing it said aloud was all it took. He put his arm around her shoulders, pulling her closer. 'Cry all you want,' he said. 'It's OK.'

But it wasn't OK. They were dead. They'd never sing *Happy Birthday* to her again. She'd never have a birthday breakfast cooked by her mum again. She'd never get another Pokémon plushie from Mhairi. She wouldn't be able to go to a club and celebrate with her either. Mhairi had suggested it every year but she'd never said yes. She wished she had just once, just so that she could've experienced it. Why had she said no? Why couldn't she have put herself before Patrick just once? Why had she been so caught up in that prick? Would he even wish her a happy birthday? Would they stay in contact now that the divorce was finalised? Did she want to stay in contact with him?

Ugh, no. But not having him say happy birthday to her when they'd known each other so long would be almost as weird as her mum and Mhairi not being around.

'Breakfast's ready!' called her dad from downstairs.

She lifted her head from Liam's chest. 'Breakfast?'

'That's what he said,' said Liam. He wiped her eyes with his shirt sleeve. 'Shall we go investigate?'

She didn't want to, but her dad had made an effort, so she

felt that she should, too. The smell of bacon, eggs, sausages, baked beans and black pudding filled her nostrils as she descended the stairs. He'd cooked a full English breakfast. Just like Mum used to. She forced back tears.

'Happy birthday, sweetheart,' her dad said, hugging her and kissing her forehead when she entered the kitchen. He still looked ill, but the coughing and sneezing had lessened over the past few days. It was a start.

'Thanks. You didn't have to do all this,' she said, hugging him back.

'Sure I did. It's tradition.'

'Where's Brooke?'

'Still in bed, probably. Typical teenager,' he said. 'So, do you want some black pudding this year?'

'No. Never again,' said Fayth. She'd tried black pudding once when she was ten. She had no interest in trying it ever again.

'Don't know what you're missing, gal.' He picked up the spatula from beside the frying pan and flipped over the bacon. 'Can I interest you in some black pudding, Liam?'

'Sure,' said Liam, sitting at the dining table. The dogs circled his feet. They still hadn't got over their new playmate.

'You like black pudding?' said Fayth.

'I don't mind it,' he said.

Fayth looked around. She suddenly realised who was missing. 'Where's Wade?'

'Being paranoid,' mumbled Liam.

'What does that mean?' asked Fayth. She sat beside him and stretched her legs out under the table.

'He's gone to the local police station to brief them on what happened in New York,' said Liam.

'Seems sensible to me,' said Fayth's dad.

'Me too,' said Fayth. 'Although I'm not sure why he didn't go yesterday.'

'They were shut,' said Liam.

Fayth stifled a laugh. The local police station shut. Who'd have thought?

The kitchen door opened. Brooke walked in, her hair dishevelled and bags under her half-open eyes. 'Happy birthday, sis,' she said, suppressing a yawn. She gave her a hug.

'Thanks,' said Fayth. 'Shouldn't you be on your way to college by now?'

'Free period,' she said with another yawn. 'Where's the bacon?'

'Who said you get any?' said Fayth.

'Fine,' she said, turning around and leaving the kitchen.

'Where are you going? Breakfast is ready now!' her dad called after her.

'Birthday girl said I can't have any. I choose sleep instead,' said Brooke.

'I'll give yours to the dogs, then,' said her dad.

Brooke had never reappeared in the kitchen so fast. 'Don't you dare.'

Fayth ate her birthday breakfast at the dining table, Liam beside her and her dad opposite. Brooke had disappeared upstairs with her food, probably to check Facebook while she ate. Phones weren't allowed at the dining table.

Liam shifted in his seat, causing his knee to touch Fayth's. He left it there. She stiffened, moving her leg away.

'Fayth! Where did you put my straighteners!' called Brooke just as Fayth was finishing off the last mouthfuls of breakfast.

'What?' shouted Fayth. 'You know I don't use them!'

'Oh, it was probably me,' said Liam, totally serious. 'My hair didn't fall right.'

'Fayth!' called Brooke again.

'All right, all right!' Fayth put down her cutlery and ran upstairs. Liam and her dad followed.

Brooke stood in the doorway to Fayth's room, grinning. Fayth's bed was adorned with presents.

Her jaw fell open.

She looked from her sister, to her dad, to Liam. They all stood smiling smugly. They'd tricked her!

'You didn't really use Brooke's straighteners, did you?' said Fayth.

'Oh he did,' said Brooke. 'He also suggested this.' She pointed to the pile of presents on the bed.

Fayth approached them. It contained not only presents from her dad and sister, but also Hollie and Astin, Liam, Tate, and Ross.

'Open ours first,' said her dad, gesturing to a large, square parcel on the bed. It was wrapped in metallic polka dot paper. Brooke had always loved wrapping presents: it had her hallmarks of cute bows all over it. She opened it, careful not to damage the wrapping paper too much.

Inside was a DSLR camera. Not a cheap one, but a fancy Canon one that Fayth had secretly been pining over for months. She'd mentioned it to her sister in passing a few times but didn't think she was listening, let alone that she'd buy her one!

'Brooke—'

Brooke looked upwards, her eyes welling with tears. She put her index finger up. 'No. No soppiness. My PMS can't handle it.'

Fayth ignored her sister, hugging her anyway. 'Thank you,' whispered Fayth. Brooke hugged her back, sobbing.

'Hey now, no tears. This is a happy time,' said her dad. He joined in on the hug. 'Do you like it?'

'I love it, Dad,' said Fayth. She pulled away and kissed his cheek. 'You shouldn't have.'

'We wanted to give you something special,' said Brooke. 'There's another one in there somewhere.'

'What?'

Brooke lifted her head in the direction of the pile. Fayth returned to the camera box. Attached to the side of it was an envelope. In it were details of photography courses all over the world.

'We didn't want to book anything because we didn't know where you'd want to go,' said her dad, 'but we found you a list and will give you the money when you do decide.'

'Dad, you don't need to do that.'

'If it's what you want to do with your life, then we want to.'

Fayth glanced over at Liam. Light glistened in his eyes, as if he, too, were about to cry.

'I don't know what to say,' said Fayth.

'Then shut up,' said Brooke, 'and open the rest. I don't know what anyone else has got you. Except Liam.'

'How do you know what Liam got me?' asked Fayth.

'Open it and see,' said Liam, pointing to another box, this time wrapped in swirly paper. 'Brooke wrapped it for me. I don't have the patience.'

'Me neither,' said Fayth's dad. 'She gets it from her mum.'

A tangible silence fell over the room at the mention of her. Fayth's hand hovered over the box. She pictured her mum's short, curly hair; her warm smile. She'd always taken such care wrapping presents. She could make the weirdest-shaped present look like a work of art when wrapped.

'I know you don't believe she's here, Fayth, but she'll always be a part of you. She'll always be the woman that inspired you to become who you are today,' said her dad.

Fayth's eyes filled with tears. Liam sat beside her and put his hand on her shoulder. She leaned into him as her sister and dad sat on the other side, their hands also reaching out to her.

'Stop it! You're making me more emotional!' cried Fayth.

'Fine then. We won't be supportive.' Brooke perched on the end of Mhairi's bed.

Her dad flashed her a *typical Brooke* smile. 'Go on,' he said, pointing to Liam's present.

She unwrapped it. Inside were several lenses to go with her new camera. She looked over her shoulder at him. He grinned. 'You can't have an expensive camera without the lenses, now can you?'

She almost reached out and kissed him. *Almost.* Doing so was a bad idea. She gave him a quick squeeze instead. 'Thanks.'

'I have no idea what any of them do, but Brooke insists they're all perfect for your camera.'

'They are,' said Brooke. 'You'd think being an actor he'd know more about cameras and lenses.'

'I just get paid to repeat lines and look pretty,' said Liam.

Fayth opened the rest of her presents in the company of Liam, Brooke, and her dad. Ross gave her a fancy tea set and Tate got her a Desigual scarf. From Hollie and Astin she had a handbag that looked remarkably like Hollie's, only smaller. She turned to Brooke. 'Hollie made this, didn't she?'

'Check inside,' said Brooke. She did as her sister instructed. A label inside said *Hollie Baxter* with a pink heart in between the two words. There was also a purse inside. She took out the purse and opened it. Inside it was a voucher. For £100 to spend…on *Hollie Baxter* designs. She jumped up, squealing.

'Since when do *you* squeal?' said Brooke, rubbing her ears.

Fayth waved the voucher into her sister's face.

'Yes, thank you, I know what it is. Hollie knew you'd feel guilty getting stuff for free now that she's got a business, so this way you can pick anything out that you like without feeling guilty.'

Hollie knew her too well. That came with having known someone more than half your life, though.

'Thank you,' said Fayth.

Her dad nodded. Liam smiled. Brooke shoved her, causing her to fall back onto the bed.

❋

The dogs scurried to keep up as Fayth walked through the park without them, too busy taking photos to pay them any attention. Liam just about managed to keep in step, checking periodically to make sure the three papillons were still behind them.

Fayth clicked away on her camera. She hadn't stopped smiling since she'd been given her birthday presents. It made Liam smile, too. She deserved to be happy, whatever it took. He was glad he could play a little part in that. If only he could do more.

Fayth stopped, looking back at the dogs. She patted her hip. 'Come on!'

They ran up to her, sitting at her feet obediently. She snapped a few photos of them, then picked up a stick from the edge of the path and threw it. The darkest of the three dogs, Paris, ran after it. The other two, Rio and Vienna, watched as their sister chased after the stick. They then watched Fayth expectantly.

She shook her head. 'Who's ever heard of a dog that won't play fetch?'

Paris reappeared with the stick, and Fayth threw it again. Vienna and Rio still didn't move. Paris returned again, the stick hanging out of her tiny mouth. Fayth took some more photos of Paris as she sat expectantly at Fayth's feet. She dropped the stick. Fayth continued to take photos. Liam bent down and picked up the stick, then threw it for the little dog. Fayth snapped some photos as Paris chased after it again. Then she turned the camera on to Liam. He barely registered the camera, but the feel of her eyes on him made him more self-conscious than any paparazzo ever could.

She let go of her camera and it fell to her stomach, swinging from its strap. As she fished a tissue from her pocket, a raging sneezing fit took hold of her. Liam continued to play fetch with Paris as the other two dogs circled their feet. He rubbed Fayth's back as she continued to sneeze. 'You OK?'

She waved him off. 'Be—' She sneezed '—fine.' She sneezed again.

After five or so minutes, the sneezing finally subsided. She stuffed the dirty tissue back into her pocket. 'Ow,' she said, rubbing her chest.

'You should really be resting,' said Liam.

She carried on walking. Her foot caught on something underneath her. Rio. She stumbled forwards, her arms outstretched ready for impact. Liam grabbed her before she hit the floor. Rio scurried off, his tail wagging.

Her skin was warm against his. They were so close he could smell her cocoa butter moisturiser and feel how soft it made her skin. She tried to stand up but slipped in the mud. Huffing, she turned around. Their eyes met. The whites of her eyes were bloodshot, her pupils enlarged. It was pretty bright out. Could it mean she was attracted to him after all? If he'd leaned in just a little, he could've kissed her. Something flickered in her eyes, almost like she wanted him to.

'Bloody dogs,' she said, straightening herself up and ruining the moment. 'I can't stop just because I've got a bit of a cold.'

'That's "a bit" of a cold?'

'I'll get over it.'

He couldn't work out if she was stubborn, naive, or determined. Either way, he found her attitude admirable. He found everything about her admirable. If only she knew.

Eleven

Hollie leaned back in her sewing chair. Her eyes hurt from all the sewing. So did her joints. She really needed coffee. And to exercise more. She stood up and tried to touch her toes, but barely reached her knees. To call her unfit would've been an understatement.

The hotel phone rang as she straightened up. There was no point waiting for Astin to pick it up, so she answered. A short break from sewing would do her some good. 'Hello?'

'Miss Baxter,' said Jamal. 'You have visitors. A Mr Cuoco and Master Mack.'

Hollie sunk on to the sofa. So Jack was finally ready to make an appearance. But with Cooper? As far as she knew, they'd never even met. And wasn't Cooper supposed to be at school?

'Miss Baxter?'

'Sorry. Send them up. And can you bring some coffee please? And whatever Cooper wants to drink, too.'

'Certainly.'

Hollie put the phone down. How would she tell Astin?

She walked in circles around the room, trying to figure it out. All was quiet from Astin's room – he was probably asleep. She hadn't heard much of him all day. He had physio the following morning so was probably resting in preparation.

A couple of minutes later, Jamal entered, Jack and Cooper in tow. 'I'll go get your drinks,' said Jamal before bowing out.

Jack stepped inside, a sheepish look on his face. Unusual. Jack's default expression was cocky.

Cooper emerged from behind him, his cherubic face somewhere between awestruck and terrified.

'Cooper wanted to see how Astin was doing,' said Jack.

'Sure, blame the kid,' said Hollie.

'I'm not a kid,' said Cooper, glaring at Jack with his bright blue eyes. They had a curiosity to them that Hollie recognised from Astin. There was no doubt that they were brothers. 'I'm ten.' His accent was also a *lot* thicker than his older brother's.

'Can you excuse Jack and me for a moment please?' said Hollie, grabbing Jack's ugly floral shirt and pulling him into her bedroom.

'Whoa there. Sleeping with you won't help me get Tate back,' said Jack.

'Ew. No,' said Hollie. She'd only met Jack briefly a couple of times when they were in New York. That had been enough. 'Did you kidnap him?'

'No! Astin's grandparents asked me to bring him,' said Jack.

Did they miss the part where he was an alcoholic that often ended up in jail?

'I don't believe you.'

Jack shrugged. 'Take it up with them, not me.'

'He's right,' said Cooper, walking into Hollie's room.

'What's going on?' called Astin.

Shit. She almost said that aloud, but stopped herself so that she didn't swear in front of Cooper. 'Now look what you've done,' she mumbled to Jack.

Cooper ran towards the sound of his brother's voice.

'Cooper, wait!' called Hollie, but it was too late. Cooper flung the door open and ran into Astin's bedroom.

'*Cooper?*' said Astin.

'Astin!' cried his brother.

Hollie reached the bedroom in time to see Cooper dive on his older brother. She cringed.

'Be careful, Cooper!' said Hollie. She hated berating him, but Astin was fragile. Cooper didn't know just how much because Astin had played it down every time they'd spoken.

Cooper snuggled up to his brother, hugging him tightly. Astin put his hand on Cooper's back.

'You look funny with a beard,' said Cooper.

Stupid more like. He hadn't shaved since being confronted by the woman in Hyde Park. Was it his way of disguising himself somehow?

'How did you get here?' said Astin, his voice full of shock and confusion. 'Shouldn't you be in school?'

'Jack brought me. I have homework.'

'*Jack?*' said Astin.

Jack stepped into the room, his hands in his pockets. 'Hi.'

'Gramma and Gramps got Jack to bring me because they can't travel and Mom and Dad won't,' said Cooper.

'What about school?' asked Astin.

'I just told you. I have homework with me,' said Cooper.

'That's not the same, Cooper.'

Cooper pulled away from his brother and sat on the bed like a scolded puppy. 'I can still learn stuff.'

'He's right,' said Jack. 'There's no better teacher than experience.'

Astin scoffed. 'You'd know.'

Hollie widened her eyes in a *not in front of Cooper* expression. If Astin noticed it, he didn't react.

'Why don't you go check out the rest of the suite? I need to talk to Hollie and Jack for a minute,' said Astin.

'It's about me, isn't it?' said Cooper.

Astin patted his brother's shoulder.

'Fine,' he said, hopping from the bed and scurrying off.

Hollie closed the door. She wouldn't make that mistake again.

Astin's eyes were filled with more rage than Hollie had ever seen in them. 'What. The fuck. Have. You. Done?'

Jack put his hands up in surrender. 'Hey, I was just trying to do the right thing. Your grandparents called the apartment and asked me for a favour. They didn't have the contact details for anyone else and your parents wouldn't pass them on.'

'He shouldn't be here,' said Astin coldly.

'He needs his big brother.'

'I'm not his big brother right now!' shouted Astin.

The three of them paused, expecting Cooper to burst in. He didn't.

'Being in a wheelchair and wearing a head brace doesn't make you any less of a person,' said Hollie. 'You'll always be his brother.'

'She's right,' said Jack.

'How am I supposed to spend time with him? I can't even move my fucking head!'

'Would you stop swearing?' snapped Hollie. 'You don't know if he's listening.'

'He is,' said Astin. 'He always is.'

A moment later, Cooper reentered the room, smiling innocently.

'You shouldn't have been listening, dude,' said Hollie.

'I don't want anyone to get into trouble because of me,' said Cooper, staring at the floor.

'They won't,' said Hollie, shooting Astin a warning look. He didn't acknowledge it.

'Will you make me go home?' said Cooper, his voice quivering.

'Not yet,' said Astin.

Cooper kissed his brother's cheek. 'Thank you!'

'Don't thank me yet,' said Astin.

The suite door opened. Jamal had returned with their drinks. Saved by the coffee.

Hollie turned to Cooper: 'Shall we go get a drink, leave these two to talk?'

'OK,' said Cooper, leaving the room.

'Don't kill each other,' mumbled Hollie before closing the door.

Astin stared at Jack, his jaw tight and his eyes hard. 'Why the fuck would my grandparents ask *you* to bring Cooper?'

'You never told them I'm an alcoholic, did you?'

'No,' said Astin. 'They would've hunted me down and dragged my ass back to Texas.'

'They knew you wouldn't tell them how bad your injuries really were, so they called the apartment hoping to get hold of me. They don't have anyone else's numbers,' said Jack.

With good reason.

'Cooper overheard and got upset, and he sweet-talked everyone into letting me bring him.'

'Were you even safe to fly?' said Astin.

'I'm sober,' he said. His eyes flitted around the room, looking anywhere but at Astin. 'That's what I've been doing the last few months. Getting sober.'

'For how long?'

Jack had been in and out of rehab for as long as Astin had known him. He didn't believe Jack could stay sober for long any more than he believed Liam wasn't in love with Fayth.

'This time's different.'

'Is it?' said Astin. 'Why?'

'It's not just therapy this time. I'm taking pills, and they stop the alcohol from doing anything. It's like drinking water.'

'You'll find something else,' mumbled Astin.

'Maybe I will,' said Jack, 'but this time it's going to be something that makes my life better, not worse. I want to be a better man. For Tate. For you. For kids like Cooper who need someone to look up to.'

Astin scoffed. 'Yeah, you're a great role model.'

'What's your deal? Would you stop shooting me down? I've only been here five minutes. I did you a favour!'

'Like hell you did!' shouted Astin. 'I didn't want him here!'

'Say that a little louder, why don't you?'

Astin breathed heavily, staring Jack down. It didn't affect him.

Astin hadn't spoken to Cooper much since the accident for a reason. They'd gone from speaking daily to once a week at most. Astin couldn't bring himself to let his little brother see him so fragile. Cooper was vulnerable himself. He needed to hold on to the image of his older brother as invincible.

'Whatever,' said Jack. 'I need coffee.'

Leaving the door open behind him, he joined Hollie and Cooper at the dining table. It was bad enough Hollie seeing him everyday, but Jack and Cooper too? Who next? His grandparents? The press? More fans from his modelling days? He was too much of a burden on Hollie as it was; he didn't want to be a burden on anyone else. Cooper was too young to understand. He didn't need to see him like that. Not when there was nothing he could do.

Jamal appeared from the living area. 'Would you like me to help you out of bed so that you can join your friends for coffee?'

'No. I'll drink it in here.'

Cooper didn't want to be too far from his brother so the hotel set up a spare bed for him in the living area. It meant Hollie couldn't get up early to sew, so she relocated her sewing machine to her room. It made things more cramped, but it gave Cooper some space to himself.

Jack, meanwhile, had a room just down the hall. He went to bed early that night, blaming jet lag. Hollie had a feeling it was more than that, but she let it go. He seemed different to how she remembered him from New York – aloof, off-kilter and high – but, aside from being sober, she couldn't work out why.

He went out early that morning, so he didn't join the three of them for breakfast either. While Cooper was in the shower, Astin said: 'Jack wants to go to continue his rehab. That's why he's being weirder than usual.'

'Oh,' said Hollie. That explained a lot.

'He won't last,' said Astin.

'That's a bit harsh,' said Hollie.

'Why is this time any different than last time?'

'I don't know,' said Hollie, 'but he's your friend, and as his friend, you should at least give him a chance.'

Astin scoffed. 'Yeah, all right.'

She furrowed her brow. If Jack was trying, he'd be more likely to succeed if his friends supported him, but given how stubborn Astin was, there was little chance of anything she said changing his mind. She let the conversation end there instead. They'd argued enough lately.

Once Cooper was showered and dressed, they climbed into Hollie's car and headed to physio. Cooper sat in the backseat staring out of the window and occasionally gasping at the sights.

'Have you been to London before, Cooper?' Hollie asked as they sat at some traffic lights.

'Nope,' said Cooper. 'I've never even left Texas before. Mom doesn't like travelling.'

Their mum didn't seem to like a lot of things.

She left Cooper to talk to Astin while she went to get a wheelchair. Cooper insisted on helping Astin into it. There wasn't much he could do – he was no stronger than Hollie – but he was adamant he was going to help.

Hollie pushed the wheelchair through the corridors while Cooper held the doors for her. She had to admit, it *was* nice having someone to help. But what would he do when Astin was inside? Would Astin let Cooper watch? It wouldn't be fun for a ten-year-old. She'd made sure he had his 3DS with him to keep him entertained, but he was more interested in talking to Astin. Most of Astin's responses were monosyllabic. Hollie tried her best to flesh them out. It was exhausting.

'Astin Mack,' called the physiotherapist. It was the same one he'd seen the week before.

Hollie pushed him to the door, Cooper behind them. Would he want them both there, or would she have to find a way to entertain Cooper in a hospital for an hour?

'I'll see you in a bit,' said Astin.

That answered that, then. He didn't want Cooper in there, and she was now the babysitter. Brilliant. She was the youngest person in her family. She had no idea how to entertain a kid!

'Ring me when you're done,' said Hollie. The physiotherapist took over pushing the wheelchair, leaving her and Cooper to wander the hospital corridors. She was familiar with the one where her mum worked, but everything was bigger and more confusing in London, hospitals included. It was a monster of a hospital. Cooper walked alongside her quietly, his gaze as curious as it had been in the car.

'That looks pretty,' said Cooper, pointing to a courtyard Hollie hadn't even noticed.

'Shall we go check it out?' She pushed open the door and they went into the empty courtyard. A few birds tweeted from the bushes. The smell of roses filled her nostrils. She sat on a bench beside a rose bush and stretched her legs in front of her. Cooper ran around, chasing a butterfly.

An old man walked past the window pushing a wheelchair. Inside it was a woman around the same age. From the way he nudged her, then whispered into her ear, they seemed like a couple. She smiled. She loved seeing old couples together. It was reassuring to know that love didn't care what age you were, or how frail you were. It was unconditional. But she sometimes wondered if what she and Astin had was. Would he ever stop trying to push her away? Would he ever accept that she was there because she loved him?

JUNE

One

'I don't like any of this food,' said Cooper as they sat at the dining table and studied the menu. 'I want Wendy's.'

Wendy's? What the hell was Wendy's?

'They don't have Wendy's over here,' said Astin.

'What do they eat then?' said Cooper.

'Food,' said Hollie.

'Bad food,' said Cooper.

Hollie bit her tongue. Her nan had brought her up to eat what she was given or starve. Cooper obviously hadn't been brought up with the same mentality.

'Hollie can take you out for something when we've eaten,' said Astin.

Hollie tightened her jaw. 'Hollie has work to do.'

'But—'

'He has food – expensive food, might I add – being offered to him. He can eat it or starve.'

Cooper slumped in his chair, his arms folded.

Just take him somewhere, mimed Astin.

No, mimed Hollie. She wasn't caving this time. Cooper was old enough to appreciate that he had food in front of him. He shouldn't need taking elsewhere because there was nothing else he liked. There was meat, chips, and vegetables. What more did he need?

Cooper stood up and headed towards the door.

'Where are you going?' said Astin.

'To Jack. He'll listen!' He slammed the door behind him.

'What did you do that for?' snapped Astin.

'Because he's old enough to eat what he's bloody given!'

'He's old enough to be able to decide what he eats!'

'He should appreciate having food in front of him. Kids in North Korea get themselves killed over a mouldy grain of rice!' Hollie waved the menu around in exasperation.

'We're not in North Korea!'

'No, but he should understand how lucky he is! Being an adult isn't always about having choices, it's about appreciating what you've got and making the most of it!'

'Says the person that couldn't handle working in an electrical store.'

'What's *that* supposed to mean?' said Hollie, waving her arms in exasperation.

'You want to talk about appreciating what you've got? You quit your job and didn't even have a back-up plan!'

'Because my boss was a dick!'

'So report him to HR!'

'It wasn't that simple!'

'Wasn't it?' said Astin.

'No! I couldn't do anything without anyone else to back up my story, and they were all too cowardly. So no, I couldn't bloody do anything about it.' She stood up. 'Nan was born right before the war. When she was Cooper's age, she had to queue for hours for a loaf of bread. She brought me up to appreciate that I could pick up a loaf of bread whenever I wanted and didn't have to worry about starving to death or malnutrition, because I had so much food to choose from. Not everyone has that luxury.' She picked up her blazer from the back of the chair. 'I'm going to eat downstairs.' She grabbed her book from the table and stormed off downstairs.

Hollie picked a spot by the stairs so that she could see everyone coming and going in the foyer. Every so often, she glanced around the room, hoping Astin would appear and join her. He didn't.

She'd almost finished eating when Jack and Cooper appeared on the stairs. The waiter led them over to her table and added another chair so that they could join her. She didn't speak. Jack winked. Cooper's head was bowed.

'I'm sorry, Hollie,' he said. 'I didn't realise how selfish I sounded.'

Hollie turned to Jack, her eyes wide. What had he said?

Jack grinned. 'So, what do you want to eat, kid?'

'Um…fish. I like fish. We don't get it much back home.'

'Why not?' said Hollie.

'Mom doesn't like the smell so won't let us eat it. Dad cooks it when she's out sometimes.'

Of course it was because of their mother. The more she heard about Astin and Cooper's mum, the more she disliked her. Some people shouldn't be allowed to breed. Then again, if she hadn't, there'd be no Astin or Cooper.

The waiter returned. Jack and Cooper ordered mains, while Hollie ordered dessert.

'Have you spoken to Astin?' asked Jack.

'Not since I came downstairs,' said Hollie. 'Why?'

'He's eating upstairs.'

'Now there's a surprise,' said Hollie.

'Why won't he leave the suite?' asked Cooper.

Hollie shot Jack a look. What was she supposed to tell him? The truth? 'He's just scared.'

'Of what?'

'Everything,' Jack mumbled.

Hollie kicked him under the table.

It's true, he mimed.

'Stop miming,' said Cooper. 'I can lip read.'

'Sorry,' said Hollie. 'Some stuff happened before you arrived that kind of put him off, that's all.'

'"Kind of put him off"?' repeated Cooper.

'She means terrified him into holding himself hostage,' said Jack.

She kicked him under the table again.

'*Ow*,' said Jack. 'Do your shoes have steal toecaps? They hurt! And it's true. He *is* holding himself hostage.'

'No, they're plastic. And I've tried to get him out, but he just won't go.'

'Are y'all going to tell me what happened yet?' asked Cooper.

He wouldn't let it drop. So Hollie explained what had happened. When they'd finished, Jack was silent. Cooper said: 'That would scare me, too. I don't like people in my face.'

'Me neither,' said Hollie. Would she have reacted the same if someone had done it to her?

Two

Cooper was a cute kid, but his presence made things awkward. Astin still refused to leave the hotel, and Jack spent half his time at therapy, so Hollie was the only one 'available' to take him out. He spent a lot of time in Astin's company playing games and eating, but he was a ten-year-old kid that had never left his home country and wanted to explore. Hollie didn't blame him. So she went with him when she could. They went to Hamley's, the Tower of London, they took a boat along the Thames…all things they should've done with Astin. It got to the point where she'd check her emails when she went to the loo, taking the few precious moments to herself to catch up on things.

It was hard saying no to Cooper's inquisitive gaze and puppy dog pout. He deserved to have fun. But she had to be careful. Things were going well with her business. She wasn't making a profit yet, but she was on track to. If only she had more time. If she wasn't careful, she'd fall so behind she'd never catch up.

She lay on the living room floor, cutting out the pattern for Tate's gala outfit, when Cooper walked in from Astin's room.

'Can we go get some ice cream please?' he asked.

He looked so cute with his big blue eyes and hunched posture, like it took all the energy he had to ask her. But she couldn't. She had too much to do, even if she did really need ice cream. 'Maybe later? I'm just working on a pattern for Tate's gala outfit.' Guilt welled up inside her. They'd spent a lot of time together since Astin's arrival. He was a cute kid and she enjoyed his company, but she was getting behind on work as it was. She couldn't afford to keep taking him to places.

'Oh. OK.' If he was disappointed, he didn't show it; his tone was neutral. 'Tate's cool. Is there anything I can do to help?'

'A pattern weight slid under the sofa earlier if you want to have a look for it,' said Hollie, struggling to think of anything else to keep him occupied that didn't involve playing more games with Astin. It was becoming increasingly difficult for her to think about things that weren't sewing-related. Every time she tried to switch off, she saw needles and fabric and thread; she heard the sound of fabric ripping, or a sewing machine buzzing.

'What's a pattern weight?' said Cooper.

She went into her sewing box and took out a flat metal ring. 'I use them to keep the pattern still when I'm cutting out the fabric. Some people use pins, but pins hurt a lot more when you stand on them than these do.'

Cooper chuckled. He knelt down behind the sofa.

'Hollie!' called Astin from the bedroom.

'Back in a minute.' She went into Astin's room. 'What's up?'

'Close the door,' said Astin.

Not a good sign. She did as he asked.

'Why did you do that to Coop?'

'Do what?'

'You brushed him off then made him do Jamal's job!'

'*I* brushed him off? You're the one who thinks you can entertain a ten-year-old by eating food and playing games! He's in *London*! Do you not think he wants to go out and explore?' she said, waving her arms about.

'I can't leave the hotel!'

'The only prison you're in is one you've created.' She left before he could respond. How dare he accuse her of not entertaining his little brother enough?

Cooper was in the living area doing a jigsaw when she returned. The pattern weight Hollie had lost sat beside her sewing things. She thanked him then went into her room and closed the door. She needed to talk to Fayth.

'I cannot believe him!' Hollie squealed before Fayth could speak.

'Who?'

'Astin!' She lowered her voice, just in case Cooper could hear. 'He just had a go at me because I said I couldn't take Cooper out for ice cream! That's his job, not mine!'

'He still won't leave the hotel? Not even with Cooper there?'

'No! He thinks it's fine for Cooper to sit playing games with him all day.' Hollie sat on the edge of her bed, her foot twitching.

'Ugh,' said Fayth.

'I'm working on the patterns for mine and Tate's outfits for the gala. I don't have time to entertain a ten-year-old right now. Twat. Him, not you. What am I supposed to do now? I can't stand to be near him, but if I take Cooper out, he wins!'

'That's pretty petty, Bea.'

'But it's true!'

'You're overthinking it. If you want to go out, go out.'

Hollie grumbled. Astin got his way too often lately. She was sick of it. They always ate what he wanted to eat (which was limited, given he still refused to go out), they watched what he wanted to watch, and they went out when he needed time alone. She had work to do. She'd thought he understood that. Obviously not. 'Ngh.'

'I stand by my previous comment.'

'On another note, have you decided on your outfit yet? There's only a couple of months to go.'

'Not really,' said Fayth.

'What about Dorothy?' suggested Hollie.

'I hate gingham,' said Fayth.

'I can work around that,' said Hollie.

'No. No *Wizard of Oz* outfit.'

'Fine,' said Hollie. 'But I need something soon.'

'What about Red Riding Hood?' said Fayth.

'I have the perfect outfit in mind,' said Hollie.

'Are you all right, Hollie?' Cooper asked as they ate their ice cream.

Her desire to get out of the hotel had surpassed her desire to go against Astin, so she'd grabbed Cooper and taken him for ice cream. He opted for chocolate chip while she went for mint chocolate. She picked a seat by the window so that they could people watch.

'Mm-hm.' She stared out of the window, watching passersby but not really seeing them.

'I'm sorry Astin yelled at you.'

Shit.

'You heard that?'

Cooper nodded. He licked his ice cream. 'He's been yelling a lot lately.'

Hollie frowned. 'Yeah, he has. I'm sorry you had to hear that.'

Cooper shrugged. 'I'm used to it.'

'You shouldn't have to be.'

'Do you think Astin will stay like this?'

'Stay like what?' She licked some ice cream from the edge of the cone before it ran down her hand.

'This angry.'

'He's just struggling with a few things right now, that's all.' It was the only answer she could come up with that wasn't blind optimism or downright pessimism.

Cooper sighed. 'Hollywood turned him into a drama queen.'

Hollie almost choked on her ice cream. Astin was a drama queen, all right.

Three

The *Pokémon* theme tune echoed through the bedroom. Liam pulled a pillow over his head. It was too early to talk to people. His phone stopped ringing. The radio played quietly in the background.

The bedroom door flung open. Wade snatched the pillow from Liam's head and shoved a phone under his nose. 'Parents.'

Groaning, Liam took the phone from him. 'Hello?'

Satisfied, Wade disappeared back into the living room.

'Liam, son, I don't want you to panic, but our apartment was broken into earlier,' said his dad's voice.

He sat bolt upright. *What?*

'Are you all right? Is Mom all right?'

'She's upset, we both are. The police are talking to her now.'

'What do they think?'

'They think it may be linked to what happened at yours.'

His nostrils flared. It was one thing to target him, but to drag his parents into it too, after everything they've been through?

'We're going to go stay in the Hamptons while things cool off,' said his dad.

'Good idea.'

His mum was a nervous wreck at the best of times. Someone breaking into their home would only make her worse.

'Liam,' said his dad in a booming, authoritarian voice. He was about to say something serious. 'The police think you have a stalker.'

Liam scoffed. 'As if.'

'I mean it, son. They think that he or she couldn't work out where you are so they broke in here to look for clues.'

'Shit.' He ran his hands through his hair. Could he really have a stalker?

'Be careful, Liam.'

His hands were clammy with sweat. He wiped them on the bedding. A stalker? A fucking *stalker?*

'I think you should stay where you are for now,' said his dad.

'Yeah,' said Liam. His eyes flitted to the door. Wade had probably already fallen back to sleep. No matter how much he paid him he couldn't be with him all the time. What was he supposed to do when he was alone? 'Do the police think this… *person* found any clues as to where I am?'

'No. There's nothing around here that suggests where you are. They trashed some of Saoirse's paintings, though.'

Tears formed in Liam's eyes. 'I'm sorry, Dad. This is my fault.'

'No, it's the fault of the person doing this, not you. Your mother's finished with the police, would you like to speak to her?'

'Please.'

There were a few muffled voices on the other end of the line, then his mum said, 'Liam, honey, are you all right?'

'Me? I'm fine. You're the one whose—'

'Has your dad filled you in?'

'Yeah. How are you feeling? Do you want me to come home?'

'No! Definitely not.'

Liam tried to fall back to sleep, but the harder he tried, the more he woke up. After an hour of tossing and turning he climbed out of bed and got dressed.

'Where are you going?' asked Wade, staring at him through one eye as Liam headed for the door.

'To get some fresh air.'

Wade was up like a shot. 'Not so fast, princess.'

'Stop calling me that!' The tone in his voice shocked even him. 'Sorry.'

'It's fine. Give me a minute to get dressed and I'll come with you.'

'OK,' said Liam as Wade grabbed some clothes from the back of the sofa and went into the bathroom.

He needed to get out of there. The walls suffocated him. He needed something – anything – to distract him. He grabbed his phone and some headphones then put on some music.

'Ready to go?' said Wade. He was in workout gear.

'Why are you wearing that?'

'Figured since you like walking to clear your head, jogging would help even more.'

Liam had jeans on, but he didn't have time to get changed.

He was too desperate to get away.

As they stepped through the pub doors and the muggy morning air hit them, he began to feel calmer. They walked at first, and it helped. A little. Then they power-walked. That helped even more. Before Liam knew it, they were jogging. The muggy air forced out all the negative thoughts, and by the time they returned to the pub half an hour later, he almost felt back to his old self.

'You were right when you said you're better off here,' said Wade as they climbed the stairs back to the flat. 'So long as you keep a low profile, I think we can wait this one out.'

Liam stared after him. 'You really think so?'

Wade unlocked the door. 'Yeah, actually. I do.'

Finally, someone believed he could make the right decision!

'I'm going in the shower,' said Wade as they got inside.

'OK.' Liam went back into the bedroom and fell back to sleep.

When he woke up, a note was on the door saying Wade was downstairs eating lunch. It was almost midday. How had he slept for so long? He still wasn't hungry, so he took out his art supplies from a cupboard by the window instead. After Fayth had told him off for wasting napkins by doodling on them, he'd ordered a sketchbook and some pencils online. They'd taken a while to arrive since they were in the middle of nowhere, but Fayth had given him one of her old notebooks in the meantime.

The last project he'd worked on was Astin's *Back to the Future* tattoo. He was proud of that design. It was of the DeLorean, with Einstein's head sticking out of the window. Not long after that, Saoirse was killed. He hadn't drawn since.

As he ran the pencil over the paper, his whole body relaxed. More tension left his muscles with every line; his mind saw nothing but the images he wanted to create. It was exactly what he needed. Why hadn't he done it sooner?

Fayth opened the flat's door a fraction and poked her head through. 'Do you want food?'

'No thanks,' said Liam. 'You can come in, you know.'

She walked into the room and leaned against the kitchen counter. 'You need to eat something. Wade said you didn't have any breakfast either.'

'Meh.'

She joined him on the sofa and leaned across to see what he'd drawn. It was the view from the flat window: houses, street lamps, rain. 'That's beautiful. You actually make that view look interesting.'

Liam gave a nervous laugh. 'Thanks. I don't draw much any more.'

'You should.'

'Right now it's the only thing that distracts me.'

'Are you still interested in bartending? We could use some help,' said Fayth.

'Yes!' He hugged her. Working behind the bar was just what he needed. He'd be too busy to worry about his parents or crazed stalkers.

'Calm down,' said Fayth, 'it's not that exciting.'

She had no idea.

'We'll pay you, of course—'

Liam stopped hugging her and stared at her blankly. 'Pay me? You're doing me a favour!'

'You're working for us, you should be paid,' said Fayth.

'I really don't need the money.'

'Well tough. It's a job. You get paid for doing jobs.'

'Fine. I'll spend it at the pub and put it back into the business,' said Liam.

'Whatever makes you happy,' said Fayth.

A couple of hours later, after lunch, Liam joined Fayth behind the bar for his first lesson in bartending.

'Do you know how to pull a pint?' she asked.

Liam stared at the contraption in front of him. He'd seen people do it before, but he'd never paid it much attention.

Fayth took a pint glass from under the bar and placed it under the nozzle. 'Put the glass underneath the nozzle and pull down slowly. You want about a centimetre's head on top. Some people will ask for more or less.' The lever reached the bottom. She let it go back up again then pulled it down again. 'Just keep going until the glass is full. If it takes more pulls, the barrel's near the bottom.'

He nodded. Sounded easy enough.

It wasn't.

Several of the regulars complained that his pint-pulling skills sucked. He was the newbie though, so they let him off. He was grateful for that – it'd been a rough could of days. Months, even.

Fayth made a few comments about how he was more determined to be good at bartending than ice skating, but she was forgetting something: when they went ice skating, he had nothing to worry about. Crazy ex-girlfriend aside. Six months later, all he could think about was his stalker. Who was it? Why did they hate him? Would the police ever catch him or her?

Being in Fayth's company for longer wasn't a bad thing, but living in a constant state of anxiety was taking its toll. How much longer would he have to go on like that?

He channelled his energy into drawing, jogging and learning how to bartend. He picked it up quickly, probably because he had nothing better to do with his time.

Word got out about where he was and people started to travel to see him. He embraced it, smiling and signing autographs, but a voice at the back of his mind warned him about photos each time he smiled for a selfie. If people posted photos and tagged him in them, how long would it be until his stalker – if he really did have a stalker – saw them?

Four

Insomnia had hold of Hollie like King Kong clutching Fay Wray. She couldn't remember the last time she'd slept without waking up several times in the night, or managed to fall asleep straight away. She tried to imagine her clothes on the runway of New York Fashion Week, Tate modelling for her and Camilla on the front row, but it didn't help. She usually gave up and read a book, played on her phone, or went back to work. Astin, meanwhile, was on sleeping tablets, so he slept just fine. She almost stole some a couple of times, but thought better of it.

She was asleep on the sofa one sunny June morning when she heard Astin's wheelchair whir to life. She opened one eye. He sat in front of the window, looking out, huffing and puffing like he'd just been to the gym for the first time in months.

'Are you all right?' she asked.

'Mmm.'

'Have you just done your exercises?'

'Mmm.'

'What's that mean?'

'It means I don't need you to nag me and tell me what to do,' he growled. He wheeled around to face her. His body was rigid. Tension like that wouldn't do him any favours.

'I'm just trying to help,' said Hollie.

'No, you're not. You're interfering. Like you always do.'

'I beg your pardon?'

'You heard me. Stop telling me what to do! I'm sick of it!' He returned to his bedroom and closed the door. If he'd been able to slam it, he probably would've. If that was the mood he was in, he could get himself into bed to play his bloody games.

She lay back on the sofa and squeezed her eyes shut. She needed to get up and get things done, but all she could hear was Astin's words echoing in her head: *Stop telling me what to do! I'm sick of it!* Did she really interfere that much? Did he really hate her trying to help that much?

They needed to talk. They kept getting into the same arguments and it was time something changed. She couldn't carry on how things were. She wouldn't.

Just as she was about to go into his room to discuss things, the phone rang. She hesitated, hoping it would stop. It didn't. There was no way Astin would answer. Sighing, she went over to the phone and answered it.

'Hello?'

'Miss Baxter,' said Jamal, 'I have a Mr Roskowski here to see Mr Mack.'

Hollie tightened her grip on the phone. What was Lawrence doing there? And what was she supposed to do about it?

'Keep him there please. I'll be down in a minute.'

'OK,' said Jamal.

She hung up and walked in circles a few times. What was she supposed to do? She couldn't let him up to see Astin. She brushed her hair, applied some lipgloss – AKA warpaint – grabbed her keys and bag, then ran downstairs. The stairs would give her chance to formulate a plan. She could try calling Jack, but he and Cooper had gone to some reading at the Natural History Museum. There was no telling when they'd be back, and what good would involving them do anyway?

Lawrence sat at a table in the foyer, his curly blond hair as scruffy poodle-like as ever. He stood up when he saw her. 'Hollie. It's good to see you.'

'What do you want?' she asked, her eyes hard.

'To talk to Astin.' He sat back down, gesturing to the empty chair opposite him. She remained standing.

'That's not a good idea.'

'Five minutes, that's all I need.'

'To do what? Don't you think you've done enough?'

'He's suing me. You know that, right?'

She nodded. Yes, she knew. But what could she do? She was his girlfriend, not his lawyer.

'Do you agree with that?' pushed Lawrence.

'It's his choice, not mine.'

'You're his girlfriend! You have a say!'

'It's not my job to tell him how to live his life; it's my job to support him in his decisions.'

'Five minutes. That's all.'

Hollie shook her head. 'No.'

'Please, Hollie. Do you have any idea how I've felt these last few months?'

'How *you've* felt? Are you seriously still trying to clear your guilty conscience?'

Lawrence fidgeted in his seat, his eyes darting around the room.

'This is on you, Lawrence. This is on your shitty decisions and crap listening skills. You're not welcome in our life.'

'"Our life",' he said with a chuckle.

'Yes?'

'Happy, are you?'

'Is that any of your business?'

'Trouble in paradise?'

'I beg your pardon?'

'Astin not the perfect boyfriend you thought he was after all?'

He was baiting her, and she knew it. Why? What reaction did he want from her?

'You're not welcome here,' she repeated.

'Just five minutes. *Please.*'

'No.' She glared at him. His face was empty of recognition and emotion. Why would he not take the hint?

'I don't have time for this.' She left the hotel and walked off towards Hyde Park in search of fresh air. Or as fresh as you could get in London.

Who the fuck did he think he was? And how dare he suggest things in their relationship weren't great? They weren't, but that was none of his business. She and Astin would work through things. It was a difficult time for them both. They were bound to project their bad moods on to one another. That was what you did in relationships.

She squinted as she crossed the road into Hyde Park. It was bright out, and she'd left her sunglasses at the hotel. The plush green grass was covered in sunbathers who had nothing better to do with their time and a higher sun tolerance than the chronically pale. It was all right for some. She moved off the path to make way for some cyclists and found a shady spot under a tree to call her nan.

'Bit early for you, isn't it?' answered her mum. It was ten o'clock. It wasn't *that* early. Not any more. It was to her old self, the one that had lived with her mum and nan a few months earlier, but not to the Hollie that lived in London. That Hollie had a business to run. The earlier she got up, the more work she could get done.

Hollie twirled the necklace Astin had bought for her between her fingers. Even the silver was warm against her skin. 'Need Nan.'

'She's busy.'

'Need Nan.'

'She's on the loo.'

'Didn't need to know that,' said Hollie. She stretched her legs out in front of her, leaning against the tree. If ever there was a good spot to nap outdoors, she'd found it.

'You shouldn't have asked. What's wrong?'

Hollie explained about Lawrence's visit, and how much of a bad idea it was for him to see Astin. Her mum listened, occasionally chiming in with 'yeahs' and 'uh-huhs'.

'What was I supposed to do?' Hollie asked when she'd finished.

'You did the right thing,' her mum reassured her.

'Thanks.' A couple of seagulls landed in front of her and argued over a leftover sandwich. The fat one nipped at the smaller one. As the smaller one recovered, the fat one grabbed the sandwich and flew away.

Her phone vibrated to signal someone else was calling her. Astin. She said bye to her mum and answered. 'Hey,' she said.

'WHY IS LAWRENCE HERE?'

She jumped to her feet. The other seagull flew away. Shit. She belted back towards the hotel. He wasn't supposed to be there. He was supposed to leave when she did. The bastard. The fucking bastard.

'WHY IS HE HERE?' Astin shouted down the phone.

'I don't know!'

She was panting by the time she reached the hotel. The lift took too long to arrive, so she took the stairs again. She was so unfit her body was ready to collapse by the time she reached their suite and pelted through the doors. Astin sat in his wheelchair, staring out of the living room window. There was no sign of Lawrence.

At the sound of the door opening, Astin turned around. His face was red. 'How dare you tell him he can come see me? I had to call security!'

'You know I'd never do that. I told him to fuck off.'

'Then how did he find his way up here?'

'How should I know? I told him to fuck off then I went and – shit.' He'd snuck upstairs after she'd gone. 'I told him to fuck off then went for a walk. He must've snuck up after I left.'

'How else would he have found our room? You had to have let him in!' His chest was heaving, his voice full of rage. He'd never spoken to her in such an angry, accusatory tone before.

'For crying out loud, it wasn't me! I'm so sick of you blaming me for things! You stay here playing the victim all the fucking time, not realising you're a fucking prisoner of your own making. Is that your way of punishing yourself? Holding yourself hostage?'

'How dare you? I'm not up to going out!'

'Yes you bloody are. You just don't want to. Admit it: you don't want to be seen in a head brace.'

Astin huffed.

'You care so much about what people think of you that you'd rather your little brother be bored of out his skull than go to a storytelling event with him, or even just for a coffee down the road. It's disgusting.'

'Leave Cooper out of this!'

'Cooper became a part of this the minute he walked through that door. You've treated him like shit since he got here. I'm not sure who's looking after whom any more.'

'You're not looking after me, that's for sure.'

'Is that so?' said Hollie. 'I've sacrificed everything for you. I spend half my time looking after you and the other half working on my business. I haven't slept in weeks. And what I do isn't good enough?' She waved her arms in the air. 'Why do I fucking bother?'

'You tell me.'

'I don't know any more. I thought I knew you. I was wrong.'

'You knew exactly who I was when you decided to stay here instead of going home!'

'I thought I did,' she said. 'I was wrong.'

'Oh what a shame. The mighty Hollie Baxter got something wrong. What will she do next?'

Hollie widened her eyes. 'How dare you? I've spent the last three months trying to help you—'

'Help me? *Help me?* All you've done for the last three months is interfere! You tell me what to do and how to do it; you try to get me out of here when I don't want to go. You won't give me five minutes' peace!'

'Because you suck at following doctors' orders! If I didn't nag you—'

'Damn right you nag,' he muttered.

'—You wouldn't be resting or about to get your fucking head brace taken off, you'd be stuck in it even longer!'

'What, and you know all that because Mommy's a nurse, do you?'

Hollie jabbed her finger in his direction. 'What the hell is wrong with you? There are far worse things that could've happened to you.'

'Don't you get it? I've lost everything!'

'Everything?' she whispered, her voice cracking. '*Everything*?'

'I'll never do stunt work again! Everything I've spent the last ten years working towards is gone!'

A lump formed in her throat. 'Is that all that matters to you?'

'It's all I have!'

Tears formed in her eyes. Her throat tightened. She tried to pull the necklace – which suddenly felt like a noose – from her neck, but it wasn't as easy as they make it look on TV. She unfastened it and threw it at him. It clattered to the floor. She didn't notice where.

She stormed into her room and slammed the door, grabbing her suitcase and shoving things into it.

Astin shouted through the door. 'If you walk out that door, don't bother coming back.'

'Don't you get it?' she called, still packing. 'I don't want to.'

She didn't bother with her strict packing regime; items were shoved where they fitted. It didn't matter what went where, so long as they went somewhere. The faster she got out of there, the better.

She dumped her bags in a pile by the suite door. There was no sign of Astin. She'd get Jamal to carry the bags to her car then leave him a tip and thank him for all his help. He'd been good to her. It was a shame she couldn't say the same thing about her boyfriend. *Ex*-boyfriend.

Her hand hovered over the door handle. Explosions from whatever game Astin played echoed through the suite. That hadn't taken him long.

She opened the door and stormed out holding only her handbag. Tears ran down her face. She wiped them away.

The lift doors opened and a couple stepped out, giggling. They were so wrapped up in each other they didn't notice the crying girl a few feet away. Once they were out of sight, she got into the lift and went down to the lobby.

What would she say to Jack and Cooper? How would she speak to them? She didn't want to ring and interrupt whatever they were doing. After everything they'd been through, they deserved to have fun.

Jamal was nowhere to be found in reception, so she left a message with the concierge then went outside to wait for her car. Jack and Cooper rounded the corner, laughing. There was nowhere to hide.

Jack saw her first. When his eyes met with hers, he stopped juggling the smoothie bottle he'd been playing with and stared at her with a look so intense she had to turn away.

'Hey Coop,' said Jack when they were within earshot, 'why don't you go get a drink and we'll come meet you in a minute?'

Cooper hesitated, but after a moment, agreed and carried on inside.

'How was the storytelling thing?' asked Hollie, barely about to form the words.

'Shit,' said Jack, guiding her a few feet away. 'What happened?'

Somehow she managed to update him on Lawrence Roskowski and the ensuing argument despite barely being able to breathe. 'I can't do it any more. I tried. I tried so hard.' She broke down, unable to see through the tears.

Jack took a tissue from his jeans pocket and handed it to her.

'Thanks.' She patted at her eyes. 'He's not the person I fell in love with. He's selfish, he's lazy, and he's self-pitying.' She shook her head. Fuck him and his stupid attitude problem. Fuck him and his hot-and-coldness. Fuck him to hell. 'Will you be OK?'

'Please. You think he's bad? You should've seen what I was like,' said Jack. 'It's you I'm worried about. You're the one he treated like shit.'

'Yeah. Well.' She ground her teeth. 'Not any more.'

'Want me to bring anything to the car?'

'No thanks. The concierge is sorting it.'

Her car had appeared a few feet away. Jamal and a couple of others began to put her things into it. She looked away.

'OK,' said Jack.

'I should talk to Cooper,' she said. She was wrought with guilt for leaving him, but what could she do? Astin was his brother. He wouldn't hurt him. Cooper was old enough to understand. She hoped. The sooner she spoke to him, the sooner she could get away. And she desperately needed to get away.

What if he appeared downstairs and tried to stop her? What would she do if he did?

Who was she kidding? He *wanted* rid of her. He'd been trying to get rid of her for months. He'd even tried to dump her right after the accident! If only she'd agreed to it back then. If fucking only.

Jack stayed outside with her car while Hollie went inside to find Cooper. He sat at a table in the foyer, studying a menu. She sat down, clasping her hands on the table as she tried to work out what to say. He reached over and put a hand on top of hers. She sniffled. If her eyes were red and puffy from crying – which she was about 99% sure they would be – Cooper didn't say anything.

'I'm leaving,' said Hollie, her voice quivering.

'But this is your home,' said Cooper.

'No, it's not. My home is with my mum and nan.' As the words left her lips, she knew it was true.

'Is this about Astin? He's been strange lately.'

Strange was one word for it.

'I understand,' said Cooper. 'I'm not sure I'd love him right now either if he wasn't my brother.'

Hollie pulled Cooper to her and hugged him. God, he was cute. 'No matter what, your brother will always, *always* love you. Got it?'

'What about you?'

'What about me?'

'Will he always love you?'

Goddamn that kid.

Five

The door closed.

Hollie was gone.

It was better that way. It wasn't her job to look after him. He didn't want her to. He never had.

He shot a few more aliens on *Doom*, turning the volume up to block out the sound of Jamal and co removing her presence from the suite. If only he knew where his headset was.

When the noise stopped, he wheeled out of his room and into Hollie's. Fabric he'd bought her for sewing projects sat folded neatly in the corner beside the sewing machine he'd given her. Never had he wanted to smash something more. He tightened his grip on his wheelchair.

The door reopened. She'd come back!

'You're an idiot sometimes, you know that?' called Jack. He found Astin in Hollie's room and leaned against the doorframe, a smoothie bottle in his hand. He held it out to Astin.

'No.'

'Suit yourself.' He took the bottle and sat on the sofa.

The glint of Hollie's necklace caught Astin's eye as he entered the living area. It had fallen by the dining table, the clock pendant on one side, the chain on the other. He turned his chair in the other direction.

Jack crossed one leg over the other and leaned back. 'Did I mention you're an idiot?'

'Thank you, Dr Phil, for your insight.'

'It's my job to be honest with you. That was part of our agreement, wasn't it?'

'What agreement?'

'Fine, an unspoken agreement.' Jack waved the smoothie bottle around as he spoke. 'You've been treating her like shit. I can't believe she put up with it for so long.'

'She shouldn't have come.'

'And what would you have done, if something had happened

to her?' said Jack.

'Gone over and—' He stopped talking, realising what Jack was trying to do.

'Exactly. She did exactly what you would've done if the situation was reversed.' He continued to wave the smoothie bottle around. Astin nearly knocked it out of his hands. 'Not only that, but she's already used to caring for someone in a wheelchair. But instead of listening to her, you kept slamming the door in her face.' He opened the bottle and drank from it. 'I'm not sure who deserves a medal more: her, for putting up with you, or you, for how much of a cunt you were.'

'What the fuck do you know? Look how you treated Tate all these years!'

Jack's jaw tensed, his grip on the bottle tightening. 'Don't you think I know she deserves better?' He walked towards the door, his hand hovering over the handle. 'Not being with her everyday is like a piece of me is missing, but goddamnit, I just drag her down. But I want to be a better person. I want to be a better person so that I don't look back on my life when I'm old and regret what a dick I was. I want to look back on my life and be proud of what I did and who I was. Because we all fucking deserve that.' He slammed the door.

Who the fuck did he think he was, lecturing someone after all the shit he'd pulled? Hypocrite.

Astin wheeled himself into his room, slammed the door, and climbed into bed. His pillow smelled of vanilla and blackcurrant: Hollie's perfume. His eyes filled with tears. She was gone. She was really gone. A tear escaped from his tear duct, followed by another. He wiped them away with his fist.

He'd made the right decision. He had. If he kept telling himself that, one day he might believe it.

Hollie's car had never been packed so neatly. Barely able to breathe, she gave Jack and Cooper one last hug then climbed in, adjusted the seat, and pulled away. A taxi's horn blared. She'd cut him up. Fuck.

The blood pounded in her ears. Her heart thudded in her chest. Pins and needles ran through her hands and feet. Her vision disfigured, as if she were looking through a fisheye lens. She had to get away. But she was stranded. If she kept driving, she risked causing an accident. If she didn't drive, she was too close to Astin.

Astin…

Tears filled her eyes. She wiped them away. She needed to pull over somewhere, but where? She was in London. There was nowhere to bloody park.

She called to Siri to find her the nearest car park, but it didn't understand what she meant. She threw her phone on to the passenger seat. Stupid piece of shit.

A sign for an NCP caught her eye. She indicated and pulled in. It'd cost a fortune, but she needed the time to recalibrate. He wouldn't think to look for her there.

But then, how could he, even if he wanted to? He could walk a few feet; he couldn't chase a car. Even at his fittest he couldn't have chased after a car.

And why would he? He hadn't even gone looking for her downstairs. He obviously didn't want to be with her.

She clutched the steering wheel, her nails digging into her palms. Breathing was hard. *Really* hard. As if she'd just ran the London Marathon.

Well, it was like a marathon after what had happened with Astin.

Astin.

Oh, Astin.

She started sobbing uncontrollably.

She loved him.

And she'd dumped him.

Had she made the right decision?

Should she go back to him and apologise?

No. He had an attitude problem. She didn't have the time or the patience to be treated that way. She was nobody's doormat. If he was that interested in her, he'd reach out to her. He was the one that had ruined things. It was his job to apologise first. He'd be sorry without her. He was a better person with her.

But then, she was a better person with him.

She cried harder, her chest tightening as bile rose in her throat.

Even though she knew she was having a panic attack, she couldn't stop it. The chest tightness, the crying, the shaking – it had hold of her and wouldn't let go. All the advice she'd been given over the years tried to force its way forwards, but the anxiety just wouldn't let it through.

Her hand shaking, she picked her phone up from the passenger seat and rang Fayth. She put it on handsfree, silently pleading her best friend to pick up. Because she was totally telepathic.

Thankfully, she did.

'Hey Bea. How's things?'

Hollie couldn't answer her. She was too busy crying.

'Hollie? What's wrong?' Fayth's voice was full of concern.

'Astin and I. We…we…we broke up.' Saying those words cemented it. It was true. There was no going back.

'I'm so sorry,' said Fayth. 'Are you OK?'

'Can't…breathe…'

'Remember what your mum always says: short, shallow breaths. Keep the carbon dioxide going.'

Hollie nodded. Remembering Fayth couldn't see her, she mumbled, 'Yeah,' and took the advice. In. Out. In. Out. In. Out.

'Do you want to talk about it now, or later?' said Fayth.

'Later,' said Hollie. 'I need to get home first.'

'Are you sure you're safe to drive?'

No, but she wasn't going to tell Fayth that. Not after what had happened to her mum and sister. 'I'll be OK. The driving will help me calm down. That and playing No Doubt deafeningly loud.'

'OK. But no *Ex-Girlfriend*. That song will *not* help right now.'

Hollie pouted. 'But it's one of my favourites.'

'And way too angst-filled for your current mood.'

'True,' agreed Hollie.

'And no *Don't Speak* either. Better yet, no No Doubt. Too many breakup songs.'

'Well what am I supposed to listen to then?' grumbled Hollie.

'Podcasts?' suggested Fayth.

'You're really not helpful, you know that?'

'Sure I am. You sound calmer already.'

She did feel a little calmer. Her hands still shook, but not as much. Her breathing had almost returned to normal. Her heart had slowed.

'Thanks,' said Hollie.

'Maybe you should stop off somewhere and get some food,' said Fayth.

'I'm really not hungry.' The very concept of food made her want to projectile vomit over the dashboard.

'What about just a drink, then? Get some sugar in you.'

'Yes Nan,' said Hollie.

'I'm just looking out for you, that's all. Is there anything I can do?'

'Could you ring Mum and Nan please? Tell them what's happened? I don't think I can bring myself to tell anyone else.'

'OK. Are you sure you'll be all right?'

'Yes! Stop worrying about me!'

'I do worry Bea, you know that. Just remember, he may be a prize twat, but you still have lots of people around you that love you.'

'I know,' said Hollie. It wasn't the same, but she was still lucky. If she said the word, Fayth and Cameron would go to Astin like an angry mob with their pitchforks and torches. But she didn't want them to hate him. She just wanted to forget she'd ever met him. But she couldn't. Everything reminded her of him. And how could it not? If it wasn't for him, she wouldn't be on the path towards her lifelong dream of being a fashion designer. She owed him more than she did anyone else, except maybe her mum and nan. But that was different. They'd raised her. Him… he'd changed her life in less than six months. And she'd given up on him. Had she really made the right decision to give up on him after just three months of him being in a wheelchair? Did breaking up with a disabled guy make her a bad person?

No. She was *not* a bad person. It wasn't the wheelchair that was the problem. Her nan was in a wheelchair, and she didn't love her any less because of it. The problem was Astin's neglect and snippy attitude. She hadn't signed up to be in a relationship with a guy who bit her head off every time she tried to have a conversation with him. That wasn't the kind of relationship she was interested in. That was part of why she'd waited so long to get into one. It wasn't even about high standards. It was just about not wasting time on arseholes. She wanted someone who complemented her. Someone that understood her. Someone that made her a better person. Someone that made her stronger.

Until recently, Astin had been that person.

But he'd fucked it up.

It was *his* fault.

Not hers.

Tears streamed down her face again, clouding her vision so that the only thing left that she could see was Astin, the first time they'd met. God, he'd been handsome. And funny. Really funny. And intelligent. And—

'Bea, you still there?' came Fayth's voice.

'Yeah, sorry,' said Hollie, snivelling. 'Zoned out for a minute.'
'Are you sure you're—'
'YES! Sorry. I didn't mean to snap. I'll get on the motorway then stop and get a coffee and text you then, OK?'
'And when you get home. And any other time you need me. Doesn't matter when. I'm always here for you.'

When Hollie finally pulled up on to the driveway of her childhood home, she burst into tears. She'd driven back in a daze. Her head hurt, her bladder hurt, her eyes hurt. She needed to get inside, to pee, then to sleep.

Leaving her things in the car, she went inside. Her nan was already on her feet. She pulled Hollie into her. Hollie cried harder. Fayth had called like she said she would, and for that, she was grateful. Hollie couldn't bring herself to repeat the words again: *we broke up*. It wasn't being alone that bothered her. She was used to being alone. It was being without Astin that bothered her. But did she even know him any more? She'd spent just a few weeks in the company of the man she thought she knew. She'd spent more in the company of a grumpy, angry boy whom she'd hoped would revert back to the person she'd first met. But he never would. She knew that now. His life revolved around his stunt work. She didn't matter to him. He'd made that perfectly clear.

George nudged the side of her leg. She put her hand down and stroked behind his ears. He licked her hand.

'Do you want some food?' said her nan.

Hollie shook her head.

'Have you eaten?'

Her stomach grumbled.

'I'll make you some beans on toast,' said her nan, starting to pull away.

'Still hugging.' She stopped scratching behind George's ear and put both arms around her nan, squeezing her as tightly as she could.

'You'll be OK,' said her nan.

'How do you know?'

'Because you're my granddaughter.'

Six

Liam's first few weeks behind the bar were quiet. The locals were always patient with new staff, especially ones they could – or already had – establish a rapport with. Liam was one such person. If he struggled with something, he flashed them his trademark smile and the regulars melted. It worked every. Time. Fayth had never seen someone so instantly likeable before. Especially not someone who could be so bad-tempered when no one was looking.

For the first time in years, Fayth enjoyed working behind the bar instead of hiding in the kitchen. She enjoyed being a part of the conversations Liam got into with the regulars. Except the ones about tennis. Andy Murray could've been from the same village as her and she still wouldn't have cared.

Sometimes Wade sat at the bar and joined in with conversations, other nights he worked the door. Occasionally he sat alone and read a newspaper. Wherever he was, he appeared casual until someone approached Liam. If Liam gestured to him that it was fine, he'd return to whatever it was he was pretending to do. If Liam ran both his hands through his hair, Wade got him out of there, stat. They had a good system going. It reassured most people that Liam was safe. Except Fayth.

As the days grew lighter, the kids stayed out later, and more of them appeared at the pub. Officially, they were a family pub, but unofficially, Fayth wasn't a fan of children. She just didn't know what to do with them. How were you supposed to speak to them? She swore too much to be about children, that was her problem. She was too afraid to say the wrong thing. Hiding behind the bar meant that she wouldn't have to go near them – whomever was on kitchen/table-waiting duty would.

Every so often there was a lull, at which point Fayth and Liam went for their breaks or chatted to some of the regulars. In Liam's case, that included talking to Abe about tennis.

'Have you ever been to Wimbledon?' asked Abe.

'No,' said Liam, leaning against the back bar with his hands in his pockets, 'but I'd love to go one day.'

'You should take him, Fayth,' said Abe, waving his pint as he spoke.

'I'm sure Liam's got plenty of friends to go with who'd enjoy it more than me,' said Fayth. She stood beside him, her eyes darting around the room looking for threats. Even with Wade there, she wanted to be on full alert. The more lookouts they had, the more likely they were to pick up on someone suspicious.

'I've never known anyone hate tennis as much as Fayth,' said Abe.

'I don't hate tennis. I just don't understand the fascination. I'm not as bad as Hollie. If you mention sports around her, she recoils.'

'How is your Brummy friend?'

'She's not Brummy,' said Fayth automatically. She had a twang. That she was in denial about. That was all. 'She's OK.' Just quiet. And teetering on depression. 'She's making me an outfit for the charity gala in a few weeks.'

'Who are you going as? The Wicked Witch of the West?' Abe sniggered at his own joke.

'Very funny. No, I'm going as Red Riding Hood.'

'And a dashing Red Riding Hood you'll make too,' said Liam.

'Who're you going as?' Abe asked Liam.

'Prince Charming,' he said, putting his hands on his hips and flashing him his biggest, cheesiest grin.

'I have to admit, you do look the part,' said Abe.

Oh god. Liam's ego was big enough. The last thing he needed was a middle-aged electrician stroking it.

'Excuse me,' said a voice so high-pitched it definitely didn't belong to someone over the age fifteen. Nobody under 18 was allowed at the bar after nine. It was well past that. Most people adhered to this rule. But there were always exceptions.

The person the voice belonged to was barely big enough to see over the bar.

She walked over to the part of the bar closest to Liam and hopped on to a stool. Little bugger. 'Can I get a photo with you please?' She gave Liam her sweetest smile.

Wade, who was reading a newspaper on a nearby table, looked up. Liam gave a small shake of his head. Wade continued to watch anyway.

'Is that a good idea?' Fayth asked through the side of her mouth.

'It's just a photo,' said Liam.

'Aren't you forgetting something?' said Fayth.

Like, having a stalker?

'What's she going to do with it? Put it on Instagram? She's barely old enough to be in middle school,' said Liam.

'I have no idea what age range that is, but she has parents who no doubt use it,' said Fayth.

'You worry too much.' He stepped forwards and grinned at the girl. 'Sure thing. Do you want any drinks while you're here?' Ever the salesman, too. Fayth and Wade exchanged disapproving glances, but what could they do? He wouldn't listen, and they knew it.

In a surprise twist that Fayth and Wade hadn't expected, the photo didn't appear on social media. Not as far as they or Brooke could tell, anyway. They checked several times over the following days, but nothing materialised. Some people still kept photos just for themselves after all. Fayth had thought that tradition had died out with photo albums. Their paranoia at finding a photo of Liam at the pub online did inspire Fayth, though.

She, Brooke, her dad, Liam, and Wade sat around the kitchen table eating breakfast. Wade had offered to make everyone American-style pancakes for breakfast. Never ones to turn down free food, the Campbells had agreed and given him the run of the kitchen. He'd said it was a thank you for letting them stay at the pub. Fayth wasn't so sure. She had a feeling it was Wade's way of apologising for Liam letting the girl take his photo. While they hadn't had any signs that Liam's stalker had found out where he was, the more evidence there was of his location, the more likely it was they'd find him.

'I've been thinking,' she said.

'You can think?' said Brooke.

'Hilarious,' said Fayth. 'May I continue?'

'You may,' said Brooke, sawing off another piece of pancake.

'Thank you.' She took a sip of tea, then continued: 'Everyone wants to know what's going on at the pub, right? What if we take control of that by setting up, say, a Twitter or something? That way we can show people Liam isn't here, so they needn't come.'

'But I am here,' said Liam.

'Curly Sue's on to something,' said Wade.

'Curly Sue?' said Fayth, horrified. Her hair wasn't *that* curly. Or '90s.

Wade grinned. 'It fits.'

'It really doesn't. I preferred "The Scot",' said Fayth.

'Boring,' said Wade.

'Back on topic,' said Fayth's dad, 'I think it's a great idea.'

'Have fun, sis,' said Fayth.

'What?' said Brooke.

'I don't know how this stuff works. You're the best person to run it.'

'I don't have time! I have exams!'

'Not for much longer,' said Fayth.

'I'll do it,' said Liam. 'If I'm taking the photos, I can't be in them, can I?'

'He's right,' said Fayth's dad.

'Timer,' mumbled Fayth. Nobody seemed to notice.

'Why don't you all run it? The more you post, the better it'll do,' said Wade.

Liam turned to his bodyguard. 'Since when did you become a social media expert?'

'Sister works in marketing. She never shuts up about it.'

'But what about when people come in and see Liam working at the bar?' asked Brooke.

'We won't mention him on there,' said her dad. 'And if someone asks us about him, we won't respond. And we'll ban punters from taking photos.'

Brooke snorted. 'Like people will listen to that. This isn't Luke's Diner.'

'Where?' said her dad.

'Never mind,' said Brooke.

'He bans phones, not cameras,' Fayth pointed out.

'If we police it closely, we can get away with it,' said her dad.

'And we risk putting off even more people,' said Brooke.

'Like we get that many millennials in anyway,' said Fayth. 'They only started coming in when they thought they'd run into Liam.'

'But the boost in business is why we can sell the pub for a higher price,' said her dad. 'We can't afford to alienate anyone.'

'I'll keep an eye on things,' said Wade. 'If anyone looks like they're taking sneaky photos of Liam, I'll have a word.'

'And if they're brazen like the girl was?' said Fayth. 'You

can't police it without taking people's phones off them.'

Wade opened his mouth.

Brooke cut him off. 'You're not doing that.'

Wade slumped. Fayth had never seen him put down so quickly. She laughed.

'So what do we do?' asked Fayth's dad.

'It's a shame we can't put him in the kitchen,' said Wade.

'Let's not even consider that,' said Fayth.

'I'm better than I used to be!' protested Liam.

'Baby steps,' said Fayth, patting his shoulder.

'We'll take things one day at a time,' said Wade. 'I worked as a bouncer at a few high-end clubs before I became a bodyguard. This is nothing compared to that. This is the easiest gig I've had.'

'You're kidding?' said Fayth.

'I worked for Camilla Persia. I've never met someone so high maintenance in my life.'

'Not even Liam?' said Fayth. She ignored the death stare he gave her.

Seven

Two weeks after leaving London, Hollie still hadn't sorted through her bags. Running low on clothes, she figured it was probably time she unpacked. She unzipped her suitcase and tipped everything on to her bed. A t-shirt at the bottom stood out. It didn't look like her size. It was *way* too big. She held it up. It was a navy blue Hard Rock Cafe t-shirt. Astin's. She'd worn it as a nightshirt a few times and must've put it into her suitcase by accident. She hugged it to her, crumpling into a heap on the floor.

They hadn't spoken since she'd left. She hadn't reached out to him, and he hadn't reached out to her. That proved to her he didn't want her back and that she'd made the right decision. They'd had some good times together, but the bad outweighed the good.

That didn't make her miss him any less.

The faint smell of his patchouli and citrus cologne still hung to the t-shirt. She sobbed. God, she missed that smell. His fluffy hair. The huskiness in his voice, especially if he was tired. The Texan twang to his voice that he refused to acknowledge was there. Having someone to have long, in-depth conversations about classic literature with. And someone to discuss *Back to the Future* fan theories with. And his tattoos.

She threw the t-shirt at the wall.

Knock knock.

'It's me,' said Hollie's nan.

Hollie opened her eyes. She'd fallen asleep on her bedroom floor, her pile of clothes unsorted on the bed in front of her. *That* t-shirt sat hanging off the end of her bed.

Her nan pushed the door open, a tray of food and drink in her hands. Noticing the state of Hollie's room, she frowned. 'What's this all about?' she said, shoving some stuff on the TV unit aside to put the tray on.

Hollie pointed to the t-shirt. Her nan picked it up, holding it in front of her. She squinted. 'Hard Rock what?'

'Cafe,' mumbled Hollie.

'What's that?'

'A cafe.'

'Well I gathered that,' said her nan, 'but what makes it special enough to warrant its own t-shirt?'

Her nan was trying to cheer her up and get her to engage in a joke or two. In most cases, it would've worked. It wasn't one of those times.

Her nan pushed aside some of the mess on the bed and perched on the corner of it.

'Did I do the right thing, Nan?'

'Only you know that, gal.' She patted the bed.

Hollie sat beside her, not caring what clothes she crumpled. She rested her head on her nan's shoulder, inhaling the scent of musky perfume and stale cigarette smoke.

'I don't know, that's the problem.'

'You'll figure it out. In the meantime, you have this room to clean.'

Hollie scoffed. Despite everything else that was going on, her nan was still going on about how messy her room was. Some things would never change, and that was a good thing.

'Just don't let him get you down. If he misses you that much, he'll come to you.'

Hollie always trusted her nan's advice, but she wasn't so sure about that. Not only had she not heard from him, but he also hadn't posted online, and nobody had given her any updates on him. She assumed that was out of courtesy, but she couldn't shake the niggling voice that wanted to know how he was and what he was up to. Was he getting better? Was he still glued to his TV?

Did he miss her?

Did he?

Probably not.

If he did, he would've at least texted.

Wouldn't he?

Her nan stood up. 'Why don't you go see Cameron for a few days? He's always good at cheering you up, and he's not as far away as Fayth.'

'Yeah,' said Hollie. She quite fancied a change of scenery. Her old bedroom was suffocating and was filled with reminders of Astin. Cameron's flat was one of the few places that hadn't been corrupted by him. 'I think I might.'

'In the meantime, you can get dressed and take me for some lunch.'

'Can I now?' said Hollie.

'Yep. I'm not having you stuck in here all day.'

Just like Astin.

Hollie pulled up outside Cameron's apartment building a couple of days later. She'd never been so happy to see that battered building and its collection of cigarette butts outside the front doors. She lifted her suitcase from her car boot and pushed open the front door. Cameron had lived in the same building since university and the front door was *still* broken. No wonder the rent was so cheap.

She made her way to his apartment, remembering the way from when they were at uni together. It felt like an age ago. She'd once pined for that time, for a better period in her life. She wasn't so bothered any more. She wanted to forget everything that had happened in the past and move on.

The door to Cameron's apartment opened before she reached the end of the corridor.

'Creepy, very creepy,' she said.

Cameron poked his head around the door and grinned malevolently. 'Heard your footsteps and saw you through the peephole.' He stepped aside to let her in. It opened out into an open-plan living room and kitchen with the bedroom and bathroom off to the left.

'Loving the new hair.'

'Thanks,' she said, dumping her suitcase by the door. She caught sight of herself in the mirror. Her wavy red hair and side fringe were gone, replaced by a sharp chocolate brown bob with a blunt fringe. It was a classic style that she could use to her advantage. It looked grown-up. The darker colour also reflected her mood. Darkness descended on her like a dementor, but the closest thing she could get to a patronus was a bottle of hair dye.

'How was the drive?' asked Cameron.

'Same as usual.' Her stomach rumbled.

'Food?' suggested Cameron.

'Let's go.'

'So,' said Hollie. 'What's the story with that guy?' She pointed to a bald man covered with tattoos, and only wearing a pair of navy Bermuda shorts. He hobbled as he walked, a carrier bag in either hand.

It was a game she and Cameron had played often when they were at university – they'd sit in the window of a cafe or restaurant, then make up stories about the people that went past. It had been their favourite way to pass the time back when they'd been students. If only she could still afford to spend all her time playing pointless storytelling games.

'Fabric irritates him. He mows lawns for a living,' said Cameron.

'Where do you get this stuff from?'

'He's cheating. It was in the local paper,' said another voice.

Hollie's back stiffened. She knew that voice. She knew that voice all. Too. Well.

Will.

She studied his reflection through the glass. His hair was shorter and less scruffy. His skin was still spotty, but not as bad as it had been. A nose piercing was covered by masking tape.

'Hey man, what're you doing here?' said Cameron.

'They're short-staffed, so my manager asked me to cover. I work at the one across town.'

Bloody typical. Last she'd heard he'd moved back in with his parents up north somewhere. That obviously hadn't stuck.

'When did you move back?' asked Cameron.

'About a year ago, I think. I live in Clifton.'

'Nice,' said Cameron, his voice dripping with sarcasm.

'So, what can I get you both to drink?'

'Lemonade for me please,' said Cameron.

'Just water for me please,' said Hollie.

Of all the times to run into him. She mostly just wanted to laugh. She didn't, though. That would be rude.

He'd once had so much power over her, but now he had so little. She'd always have a soft spot for him, but the way she'd once felt about him paled in comparison to how she felt about Astin.

Once Will had left with their orders, Cameron put his hand on Hollie's arm. 'I had no idea he'd be here, I swear.'

'It's fine,' said Hollie, giggling. 'Really. It's funny.'

'It is?'

'Yeah. I don't feel anything. I just want to laugh.'

'Why?'

'Compare the two,' she said. She couldn't say Astin's name aloud; it was still too raw. Despite the way Astin had treated her, he'd always been upfront about his feelings for her. Will, on the other hand, had led her on for years, and she'd fallen for it. She'd given up on him when she saw him making out with a randomer at a house party. You don't tell someone you love them then make out with someone else.

'Will's a nice guy, but yeah. You upgraded. Next time you'll upgrade again.'

Next time. She wasn't ready to think about next time yet. If ever. Her career was her greatest love. It had to be.

Will brought their drinks over, took their food orders, then left again. Hollie picked up her drink and sipped it. 'Oh my god.'

'What? Is it vodka?' said Cameron. He leaned over, a hopeful note in his voice.

'No. It doesn't have ice in. I forgot to mention it. He remembered.'

'Funny how he remembers that but forgot your birthday.'

Hollie laughed. 'Yeah.'

'He has a girlfriend, by the way. If his Facebook is still up-to-date.'

'Who?'

Cameron shrugged. He took out his phone and found Will's profile. His profile picture was of him and a redhead with a button nose and pale blue eyes. She looked eerily like Hollie. She shuddered.

'Apparently you have a doppleganger,' said Cameron.

Hollie shoved his phone back at him.

'Some people definitely have a type,' said Cameron.

Astin looked so different to Will it was ridiculous. The only similarity they had was their height.

'I need to piss. Will you be all right?' said Cameron.

'Go for it. I don't want to get blamed for you having an accident in the middle of a restaurant.'

'You sure? I mean…' He looked around.

'I'll be fine. What's the worst he can do?'

Cameron got up and left her alone.

Hollie took out her phone and texted Fayth: *Of all the places for Will to work, it had to be where Cam and I picked for food, didn't it? *rolls eyes**

It had hurt at the time, but she knew she'd made the right

decision to cut Will out. If she hadn't, she may never have met Astin, or Tate, or started her fashion line. She missed Astin and felt empty without him, but one day the pain would be easier. She hoped.

'Hey.' Will slid into the seat Cameron had vacated. Was he allowed to do that?

'Hi,' said Hollie, not taking her eyes from her phone.

'How's things?'

'You know,' said Hollie.

'I hear you're mingling with the rich and famous now.'

'Something like that,' said Hollie.

'I saw that outfit you made for Tate Gardener. I knew it was yours right away.'

Hollie widened her eyes. 'You watched a Tate Gardener video?'

He'd always moaned about Hollie's taste in music when they were friends, saying she only listened to 'the cheesiest of pop music'. Tate was right at the top of his list of hated artists.

'I saw a post Cameron put on Facebook, bragging about how talented you are. I still think you would've looked better in that outfit than her, though.'

He wasn't actually trying that one, was he?

'How are things with your stunt man?'

Her stunt man. What a way to put it.

'How are things with your girlfriend?'

'They're OK. Yeah. OK.'

Just 'OK'? That sounded enthusiastic.

'I wish we'd kept in touch,' said Will.

Oh god.

She looked down at her phone. *Where* was Cameron?

'I still think about you,' he continued.

WHERE WAS CAMERON WHEN SHE NEEDED HIM? She thought her piss breaks were badly timed.

'What happened was a long time ago. We've both moved on since then,' said Hollie.

'Things can still happen,' said Will.

'Can they?' said Cameron. He finally reappeared, standing beside them like a disapproving father. He crossed his arms, staring Will down.

Will jumped out of his seat. 'Talk to you later.'

'Please don't tell me he just hit on you,' said Cameron. He slid back into his seat.

'OK,' said Hollie. 'I won't.' She looked back down at her phone.

After a few moments of relentless fidgeting, Cameron said, 'He hit on you, didn't he?'

'Not blatantly, but he said he wished we'd kept in touch and that he still thinks about me. Then the bit you heard.'

Cameron shook his head. 'What a bastard.'

'Whatever. I'm not interested anyway.'

'That's my career girl,' said Cameron.

Eight

'I've been thinking,' said Liam one morning as he and Fayth took the dogs for a walk. They scurried around the local park, pushing each other over and into puddles of mud. It had rained heavily the night before, so Fayth had on her wellies while Liam was stuck wearing Nikes. They soaked up the water, staining the fabric, but he didn't complain about them being ruined *or* his feet being wet. Fayth was impressed.

Wade jogged around them, pretending to look casual and not as conspicuous as bodyguards often looked. He mostly looked stupid, since he jogged in circles.

'About what?' said Fayth.

'What if Patrick's my stalker?'

Fayth stopped walking. A crippling, uncontrollable laughter took over her. She grabbed on to a tree to steady herself as she carried on laughing. 'I – I'm sorry. That's the funniest thing I've heard in ages.'

Liam pouted, giving her that puppy dog look that was so damn cute. 'Why is it?'

She straightened herself up, still giggling. 'He – he couldn't afford to get a ferry to Northern Ireland, let alone a plane to New York. Not to mention…he couldn't pull off a plan like that if he wanted to. He's not smart enough. We'd have figured him out ages ago.'

'How do you know?'

'He once tried to surprise me for my birthday and he left my present in the living room.'

'Could've been an accident.'

'He did the same thing for Valentine's Day.'

'Oh.'

'Sorry.' She took a few breaths to slow her laughter.

Liam pouted.

'The police will find whoever it is, don't worry. In the meantime—' Fayth opened the rucksack she always took dog walking and fished out a poo bag. '—Vienna's left a present for you.' She gestured to a pile of poo a few feet away. Vienna stood near it, kicking up the dirt to try and cover it.

It started to rain again while they were out, so Fayth and Liam ducked into the pub to dry off. It was between lunch and dinner, so everywhere was quiet. Wade went upstairs to shower, leaving the two of them alone. Liam took out his sketchpad while Fayth got out her camera and pointed it at him. Each time she closed the shutter, he twitched.

'Oh my god, you can't sit still, can you?' she said, lowering her camera.

He looked up from his sketchbook, propped his head up with his hand, and tried to look 'sophisticated'. She pressed the shutter then checked the display. She didn't look impressed.

'OK, let's try this.' She put her camera on the bar and spun his barstool around. 'Focus on me, and *only* me. Not the camera. Not the pub. Just me.'

'OK.'

Fayth picked up her camera again. 'Wherever I'm standing, look at me.'

'But you have a camera in your face.'

She sighed. 'Pretend you have a good imagination and it's not there.'

He glared at her.
She snapped a photo.
He shook his head.
She took another one.
He laughed.
She took another.

Each time he reacted to her taking the photo, she pressed the shutter again.

After a few minutes, she stopped taking photos and flicked through them. She smiled.

'What're they like?' he asked, hopping off the stool.

She pulled the camera from his view.

'You have to show the subject your photos, that's the rule!'

She pulled her camera closer, eyeing him warily. 'Says whom?'

'Me,' he said, trying to reach it.

She pulled it away. He wrapped his arms around her, trying to get to the camera. She giggled, squirming in his grasp.

He perched his head on her shoulder. She turned her camera so that he could see the display.

'Damn, I'm handsome.'

'How does your ego fit through doors?' wondered Fayth.

'It struggles in old pubs like this.'

'I'm not surprised,' said Fayth, flicking through the shots.

'Wait. Go back a minute,' said Liam.

'That one?'

'Yeah.' It was one she'd taken when he looked straight at the camera – at her. He'd thought about her and nothing else. How beautiful she was, inside and out, and how she didn't even know it. She no longer just smelled of cocoa butter; there was a hint of rain, but that only made him want her more. She didn't care if she didn't smell like a perfume advert, or if he saw her looking less-than-perfect. Unlike the people he'd spent more than half his life around, she was normal. She was just what he needed to stop Hollywood from taking over his life again. But did she need him?

'I like that one,' said Fayth.

'Nice work, Campbell.' He let go and gave her a playful shove.

'Thanks. You weren't such a bad subject after all.' She nudged him back and placed her camera on the bar, then hopped up on to a stool.

'Mind if I use it?' He picked up the camera and flicked through the images.

'For what?'

'Social media, duh.' He sat on the stool beside her. 'I'll credit you, of course.'

'That could be…awkward.'

'Why?'

'The rumours. You know.'

'It really bugs you, doesn't it? People talking about you.'

She stared into her lap, fiddling with her hands. 'A little.'

He reached out and rubbed her arm. Was that what stopped her from giving him a chance, or was there more to it, like what had happened with her ex-husband? Or her mum and sister? He wished he could dissect her mind and figure out how it worked; how to get past her guarded heart and prove to her that he'd protect her.

She'd probably hate that. She was too independent for that. But what *did* she want?

'Then I won't use it. We'll keep it between you and me.'

She squeezed his knee. 'No, it's OK. You can use it, just don't credit me. Maybe in a few months I'll feel differently.'

'Um, Dad? I think you should see this,' said Brooke. She entered the kitchen and handed him her phone.

Fayth sat at the dining table, researching photography schools on her laptop. Rio was curled up on her lap, fast asleep. 'What's up?'

Her dad looked at Brooke's phone. His face fell.

'*What?*' said Fayth.

Brooke snatched her phone from her dad and shoved it at Fayth. The pub's social media accounts had barely been open a few weeks, but that hadn't stopped the negative comments. Someone had sent them a string of abusive tweets. Threatening violence and rape. Fayth threw the phone across the table as if it were contaminated. 'What's wrong with people?' She felt sick. Most of them weren't even tweets about the pub, but tweets about its employees. How dare someone threaten to rape her sister just because of where she worked? Or to kill her dad because he owned the pub?

'Can you delete those?' asked her dad, his face forlorn.

'No,' said Brooke. 'That's not how Twitter works.'

'Do whatever you can do with them, then. And tell Wade so that he can pass it on to the police,' he said.

'You think this has something to do with Liam?' said Fayth.

'I think it's possible,' he replied.

The one thing Liam hated about working behind the bar was taking phone calls. The mysterious phone calls he'd had in New York still haunted him, and whenever he heard a phone ring, he expected it to be his stalker.

Thankfully the phone didn't ring often, but whenever Liam did answer it, he put on a fake accent – usually a Scottish one – so that nobody suspected it was him. He'd never used his Scottish accent on camera, so the only people who'd know it was him were the Campbells and his family.

He was just about to go on his break when it rang for the first time in almost a week.

'I'll get it,' said Liam, reaching for the receiver.

Fayth was a few feet away, serving a customer and looking as amazing as ever in tight-fitting jeans and a Snoopy t-shirt.

'Good evening, Cock and Bull,' he said.

'Is that Liam?' asked an excited female voice.

'No, Liam's not here right now. How may I help you?'

'Don't lie to me; I know it's you!' she squealed.

'Would you like to book a table at our restaurant? The chef's special this week is deconstructed haggis with piped mashed potatoes and fresh seasonal vegetables. I can highly recommend it.' For dog food. He'd tried haggis at his grandparents' once. Once was enough.

'Why are you pretending? Why won't you be honest with me?'

Goosebumps formed on the back of his neck. Who was it, and how did they know he was putting on an accent? It wasn't that bad, was it?

'Why won't you tell me?' she cried.

Was it his stalker? Had they found him?

No. The pub got weird phone calls all the time. Fayth said so herself. With her only a few feet away, he had to stay calm. Or at least pretend to be calm. She worried enough as it was.

'We also do a vegan version of our special, made with tofu,' he said, trying to sound cool. He glanced up at Fayth. She was serving another customer, paying him no attention. For once, he didn't mind.

Beeeeeeeeeeeep.

Fuck.

He put the phone down and lifted up the end of the bar, suddenly in desperate need of a break.

'Who was it?' asked Fayth. She pressed a shot glass up to the whisky.

'Sales call.'

Nine

'Looking forward to your last day of wearing this thing?' Declan asked, gesturing to Astin's head brace as he helped him out of the bath. It stood a few feet away, leaning against the wall. He didn't wear it all the time any more – like when he had a bath – but he still wore it more than he would've liked.

'That's today?' said Astin as Declan began to dry him off. He wouldn't be completely free – he'd still have to wear a foam collar – but his upper body would no longer be in a vice. While he resented the head brace and everything that it meant, he was used to it. Would his body be able to cope without it?

'Yeah. I reminded you yesterday. And last week. And I think it's in your calendar.'

The calendar Hollie had set up on his phone with all his hospital appointments in. He'd barely checked his phone since she left. It hurt too much that she hadn't contacted him. He wasn't interested in talking to anyone else.

'Oh. When do I get my crutches?'

'When physio think you're ready,' he answered vaguely.

Declan helped him put his head brace back on for the last time, then get dressed again. When they left the bathroom, Jack and Cooper were talking to Jamal.

'I'll organise a car to pick you up at lunchtime,' said Jamal.

Was he the only one who'd forgot his appointment?

'Thanks,' said Astin. Since Hollie had gone, they no longer had a car or a driver. Jack liked cars and knew how to take one apart, but he had no interest in driving them. He rode bikes, but a bike wasn't suitable for Astin. Or big enough for all three of them.

'Right then. Unless you need me for anything else I'll see you later on,' said Declan.

'Bye,' said Astin.

'Later,' said Jack.

Jamal left to go organise the car. Astin, Jack, and Cooper sat silently in the living area. There was a vacant spot on the table in the corner, where Hollie's sewing things had once been. Astin had had Jamal put them into storage along with anything else Hollie had left behind.

Cooper took his 3DS out from under a sofa cushion and began to play on it. He'd always been quiet, but since Hollie had left, he'd been even quieter than usual. He spent most of his time with Jack or playing on his 3DS.

Jack went over to the window and stared up at the sky. Astin pushed forwards the gearstick on his wheelchair and joined him. It was a grey day, like most in England. The sky was overcast and it spat with rain.

'The weather around here doesn't do much for your mood, does it?' said Jack.

'No,' agreed Astin. He missed the dry heat of Texas. England didn't get heat like that. On the rare occasion England was warm, it was also muggy.

'I think I might go travelling, once you're back to being you again,' said Jack.

Astin would never be the person he was before the accident again, but Jack wouldn't accept that. So instead of arguing, he asked, 'Where?'

'Wherever I can. I want to go out and live. Really live, without the drink or the drugs. Maybe if I learn how to live without it, I'll find out what's really important to me.'

'I hope you do, man, I hope you do.'

Astin returned to his bed after getting his head brace off. Hospital exhausted him, and he wanted chance to get used to his new foam collar. It was less restrictive than the plastic thing he'd had to wear, but it was itchy and uncomfortable. He opened *The Witcher* to where he'd left off the day before. Playing games was the best way he'd found to relax. Even if he couldn't move, he could still exercise his mind.

Cooper burst in and started bouncing on the bed. 'Can we go see the new *Teenage Mutant Ninja Turtles* movie please? *Pleeeeeeeease?*'

Astin cringed, his grip tightening on the controller. Cooper's jumping on the bed caused ripples that hurt his back. 'Why don't you go with Jack?'

Cooper sat still, crossing his arms and legs. Astin exhaled. 'I want to go with you. We never do anything together.'

'We play games together,' said Astin. Even though *The Witcher* wasn't suitable for a ten-year-old, he carried on playing as he spoke to his brother.

'We never go out,' said Cooper.

'I told you I couldn't when you got here.'

'But you've got your head brace off now! You can go out!' said Cooper.

'Drop it, would you?' Astin tried to focus on the game, but his little brother shoved his head in front of the TV.

'No! You won't do anything with me and I hate it! Gramps does more than you do!'

'Then go back to Gramps!' shouted Astin.

Cooper ran out of the room crying.

Hollie lay on her bed, updating her website. Websites were annoying, but they were a necessary evil. They were where she made all her sales, so keeping it up-to-date – and updating any items that weren't selling well – was crucial.

Her phone began to ring on her bedside table. It was Cooper. She hadn't spoken to him since she'd left. Had something happened?

'He's horrible, Hollie!' sobbed Cooper as soon as she picked up. 'I asked him to go see the new *Teenage Mutant Ninja Turtles* movie with me, and he won't even do that!'

What did he want her to say? She'd broken up with Astin because he was incorrigible. She'd hoped he wouldn't be as bad with his little brother. Apparently she was wrong.

'Can't Jack take you?' she suggested.

'It's not the same!' said Cooper. '*He's* not the same! He doesn't care about anything any more!'

Oh, he cared all right. About his stunt work.

'I wish there was something I could say to make you feel better, Coop. I really do.'

Cooper sobbed down the phone.

'Where are you?'

'In Jack's room. He's at one of his meetings.' He sobbed some more. Hollie wished she could reach through the phone and hug him. Then strangle Astin. 'Should I go home?' asked Cooper.

'Back to Texas?'

'Uh-huh.' Cooper continued to cry.

'It's up to you,' she said.

'I don't think he wants me here,' said Cooper. 'I don't think he ever did.'

She couldn't lie to him, but she wouldn't admit that either. Knowing that would destroy him.

'Do what feels right for you, Cooper. Don't stay because you feel you have to. He has plenty of other people who can look after him. Sometimes you have to put yourself first.' Even if you spent the following weeks second-guessing yourself and would never be sure if you'd made the right decision.

'How was your first night's sleep without your head brace on?' Declan asked as he helped Astin out of bed.

'You mean wearing my dog collar instead?' said Astin, touching the itchy foam collar around his neck.

'If that's what you want to call it,' replied Declan.

'Uncomfortable,' said Astin. He tugged at it to try and loosen it, but it didn't work.

Declan chortled. He lifted Astin up and on to his walking frame. 'It'll take some getting used to again. It all will.'

Using his frame, Astin made his way towards the bathroom. The living area was empty.

'Where's Cooper?' said Astin.

'Dunno. He wasn't here when I arrived.'

Jack walked out of his room – formerly Hollie's room – yawning. He'd moved in after she'd gone. Every time the door opened, Astin still hoped Hollie would walk out. 'Morning gentlemen. Cooper's in my room. We fell asleep watching *Rocky Horror*.'

'You made my ten-year-old brother watch *Rocky Horror*?' Astin continued to edge towards the bathroom. Every step drained him; he had to stop after each to regain his breath. He refused to give up, though. He'd make it to the bathroom. Eventually.

'It's called giving him an education.' Jack yawned again. 'He's still asleep, by the way. He's still thinking of going home, too.'

Astin reached the bathroom door. 'If that's how he feels, then take him.'

Jack and Cooper left a couple of days later. Cooper didn't say goodbye. Jack did, but Astin barely acknowledged him. He couldn't. Saying goodbye to Jack meant that he was on his own.

For a while, at least. He didn't know when – or if – Jack would return from the States. The only people left to put up with him were paid to tolerate him. He was more isolated than ever.

But he didn't want company anyway. He wanted to be alone. He wanted to play games and watch daytime TV and not have to put up with people.

Before the accident, he'd liked people, but since then, he couldn't stand their pitying stares or constant questions. He'd lost count of how many times he'd been asked how he was since the accident. He could hardly walk or move his head. How did they *think* he was?

Everyone liked to remind him how lucky he was. That didn't help either. It didn't change that he'd lost everything. Every*one*.

He'd told Hollie that he'd lost everything. That was why she'd left. It wasn't until she was gone that he'd realised the accident hadn't taken everything away from him. He'd still had her. Until she'd given up on him too.

Part of the reason he'd stayed in London so long was her. The doctors had said he could fly at his own risk. He'd have risked it to be back home in New York if Hollie hadn't offered to care for him. She was the only person who'd made him feel better the last few months. No matter how bad he felt, seeing her everyday gave him a reason to keep going. But she was better off without him – not caring for him meant she had more time to spend on her business. As much as he missed her, she was right to leave.

Who'd even look after him if he went back to New York? He had friends there, sure, but would they really sacrifice everything to care for him?

He reached into the bedside drawer and took out Adrian, the dumb-looking teddy bear she'd bought him from the hospital. With its brown eyes and Mohican, it was cute, in a weird sort of way. Hollie hadn't known it when she'd given it to him – she probably still didn't know – but that small gesture on the day of the accident had given him hope. It had made him feel loved, even when he'd felt ugly and like a failure.

The bear stared at him with big, brown eyes. It stared into his soul, mocking him for his bad decisions. For letting Cooper leave. For letting Jack leave. For letting Hollie leave. For slipping on the ledge. For trusting Roskowsi's leadership.

He threw the mocking bear at the wall. It bounced off, landing on the floor a few feet away, unharmed. Piece of shit.

JULY

One

For once, it was hot outside. The Cock and Bull didn't have any air conditioning – what was the point, when it was always cold? – so desk fans were dotted around the pub to try and keep it cool. It didn't work. The bar was roasting and the sticky heat only exacerbated Fayth's almost constant nausea. She didn't mention it to anyone because they'd either ask if she was pregnant (not unless it was Jesus), or tell her to go to the doctors, and she didn't have time for either conversation. If it really was stress, it would go away on its own. Eventually.

It was worse in the kitchen. Fayth checked on Ross regularly to make sure that he drank enough, and they switched places every so often so that they could have a break from the sweltering kitchen conditions. Fayth didn't like Liam being behind the bar without her, but she had to trust him. He was good at it, the punters liked him, and Wade was there. He'd be fine. He had to be.

After having spent her hour in the kitchen, Fayth went for a break then returned to the bar. Most of the punters were in the picnic area outside, with the exception of those that didn't like being outdoors or couldn't get a table. That made the pub look quiet, when actually, it was busier than usual. Fayth sent Liam on his break and struck up a conversation with Wade.

A woman with brown hair in a green cardigan walked in as they talked. She smiled at Wade. 'Hey,' she said to them both. Her accent was partially Scottish, but there were hints of other places in there too. Fayth couldn't place it.

'Hi,' said Fayth. 'What can I get for you?'

'What's good here?' she asked.
'What do you usually drink?' said Wade.
'Vodka cranberry,' she replied. She hopped on to a barstool beside Wade and tossed her mousy hair.

He leaned into her. 'A vodka cranberry. How old are you?'

She tucked her hair behind her ear. 'Wouldn't you like to know?'

Fayth backed away, pretending to busy herself by rearranging bar towels. She suddenly felt like she was intruding. Was she actually hitting on Wade? Of all the times for Liam to be on his break!

'Are you local?' asked Wade.
'Kind of.'
'You don't give much away, do you?'
'Where's the fun in that?'

Fayth was used to seeing people flirt. It happened all the time when alcohol was involved, but this was Wade. Mr Workaholic.

'We'll have two pints of your guest ale,' decided the brunette. She put some money on the bar.

'I'm working; I can't drink,' said Wade.
'You're sitting at a bar. How is that working?'

Fayth turned back to Wade, a wary expression on her face. Wade looked at her as if to say, *what should I do?* She shrugged. What did he want her to say? They tried to keep it quiet that he was Liam's bodyguard. The less people that knew, the easier it would be for him to spot the stalker. Apparently walking around in a suit all day didn't make him conspicuous. It was a good job most of the punters wouldn't know the difference between a designer suit and a Primark one.

'I guess a pint can't hurt,' said Wade.

'Man, how many pints have I had?' Wade yawned. 'I'm wiped.' He rested his arms on the bar and lay his head on them.

He'd carried on drinking at the suggestion of his new lady friend and the encouragement of Liam. Fayth hadn't liked it, but Liam kept telling her not to be so paranoid. She gave up in the end. She didn't want to be a nag. What Wade did wasn't her business.

Wade's new lady friend left about an hour before closing, promising to add him on Facebook. So far, she hadn't.

'I've drunk more than you, you lightweight,' said Liam. He

leaned against the back bar, watching his bodyguard.

'How many have you had?' said Fayth, changing the gin bottle. She didn't mind him having a few, but she didn't like the idea of half their booze going to staff. Punters paid. Staff didn't.

'Some fans bought me a couple. It's no big deal,' said Liam with a shrug.

Well. That was something.

Wade yawned again. 'I think I'm gonna go lie down.' His forehead dripped with sweat; he wobbled as he stood up. It was warm for July, but it wasn't *that* warm. Not compared to New York.

She grabbed Wade and dragged him to a quiet corner. 'What are you doing? You're supposed to be looking out for Liam! I can't run the bar and babysit him!'

Wade wiped his forehead with the back of his hand. 'You managed that first night he was here.'

'When word hadn't got out that he was here!'

Wade tugged at his shirt collar. 'It's just one night. You can manage. Hey, have you always had two heads? You look like you have two heads.'

Fayth stepped aside. There was no point keeping him downstairs; he was in no state to do anything.

Wade yawned again then disappeared upstairs.

Fayth returned to the bar, trying her best to hide her disapproval.

'He's not usually such a lightweight,' said Liam.

'What're you saying?' asked Fayth.

'Your "real ale" must've poisoned him.'

Fayth shot him a sarcastic smile. 'Thanks.' She rang the bell for last orders and the bar was bombarded once more. It wasn't easy keeping her eye on Liam and serving punters, but she did her best. Multitasking wasn't her thing; it never had been.

Last orders were as uneventful as they always were, and for that, Fayth was grateful. Everyone served their final drinks, she and Ross began to clear the restaurant while Liam tidied up the bar. She hadn't even asked him to.

Fayth and Liam went upstairs to check on Wade once the pub was tidied. He was flat out on the sofa, his arm over his face. A blanket was wrapped around his feet.

'Should we move him?' said Liam.

Wade let out a loud snort.

'Nah, he's fine,' said Fayth. 'Looks like he's out.'

He rolled on to his side, his face smushed against the sofa cushion.

'Tea?' said Fayth, filling the kettle.

'Please,' said Liam. He yawned.

Fayth flicked on the kettle then yawned too. 'That was a long night.'

'Yeah,' agreed Liam, grabbing a couple of mugs from the cupboard, 'but you only have to do it for a few more weeks.'

'Mmm,' said Fayth. She unfastened her ponytail and let her hair fall around her shoulders. It had been pulled so tight for so long that her hair hurt.

'Are you not glad?' His arm brushed hers as he reached past her to get some teabags from the box on the side. Her skin tingled.

'I don't know. It's bittersweet. I'll miss this place, but at the same time, I can't wait to get away,' she replied.

'I know what you mean. I felt the same about *Highwater*.'

'You did?'

'Yeah. I really enjoyed working on the series and meeting all the fans, but I didn't enjoy all the attention or hype. All the hype put a lot of pressure on us, and in turn, we put too much pressure on ourselves.'

Fayth rubbed his arm. She'd never been in a situation where she needed to put pressure on herself, not in the same way that Liam had, or Hollie or even Astin. Her life was tame and boring compared to theirs. How had she got to 24 and never really lived? How had she been so comfortable coasting when her parents had always pushed her to be better, to do better?

'Have you thought any more about what kind of photography you want to do?' asked Liam. The old kettle began to boil; they almost had to shout to be heard over it.

'A little. I like taking photos of landscapes, but it's people that really interest me. You can show so much in a photo if it's taken right. What's their story? How can I show what they're really thinking?' said Fayth.

'By recording a video?'

'Funny.'

The kettle finished boiling and she poured the water into the cups.

'You know what I mean,' said Fayth.

'No I—'

The lights went off.

Fayth flicked the switch on the kettle. Nothing. Bloody brilliant.

'Power cut?' said Liam.

Fayth looked out the window. The street lamps outside were still on. 'More like shitty pub power cut.' She grabbed a torch from under the sink.

'Where are you going?'

'Basement. That's where the fuse box is.'

'You know what happens in horror movies, don't you?'

'You do know they're fictional, don't you?' She headed for the door. 'You coming?'

'I'm good,' said Liam.

'Suit yourself.' She headed down into the basement, her least favourite part of the pub. It was dark, dank, and the concrete stairs were steep and uneven. It was even worse at night with no power, but Liam and Wade couldn't go all night without it. They'd melt.

She automatically tried to switch on the light as she opened the doors, but nothing happened when she pulled the cord. Torch in one hand, the other on the rails, she descended. The plastic curtain at the bottom of the stairs stopped her from seeing anything until she pushed past them. They helped regulate the temperature and keep it cold enough for the beer barrels. Whose stupid idea it was to keep the fuse box down there she didn't know. Whoever they were, they were an idiot.

A sweet, unfamiliar smell invaded her nostrils as she pushed through the curtain. It was sickly sweet, like artificial strawberries. It was nauseating. She hesitated. Brooke didn't like strawberries. Her dad wouldn't spray something like that. She was pretty sure Liam and Wade wouldn't, and Ross hated strawberries. Nobody else had access.

She swallowed. Something wasn't right.

The fuse box was just around the corner. Just a few feet. The basement was small. If someone was in there, she'd see them. Wouldn't she? She raised her torch and shone it around the room. Nothing. She exhaled.

Her hands still shaking, she rounded the corner to the fuse box. The door was open. It was never open.

She crouched down in front of the fuse box. A sharp pain shot through her as something heavy hit the back of her head.

Two

Liam checked the clock. Fayth had been gone ten minutes. It didn't take that long to flick a switch on a fuse box, even he knew that. Even if he didn't know what one looked like.

If he had to go down to the basement, he didn't want to go alone. He poked Wade's cheek. He didn't budge. He poked his cheek harder. Wade waved his arms around his face like he was trying to swat a fly, then rolled over so that his face was so smushed against the sofa it'd be a miracle if he didn't suffocate.

Liam shook his head. 'WADE!'

Wade snuggled into the sofa.

Admitting defeat, Liam pulled the blanket over his friend and bodyguard and left him to sleep. The one time he might've been useful.

He'd never admitted to anyone that he was afraid of the dark. Having grown up in a city that was always so bright it was hard to comprehend real darkness. He was filming in a small village in Ireland when the fear took hold. The village was beautiful with its poplar trees trees and the smell of freshly cut grass filling the air. But at night, the poplar trees vanished. So did the lush green grass. There was nothing but darkness. He couldn't see who was behind him or approaching him. He had no idea if someone was watching him. He couldn't see where he was going – if he was about to jump off a cliff or walk into a wall. Or if his stalker was right behind him…

The light from the street lamps were due to go off in a few minutes: the council's way of saving money.

He needed to make a decision fast.

He shook his hair out then tucked it behind his ears. Fayth had been gone way too long. What if something had happened to her?

He rooted around under the sink for another torch. There were a few candles and no lighter, but not much else. Then something caught his eye. A penlight. It'd barely light a few feet in front of him, but it was better than nothing. If there was a bogeyman in the basement, at least he'd be able to see him. Or at least, part of the bogeyman. Provided it worked. He pressed the button. It flickered a few times, then went off. Brilliant.

There had to be some batteries around somewhere. He turned the penlight upside down and tried to prize it open, but the end was rusted shut. He threw the penlight across the room. It hit the wall with a metallic twang, then bounced off the faded carpet. Still rusted shut.

The lights went off outside. The pub fell into darkness.

Liam jumped on the spot a few times. If something really had happened to Fayth, she'd need him. Afraid of the dark or not, he had to go find her. And if he did find her, she'd have a torch.

His eyes adjusted to the darkness, but he could only make out a few shapes around him. He tried to use the light on his phone, but it was out of battery. Fucking brilliant. He plugged it in to charge then headed for the door.

Time to go face the bogeyman.

The pub was dark and creepy. He flinched each time the wind echoed through the old building. There was no such thing as ghosts. Nobody was out to get him.

Except his stalker.

But his stalker was in New York. He'd gone to Scotland to get away from his stalker. His stalker wouldn't follow him.

He was safe.

Wasn't he?

A floorboard creaked.

He jumped, turning around to see who was behind him. Nobody was there.

He reached the basement door and hesitated. They were just movies. Really good, psychologically draining movies.

There was nothing to be afraid of.

Behind the plastic curtain in the basement was a faint glow. He ran down, calling out to Fayth.

He didn't get a response.

Her torch was at the bottom of the stairs, abandoned. He picked it up and shone it around the room. 'Fayth? Where are you?'

'Ngggh.'

'Fayth?' Shining the torch in front of him, he rounded the

corner. Fayth lay on the floor by the fusebox, unconscious.

'Fayth!'

A figure stepped out of the shadows and stood between them. 'Don't move.'

He raised the torch. It was the woman Wade had flirted with earlier in the evening. She no longer spoke with a Scottish accent; she spoke with a Brooklyn one. She still had on her unassuming green cardigan that made her look like a kindergarten teacher. Except kindergarten teachers didn't carry guns.

'Step away from your girlfriend,' she said, pointing the gun right at him.

'Whoa. Whoa.' He took a few steps back, holding his hands up. The light from the torch reflected off the ceiling. He had no idea why she was there, or why she had a gun. He'd never seen her before that night. Blood pounded in his ears.

'Who are you?' he said. The best tactic was to keep her talking. The more he kept her talking, the less chance she had to think about shooting anyone.

'I'll ask the questions,' she said.

He gulped.

'Stay,' she barked. Her stilettos clicked on the concrete floor as she stepped over Fayth and went over to the fusebox. Gun still pointing at Liam, she used her heel to flick the lights back on. Liam forced his eyes to stay open as they adjusted. He needed to keep his gaze on her. It was the best chance they had.

Liam switched the torch off but kept hold of it.

The room came back into focus. Fayth's fingers twitched. She was still alive. Good.

'Drop the flashlight,' she ordered.

Liam put it on the floor and kicked it. It rolled across the floor, past the crazy woman, and over to Fayth.

'Recognise me yet?'

No. Nothing. He couldn't even come up with a good lie.

She reached into the pocket of her jeans and held up a photo from the Hard Water meet-up. She was the one who hadn't smiled; who couldn't have looked less enthusiastic about meeting him. Her hair had grown and she had less make-up on than in the photo, but it was definitely her. He'd thought something was off with her at the time. He hadn't expected to be right.

'I followed you to London, but you were always surrounded by people,' she said. 'It was impossible to get you alone. Then you disappeared, and I couldn't figure out where you were. Even your parents' place didn't offer any clues.'

At the mention of his parents' place, he curled his hands into fists. So it was her. It was *all* her.

'But then photos started to appear online of you here. It was perfect. Quiet and secluded. Just what I needed. I had to save some money first – following you to London had taken most of my savings – but it was worth it. *This* makes it all worth it.' She twirled the gun around her fingers.

'Why me? Why do you hate me so much?' said Liam. If she was going to kill him, he had to know why.

Her expression grew whimsical. 'Trinity and I, we have a special bond.'

Trinity?

What the fuck did Trinity have to do with it?

A logo on her blouse glistened in the light. Diesel. Trinity had modelled for them a few years earlier. She also had a penchant for heels she couldn't walk in. So far, the woman in front of him had proven herself to be better at walking in them than his ex-girlfriend, but her heels were still unnecessarily high.

Shit.

But what was their 'special connection'?

'How do you know Trinity?' he asked.

'Didn't I just say that *I'll* be the one asking the questions?'

'I'm sorry,' said Liam in his best soothing voice. As much as he wanted to lash out, he couldn't. He knew nothing about her – if she had any fighting skills, if she was smart enough to take the safety off the gun – and pushing her could end up with someone getting hurt. Or killed. He had to keep her calm – and somehow keep calm himself – until he figured out what to do.

'Trinity's been sending me secret messages for years. Sometimes she asks me to do small things, like get a picture of something, other times, it's bigger, like breaking into your dressing room or your apartment. It's all in her music.'

Reading nonexistent secret messages into song lyrics. How Charles Manson of her.

'It's time you and your girlfriend paid for what you did to Trinity! After she saw you at the Rockefeller Center she posted a video asking her fans to help her, but I'm the only one who knows what she really meant. I saw the video where Fayth confronted her and you didn't even react. How she got away with upsetting Trinity like that, then caused her to meltdown on live

TV and—' She fanned her face with her spare hand and took a few breaths. 'This is your fault! She's a good person. She doesn't deserve any of what happens to her!'

Liam resisted the urge to scoff. Yeah. Trinity was a *great* person. 'Trinity's outburst was drug-fuelled.'

She waved the gun at him. 'Don't say that! She doesn't have a drug problem! She's too pure and good!'

Delusional, much?

But she still had a gun. And therefore all the power. His eyes darted around the room. Fayth stirred again. He needed to keep the woman talking. That way she wouldn't notice Fayth and she'd be too distracted to think about firing the gun. If he could distract her enough, she might even lower it. Then he'd seize his opportunity.

Fayth opened her eyes. Fuck, her head hurt.

Someone talked nearby. The voices were muffled at first. Then they became clearer. Liam. But who was he talking to? She didn't recognise the second person. She rolled on to her side. A female figure stood between her and Liam, pointing a gun at him.

Shit. She wouldn't actually shoot him, would she?

No.

She wouldn't let that happen. She couldn't. She'd lost too many people already.

But what to do?

She was stuck in a corner with nothing but a fusebox and a torch within her reach. Almost everything else involved walking past the woman with the gun.

If she stayed quiet enough, she had surprise on her side. But she didn't have her phone, and if she moved too much or too quickly it would echo through the basement. Her rubber-soled shoes wouldn't make too much of a noise, but it was still a risk.

She catalogued the contents of the basement: wine bottles, beer barrels, snacks, gas bottles. Oooh! A gas bottle. Those things were lethal. But they'd also blow the whole place up. And they were right beside where the crazy lady stood.

The torch *could* work, but if she caught the woman at the wrong angle with it, it could also cause her to fire the gun.

She scanned the shelves above her head. Anything heavy, glass or metallic would make a noise. Her eyes stopped as she saw something out of place on one of the shelves. Bar towels. They were supposed to be tucked away in a cupboard, but Brooke could never be bothered to put them away properly. For the first time ever, her laziness had an upside.

She rolled on to her front and began to slide forwards.

'Trinity loves me,' said the crazy woman. 'She wants me to avenge her for what you did.'

Avenge her?

Liam kept her talking, his voice soothing. Damn, he was a good.

Fayth reached the shelves. The room spun as she stood up. The urge to vomit rose within her. She clutched a shelf to steady herself. Her body needed to play along. If it didn't, they were doomed.

She snatched a bar towel and clutched it to her.

Her plan had to work. It was the only chance they had.

Holding the bar towel out on front of her, she crept towards their captor and avoided all eye contact with Liam. They couldn't risk it. She was about Fayth's height. Perfect.

Fayth threw the towel in the woman's face and elbowed her in the side. She pulled her gun-holding arm out, and tried to wrestle the gun from her grip. She wouldn't let it go. Liam ran towards them and tried to get hold of the gun, but the woman's grip was like a vice.

Fayth tugged at her arm, kicking her in the back of the knee and forcing her to the floor. Liam seized the gun from her grip. Fayth pressed her foot into the woman's back. The woman flailed. Fayth grabbed the woman's arms and held them behind her. The woman kicked her feet, screaming out. Fayth pulled her up so that she could speak in her ear. 'Sit the fuck still.'

The woman jutted her head backwards and head butted Fayth. A sharp, searing pain reverberated through her head.

She lost her grip and fell on her side. Her vision blurred. Shit. Someone – she assumed the crazy woman – pinned her down and tried to wrestle her. Fayth fought her off the best she could, aiming for vulnerable spots like the stomach or back of her knees, but not being able to see properly made it difficult.

She smelled Liam near her. It contrasted with the vile artificial strawberries emanating from the crazy woman. He was nearby. To her left, maybe? He pulled the woman from her. The woman groaned as he shoved her against the wall.

Fayth rolled on to her front.

A blurry Liam pointed the gun at a blurry crazy woman.

Fayth went to stand up, but she slipped on the torch. She thudded to the floor. Liam ran to her.

A guttural growl escaped the woman's lips. She ran towards them. The gun fired. Everything went black.

Three

When Tate had suggested stopping by Hollie's place to check out her outfit for the charity gala, Hollie had thought she was joking. Turned out, she wasn't.

It wasn't until a Rolls Royce pulled up outside their house that Hollie realised it. A long-haired, honey-blonde Tate got out with Moxie, waved goodbye to the driver, then headed for the door. The driver waited until Tate was inside to drive off.

'Hollie! It's so good to see you!' said Tate. She hugged her, then the two of them stepped into the living room. 'You must be Hollie's nan.' Tate stood in front of the chair, a broad smile on her pink lips.

'Why? What's she told you?' said her nan.

'Nothing bad, don't worry!' Tate said with a giggle.

Hollie smiled. The two of them would get on just fine.

Moxie yelped.

'What's that thing!' said Hollie's nan.

Tate lifted Moxie up. 'This is Moxie, my morkie.' She held her closer to Hollie's nan. Moxie wriggled in her owner's arms.

'She looks like a rat,' said her nan.

'She doesn't mean that,' said Hollie. 'She loves all dogs.'

Moxie yelped again.

Awoken by the smell of another dog, George emerged from the kitchen. He watched for a few moments.

'Is he OK with other dogs?' asked Tate.

Hollie nodded. George was so placid another dog could bite off his nose and he wouldn't retaliate.

Tate let Moxie off her lead and she crept towards George. They did the usual arse-smelling thing, decided they were happy with one another, then proceeded to chase each other around the living room.

Meanwhile, the humans drank coffee and exchanged stories. Hollie was worried about what Tate would think of their house with its old-fashioned decor and run-down estate, but Tate never said anything. She made out like she had all the time in the world for them, and that meant more to Hollie than Tate wearing her clothes.

Hollie made some vegetable soup for dinner, then she and Tate headed upstairs so that Tate could check out her outfit. Hollie didn't want to risk taking it downstairs and getting it covered in dog fur. George and Moxie were crashed out on the rug anyway, having tired themselves out playing chase.

Just in case Tate did actually show, Hollie had tidied her sketches and paperwork into her desk drawer. Everywhere was still covered in rogue bits of fabric and cotton, though. It didn't matter how many times she vacuumed. The damn things got everywhere.

She took the dress from the back of her bedroom door and unzipped the black garment bag. Nerves didn't control her any more. Nothing controlled her. Except emptiness. She didn't care if Tate didn't like the dress. She didn't care about anything. The only reason she'd finished it was because she had to, and the only reason she kept going was because she didn't want to let her family, Fayth, or Tate down. A small part of her was determined to keep fighting, but it grew weaker each day.

Tate pulled the dress out. It was covered in glitter, sequins, and butterflies. There was only one way to do a fairytale outfit, and that was to go all-out. And in Tate's case, to make it sparkle. Hollie had even made a wand out of MDF to go with it.

Tate's lips curled into a grin. 'It's perfect!'

'Thanks,' said Hollie. Her voice was flat; devoid of emotion.

Tate wrinkled her nose. 'What's wrong? You've done an amazing job!'

'It's not that,' she said. She sat on the edge of the bed and played with her cuticles. 'It's hard sometimes.'

'What is?'

Hollie pulled her legs to her and hugged her knees. 'If it wasn't for him, none of this would've happened. It's hard to shake that association and keep going sometimes.'

She still couldn't say Astin's name aloud. It was poisoned. Saying it unleashed tears, and she didn't have time for tears.

Tate returned the dress to the garment bag and sat beside her. 'He is proud of you, you know.' She put her arms around Hollie.

Hollie scoffed.

'I mean it. He's always asking how you are.'

'Sure he is.'

Tate let go, waving her arms in exasperation. 'He *is*!'

'Well he's got a bloody funny way of showing he cares, then.'

If he really cared, why didn't he just ask her how he was herself?

'Yes,' agreed Tate. 'But none of us are perfect.' She stood up, taking the dress out again and holding it at arm's length. She tilted her head, sticking her tongue out of the side of her mouth.

'What?'

'It looks like a cross between a fairy godmother outfit and Tinkerbell outfit.'

'Is that a bad thing?'

'No! I love it! I thought I already said that?'

Hollie shrugged.

Tate lowered the dress and sat back down. 'He really hurt you, didn't he?'

Hollie nodded. 'I thought—'

'You had a future together.'

She nodded again.

'I felt the same way about Jack. Truth is, we never know who'll be in our lives a week from now, let alone in a few years' time. But you and Astin? You're both full of fire. It was always going to end with fireworks.'

Hollie sighed. It'd ended in fireworks, all right.

'And the thing with fireworks is that they can be beautiful, but they can also be destructive.'

There was no denying that.

'At the end of the day, your relationship with Astin may not have lasted, but it all led you here. And you live with a family that loves you, you have great friends, and, with my investment, you're about to start your global fashion empire. From where I'm standing, you're in a pretty good place.'

Hollie raised an eyebrow. *Tate Gardener* thought she was in a pretty good place?

'What? I like my life, but it wouldn't suit most people. You're luckier than you think.'

Hollie sighed. 'I guess. But where do I go from here?'

'You'll work it out. We'll figure it out. If we make a few mistakes along the way, so be it.' She clapped her hands together and stood up. 'Right, I'd better go try this on!'

'Bathroom's next door,' said Hollie.

Tate disappeared into the bathroom with the dress, leaving

Hollie to continue picking at her cuticles.

From the outside, her life did sound pretty good. So why did she feel so low? Why did she want to be in bed all day? Why did it take every amount of strength that she had to spend just a few hours in the company of Tate, her friend, the woman making her career possible?

Tate emerged from the bathroom. She spun around. The dress sparkled in the light, just like Hollie had planned. She pointed her wand at Hollie. 'I'll grant you one wish! What will it be?'

Hollie laughed. If only it were so simple.

Since it was a nice day, Hollie and Tate took George and Moxie for a walk down by the canal. It was overgrown in places, but its beauty couldn't be denied. It was as close to the English countryside as Hollie cared to get: pretty, but not too far away from the nearest coffee shop.

They let their dogs off their leads to run ahead of them, but neither dog strayed too far. George was too neurotic and Moxie too well-trained – and short – for that. Tate hooked her arm through Hollie's as they strolled down the footpath.

'When do you arrive in London for the gala again?' said Tate, pushing past an overgrown tree branch.

'I'm not sure yet. I haven't booked it,' said Hollie. She kicked a rock. It plopped into the stagnant water. 'I haven't had chance to look up B&Bs—'

'B&Bs?' Tate scoffed. 'You can stay with Moxie and me.'

At the mention of her name, Moxie's ears pricked up. Tate gestured for her to carry on, and the little dog chased after George into the trees.

'I wouldn't want to put you out,' said Hollie. Not to mention her favourite hotel was where a certain person still lived.

'Don't be absurd!'

'Aren't you staying with Camilla?'

'She's on tour so can't make it.'

Hollie was running out of excuses. 'What about…'

'What?'

Hollie kicked another rock into the water. She couldn't say his name.

'Is this about Astin?' said Tate.

Damn her.

'Why would it be about him?'

'Sweetie, you just broke up. *Everything* is about him.'

She was right there.

Tate patted her arm. 'I'm staying at the Beaumont – Claridge's was fully booked. And as for at the gala, I'll make sure he's at a different table.'

A table far, far away. Like in a different galaxy, maybe.

'I just don't know if I can face him,' said Hollie. 'I can just about face Nan right now, let alone anyone else.'

'Hey!' said Tate.

'Sorry,' said Hollie, 'it's just hard. I want to lock myself in my room and never come out again, but I know I can't.'

'No, you can't. But you're allowed to feel that way.'

Four

Ugh. What was that smell? Bleach? No. Disinfectant? Why could she smell disinfectant?

Oh no.

There was only one place that smelled that strongly of disinfectant.

Someone squeezed her right hand.

Fayth forced her eyes open. White ceiling. Beeping noises. Needle thingy in the back of her hand. Oxygen monitor on her finger.

She was in hospital all right.

Shit.

'Fayth!' Liam took his hand from hers and hugged her.

'How long was I out?' She coughed. Her throat felt like someone had ran a cheese grater over it while she was asleep.

Liam handed her a glass of water from the bedside cabinet. He moved the straw so that she could sip from it. 'Few hours. You scared me.'

Fayth took a few sips. Swallowing hurt. The water did nothing to get rid of the nausea that grew the longer she was awake. She was used to being nauseous thanks to stress, but a whole new layer had been added that made her never want to eat again. What was *wrong* with her? 'I'm not the one who had a gun pointed at me. What happened?'

'What's the last thing you remember?' He took the glass from her and sat back down.

'Some crazy woman was in the basement, pointing a gun at you. I tried to fight her off. Wait. Was there a gunshot? Did someone get shot?' She patted her body, trying to find a wound.

'Relax, you didn't get shot. You just have a concussion.'

'Did you get shot?' She coughed again.

Liam passed her the glass. She took a few more sips.

'No, I'm fine. I shot her,' said Liam. He couldn't have sounded more laid back about the whole thing if he'd tried.

'*What?*'

Liam ran his hand through his hair. He looked over at the door, as if hoping someone would enter and prevent him from having to explain. They didn't. 'I had the gun pointed at her when you slipped. I went to check on you and she took it as an opening and ran towards us. I shot her in the leg to keep her away. You passed out as the gun went off. I made sure you were OK, then tied her up with some string I found in the basement.'

Fayth widened her eyes. He'd shot someone? He'd almost *killed* someone?

'She's fine, by the way. She intends to sue, but the police don't think she'll get away with it.'

'Why?'

'Because it was her. She was my…stalker.' He said the last word as if it took all the strength he had.

'Oh my god,' said Fayth.

He held her hand. 'I didn't have a choice. She was running towards us, and all I could think was that she might hurt you. I couldn't let that happen. I'd do it again, if I had to. I'd always choose you.' He put his hand on hers.

What had he just said? What did that even mean?

'Ah, I see you're awake.' A nurse walked in, a friendly smile on her round face. 'How are you feeling?'

Liam removed his hand.

'Groggy,' said Fayth. 'And my head hurts.'

'It will for a while.'

'How long am I being held hostage for?'

'Just overnight,' she said, 'so long as you've got someone to keep an eye on you when you get home and make sure you take it easy.' She looked over at Liam.

'I will, don't worry.'

'Surely you have better ways to spend your time?' said Fayth.

'Than spending time with you? Never.'

The nurse gave her some paracetamol then went to find some food for her. Fayth and Liam continued talking, but she couldn't let go of his words: *I'd always choose you*. What did that *mean*?

'Miss Campbell? Have you got a minute?'

Fayth turned her gaze to the door. A police officer stood in it. 'I'd like to ask you a few questions if you're up to it,' he added.

'Um, OK,' said Fayth.

'Do you want me to go?' said Liam.

'No, it's OK,' said the police officer. 'I'm Constable Doyle.' He entered the room and closed the door behind him. 'How are you feeling?'

'Not bad, considering,' said Fayth.

Liam stood up from the plastic chair and relocated to the armchair. Constable Doyle sat in the vacated chair and took out a reporter's notebook. 'Just tell me what you remember.'

Fayth recounted what she could remember, but a lot of it was a blur – she was as unreliable as they came. She had a concussion. It was a valid excuse. The police officer made notes as she spoke, occasionally asking her questions to fill in any gaps.

'Will Liam get into trouble?' said Fayth when the officer had finished his questions.

'No. It was self-defence. We have significant evidence of her stalking both here and in New York.'

'You do?' said Fayth.

'We've already looked at her phone records and internet search history. She's called your family's pub, sent you emails, sent you threatening messages on social media, and, as you know, broken into Liam's apartment and dressing room, as well as his parents' apartment. She was also in London when you were a few months ago.'

'She *was*?' said Fayth.

Liam nodded. 'She posed for a photo with me at the Hard Water meet-up.'

'Ugh,' said Fayth. 'Wait.' When they'd been in London, a woman had barged into her and Wade had scared her off. Could it be…? 'I think I saw her in London. I didn't see her face properly this time – it all happened so fast and the room kept spinning – but the hair, the schoolteacher dress sense…it could've been her.'

Constable Doyle reached into his jacket pocket and took out his phone. After a few minutes of him scrolling through, he turned the display to Fayth. 'Was this her?'

'Yeah, I'm pretty sure. Wade saw her too. She tried to pick a fight with me but he scared her off,' said Fayth.

'You never said anything,' said Liam.

'I didn't see the point at the time,' said Fayth. 'But now…'

'I'll speak to Wade and see if I can find some footage,' said Constable Doyle, scribbling some more notes. 'There's no doubt she was stalking and harassing you both, so it's possible.'

Stalking them both. Fayth shuddered. What had she found

out about her? About her family?

'We've got her in custody,' he added.

Fayth lay her head back on the pillow. Phew. That didn't change that someone had tried to kill them, though.

Constable Doyle stood up. 'Thank you for your time. If we have any further questions, myself or a colleague will be in touch.'

'Thanks,' said Fayth.

'I'll show you out,' said Liam. He followed the officer out then returned a few minutes later with Wade beside him. He had on a grey hoody and jeans instead of his usual suit. His shoulders were hunched, his hands stuffed into his hoody pockets. The poor guy. After everything he'd done to protect Liam, it still wasn't enough. But what happened still wasn't his fault. He knew that, didn't he?

'Hey,' said Wade to the floor. He leaned against the door frame. 'Man, my head hurts.'

'Don't tell me you've got a concussion too,' said Fayth. She shuffled up in bed a few inches. Her head pounded. She put her hand to it and closed her eyes for a second. Everything seemed to settled. She reopened them.

'No.' He rubbed his forehead. 'The crazy bitch spiked my drink. That's why I crashed out. Didn't hear a thing. Doctors say I should be fine. The amount of pills in my system was pretty crazy, apparently. If she'd given it to someone smaller than me they wouldn't be here now.' He shifted positions, still staring at the floor and only looking at Fayth and Liam intermittently.

'Shit,' said Liam. He returned to the plastic chair beside Fayth.

'Yeah. Like I said, crazy bitch. This is why I like being single.' He rubbed his forehead again.

'Why don't you go lie down?' said Fayth.

'You look like you need it,' said Liam.

'You really know how to flatter a guy, you know that?' He walked over to the armchair beside the bed. It almost seemed like his legs could barely hold him as he fell back into it. 'I spoke to Thalia and Ola, by the way. Ola says you need to speak to Jim.'

'I've had other things going on,' said Liam.

'Is that the only reason?' asked Wade.

'What other reason would there be?'

'I don't know. You tell me.' Wade leaned back in the chair.

'How about I don't and you make something up?' said Liam.

How long had Liam been ignoring his agent's phone calls?

Wade sat up. 'You're allowed to take some time to recharge, you know. Nobody would blame you.'

'Wouldn't they?'

'No. Not if you're honest with them.'

Liam sighed. He didn't look convinced.

'Just tell them you need some time to process everything that's happened the last few months,' said Wade.

'Will that be good enough?'

'If it's not, it's their problem. At least then you've given them a reason and you're not just hiding from them and playing *WoW*,' said Wade.

'Yeah,' said Liam. He clasped his hands and leaned forwards, his expression turning pensive. Whatever his reasons were for avoiding his agent's phone calls, he couldn't do it forever. Not if he wanted a career to return to when he went back to New York.

Wade rubbed his face with his hands. He looked more tired and withdrawn than Fayth had ever seen him. He was usually a beacon of sarcasm and energy. Not any more. 'I failed you. I'm sorry.'

'It wasn't your fault. How were you supposed to know it was her?' said Liam.

'I slacked off, and you could've been killed because of it.' He shook his head. 'Please accept my resignation.'

What?

Liam sat up. 'No.'

'"No"?' echoed Wade.

'No,' said Liam. 'What happened wasn't your fault.'

He waved his arms, his hands in fists. 'It's my job to protect you!'

'And you do. But you can't be there for me 24/7.'

'I should be!'

'That's impossible. And weird. I don't want you to follow me to the bathroom.'

Wade gave a small laugh. He crossed his arms over his stomach. 'You deserve better.'

'I don't "deserve" anyone or anything in my life. I pick the people I want in my life, and you're one of them.'

Fayth smiled.

The light glistened in Wade's eyes. 'I failed you.'

'Shouldn't that be for me to decide?' said Liam.

Wade didn't respond.

'If you really want to quit I won't stop you, but just think about it first. Please?' He stared into his lap, his hands resting on it. He looked so sad. 'I trust you. Whether you trust yourself right now or not.'

Wade was one of the good guys. She hated seeing him beat himself up. How was he supposed to know the woman that he'd spent the night flirting with was Liam's stalker?

Wade nodded. 'OK.' He wiped at his eyes again before getting up and leaving.

Liam lay back in the crappy plastic chair and rubbed his face.

Fayth reached over and rubbed his arm. The room swam, but she forced herself to focus on Liam. 'He cares about you too much to leave you.'

'Does he?' said Liam, meeting her gaze.

'You know he does,' said Fayth. She returned to her spot on the bed. The room was stable there.

'What if he does leave?' he asked, his voice trembling.

'Then you'll find a new bodyguard. But he'll always be your friend.'

Five

Fayth stared at the ceiling of her hospital room. Nothing stared back at her. It was visiting time soon. She'd never been a patient during visiting time before. She hoped to never be one again. It would be her only one before she was free to leave, thank god. The doctor insisted on keeping an eye on her overnight, but so long as that went well – and she was determined that it would – she'd be home in less than 24 hours.

Satisfied that Fayth was awake and alive, Liam had gone in search of food. Fayth fell back to sleep, but she didn't sleep well. She dreamed of what had happened at the pub, and what could have happened if she and Liam hadn't thought fast. How badly could things have gone? Would her dad and sister have had to prepare for another funeral in less than a year? Would Liam have returned to New York in a bodybag?

The sound of heavy breathing jolted her from her nightmares. She only knew one person that breathed so heavily and wasn't a smoker: Patrick.

His stood in the doorway, his hands in his pockets, his head bowed. It was a far cry from the guy who'd burst into the pub and demanded to know what the deal was between her and Liam.

'May I?' He gestured to the room.

'Yeah.' Fayth shuffled up in bed.

He stepped inside, but stayed near the door. 'How are you? I mean, aside from being in here.'

'How did you find out?'

'Village gossip.' He reached into his pocket and took out a packet of cookies. 'Thought these might help.'

She smiled. 'Thanks.' Chocolate chip cookies were her ultimate comfort food. She took the packet from him and opened it, then offered him one.

'No thanks. I never liked them,' he said.

'You didn't?'

'Nope.'

You can know someone your whole life and never really know them.

He rocked on his heels, his eyes glued to a spot on the floor. 'This fancy celebrity lifestyle of yours, it worries me.'

'It's not really a fancy celebrity lifestyle,' said Fayth in between cookies.

'So you two aren't…?'

'No.'

'Oh,' said Patrick. 'Then why did that woman…?'

'She was delusional,' said Fayth. Her head throbbed at the thought of the gun hitting her, almost as if it were happening all over again. She rubbed her forehead, wishing she had a pair of sunglasses to protect her from the bright hospital lighting.

'Aren't we all?' said Patrick with a forced laugh. He rubbed his face. 'I'd hate it if anything happened to you.'

She twirled a cookie between her fingers. While she hadn't liked Patrick much in the last couple of years, she would've hated it if something happened to him, too. 'Me too.'

Patrick shoved his hands into his pockets and rocked on his heels, his face contorted. That was the look he got when he wanted to say something but didn't know how to say it. After a few moments of thought, he said: 'Why couldn't we make it work?'

Something tugged at her heart. 'We grew apart.'

He reached into his pocket and handed her a white envelope.

'What's this?'

'Open it.'

She tore it open. Inside was a cheque.

'The money for the bike. I never should've used our savings like that,' said Patrick.

She shoved the cheque at him. 'You don't have to.'

'Yes I do. Please, take it. You'll spend the money better than I will. It's the only thing I can think of to prove to you that I've changed.'

Fayth laughed.

'What?'

'You've already proven that.'

He flashed her an embarrassed smile. 'I've started working again, too.'

'That's good.'

'Yeah. I feel better for it. Like I'm making a difference.' He laughed, rubbing his face self-consciously. 'What am I saying? I'm a plumber, not a doctor.'

'No, but people need running water. We don't realise how much we take it for granted until we don't have any.'

'Like that time the sewage pipe in your house burst and nobody could shower and the pub didn't have a working bathroom at the time? You came to mine to shower.' He chuckled.

'Yeah. Your shower was crap.'

'Still is,' said Patrick. 'Parents refuse to acknowledge the existence of a power shower.'

'You need to take them on holiday and introduce them to one,' said Fayth.

'I've tried. They're too settled into what they know. They think new equals bad.'

Fayth had thought the same thing not long ago, too. 'You can't force them to change if they don't want to.'

'I know. I tried. Some of us are just like to stay within our comfort zones. You were always destined for bigger things.'

'I wasn't.'

'You were,' insisted Patrick. 'I held you back.'

'No you didn't.'

'I did. If we hadn't got married you would've gone off to university. I proposed because I was scared of losing you. I couldn't imagine my life without you.'

Fayth reached over and touched his arm. It was the most honest he'd been with her in years.

'Do you know why I got so angry when I found out you'd met Liam?'

'No. Why?'

'I knew we were really over.' He sighed. 'I can't compete with him.'

'Patrick—'

He held up his hand. 'I know you said you're not together. I believe you. But if you wanted to be…I'd be OK with that. I'd prefer you to be happy with him – or on your own – than miserable with me.'

She pulled him into a hug. He flinched, as if the gesture had surprised him. It had surprised her. The person she'd fallen in love with as a teenager would always be a part of him, even if she was no longer compatible with him.

They pulled apart. Patrick rubbed at his eyes with his fists. 'Take care, Fayth.'

'You too, Pat.'

He wiped at his eyes again. She used to call him that when they were younger, whether they were a couple or not. She hadn't used it since she'd filed for divorce. He turned to leave.

'We have a buyer, by the way.'

He turned back. 'Good. I'm happy for you.'

'If you want to come in for a pint in the meantime…I wouldn't stop you.'

He nodded, then left.

Fayth hugged the cookies to her. Was it possible that she and Patrick could be civil towards each other after all?

Liam had wanted to get Fayth some flowers to brighten up her hospital room, but they were apparently banned for 'health and safety reasons'. Health and safety gone mad, more like. He settled for getting her a bottle of Irn Bru instead. It was bright orange and she liked the taste. And they wouldn't have to worry about getting it home.

Home. He didn't have a home any more. The closest he felt to home was the Campbell house. It was the one place his stalker hadn't touched. As far as he knew. Would he ever feel safe again? Without Wade nearby he was jumpy even though he knew he was safer than he had been the day before. What if his stalker had an accomplice? What if they were still nearby?

Each time he was stopped for an autograph he flinched. That caused his shoulder – which was still store from firing the gun – to tense up, and he'd have to massage it to relax it. When he realised the person was harmless – as most were – he put on his usual facade and pretended he was fine.

After being stopped by one of the agency staff for a selfie, he rounded the corner to Fayth's hospital room. Patrick was just leaving.

Liam tightened his grip on the bottle of Irn Bru. He'd never met Patrick sober. He hadn't seen him since he'd tried to pick a fight in the pub. Impressive, given how small a place they lived in.

There was no way of avoiding each other. They had to at least walk past each other. Liam bowed his head and sped up his pace.

'Hi,' said Patrick as they approached.

Damnit. He'd hoped he wouldn't speak. 'Hi,' said Liam.

What had he said to Fayth? Had he upset her?

'I took her some cookies,' said Patrick, staring at his shoes. 'They're her favourite food.'

'Oh. That was nice of you.'

'It's crazy to think someone came all the way from New York just to—'

'How do you know that?'

Patrick laughed. 'There are no secrets around here.'

'I'm not used to places like this.'

'I'm not sure a guy like you is a good fit long-term, but then, I never thought Fayth was.' Patrick stuffed his hands into his pockets.

'Then why'd you marry her?'

Patrick sighed. 'Because I thought I could convince her. She thought she wanted to stay, but the only thing holding her back was me.'

'I'm sure it wasn't that,' said Liam, although he was pretty sure it was.

'I may not be the guy she needed or even wanted in the end, but I'll always be there for her.'

'You're a good man, Patrick.' The words escaped Liam's lips before he could stop them. But oddly, he realised, he meant them. Patrick *was* a good person. Somewhere very, *very* deep down.

'No, I'm not,' said Patrick. 'Maybe one day.' He rubbed his face. 'You fit so much better into Fayth's life than I ever did.'

'We're not—'

'I know. But I also know she cares about you, whether she'll admit it or not.'

Liam ran his hand over his hair. Was Patrick giving them his blessing?

His phone – which was set to vibrate so that it didn't break out into the *Pokémon* theme tune in the middle of a hospital – vibrated in his pocket. He took it out and checked the ID. It was Jim. He'd taken Wade's advice and tried calling him, but it had gone to voicemail.

'Sorry, I've got to take this,' said Liam.

'Yeah, of course,' said Patrick. 'See you later.' He flashed him a downturned smile then rounded the corner out of sight.

'Liam! Long time no speak! How are you doing after, uh, what happened?' asked Jim.

'We're managing,' said Liam, pacing the small corridor.

'Good. That's good. I have some good news for you, actually.'

'You do?'

'Uh-huh. Remember the audition you went to in London for the animated dog movie?'

'That was months ago.'

'I'd forgot about it, to tell you the truth, but they rang up and said that the person they'd cast had a scheduling conflict and can't do it. You're their second choice.'

He was the back-up plan. He wasn't good enough as the first choice, but he was just fine as a back up plan.

But he got to play the villain. And it was minimum work for maximum payout! Sweet.

'You still there? The line's crackling,' said Jim.

'Sorry. Yeah. Bad signal. When's the recording?'

'October. They'll want to do a few tests before then, but it's looking good!'

'Wow. Thank you.'

'Just doing my job. I know things haven't been great between us lately, but I hope we can work through things. I like working with you. You're a talented guy, Liam.'

'Thanks.' The line crackled. 'Can you email me with the details please? The signal's going dodgy again.'

Jim chortled. 'You've spent too long in Scotland, my friend. I'll email you later. Have a good day.'

Six

After having spent a night in hospital, Fayth almost understood why Astin was so moody after the accident. There was nothing comfortable about a hospital bed, and even when you had your own room, the beeping of machines and sounds of people coming and going all night didn't help you to get any sleep.

She'd spent most of the night texting Liam. He spent most of the night apologising. No matter how many times Fayth told him it was OK so long as they were both OK, he wouldn't have it. The guilt followed him like a snow cloud above Olaf.

When he and her dad arrived to pick her up, he looked more sheepish than she'd ever seen him. Whatever she'd said to him in the night, it hadn't helped any.

As soon as they pulled up at the house, both men insisted Fayth go straight to bed. She was more than happy to do as she was told for once.

A couple of hours later, Liam appeared with a mug of tea and slice of toast. 'How are you feeling?' he asked, perching on the bed opposite.

Fayth yawned. 'Like I got hit in the head.'

'Appropriate,' he said as he helped her adjust her pillows so that she could sit up. He'd recently resprayed his cologne, and the smell of cinnamon and sandalwood took her back to the night in New York where they'd first met. She'd barely been able to say her name, and seven months later, he was fluffing her bloody pillows and making her tea and toast. She laughed.

'What?' He stopped fluffing the pillows but hovered near the bed.

'Just thinking about when we first met.' She picked up the slice of toast and took a bite. Its sweet, buttery goodness was just what she needed.

'You were cute,' he said.

'No I wasn't.'

'You were so starstruck,' he said with a teasing smile.

'I was not!' She sipped her tea. She had been. She just didn't want to admit it.

'No? Then why did you keep getting confused?'

'Crap memory,' said Fayth.

'You have a better memory than me. Try again.'

She scowled at him. Not lately, she hadn't. Bastard stress.

Then again, he was still right. She *had* been starstruck when she met him.

'N'aww. You're just mad because I'm right.'

She stuck her tongue out at him.

There was a rapid knock at the front door. Fayth rolled over in bed. Someone else could get it.

And they did.

The sound of the front door opening was followed by someone stomping up the stairs. Only one person stomped up stairs like that.

Fayth sat up in bed, flattening her bedhead as best she could.

Tap tap tap.

'Come in.'

Hollie walked in, shaking her head. 'I can't trust you, can I?'

'I didn't tell Liam to get a stalker!'

Hollie put her Jackie-O-style sunglasses on top of her head and perched on the end of the bed. 'How are you?' She crossed her legs.

'All right, considering,' said Fayth. 'You didn't need to come all this way to make a fuss, you know.'

Hollie grinned. 'Liam flew me in on his private jet.'

Right on queue, Liam entered carrying some of Hollie's bags. Fayth's dad followed carrying the rest. One day Hollie might actually pack light.

'How long are you staying for? There's enough for a year there,' said Fayth.

'This way I can check up on you and work on your outfit at the same time. Most of it's sewing stuff in case I need to alter your outfit. Also wanted your thoughts on a few fabric samples for your accessories.' She turned to Liam and Fayth's dad. 'Thanks.'

'I wish you'd learn how to pack light, lass,' said Fayth's dad, breathing heavily.

Hollie grinned. 'I did try. Kind of.'

'I brought a backpack with me when I packed light. Four

bags and a sewing machine isn't light,' said Liam.

Hollie shrugged. 'Sewing stuff takes up a lot of room.'

'Four bags' worth?' said Liam.

'Some of it's mine, obviously,' said Hollie.

'You mean most of it?' teased Fayth.

Hollie stuck her tongue out at her.

'Does anyone want a drink?' offered Fayth's dad.

Fayth nodded. 'Usual please.'

'Ditto,' said Hollie.

'I'll come help,' said Liam.

The two men left the room. Hollie turned back to Fayth. 'He even organised transport from the airport. Well, I think his assistant did actually. Have you met her?'

'Don't think so. She's called Ola, isn't she?'

'Yeah. She seems sweet. Like a nagging sister. She called me with all the flight arrangements. Very organised. Just what he needs. Anyway, what do *you* need?'

'People to stop making a fuss of me!'

Hollie put her hands up in surrender. 'All right. No more fuss.' She approached one of the bags Liam had carried up and took out a garment bag. She lay it on the spare bed, unzipped it, and lifted out a red satin jumpsuit with a hood. She held it up so that Fayth could see it. It was almost as tall as she was.

'I love it!' said Fayth.

Hollie gave a small smile. 'Are you all right to try it on?'

'Um…maybe?' She pulled the covers off her and swung her legs round. The room spun a little. Fayth hesitated, waiting for the room to steady itself.

'We can try later if you want,' said Hollie.

Fayth held up her hand. 'I'll be fine, so long as we don't rush.'

'No rush,' said Hollie. 'I won't even help if you don't want me to.' She sat on the bed opposite, her arms folded and the jumpsuit beside her.

Fayth took her jeans off while sitting down. It seemed safest. Hollie passed her the jumpsuit and she put it on, pulling the hood up over her head. The satin fabric was soft against her skin, the hood so big it blocked her peripheral vision. The two of them walked to the mirror at the end of the room. 'It might need to come up a bit at the bottom if you're not wearing heels,' said Hollie, pulling it up at the waist. 'But other than that, it's not bad.'

'That's because you're good,' said Fayth.

'And I've made enough clothes for you in the past. What do you think to it?'

'It's great, Bea. Honestly. What're you wearing?'

'I'm glad you asked,' said Hollie. She took her phone from her pocket and showed Fayth a photo. It was of a blue strapless dress with a puffball skirt and black lace around the waist.

'*Alice in Wonderland*. Appropriate,' said Fayth.

'Isn't it?' said Hollie. 'I'm thinking of getting a blonde wig.'

'You are so not a blonde.'

'It's just a wig!'

'Is it safe to come in?' said Liam. 'I have tea and coffee.'

'It's safe,' said Fayth.

Hollie opened the door for him. He balanced the tray on one of the beds then turned back to Fayth. He nodded. 'I like the modern interpretation.'

'Thanks,' said Hollie. 'Are you still going as Prince Charming?'

'Yep,' he said with a grin.

Fayth shook her head.

'What?' said Liam. 'You don't think I'm charming?' He mock-pouted.

Hollie stifled a giggle.

Hollie set up her sewing machine on the desk in Brooke's room. Brooke was staying at her friend's for the night, so Hollie had her room. Liam returned to Mhairi's old bed so that he wasn't on his own. Fayth sat on Brooke's bed, flicking through Hollie's website.

'Some of these photos are really great Hollie.'

They were all of her mannequin on a white background: nothing inspiring.

'Have you ever thought about using models instead?'

Hollie lifted her foot from the sewing machine pedal and cut the red cotton. 'Why? You offering?'

'God, no,' said Fayth. 'I just think it would help bring the outfits to life.'

'Like I'm going to be able to find a decent model outside of London,' said Hollie. She turned around to face her friend.

'You never know until you look,' said Fayth.

'True,' said Hollie, 'but then I also have to pay them. This works for now. When things get a bit bigger I'll look into it. Tate has mentioned it. She's offered a few times, but I feel like she's done enough already.'

'It's not a bad thing to have a few more photos of Tate in your outfits online, though. I mean, she is technically the face of your brand. And as an investor, she wants to do things that will boost it.'

'I guess,' said Hollie. She swung her feet from the swivel chair. 'I just don't want to rely on her too much, you know? She's great, but what if something happens to her?' Like it had to Astin.

'Then you've got the rest of us to back you up,' said Fayth. She'd offered to invest in Hollie's line when Hollie had set it up, but Hollie had refused. She didn't want to mix her personal and professional relationships. But then, hadn't she done that – at least a little – with Tate already?

Hollie joined Fayth on the edge of the bed.

'Are you…coping?' asked Fayth.

'I'm managing.'

'If you need to talk, I'm here.'

'Thanks. I know. I just don't know what to say. I mean…I don't know. I feel like I've said everything I have to say, but I still can't let it go. I feel like George chasing his tail.'

'Don't do that. You end up crashing into the fireplace,' said Fayth. George did that often.

'It's not like I'm doing it intentionally. I'm trying to keep going, but…anyway.' She slapped Fayth's leg. 'We're not here for me. We're here for you.' She picked up the jumpsuit, on which she'd just finished raising the hem. 'Ready to try on the finished article?'

Fayth didn't go out for a meal often, so her dad insisted that she used Hollie's visit as an excuse. The nearest decent restaurant was in Edinburgh, a half an hour drive away, so Hollie took over Fayth's car for the evening. Fayth and Liam had visited Edinburgh a couple of times since his arrival, but they hadn't stayed long out of fear of being recognised.

Hollie's sense of direction was terrible, so they got lost several times despite having a satnav – which Hollie preferred to call a twatnav – on the dashboard. Half an hour soon turned into an hour. When they finally descended the stairs into the basement restaurant, they were starving.

Liam had tried to disguise himself by changing his parting and putting on some glasses, but it was a worse disguise than the

Yankees hat with blond hair poking out of the sides that he'd worn in London.

Even with Liam with them, they couldn't get a table any faster, so they sat around the bar and studied the menu.

Each time a chair skidded across the wooden floor, the noise grated on Fayth. She curled her hands into fists, trying to focus on what Hollie and Liam said instead of the noises all around them. Her sense of hearing had gone into overdrive and she had no idea why. She shouldn't have listened to her dad when he'd insisted she get a change of scenery. She should've stayed home, in bed, where it was warm and safe. For all she knew, their stalker had an accomplice who'd followed them to the restaurant and was about to blow the whole place up.

Someone screamed. Fayth and Liam jumped, reaching out to each other.

'Relax, it's just someone's birthday,' said Hollie. She gestured to a table by the window. A teenager wore a tiara with a huge *18* on it, surrounded by friends and family. They broke out into *Happy Birthday*.

Fayth and Liam let go of each other.

Hollie pursed her lips.

It was just a reflex.

Seven

Hollie left the following day, not wanting to impose any more than she already had. There was something off about her, but Liam didn't know her well enough to work out what it was. He did know that whatever it was, she'd talk to Fayth when she was ready, though.

After she'd gone, Fayth and Liam spent most of the day sleeping. Darren refused to let them back to the pub yet, so when they weren't asleep, they tried to watch *Fawlty Towers*. Streaming was no easy feat with 2MB internet. The stream stopped to buffer countless times, but they were determined to watch it. They curled up together on Fayth's bed, falling asleep with their arms around one another before it had even finished buffering. He wasn't complaining. Being close to her after what had happened soothed him. He hoped he had a similar effect on her.

There wasn't much room in a single bed, but he didn't care. She smelled of cocoa butter, and it made him hungry. Hungry for chocolate, and hungry for her. She was so fragile, but she put on such a tough facade that he'd only just begun to penetrate the surface. Would what happened make her realise that he needed her? That they were a good team? That life was too short not to take risks?

'No!' she called out. 'No! Don't do it! No! Please!' Her eyeballs twitched under her eyelids.

Liam nudged her. 'Fayth, wake up. You're having a nightmare.'

'No! No, please! Please I—'

'Fayth! Fayth!' He spoke louder, worried her shouting would wake the rest of the house.

'No!'

'Fayth!' He almost shouted.

Fayth sat up with a start. 'Wha – where—'

'You're home. You're safe.'

She curled into him. 'I had a nightmare. The crazy bitch

was there. She ran the car off the road. You were in it too.'

'I'm fine.' He patted his body. 'See? All in one piece.'

A door creaked open. A few seconds later, Fayth's dad asked through the door, 'Everything all right?'

'It's OK Dad, I just had a nightmare,' said Fayth.

'You sure you're all right?'

'Yeah.'

'All right, if you're sure.' His door creaked shut a few seconds later.

'You were shouting in your sleep,' said Liam.

'Was I?'

'Yeah. I practically had to shout to wake you up.'

'Shit,' said Fayth.

'Are you sure you're all right? What happened to us—'

'I'm fine, really. Don't worry about me.'

'Will you at least consider talking to someone?' said Liam.

'I'm talking to you,' she said.

Liam shook his head. His hair fell into his eyes. He pushed it away. 'A professional.'

'About what?'

'What happened.'

'I don't need to,' she said. She snuggled back into him and closed her eyes.

Fayth lay awake, staring at the ceiling. The paracetamol had kicked in and her headache had almost gone, but she couldn't shake the nightmare. The crazy woman had ran her mum and Mhairi off the road. But it wasn't just them in the car. Liam was in there too.

No.

It was just a dream.

And the real car crash was an accident.

Wasn't it?

Liam's head rested against hers, his arm around her shoulders. Being close to him comforted her, but she couldn't allow things to carry on as they were. Someone had almost killed them. She'd lost too many people already. It wasn't worth the risk of letting someone else in.

Lifting his arm from around her, she crept out of bed, grabbed her diary and a pen, and went downstairs.

The dogs flinched when she turned on the kitchen light. When they realised it was her and it was safe, they covered their faces with their paws and fell back to sleep.

After making herself a cup of tea she settled down on the sofa, pen poised and ready to write. But where the hell was she supposed to begin? The nightmare? The conflicting emotions? The pub? The *gun*?

She dropped the pen and notebook on to her lap.

'Hey,' said Liam. He'd changed from the jeans and shirt he'd fallen asleep in to a pair of stripy pyjama bottoms and a Batman t-shirt.

He stretched. His pyjama top raised to reveal well-toned muscles and a dark treasure trail that started at his belly button and disappeared inside his pyjama bottoms. She bit her lip. She'd fantasised about waking up beside him a million times, but she'd never expected it to happen. And when she had imagined it happening, she hadn't imagined it feeling so natural, or him being so protective of her. Or of her being so protective of him.

'Are you OK?'

'Just not tired, that's all,' she said, looking away. Had he noticed her staring? No. She wasn't staring. She was checking him out. Shite. 'You should go back to bed.'

'That your diary?' he said, nudging her so that he could sit on the sofa beside her. She lifted her feet, then lowered them on to his lap when he sat back down. There was something surprisingly normal about doing so. He rested his arms on her legs.

'Yeah.' She closed it and hugged it to her. Nobody was allowed to read it. She didn't even read back what she'd written: it was about getting her emotions out in the moment, not looking back on the past.

'It's pretty,' he said.

'Thanks. It was a present from Hollie.'

He gave a small smile. He fidgeted even more than usual as he sat beside her.

'What?' She'd narrowed her eyes at him without even realising it. She relaxed her face. There was nothing pretty about scowling like that. Then again, there was nothing pretty about her at all, and according to the press, she was fat, too.

Liam took a deep breath. 'About what I said at the hospital. You know what I meant, right?'

She swallowed. She'd hoped he'd forgot. 'Which part?'

'The part where I said I'd always choose you.'

Fayth shifted, her feet still resting against him. Yes, she knew what he meant. 'We can't, Liam.'

'Why not?' He turned so that he could face her. She pulled her legs from over him, sitting on them instead.

'Because of what just happened? You're you, Liam. The whole world loves you, and I'm just—'

'Important to me?'

Bugger it. He always knew what to say.

'Doesn't what just happened prove why we *should* give things a chance? If she'd have killed me, how would you have felt?'

'That's not fair,' she said. She put her diary on the floor and hugged her knees.

'If she'd killed you, I would've spent the rest of my life wondering what it was like to kiss you.'

'Liam—'

'I get that my life isn't for everyone but I can't imagine mine without you in it. Tell me you want to just be friends, and I'll stop. It'll be like we never had this conversation.'

Except it wasn't that simple. Not acting on underlying romantic feelings had ruined Hollie and Will's friendship. Would it do the same to her and Liam one day? She didn't want to let him in, but seeing him there, offering his heart to her, she couldn't bear to lose him. But she also didn't want to live her life under public scrutiny. But she really wanted Liam. But, fuck. 'It's too complicated.'

'No it's not. There's you, and there's me.' He put his hands on hers. Her heart skipped. 'I don't care what the rest of the world thinks of us.'

'I do,' she whispered.

'They won't hurt you. They're just overgrown school bullies letting off steam at any easy target that can't fight back. Not to mention they're just jealous.'

She snorted. 'Of what?'

He tucked her hair behind her ear. 'You being with me.'

Hollie's words echoed in her mind. *You're already being punished for the crime.* And there were worse crimes than being in a relationship with Liam York. He'd shown himself to be nothing but kind, considerate, talented and funny. Why was she so desperate to come up with reasons to keep him out?

'Long distance is hard,' she said.

'All relationships are. Some are worth it.'

Patrick had never had the right answers to her excuses. He just lost his temper and told her to get over herself and stop worrying. Liam lay his heart out on the chopping board while she held a cleaver above it. And no matter how much her fears wanted her to lower that cleaver, there was a stronger part of her that couldn't do it. That *wouldn't* do it.

He was too good to her.

She reached out and placed her hand on his cheek. The skin was rough, a five o'clock shadow forming.

He kissed her hand. 'I meant what I said. I'd always choose you.'

She leaned forwards and kissed him. Her fear hadn't gone, but those words struck something in her. Patrick had never put her first: he'd always chosen himself. How had she mistaken that for love? For any kind of affection?

Seeing the sacrifices Hollie had made for Astin made her realise what she wanted in a relationship, but what she hadn't realised was that she already knew the person capable of giving it to her. She placed her hands on his shoulders, kissing him hungrily. He kissed her back with the same urgency, his arms wrapping around her waist and pulling her into him. They fell back on the sofa. His skin was warm, his chest rising and falling with the rapid pace of his breathing.

How had she ended up like that? Would she have met Liam if it hadn't been for the death of her mum and Mhairi? Would she still be tethered to Patrick if it wasn't for them? A tear escaped her eyes before she could stop it. Liam wiped it away. 'I'm not that bad, am I?'

'No. God, no. It's just…next week is the anniversary of Mum and Mhairi's death. If it hadn't happened, would we be here now?'

'I don't know,' he said, tucking her hair over her shoulders and away from her face. 'But we're here now, so does it matter?'

He'd had too much therapy for his own good. They couldn't bring her mum and sister back, but they could look forwards to a future together. She wiped another tear from her eye.

'Just promise me something,' she said.

'Anything.'

'Don't break me. I can't take any more.'

'I promise.'

Eight

'So how does it feel having slept with the guy you had a poster of on your wall?' said Liam as he lay beside Fayth in the bed she'd had since she was ten. Oh, how things had changed.

'Was I better than your teenage fantasy of me?'

'You're loving this, aren't you?'

'A little,' he admitted. He rolled over and kissed her cheek. She tickled his naked stomach; he tickled her back.

How had she gone from barely sleeping – let alone *sleeping* – with Patrick, to *sleeping* with Liam York less than a year after she'd filed for divorce? She'd fantasised about Liam plenty as a teenager – even a little after she got married – but she'd never actually thought it could happen. He was Liam York, for crying out loud. And to be fair, most of her fantasies had been about his characters, not him. She hadn't even known what he was like as a person until she'd met him a few months ago, but she was glad she had. She hadn't felt so happy or so calm in—

The door flung open, and in walked Brooke. Her eyes were red and puffy, her body shaking as she convulsed from crying.

Fayth and Liam froze. Their nakedness was covered by the quilt, but enough of their flesh was visible that it was obvious what had happened.

Brooke's eyes widened. 'Oh my god. I'm sorry. I'm so sorry.' She covered her eyes and ran out of the room.

'Shit,' said Fayth, jumping over Liam and pulling on her dressing gown.

Liam laughed. 'It's fine.'

'It's not fine,' said Fayth. She rubbed her face. 'Shit.'

Liam stood up and put his arms around her. He was still naked, and it took all he strength to ignore it. 'Go talk to her. I'll make a drink.'

'Thanks.' She gave him one last squeeze then went to Brooke's room. She knocked, hoping it'd teach her sister to do the same.

'Mmm,' was the sound that greeted her on the other side.

Fayth opened the door. Brooke was curled up on her bed, hugging her knees. 'Don't mind me,' she said, still crying.

Fayth trudged through the mass of clothes on the floor and sat on the edge of the bed. Sloppy teenager. She put her hand on her sister's knee.

Brooke shoved her hand away. 'You're not missing Mum and Mhairi at all, are you?'

'That's not fair,' said Fayth. 'You have no idea how I feel.'

'I'm bawling my fucking eyes out because I dreamed about them and you're having sex with your handsome Hollywood boyfriend right next door. That's messed up.'

'I get it, you're pissed off, but don't you think you're reading a little too much into this?'

'Am I?' snapped Brooke. 'What should I be reading into it, then?'

'I couldn't have got through these last few months without him.'

'And what about the rest of us? Why didn't you lean on us?'

Fayth clutched her nose. 'Did you talk to me about it?'

Brooke shook her head. Her dark hair tickled her shoulders. 'I couldn't.'

'Exactly,' said Fayth. 'We're both guilty of the same mistake.'

'That doesn't explain you jumping into bed with Liam!'

Fayth pushed herself from the bed and walked to the door. 'You know what? I don't have to defend my decisions to you. After everything that's happened, I deserve to be happy. And so do you.'

'Happy? *Happy*? What the hell is that supposed to mean?'

'It means not living in the past. It means remembering why Mum and Mhairi were important while still moving on with our lives. I love you, Brooke, but we can't stay the same forever. We can't spend every moment mourning. It's been almost a year, and I'll always feel like a piece of me is missing, but I'll never get that piece back. I just need to find a way to make my life work without them.'

'And what about me? What about Dad?'

'Dad's moving on, too. Why do you think he's selling the pub?'

Brooke cried even harder. She wiped the tears away with her fist. 'I need them. I can't do this without them.'

Fayth sat back down beside her baby sister. 'You can. Your

exams are over now. You'll be going to uni soon.'

'I don't know if I want to go any more. I don't think I could be a nurse like I planned. I couldn't go through seeing people everyday like—' She cut herself off, lowering her head and sobbing into her knees.

Fayth pulled her into a hug. 'There seems to be this rule nowadays where our parents' generation expect us have to have our whole lives mapped out by the time we're 18, and if we don't, we're a failure. And you know what? That's bullshit. You don't. You're allowed to change your mind.'

'College would disagree.'

'Bugger college. It's your life, not theirs. You do whatever you want to do. Dad and I will always be here for you.'

Brooke buried herself in Fayth's neck. She'd cried a lot since the accident, but she'd never done it in front of anyone before. Her finally having done so was a sign of trust that Fayth wasn't going to ruin.

After a few minutes of sobbing, Brooke lifted her head. 'So…how was it?'

'How was what?'

'Liam.'

Fayth smiled. 'Do me a favour?'

'How does this relate to Liam?'

'I learned something last night.'

'That he's all talk and shit in bed?'

Fayth laughed. 'No. If you ever sleep with a guy who makes it all about him, run.'

'Why?'

'Because the guys like that are only interested in themselves. They'll never put you first. In bed or anywhere else.'

'Sage advice, sis,' said Brooke. 'So are you and Liam now…?'

'I don't know,' said Fayth with a sigh. 'It's complicated.'

'Is it?' said Brooke.

'Sure it is. He's *Liam York*.'

'So what?' said Brooke. 'You love him, don't you?'

Fayth nodded. She did.

'Right after I broke up with my first boyfriend, Mum gave me some advice. She said, "love with all you have, but if one day you realise they don't deserve your love any more, don't be afraid to take it back".'

'That sounds like Mum.'

'She and Dad were soulmates. I hope one day I can find something like that too.'

'You will,' said Fayth, giving her sister a squeeze.

'Will I be old like you when I do?'

'Oi!' She shoved her.

Brooke grinned.

Liam looked up from his phone and smiled as Fayth reentered the bedroom. He'd changed back into his Batman pyjamas, but even just the sight of him in those gave her goosebumps. Did she and Liam really have what her parents had had? Was it really that simple?

'Is Brooke all right?' said Liam.

'I think so,' said Fayth. She picked up a mug of tea from the bedside table and sipped it. It was just right.

He could make tea. And Brooke approved. And her dad liked him. And so did Hollie. And he'd helped out at the pub more than he'd needed to. He'd learned to clean tables and even improved his cooking skills. Not enough to work in the pub kitchen, but enough to not set the fire alarm off when making toast. It was a start.

Was it really as simple as Brooke said?

Well. They'd had sex. They had to define their relationship at some point. Better to get it over with.

She put the mug down. 'No public appearances. Not yet.'

'Define "public",' said Liam. He put his phone on the bed beside him.

'Tate's gala. No red carpet crap.'

'I reserve the right to hold your hand when there aren't cameras around,' he said.

'There are always cameras around.'

'Paparazzi, then.'

'Fine. And cheating is a deal breaker.'

'Agreed,' said Liam. 'And no paparazzi tip-offs.'

Fayth snorted. 'I wouldn't even know who to call to tip them off.'

'Good. Any other deal-breakers for you?'

'No. No.' She paced the room. 'It has to be about what *we* want. It has to be about compromise. That's what went wrong with my marriage, and that's what went wrong with Hollie and Astin. We *have* to learn to compromise, else it won't work.'

'All right, all right. I want to hold your hand in public, but

I'll only do it in places we're not likely to be outed, like around here.'

'Or *inside* Tate's gala, where most people will know us anyway,' said Fayth.

'Deal,' said Liam. 'What about social media?'

'I don't use it. That's your problem,' said Fayth.

'Am I allowed to mention you on mine?'

'Depends what you say.'

'If I mention you, I'll check with you before I post it. Sound good?'

'Sounds good, although why you'd want to mention me is beyond me.'

He walked over to her and hugged her. 'Because I love you, that's why.'

'You love me?'

'Yes,' he whispered into her hair.

She turned to face him, grinning. 'I love you too.'

'I'd shout it from the rooftops if it wasn't so cheesy,' he said with a shy smile.

'I'd prefer it if you didn't. It'd attract even more attention.'

'No shouting from the rooftops, then,' said Liam. 'Or on social media, which is the modern-day equivalent. We'll keep things low key. Anything else?'

Fayth hugged him tighter. What had Patrick done in their marriage that had annoyed her so much? What had led to their break up? What compromises could she and Liam put in place now that would set the tone for the rest of their relationship, however long that might be? She raised her head. 'I don't want to mother you.'

'I already have a mom.'

'And I don't want to replace her or be a substitute for her. I want to be your partner, not your mother.'

Liam held his hand out, and they shook on it. 'Deal.'

Nine

Liam hadn't felt safe since Wade left. He tried his best to hide it from Fayth, but the truth was, he was scared to be alone. He threw himself into drawing, turning his stalker's wispy brown hair into Medusa's snakes and that green cardigan into alien skin.

Jogging helped, too, but he couldn't just stick in some headphones and head off any more. He needed to be aware of his surroundings: hear every footstep; every rustle of the trees. He jogged for hours each day: it helped him burn off the anxiety and relax enough that he could act like everything was fine. It was the only time he could handle being alone. No wonder Astin was so crabby when he'd gone from spending hours at the gym everyday to twitching his foot as exercise.

Returning from his daily jog, Liam headed for the kitchen.

'Your protein shake stuff is in the pantry,' said Fayth. She sat on the floor, playing with the dogs. It was the calmest she'd seemed all week. 'It kept getting in the way so Dad moved it.'

'Thanks,' said Liam, panting. The last few months had left him seriously unfit. He needed to get back into things again. Even if he didn't go back into acting he still wanted to look – and feel – good.

He got his vanilla-flavoured protein powder from the pantry and made himself a shake. The dogs ditched Fayth to sit at his feet and stare at him. Even though they liked the smell, he doubted they'd like the taste. He wasn't a huge fan.

Fayth got up. 'I don't know how you can drink those things.'

Liam shrugged. 'They're quick and easy. More interesting and higher protein than salad.'

'That's one way of looking at it,' said Fayth.

There was a knock at the front door. Fayth flinched. After a few calming breaths, she went to answer it.

Liam sat at the dining table and crossed his legs. The dogs continued to watch him.

'Delivery guy said to give you this,' said Wade's voice.

The protein shake halfway to his lips, Liam froze. Wade hadn't said he was coming back. He hadn't been in touch since he'd left. Was he there to resign, or had he changed his mind?

'Thanks,' said Fayth. 'I'll leave you two to talk,' she called. The front door closed.

Liam went into the living room. Wade stood near the front door, his hands in his pockets. He still didn't have on his usual suit, but he'd upgraded from a hoody and jeans to chinos and a shirt. It was an improvement.

Wade sat on the sofa and stared into his lap, his hands clasped. 'So.'

'So,' said Liam, sitting beside him.

'I thought about what you said.' He curled and uncurled his fists as he spoke, never looking up at Liam. 'You were right. But that doesn't make me feel like less of a failure.'

'Wade—'

Wade held up his hand. 'Hear me out. I like you, and I like working for you, but I can't afford to fail you like that again.'

'I don't plan to get another stalker.'

'You never know in a job like yours.'

Liam sighed. He'd been taught that lesson. He wasn't sure how much longer acting would be his line of work, but he didn't want to tell Wade that yet. He wasn't ready to tell anyone that yet. 'What did you decide?'

'I still want to be your bodyguard, but I understand if you don't want me to.' He wiped the side of his nose with his fist.

Liam smiled. 'You know I do.'

'Are you sure?'

Liam put his hand on Wade's shoulder. 'Yes.'

Wade gave him a small smile. He straightened himself up, lifting his head again. 'On to more important things: are you two together yet?' He jerked his head towards the window. Fayth was in her car, doing something to the dashboard.

'Fayth and me?' Liam grinned.

'I'm happy for you, really,' said Wade. 'It's about time you dated someone normal.'

'Um, thanks for the support?'

Fayth knocked on the living room window and gestured for them to join her outside. They went outside and found her fiddling with something on her car's dashboard.

'What's that?' said Liam, pointing to his helmet. Something was stuck to the side of it.

'A helmet cam,' said Fayth, climbing out of the car.

'It looks dumb.'

She shrugged. 'If it keeps you safe.'

'I'm with her on that,' said Wade. He grabbed the helmet from the roof of the car and dumped it on Liam's head. 'Very attractive.'

'Isn't it?' said Fayth.

Liam shook his head and removed the helmet. 'I'm not wearing that.'

Wade took the helmet off him. 'Then no bike.'

'You know I'm the one that pays you, right?'

'And you pay me to protect you. And your girlfriend is on my side.'

Fayth stood beside Wade. Traitor.

He snatched the helmet from Wade. 'Fine.'

'If it makes you feel better,' said Fayth, grabbing the passenger helmet – which didn't have a camera on it – 'I've got a dash cam too.'

'That's in a car. That doesn't look as stupid.'

'Better to look stupid and be safe,' said Fayth. Liam wasn't convinced.

Just so long as they didn't make him wear one back in New York, where more people were likely to recognise him.

'I'll see you there,' said Wade, climbing on to his Yamaha. His helmet also didn't have a camera on it.

'Do you know the way?' said Fayth.

'Two left turns and a right.' He fastened his helmet then switched on the engine, revving it a few times as Fayth and Liam put on their helmets and climbed on to the Ducati. His way of telling them to hurry up. Liam glared at him. They'd leave when they were ready. The helmet camera was awkward and made him feel lopsided, but if it made Fayth feel safer, he'd wear it. For now. Things were still raw, so anything he could do to make her feel safer, he'd do.

He switched on the engine and rode off, Wade close behind them. He felt better knowing that Wade was by his side again.

Fayth hovered in the doorway of the pub. She hadn't been back in over a week. It was the longest she'd ever spent away from it, trips to New York and London not included. The doctor had cleared her to go back to work, but that didn't mean she wanted to. Even the presence of Liam, Wade, and Ross did nothing to make her feel better. Every time she thought of the Cock and Bull she felt the gun as it hit the back of her head; pictured the crazy woman as she ran towards Liam; heard the gun firing. Her head throbbed.

Liam squeezed her hand. He hadn't been back either. He didn't seem nearly as fazed by what had happened as she was, though. Why was he dealing with it better than her? Or was he just acting?

Ross huffed behind them. He'd been to pick up some potatoes from the local farm on his way in, and was in the process of unloading. 'Are you going to stand there all day?' He dumped the sack on the floor. 'This thing's heavy, you know.'

'Sorry,' said Fayth. It's just…'

Ross patted her shoulder. 'Take your time. Just don't block the door for the punters.'

Fayth let out a forced laugh. She wouldn't stand there all night. Just for a little longer.

Wade stepped out from the pub. He'd gone in first to check things. The police on both sides of the Atlantic were certain they'd found the right person, but Wade was more vigilant than ever.

'All good.' He picked up the sack of potatoes from beside Ross and carried them like they were the lightest thing in the world.

'Show off,' mumbled Ross before following him inside.

Fayth and Liam laughed.

Much as she wanted to, they couldn't stand out there much longer. She gulped, curling her empty hand into a fist inside her jeans pocket.

The inside of the pub still looked the same. It still smelled the same. But the air was tainted. Even more than it was before. It was no longer just a place of bad memories: one of her places of safety, of sanctuary, had been corrupted and would never be the same again.

Provided the offer didn't fall through, within weeks they could be free.

Tick tock.

Fayth gravitated to her old haven of the kitchen. It didn't feel so safe any more. She had no idea whereabouts in the pub their stalker had been. Had she touched the cooker? The fridge? The sink? The island? The doors? Where in the pub had she been before she'd turned the lights off? Had she found a way into the flat upstairs? As far as Fayth was concerned, the whole pub was corrupted. She'd never feel comfortable there ever again. The sale needed to hurry up and go through.

'Hello?' called a voice. 'It's Constable Doyle.'

Fayth emerged from the kitchen.

'Sorry to bother you, but I have some new information I'd like to share with you,' he said.

Fayth nodded, wiping her sweaty hands on her jeans. What else had they found out? Did she really want to know?

She, Liam, and Constable Doyle sat at a table while Wade continued his inspection. Ross set the tables in the dining area.

'Her name is Tawny Germanotta. She grew up in Brooklyn and trained to be a teacher.'

A teacher? Weren't teachers supposed to be nice?

'After speaking to some of her old acquaintances, it seems she's been obsessed with Trinity Gold since she first entered the limelight. She's followed her career in great detail and has a diary all about Trinity and her relationships.'

Liam tensed. Fayth put her hand on his leg.

'She had a particular dislike for you, Liam.'

'Me? What did I do?'

'She didn't feel you were good enough for her.'

Not good enough for *Trinity*?

'She writes in great length about how you and Trinity got together during the first *Highwater* film, not after the trilogy had finished as you claim. She blames you for a lot of what's happened to Trinity. After Trinity's breakdown on live TV, she read hidden meanings into some of her more recent social media posts. She thought Trinity wanted her to get revenge.'

Liam curled his hand into a fist. Fayth forced it open, sliding her hand into his.

'That's when she began to send you threatening messages. I believe she also rang you a few times?'

'Yeah,' said Liam with a sigh.

'From what the NYPD have told me, when she broke into your apartment, she claimed she was visiting a friend. She went upstairs to check you were out, then returned a few minutes later claiming her friend wasn't in. She'd bought her imaginary friend a coffee that she didn't want to go to waste, so she gave it to the security guard. It was laced with laxatives. She waited until he was stuck in the bathroom, then stole his spare key.'

'Fuck sake,' said Liam, resting his head on the back of the

chair.

Fuck sake indeed. Weren't those things supposed to be safe?

'Your assistant has filed restraining orders for both of you, here and in New York.'

'Does that mean she's out of jail?' asked Fayth, her hand growing slippery with sweat inside Liam's.

'She couldn't afford the bail, so no. She's in jail at the moment and faces prison time for attempted murder and GBH.'

Liam shifted beside her. He ran his hand over his hair again. Something was bothering him. He huffed. 'What about…what about my photos and comics?'

'They were found stashed in her apartment, but for now they need to be kept as evidence.'

Liam sighed.

Fayth rubbed his arm. Those photos and comics had meant a lot to him. Some of them were first editions he'd spent years tracking down. If she'd trashed them…

Constable Doyle shook both their hands. 'Thank you for your time. If you think of anything else, please give me a call. I'll keep you posted.'

'Thanks,' said Fayth.

Liam leaned back and closed his eyes. She knew how he felt.

Wade showed Constable Doyle to the door. Ross approached them. 'You sure you're up to this?'

No, but what choice did she have?

Ten

The return to working at the Cock and Bull wasn't as bad as Fayth had envisioned, but every time she started another shift, she was more eager for the sale to go through. She was ready to move on, to get away from the place where she'd found out her mum and sister had been in a car accident, away from the place where she and Liam had nearly been killed.

They still didn't have a date, though – there was too much paperwork to do. All they knew was that they had a buyer and that he hadn't pulled out yet.

He wouldn't do that, would he?

Fayth rolled over and stared at the bedside clock. One minute to go. One minute until the anniversary of her mum and sister's deaths. The day that changed everything.

00:00 flashed up on the neon green display.

She sat up.

She'd spent over an hour trying to sleep, but she just couldn't. It was her night off, so she'd hoped to get an early night, but her brain had had other ideas.

Liam stirred beside her. Noticing she was awake, he stroked her arm. 'Do you need to talk?'

She sighed. 'I don't know.' She pulled her legs to her chest and leaned against the wall. 'I don't know.'

Liam had taught her it was best to talk about things, but it still wasn't easy. She wasn't trained to talk about things, she was trained to bottle them up. Which had done her a fat lot of good. If she hadn't bottled everything up, parts of the last year might've been easier. Almost bearable.

Or not.

He rested his head on her lap. She stroked his hair. He was so patient with her, so willing to let her open up when she was ready. She'd never had that before. Not in a relationship, anyway. She'd also never had someone who understood her as much as he did. He'd lost a close family member too. He'd been through the pain and come out the other side. Somehow. If only she could've bottled up how he'd done it and found a way to use it herself.

Then again, he had had to become an addict then go to rehab to find acceptance. Maybe that path wasn't such a good idea after all. Maybe talking was the best way to deal with things instead.

'Some days I feel numb, like I'll never be able to function again, then others I almost feel normal again. Then I hear Brooke crying in her sleep, or Dad calling Mum's name and I feel guilty. I spent months suppressing how I felt, like if I dared to feel anything I'd explode. I carried on and pretended I was fine. I had to, for Dad and Brooke. I know they pretended they were fine too. Dad's the worst for it. Brooke cried herself to sleep for months. She still does sometimes, or she wakes up in the night crying.' Tears formed in her eyes. She wiped at them with her sleeve. 'It feels like a part of me has been torn off and like the wound will never fully heal. Like it was yanked off by The Hulk. And if the crazy woman had done what she intended to…' She reached over to the bedside table and grabbed a tissue. 'It would've destroyed them.'

Liam sat up. 'But she didn't. We're still here.'

'But if it had—'

'But it didn't. You can waste you life on the what ifs and the buts and the maybes, but once something's happened, we can't change it.'

'That's very zen of you,' said Fayth.

Liam chuckled. 'Rehab.' He tucked a piece of Fayth's hair behind her ear.

'But why can't I let it go?'

'Two people were ripped from your life and you never got chance to say goodbye. That'd hit anyone hard.'

'But I should be over it by now. It's been a year.'

'You can't put a time limit on grief. It never fully goes away, you just learn to live with it.'

Liam wiped a tear from her cheek. She sobbed even harder. He was so good to her. How could she have spent so long pushing him away?

'I'm sorry,' she sobbed.

'You don't need to apologise.'

'I should've talked to someone. I should've got counselling, I should've—'

'You can't change what you did or didn't do. Even Astin's

DeLorean can't do that.'

Fayth let out a small laugh. Something tugged at her heart.

'We just have to accept what's happened and move on,' said Liam.

'But how? How do you move on from something like that?'

'You keep living,' he said, 'and one day, it gets easier. You'll still think about them, and you'll still feel like a part of you is missing, but you keep living not just for those you've lost, but for those that you still have. Those you *will* have. I can't lie to you and pretend I believe in heaven or the afterlife or any of that, but death is as natural as breathing, and it comes to us all some day. It's the fear of death that keeps us living.'

'More like what cripples us,' corrected Fayth.

'Sometimes. Depends how you react to it. But can you honestly say that your mom or sister would want you to spend the rest of your life feeling numb? Would they not be proud of you for divorcing Patrick, or falling in love with me?'

She laughed. Yes, Mhairi would be *very* proud of her for that one.

Fayth slept little that night. Having Liam beside her helped, but it didn't quieten her racing mind. She woke up every hour or so, and when she did fall asleep, she saw her mum and Mhairi. Hollie texted her as she lay in bed reading on her phone: *How are you? Need to talk? x*

She left Liam to sleep, crept into the hallway, and dialled Hollie's number.

'How are you holding up?' said Hollie.

'Better than I thought I would,' said Fayth. Her instinct had been to say 'fine'. She suppressed it. It was time she started owning her emotions instead.

'What about your dad and Brooke?'

'Dad went out early this morning. Brooke and Liam are still asleep.'

'Still? Does that guy not have a job?'

'Not currently, no, but I'm glad he's here.'

'Me too,' said Hollie.

She was silent for a moment. A moment too long.

'You being quiet is far scarier than you speaking,' said Fayth.

'Liam's helped you more than I ever thought he could.'

'Well it was your idea. We never would've become friends if it wasn't for you.'

Technically it was because of Astin, but bringing his name up wasn't a good idea, all things considered.

'We both know it wasn't me.'

A tangible silence filled the phone line.

'Are you doing all right, after everything?' asked Fayth.

'I'm focusing on the future, not the past. I have my designs, I have my business, and I'm still trying to get my head around all of that right now. I wouldn't be here if it wasn't for him, and I'll always be grateful for that, but my future is up to me. I don't owe him anything.'

'That's my girl,' said Fayth.

'Thank you,' said Hollie.

'For what?'

'Thinking of me, even today. You always put other people before yourself.'

'What can I say? I'm a masochist.'

'It's not masochism and you know it. You're a good person, Fayth. Don't let anyone ever tell you otherwise.'

Eleven

Liam entered his apartment. He'd barely been back since the break-in. Knowing his stalker was in jail didn't make him feel much better. What if she had an accomplice? He didn't want to own a gun, but when he didn't feel safe in his own home, what else was he supposed to do? How would he ever feel 100% safe again?

Something in the apartment was off. He couldn't work out what. He walked farther inside the apartment, staying close to the wall. At least one side of him was protected.

Or not.

Someone came up behind him and tied up his hands. He tried to shove them away, but they were too strong. They pulled the rope around his wrists tighter. Once he was tied up, they stepped in front of him. Tawny.

'What are you doing here?'

'I came to finish what I started,' she said. She held up a handgun and pulled the trigger.

He woke up.

He couldn't breathe. He could hear the gun firing and smell the gunpowder.

How close had she been to firing the gun that night in the basement? Would she have fired it, had she had the opportunity?

He left Fayth to sleep and crept downstairs. She had more nightmares lately than he did; he didn't want to wake her on a rare occasion when she was asleep. His laptop was on the dining table, so he opened it up and started looking at apartments in New York City. Ola had sent him some over the past few months, but they'd all sold before he'd had chance to view them. He hadn't wanted to buy somewhere he hadn't viewed, but he was too scared to go back to New York. But he couldn't avoid it forever. It was time to seriously start apartment hunting. He couldn't go back to his old place. He couldn't live with his parents for any longer, either.

Most of the apartments looked the same or had offers on them already, but one caught his eye. It was in a recently refurbished building in Tribeca, and a total blank canvas: white walls, cream carpets, no furniture. His antique furniture collection would look awesome. As would his OLED TV. And he'd have room for more furniture, as it was bigger than his current place.

He called Ola. 'I've found a place. Can you go check it out?'

Ola yawned. 'Um, you know it's two o'clock in the morning here, right?'

Liam glanced up at the kitchen clock. It was just past seven on a Saturday. That explained why everyone was still in bed. 'Shit. Sorry.' Did that mean she couldn't view it until Monday too?

'I'll contact them first thing and book a viewing,' said Ola.

'Thanks.'

'Do you want me to organise a flight for you?'

'Yeah. Wade too.'

'What about Fayth?'

'No, she needs to stay here. She's sacrificed enough for me already. I won't stay long; just long enough to see the place and visit my parents.' They'd returned from the Hamptons a few days after he'd told them his stalker was behind bars. They had no intention of moving; they felt safe again knowing Tawny was locked up. Liam was still afraid it wasn't over, but he couldn't tell them that, not when he had no proof.

'All right. I'll organise lunch with them too.' She yawned. 'Email me the details?'

'Will do. Sorry for waking you up. Talk to you later.'

'Night.'

New York was so much warmer than Scotland. Humid too. Being back after so long, it didn't feel like home any more. Especially without Fayth.

Liam and Wade slid into the Jag. Thalia sat in the front, her dark hair over her eyes. 'Long time no see. I was starting to think I was out of a job.'

'No way,' said Liam. 'If I ever move from New York, I'm bringing you with me.'

'Just so long as it's not closer to my parents,' said Thalia. She hated her parents. It was part of why she lived in New York and not Greece. 'Ola is already at the apartment looking around.

Lunch with your parents is in a couple hours.'

'Have you seen the place yet?' asked Liam.

'Only from the outside,' said Thalia. 'It looks nice.'

'You have to remember it's not just about what it looks like. We need to think about security too,' said Wade, the killjoy.

They got stuck in traffic on the trip to Tribeca, so it took them almost an hour to get there. When they finally arrived, Ola was in reception talking to the realtor, whose name was Anne. The power suit she had on reminded him of Hilary Clinton.

'Sorry it took us so long,' said Liam.

'Don't worry,' said Anne, shaking his hand. 'Shall we go up and see the apartment?'

'Sure.'

Wade stayed downstairs to interrogate the security guard. Thalia stayed to babysit him.

Anne made them put on shoe protectors before entering as the carpet was so new. Promising. The door opened out into an open-plan living/dining/kitchen area with views over the Hudson River. He gravitated to the window. The sun sparkled over the busy river.

'It's beautiful, isn't it?' said Anne. She stood just a little too close to him. He shuffled away, hoping he wasn't too obvious.

'Yeah,' said Liam.

'Two bedrooms come with their own ensuite while the third bedroom is right next to the guest bathroom,' said Anne.

He followed her into the third bedroom. It was just the right size for a pool table. And a desk. And a dart board. Perfect as a games room.

The door flung open and Wade barged in. Anne ran out of the games room and help up her hands. 'Shoe protectors!'

Wade stopped, one leg hovering in the air. 'Eh?'

Anne pointed to a box by the door. Wade crouched down and picked up a couple of shoe protectors. He shot Liam an *are you serious?* look, but he put them on and apologised anyway.

'How's the security?' asked Liam. He was desperate to find out. If the place had Wade's approval, he was putting in an offer.

'Could use some improvements, but they've agreed to them if you put an offer in,' said Wade. 'What are the neighbours like?'

'Quiet,' said Anne. She put her index finger up to silence them. They listened. Footsteps. Cars. People talking. It wasn't noisy, but it wasn't quiet either. Just how he liked it.

'I'd like to make an offer.'

AUGUST

One

Fayth shifted in her seat. Even though she'd flown in Liam's private jet before, she couldn't shake the feeling of entitlement that went along with it. It didn't sit right with her.

Liam, on the other hand, was the picture of relaxation. He sat opposite her, his legs outstretched and his phone in hand. Once the offer had been accepted on his new apartment, he'd left Ola to deal with it and returned to Scotland to help out with the pub. She wasn't complaining. She'd got used to having him around.

Wade sat across from them, his head lolled to the side and his mouth hanging open.

According to her phone, it was nine o'clock. Ten hours until the gala. Until she and Liam made their couple debut. They weren't arriving together, but everyone inside would know that they were a together. Relationships didn't stay secret in Hollywood for long.

No pressure.

She looked down at her nails. They were unpainted, but she'd done her best to file them at least. Her eyebrows were so thin they might as well have been drawn on. And as for her hair…well, it had a mind of its own at the best of times. If much more of it fell out she'd have to cut it shorter so that it didn't look so thin. And as for her skin…it had never been so bad. They'd need to apply foundation with a shovel to disguise all the spots on her face.

Tate had insisted someone would help her with all of that when she got there, but Fayth wasn't keen on being poked and prodded by a beautician she'd never met before. The last time she'd had her make-up done her eyes had twitched so much they'd had to redo it three times.

Hollie loved having her make-up done. She relished in the chance. But how would she cope when she was about to see Astin for the first time since their breakup?

'Are you sure you're all right with me going with Hollie and Tate?' said Fayth. She wanted to be there for Hollie, but they were a couple now. Things were different.

Liam looked up from his phone. 'Yeah. Why wouldn't I be?'

'Well, you know. We're together now.'

'So? It's what we agreed. I'm cool with that. I prefer it, actually. I'd go in the back way if I could. I doubt Hollie will be able to avoid the cameras, though. There may not be a red carpet but there'll definitely be press outside.'

'She might not be up to it,' said Fayth.

Liam knitted his brow. 'Why?'

'She's not been herself lately. It's like she's gone backwards since—' The rest of the sentence hung in the air. *Since she and Astin broke up.*

Liam nodded. 'Astin's off too. He's functioning even less than he was before. Fuck knows what state he'll be in when I get there.'

'He's got Jack, hasn't he?'

Liam scoffed. 'Yeah. Some help he'll be.'

'He's been going to rehab though, and Hollie said he was taking some tablets that are supposed to change how his body reacts to alcohol.'

'I don't see this time being any different than the last.' He leaned forwards, resting his arms on his lap. 'I'll meet you inside. That way we can still spend some time together without the attention. Tate's promised me we're sat together.'

'What about Hollie?'

'She and Tate are on our table. Astin and Jack are the other side of the room.'

'Good. That's good. Thank you.' She smiled. It couldn't be easy for Tate to be sat away from Astin and Jack, but Hollie was her date. Hollie and Astin had been through enough drama. The last thing anyone needed was for them to cause a scene at a charity gala for orphaned children.

Fayth picked up her camera from the seat beside her and flicked through some of the photos. Most of them were of the dogs – her dad was camera shy, and Brooke would only let her take her photo if she had on a full-face of make-up. Which she never did.

'I've been thinking about going to uni and studying photography,' said Fayth.

'Oh?' said Liam.

'But I really don't want to commit to something for so long. I want to get out more. Travel. See the world. I've never had the chance before.' She put her camera down and picked up her phone, flicking through to a website she'd looked at the night before.

'Why don't you learn from experience, then?'

'I had a look online at some of the courses Dad and Brooke suggested. There's one in New York.' She showed him their homepage.

'Huh.'

She frowned. 'That's it?'

'What do you want me to say? New York has everything.'

'But is it any good?'

'Isn't that what Google's for?'

'Thanks. I really appreciate your help.' She scrolled through the website. She'd always planned to go back to New York one day, but had originally planned to check out some other places first. But if it had a great photography school and she could study there for a few months, why not? She'd be able to spend more time with Liam, and maybe make some more – non-famous – friends Stateside too.

She had the money to cover it, but she couldn't justify going until the pub was sold. She'd done a shite job of helping out the last few months as it was; she couldn't afford to leave them short-handed any more than she already had. Not when the main attraction seemed to be her and her boyfriend.

Boyfriend.

She had a boyfriend.

It was like being a teenager again.

She opened the gallery on the photography school's website and flicked through the images. Some of them were of people around New York, others of the beautiful skyline. There were even some aerial shots.

She and Hollie had been so busy running around and avoiding Trinity/other unwanted attention that she'd hardly taken any photos when they were there. Was a photography school in New York the perfect excuse to take photos she'd missed out on the first time around?

She picked up her camera again and took a photo of Liam. He looked up from his phone, his eyebrow raised. She took another. They were good, if she didn't mind saying so herself. 'How come I can take great photos of you but most other people won't work with you?'

He smirked.

'Oh my god. Do you do it on purpose?'

His smirk grew. 'A little.'

Liam barely recognised his best friend when he entered the hotel suite. Astin lay in bed playing *Resident Evil*. His hair was longer than Liam had ever seen it, and his beard was so big he risked being mistaken for a younger Santa Claus. A thick foam collar was wrapped around his neck, suppressing his movements. For the first time in his life, Astin looked scruffy.

'You look like one of Hell's Angels,' said Liam. He stood beside the bed, frowning.

'Thanks,' said Astin.

'That wasn't a compliment. If Tate sees you like this, she'll cut both our balls off and feed them to us *I'm a Celebrity*-style.'

Astin shrugged, concentrating on *Resident Evil* over their conversation.

Liam clenched his jaw. Jack sat on the sofa in the living room, reading a magazine. 'You were supposed to look after him!'

Jack glanced up from his magazine. 'He made his appointments on time, didn't he? It's up to him when he wants to go for a shave.' He crossed his leg over his lap and returned to his magazine.

'Are you fucking serious? Look at him!'

'I have. Every day for the last two months. Where've you been?'

'Hiding!'

'Yeah, in Fayth's panties.'

Liam jabbed his finger at Jack. 'It wasn't that simple and you know it.'

A wry smile crept over Jack's lips. He stood up. 'But you don't deny it.'

Liam's blood boiled. His nostrils flared. 'How fucking dare you? I had other things going on!'

'And I didn't? Or does my rehab mean nothing to you?'

'No, not really. Why is this time any different than the last? Or the one before that? Or the one before *that*?'

'I don't have to justify myself to you,' said Jack. 'I don't owe you anything.'

'Like hell you don't!'

It was Jack that had suggested he handle his grief with drugs. Had Jack not suggested it, he wouldn't have got addicted to heroin and been arrested for DUI. But Jack wouldn't accept responsibility for any of that. Jack didn't accept responsibility for anything. He was selfish and careless, and he'd never change. Liam raised his fist.

The suite door opened. Jamal walked in. 'Good afternoon, gentlemen. Can I get you anything?'

Liam huffed.

'No thank you, Jamal,' said Jack, stepping away. 'I'm going out.' He grabbed his trilby from the edge of the sofa and left.

'Anything for you, Mr York?'

'No. Thank you,' he replied through gritted teeth. That was some fucking good timing. He returned to Astin's room. The game was paused, his phone in his hand. 'You called your butler so that I didn't kill your babysitter.'

'Something like that,' said Astin. 'Speaking of which, where's yours?'

'Downstairs in the foyer. He wanted to give us some space.'

'No need,' said Astin, shuffling farther up in bed. 'I like Wade. And he might've stopped you from killing Jack.'

'Or done it himself,' mumbled Liam. He closed his eyes and took a few deep breaths, picturing Fayth to calm him down. Getting riled up wouldn't get Astin out of the hotel and to the gala. He needed to play it cool. 'What are you going as to Tate's gala?'

'What gala?' said Astin.

Liam's nostrils flared. 'Don't bullshit me. Tate's been organising it for months, and you're living with the guy she's in love with. I know you know what I'm talking about.'

'So? She throws them all the time.'

'It's for orphan children. How can you say no to that?'

Astin grunted. He may not have wanted to have a heart, but it was still in there somewhere. Liam just needed to find a way to tap back into it.

'You're not going, after everything Tate's done for you?'

'After everything she's done for me? She's the reason I'm here!'

Drama queen.

'She got you into stunt work. If you're going to blame her for the accident you may as well blame me for you meeting Hollie,' said Liam.

Astin grunted again, his eyes turning back to the TV. He switched off the XBox and put *Jeremy Kyle* on. Liam snatched the remote from his hand and turned the TV off.

'You're not my fucking parent,' snapped Astin.

'Then don't act like a fucking child.'

Astin stood up. 'You don't know anything about what I'm going through.' His legs wobbled. He stood his ground.

'I know you're making it worse for yourself.'

'Whatever,' said Astin. His legs buckled. He fell back on to the bed. Liam went to help him, but Astin brushed him off.

'Give yourself a break, would you? You can't punish yourself forever.'

'I'm not punishing myself!'

'Yeah, and I'm not an addict,' said Liam. 'Wake up, Astin. You're one of the lucky ones. So you can't scale buildings any more. So what? There are more important things in life.'

Liam stormed out of the room and down the stairs. When had Astin turned into such a grumpy old man? No wonder Hollie had dumped him.

Wade sat at a table at the bottom of the stairs, reading a broadsheet.

'Aren't you supposed to be looking for threats?' said Liam.

'They've got a doorman,' said Wade with a shrug. 'Saw Jack come down without a scratch. I'm impressed.'

Liam sat down beside him. 'Saved by the butler.'

'Sounds like a game of Clue gone wrong.'

'Tell me about it.'

'Did you get through to Astin?'

Liam took a pen from his pocket – he always carried one in case someone wanted an autograph – and doodled on the corner of Wade's newspaper.

'I'll take that as a no, then.'

Liam pressed harder on to the paper. How was he supposed to get through to someone who was more interested in daytime TV than spending time with his friends? He stopped drawing a house and scribbled on the page.

'Excuse me gentlemen,' said Jamal.

Liam flinched. The paper ripped. He apologised to Wade, putting the pen down.

So far, Liam wasn't a huge fan of Jamal. He wasn't a fan of anyone that stopped him from punching Jack.

'Astin asked if you would go up and see him,' said Jamal. 'Again.'

'Want me to come?' asked Wade.

'Maybe just wait on the sofa as back up.'

'Gotcha.'

The two of them returned to the suite. Astin was out of bed, dressed, and sat at the dining table, his crutches propped up against it. The light glistened in his eyes when he turned to see who was at the door. 'Will she be there?'

'Hollie?' said Liam.

Astin squirmed.

'She's Tate's date.' He inched closer to his friend, worried that if he got too close Astin would back away like a scared kitten. Wade remained by the door, as stoic and silent as he could be.

'I can't face her,' said Astin, sotto voce.

'You're going to have to some day,' said Liam.

'But today?'

'She's not on the same table. You might not even see each other.' He doubted that, but he'd say anything that could reassure Astin.

'Who am I with?'

'Jack and some other people. I don't know.' Liam pulled up a seat opposite him. 'But you need to get out of this funk that you're in, man. You can't hide forever.'

'Look at me, Liam.'

'So you've got to wear a squishy dog collar and use crutches. The only reason you're ugly right now is because you look like a yeti.' And because he was incorrigible, but they'd get to that later. Baby steps.

Astin laughed. Liam had a feeling it was the first genuine laugh to escape his lips in a long time.

'We'll make sure you go in through the back, that way nobody will get any photos,' said Liam.

'But people will have cameras inside,' said Astin.

'Whatever happened to the all or nothing guy? Aren't injuries like this supposed to make you want to live more?'

Astin sighed. 'I thought I knew what was important to me. I was wrong.'

'So let's fix it. Now may be the only chance you have.'

'OK,' Astin whispered.

Liam smiled. 'Come on. Let's get you to a barbers. We can't have you scaring the orphans.'

Two

The Beaumont hotel was clean and modern, and, most importantly, didn't have Astin. Hollie's room was painted a medium grey with views out on to the streets of Mayfair. Usually she liked cityscape views, but as she looked out of the window at the cars and the people below, she felt nothing.

A knock on her door echoed through the room. She checked through the peephole: Tate. Forcing herself to smile, she opened the door. 'Hey.'

'Hey!' said Tate, hugging her. Hollie hugged her back half-heartedly. 'What's wrong?' said Tate. She held Hollie at arm's length and examined her. 'Come on. Let's get you out of here.'

She allowed Tate to drag her down the corridor and into the lift, too weak to argue. They reached the lobby and came face-to-face with the one person who could put Hollie in an even worse mood than she was already in: Trinity Gold.

Hollie curled her hands into fists. Tate's eyes widened and her back stiffened. What was Trinity, the world's biggest bitch, doing in London?

Trinity beamed. 'Tate! So good to see you!' She air-kissed Tate's cheeks. Tate didn't reciprocate.

A cloud of musky perfume filled the air making Hollie want to gag. Trinity's transparent Moschino t-shirt revealed a black bra underneath, but that was nothing compared to the obnoxious red of her hair. It kind of worked with her olive complexion, but it would've worked better if it had been a more muted shade of red and not something from The Little Mermaid.

As usual, Hollie was invisible to her.

'What are you doing here?' said Tate.

'My girlfriend and I have got tickets to your charity gala! We couldn't let the orphans down, now could we?'

Tate's jaw dropped. Hollie tightened her fists. What would running into Trinity do to Fayth and Liam after what had happened? She grabbed Tate's arm and dragged her out of the hotel. They needed to get out of there and cool off before it turned into a scene. They jumped into the first taxi they could find.

'Where to?' asked the driver.

Tate named somewhere Hollie hadn't heard of.

'That bitch!' growled Tate as they drove off.

Hollie still couldn't form words. Being around Astin was bad enough, but Trinity too? The woman who'd bullied Fayth, broken Liam's heart, and created the first argument between her and Astin?

The only thing that could make things worse was Lawrence Roskowski showing up.

'Ugh, I almost need my inhaler from the amount of perfume she had on.' Tate crossed her arms over her chest. 'The only reason she's here is to cause trouble.' She huffed. 'She didn't even get an invite. She probably wrangled one from somewhere because she's got a new record coming out. Now what do we do?'

'I don't know,' said Hollie. She was too weak to come up with ideas.

They pulled up outside a bar, paid the driver, then went inside. It was a bit of a dump, but it had a welcoming atmosphere. With its car and motorbike parts on the walls and hairy middle-aged men hanging about, it was the last place anyone would expect to find Tate Gardener, and the last place she'd be recognised. Tate hopped up on to a barstool and ordered a piña colada. Hollie went with water.

Tate slammed her empty glass on to the bar and ordered another. 'Do you know why Trinity hates me so much? It wasn't even my fault. She wrote this really beautiful song called *Eclipse*, but the record label said that if she sung it, it would sound too grown-up because it showed off her vocals so well. So they changed the key and gave it to me. She saw it as this massive betrayal even though I couldn't have stood up to the record label if I'd wanted to.'

'Why not?'

'Why didn't you stand up to your old boss sooner?'

'Point taken. Surely she'd understand that though?'

Tate laughed. 'Empathy isn't her thing. Revenge is.'

'Worrying.'

'She's always trying to sabotage things I'm involved in. She can't let it go, and it was like, five years ago. She really hates me for it. She just wants to see me burn.'

'Because that's not over the top at all.'

'It's not for Trinity. You think I had a lavish upbringing? I had nothing on her. My parents made me work for my living. She chose to. Her dad gave her whatever she wanted out of guilt for her mom's death, but no amount of money can make up for being a shitty parent. That's why she's emancipated.'

'She is?'

'Yeah. Since she was about 15. I don't blame her. I got lucky: I may be adopted but I couldn't have picked better parents. But her birth parents were bigger train wrecks than she is.'

'Is that possible?'

'Oh honey, you've got no idea.' She sipped her cocktail. 'Then I got the Calvin Klein campaign that she wanted.'

'The one that you were in with…'

'Yeah. She hated me even more because every time she tried to flirt with Astin, he brushed her off. She's too in-your-face for him.'

'I thought she was in love with Liam?'

'Oh, she is, but Trinity sees all men as conquests.'

Hollie scoffed. Ironic. She'd referred to Hollie as Astin's latest 'conquest' in New York and predicted their relationship wouldn't last. She couldn't have been more right.

'To her, Liam is the ultimate conquest because he can boost her career so much. Or at least, he could. It's pathetic.'

'I agree,' said Jack's voice, 'drinking in the middle of the day bitching about your former best friend *is* pathetic.' He kissed Tate's cheek.

'What're you doing here?' said Tate.

'I got you some flowers and wanted to give them to you in person but ran into Trinity instead. Figured you'd come here. The concierge put them in your room, by the way.'

'Thank you,' said Tate, resting her head on his shoulder. A dreamy, loved-up expression washed over her face. Hollie looked away, still unable to stomach loved-up couples – or couples-in-denial, like Tate and Jack.

Jack turned to Hollie: 'This is where we come when we want to be anonymous.'

'I can see why,' said Hollie.

Jack pulled up a barstool beside Tate but didn't order anything.

'What did she say to you?' said Tate.

'Just that you were rude and she didn't understand why.'

Sure she didn't.

'She's not worth it, babe, you know that,' said Jack. He rubbed Tate's arm.

'I know,' sighed Tate, 'but trouble follows her everywhere. She'll cause trouble, I guarantee it.'

'We won't let her,' said Jack. 'Will we Hollie?'

'Nope.'

'What time does Fayth's flight land?' said Jack.

Hollie checked the time on her phone. 'Not for another hour. Why?'

'Come on,' he said. 'I know just what you need.' He held out his hands. Hollie and Tate took them and followed.

'Where are we going?' said Hollie.

He hailed a taxi. 'Dancing.'

'I can't dance,' said Hollie.

'Dancing isn't about if you can or can't do it. It's about having fun. It's the second best form of stress-relief I know.'

'What's the first?' asked Hollie.

Jack smirked.

Tate nudged him and giggled.

'Oh! *Oh*!' said Hollie. She flushed.

When a taxi arrived, Hollie got in first, then Tate, then Jack. Tate and Jack flirted beside her as she stared out of the window. For two people who weren't together they acted an awful lot like a couple.

She'd got used to the hustle and bustle of London when she'd lived there, but returning to it after what had happened she didn't feel so fondly towards it. Everywhere she looked she saw Astin, or saw his name written somewhere, or heard someone mention him. She didn't, of course, but that's how it seemed. She could run into him at any moment. Would the gala be the last time she'd ever see him? She couldn't decide which would be worse.

The taxi dropped them off in a seedy-looking part of London that made Hollie nervous. They went up a flight of stairs and into a club where salsa music blasted through the speakers as people swayed their hips to the rhythm. She may have gone for dancing lessons as a child, but ballet was a far cry from salsa. Not to mention she'd been told off by her ballet teacher for being too wooden. Salsa was the worst dance for her.

Jack led them straight to the dance floor.

'I have no idea how to salsa,' Hollie mumbled to Tate.

'Just copy Jack,' said Tate.

She watched Jack as he began to dance. He stepped forwards a couple of times, then back a few times. He stepped without going anywhere. And forward. And back. And what? Oh, fuck. It wasn't as easy as they made it look on *Strictly*. She shook her head. She couldn't do it. What was the point? She went to the loo and stared into the mirror. She had hardly any make-up on. The bags under her eyes were huge. She hoped Tate's make-up artist would be able to cover them up. The last thing she needed was to turn up to her first red carpet looking like a zombie. It wasn't like she could avoid it if she wanted to boost her profile, either. She banged the edge of the sink. It didn't help much. It just made her hand hurt.

She wasn't in the mood to dance. She was in the mood to curl up in her duvet and never be seen again. That would make life *so much* easier. But it wasn't an option.

Tate and Jack looked *very* cosy on the dance floor when she emerged from the toilets. She left them to it, choosing to order a lemonade and people watch instead of play third wheel.

There was nothing worse than playing third wheel when your heart hadn't fully healed. Was that how Fayth had felt in New York? She'd had Liam, but was that the same? Wow, she'd been a bitch in New York, forcing Fayth to spend time with Liam so that she could spend time with Astin. And what difference had it made?

She sipped her drink. It was watered down and almost flat. She gagged a little, putting the glass down and glancing up at Tate and Jack. It was obvious from the way they danced that they had a history, and obvious to everyone but them that they had a future. It was intimate; they knew how each other's bodies moved in a way that only those who've known each other a long time can. Tate had said numerous times she still loved him. How long would it be until she let him in again?

To the left of the dance floor she noticed a guy holding up his phone and pointing it in their direction. Did nobody deserve any privacy any more?

She opted to ring Tate, as it was more subtle than going over. It also meant they wouldn't try to get her to dance again.

Surprisingly, Tate noticed her phone ring. She took it from her pocket and checked it, then looked over at Hollie, a confused expression on her face. Hollie directed her gaze at the man with the camera. Tate saw him and nodded, then returned her phone to her pocket. She put her hand on Jack's arm and whispered into his ear. He said something to her, then the non-couple joined Hollie at the bar. A few seconds later, the man put his phone away.

'Thanks,' said Tate.

'I could have got the bartender to say something,' said Hollie.

'No, it's OK. We need to head back anyway – Fayth should be landing any minute.'

Hollie couldn't wait to see her best friend again. Maybe then she wouldn't feel so isolated.

'So what's the deal with you and Jack?' Hollie asked when they got back to their hotel suite. She pulled off her hoody and draped it over the back of the sofa. Moxie scurried over to them from her bed in the corner.

'What do you mean?' Tate picked up Moxie and scratched behind her ears.

'You were practically dry humping on the dance floor,' said Hollie.

Tate blushed, sitting on the sofa. 'We were, weren't we?'

Hollie nodded, sitting beside her.

'I don't know,' admitted Tate. She put Moxie down. The dog sat at her feet, staring up at her owner expectantly. 'I love him, but it's hard. He's screwed up so often.'

'Do you really think he's changed?' Hollie asked. People could change for the worse, so why not change for the better too? It'd be ironic if Jack became one of the good guys as Astin turned into an arsehole, but not impossible.

'A little. But he's done it before then reverted to type again. It'll take time before I believe it's permanent.'

'And if it is?'

She shrugged, stood up, and looked out of the window. Moxie followed. 'Who knows?'

Hollie and Tate were already getting ready when Fayth arrived. Tate gave her a hug and whispered, 'She's been very quiet. She's barely even spoken to Moxie.'

They looked down at the black-and-tan dog that circled their feet. She was about the size of a robot dog toy Fayth and her sisters had had as kids. But much cuter. Tate bent down and picked up the little dog. She licked Fayth's face. Fayth smiled.

'You're cute. You'd fit right in at the pub.'

Tate chuckled. 'Nice try.'

'Where is she?'

'On the terrace,' said Tate, scratching behind Moxie's ear. 'I don't know what else to do.'

'She's probably nervous about seeing Astin. I'll go talk to her.'

'All right. Hair and make-up will be here at two.'

'*Two*? How long does it take you to get ready?'

Tate giggled.

A butler emerged from the bathroom. 'Miss Gardener? Your bath is ready.'

'Excuse me,' said Tate. She gave Moxie one last head scratch, put the dog down, then went into the bathroom.

'Can I get you anything?' asked the butler.

'Ice cream, please. Preferably cookie dough flavour, but I'll take whatever you can find,' said Fayth.

He nodded, then left the suite.

Time to deal with Hollie.

Moxie close behind her, Fayth joined Hollie on the terrace. She sat on one of the chairs, staring out across London. Fayth resisted the urge to go fetch her camera from her handbag. It wasn't the time for photos.

Neither of them spoke as she sat down. Fayth knew she couldn't push her. Push her too much, and she risked exploding, or worse, shutting down. At least if she exploded she'd get her emotions out. If she shut down the lid would be on so tight that said emotions risked never emerging again.

Moxie pawed at Hollie's leg. For a well-trained dog, Moxie was very cheeky. Could she sense that Hollie needed cheering up?

Hollie picked up the small dog and placed her on her lap. Moxie walked in circles a few times, then lay down. Hollie stroked her. The tenseness in her joints seemed to lessen, her face relax. The power of a good pet.

'Little attention seeker,' said Hollie.

'She seemed pretty well-trained the last time we saw her,' said Fayth. 'Maybe she just wants to help.'

'Help with what?'

'We both know how perceptive dogs can be,' said Fayth.

Hollie's shoulders slumped. 'Am I really that transparent?'

'You're not doing much to cover it up right now.'

'No, that's true.' Her voice was quiet when she spoke. It had lost the animation that coloured her voice. Everything was monotonous, like it took all the energy she had to form words.

'Is there anything I can do?' said Fayth, desperately wishing she could fix her best friend.

'I wish,' said Hollie. She stopped stroking Moxie. The dog stirred, nudging Hollie's hand until she stroked her again. 'What if I run into him later?'

'You'll make him regret ever letting you go,' said Fayth.

'Sure I will,' said Hollie.

'You will! You'll look amazing, while he'll look like the Beast from *Beauty and the Beast*.'

'How do you know what he's going as?'

'Liam picked it for him. He thought it was appropriate. He's still growing that beard of his, apparently.'

Of course he was. Lazy sod.

'It says a lot, don't you think?' said Fayth.

'He gave up long before I left, Fayth. And if anything, he *wanted* me to go.'

'Why do you say that?'

'He tried to dump me, right after the accident.'

'You never told me that!'

'I tried to forget about it.' She looked out across London for a few seconds, then continued: 'When I said he might be better off without stunt work, he said it was all he had left.' Her eyes filled with tears.

Fayth moved her chair closer and put her arm around Hollie's shoulders. 'Dick.'

Hollie gave a small laugh. 'Yeah.'

'Even if he only said it in the heat of the moment, he's still a dick. You did the right thing.'

Hollie looked down at Moxie. The little dog's feet twitched as she fell asleep. 'My head says I did, but my heart disagrees.'

'For a relationship to work, you need to think with both.'

'When did you get so wise?'

'The last eighteen months. Something good needed to come out of it all,' said Fayth.

'And you and Liam aren't enough?'

'Yeah, that's good too,' said Fayth, a smile creeping over her face.

'Is he OK with you arriving with us?'

'Yeah. It works out better, actually. I want to get used to

things between us and work out who we are as a couple before the rest of the world decides for us,' said Fayth.

'You mean they haven't decided already?'

'It's different now though. Before they were just rumours. Now it's the truth.'

'Well, at least now you're guilty of the crime you're being punished for.'

'I wouldn't call going out with Liam a crime,' said Fayth, smiling.

'Someone's got it bad,' said Hollie.

Fayth blushed.

'I'm happy for you,' said Hollie. 'You deserve it.'

'Thanks,' said Fayth. 'I hope you find it too some day.'

She'd thought she had, that was the problem. How was she supposed to let that go? To say goodbye to their dogs and house filled with gadgets? To their holidays in Italy and Australia? They'd had everything mapped out. Until he'd turned into an arsehole.

Hollie stroked Moxie, then picked her up and placed her on the floor. The dog growled. 'I've got what's important to me. I should've known better than to let a boy get in the way of that.'

Three

The charity gala was at Nobu, not far from where Hollie and Tate were staying. Had their car not stopped right outside it, Hollie wouldn't have even noticed it. It was tucked away beside a Land Rover dealership, surrounded by press. Photographers blocked most of the street, snapping photos as people left their cars. If it was someone uninteresting, they got bored and moved away. But she shared a car with Tate Gardener, and Liam York's girlfriend. There was no chance of them getting bored.

Tate climbed out first, greeting some of the paparazzi by name and asking how their kids were as she posed for a few photos. Fayth checked her hood in the mirror, then followed her out. Hollie wiped her sweaty palms on the seat of the Tesla. It didn't make much of a difference. Despite wearing heavy-duty moisturising lipstick, her lips were dry. Her throat was even drier. She let out a weak, feeble cough.

'Excuse me, but I have to move. I'm blocking the road,' said the driver.

'Oh. Sorry.'

It was time. Clutching on to the edge of the car to steady herself, she climbed out. Lights flashed so brightly it was like staring at the sun.

'Who are you wearing, Tate?' shouted a photographer.

Tate beamed. 'Hollie Baxter,' she replied, twirling in her knee-length gown. It glittered in the light. 'Aren't her designs gorgeous!' She pulled Hollie to her. 'This is Hollie. She's super talented.'

'We love you Tate!' cried a fan from across the street.

'Excuse me,' said Tate to the photographers. She hurried over to her fans, waving her magic wand.

Hollie was exposed. She stood awkwardly, staring at her Mary Janes. Her bright blue Alice dress contrasted with the blonde wig she'd bought, and her rosy cheeks made her look cute and innocent. Her favourite part was the clutch she'd made to look like Dinah. The fur kept getting caught in the zip, but that was the downside of working with fur. It only needed to last the night anyway.

'Didn't you design the outfit for Tate's video for *Comet*, too?' asked another photographer.

'Yeah,' she said, her eyes still glued to her shoes.

'Hey, aren't you dating that stunt performer who got injured filming *Knight of Shadows*? How's he doing?' asked a third.

The hairs on the back of Hollie's neck pricked up. How did they know that? How had they found that out and not that they'd broken up two months ago? She couldn't breathe. An invisible hand wrapped itself around her throat. What was she supposed to say? Could she tell them they'd broken up? Would they ask why? Was any of it their business?

'I'm sorry, but Hollie doesn't discuss her personal life. You can check out more of her designs on her website. I highly recommend it,' said Fayth, putting her arm around Hollie's waist and guiding her inside.

'Thank you,' said Hollie, hugging her friend once they were safely inside and away from the doors.

Fayth gave her a squeeze. The silky red fabric of her jumpsuit complemented her dark hair and red lips. She had the hood up, clipped to her heavily sprayed hair that had been fastened into a low bun. Hollie had sourced a wicker basket for her to use as a bag and snuck in some gingham fabric to cover the top. 'I would've saved you sooner but I kept getting asked stupid questions about Liam. I dread to think what it would've been like if we'd arrived together.'

'At least I would've got less attention,' grumbled Hollie.

Fayth rubbed her arm. 'You survived, didn't you? And you got some exposure from it! It was your first press event. You were bound to be awkward.'

'You weren't!'

'I'm used to dealing with weird, annoying people. Grew up with it at the pub.'

Hollie couldn't work out if that was a good or a bad thing. It had certainly come in handy.

'Did you get on all right?' asked Tate, joining them. She ran her hands over her fishtail braid. 'Is my hair OK?'

'Tate you've got so much hairspray on that thing it's not moving unless you chop it off,' said Hollie.

'Good,' said Tate, grinning. 'What do you think?' She

gestured around them to the lounge bar. It was bright and airy with wooden floors and a bar to the right. Tables and chairs were dotted around the room, some occupied, some empty. They gravitated to an empty table and sat down.

'It's awesome,' said Hollie.

A waiter appeared and took their drinks orders, then disappeared.

'Isn't it?' said Tate. She took her phone from her clutch and paused, reading something on it. 'We've got about an hour before my speech, then we move upstairs for the food. Would you be all right if I go talk to some of the other organisers, go over my speech?'

'Sure,' said Fayth.

Tate air-kissed Hollie's cheek, then Fayth's. 'Send my drink upstairs please?'

'Will do,' said Fayth.

Tate headed for the stairs, but she was stopped every few feet by someone wanting her attention. She greeted everyone warmly, nodding and smiling. It looked exhausting.

'How are you feeling?' said Hollie. 'I mean, after what happened…'

'I prefer crowded places, actually,' said Fayth. 'It's easier to blend in. There's so much security and press lurking about it'd be difficult for someone dodgy to get near anyone.'

'True,' said Hollie. 'But how are you coping? Really?'

'I'm managing, like I always do.'

'Good. What about Liam?'

'God knows. One day he wears his heart on his sleeve, the next he's in actor mode and won't give anything away. Speaking of which, have you seen him?'

The crowds had picked up, making it difficult to spot anyone.

'Why don't you go look for him?'

'He's probably caught up outside. The press haven't found out what happened at the pub yet, but they still like to quiz him about Trinity,' said Fayth with a sigh.

'It's been eight months,' said Hollie.

Fayth rolled her eyes. 'Tell me about it. They won't let it go.'

'Ugh.' She grumbled about the press not being able to let go of Eric and Melitha, but she couldn't let go of Astin. Two months on and she still couldn't say his name. Just thinking it hurt. Knowing that he could be in the same room as her tied her insides into knots. She ground her teeth, hoping it'd stop. It didn't. 'Do you know where the toilets are?'

'You can't need to pee already,' said Fayth.

'I pee more when I'm nervous,' said Hollie.

'They're by the door, I think,' said Fayth.

'Cheers.' She went to find the toilets and left Fayth to wait for the drinks. Liam stood just outside the door, talking to press, as Fayth had predicted. He and Fayth were a good couple. But then, she and Astin had been when they'd first started going out. A sharp pain shot through her chest. Every time she thought of him, it felt like someone took a voodoo doll of her and stabbed at her heart. When she thought of him being her ex, they twisted the knife and dug it in deeper. The wounds caused by their break up hadn't healed, just been buried.

'Boo.'

Fayth turned her head. Liam leaned over her shoulder, his hair falling into his eyes. He flicked it away and kissed her. 'Where are Hollie and Tate?'

'Hollie's gone to the loo and Tate's practising her speech,' said Fayth. 'Where are Astin and Jack?'

'Astin's avoiding Hollie and Jack's keeping him company.'

Coward.

'Did the press bother you?' he asked as he slid in beside her.

'A little. I handled it.'

She still didn't know how she'd managed it. She hated the press, and they hated her. But, after everything that'd happened, their presence almost comforted her. No, not just their presence. *Everyone's*. It was when she was alone or somewhere quiet that the fear and the nightmares crept in. That she relived the feel of the gun on the back of her head; the sound as it fired. How much longer would she have to put up with the flashbacks? With reliving the mental and physical pain of that night?

The only comfort she found was in Liam. He knew what she was going through, but he seemed to be dealing with it so much better than she was. How did he do it? Was he pretending, like he did when the press asked him daft questions, or was he really OK?

'I knew I should've sent Wade with you instead of giving him the night off,' said Liam.

'That would've just attracted more attention,' said Fayth. 'They all know Wade's your bodyguard.'

'I suppose,' said Liam, clearly unimpressed. He adjusted one of the shoulder pads on his Prince Charming costume.

'Liam! It's so good to see you!' cried a shrill, husky voice.

Fayth nearly choked on her drink. Trinity fucking Gold stood before them, her cleavage forced into a shell bra and her legs squashed into a mermaid skirt. Her hair was a bright, obnoxious red. Fayth couldn't tell if it was real or a wig. She desperately hoped it was a wig.

'Trinity,' said Liam through gritted teeth.

Trinity draped her arm around the neck of a woman dressed as Sleeping Beauty. 'This is my girlfriend, Kia. She's a yoga instructor.'

Of course she was.

'Nice to meet you,' said Kia, her voice quiet and unassuming. Perfect for Trinity to control.

Liam gave a small nod.

Fayth remained silent. Trinity was no longer just the cause of her problems in New York. She was the reason Fayth and Liam had had a stalker that had followed them all the way to the pub. She was the cause of all their problems whether she knew it or not. No matter what she did, Fayth just couldn't escape her. If it wasn't Trinity being crazy it was one of her fans.

'I heard about what happened. How are you coping?' said Trinity.

'Fine,' said Liam.

'Are you sure? I mean, someone pointing a gun at you like that, it's bound to leave scars.'

What was she trying to do? Make them feel worse?

'What do you want, Trinity?' growled Fayth. She didn't have time for Trinity and her games.

'Nothing!' said Trinity, but the smirk that played across her orange lips said otherwise.

Fayth sought Liam's hand out from under the table. They stared at Trinity. Nobody spoke. She continued to smile like she'd hatched some evil plan while Kia gazed around the room. Her expression was airy-fairy, as if she wasn't all there.

'Well,' said Trinity finally, 'we'd better go get a drink. We'll see you both soon.' She and her new girlfriend sauntered away.

Fayth and Liam didn't let go of each other's hands.

'Bitch,' mumbled Fayth.

'How didn't I see it?' said Liam.

Fayth rubbed his arm with her spare hand. 'We see what we

want to see.'

He shook his head, causing his hair to fall into his eyes. He jerked his head. Fayth giggled.

'I really need to get it cut,' said Liam.

'Cut as in a bit off the end or a new style?'

'I'm almost 26. Maybe it's time for a change. Maybe the reason no one takes me seriously is because I look the same as I did ten years ago.'

'You don't look the same.'

He scratched his chin. 'Or I could grow a beard.'

'So long as it's not as bushy as Astin's.'

'I couldn't grow that if I tried. I barely manage stubble.'

'Looks aren't everything,' said Fayth.

'They are in Hollywood.'

Hollie studied her reflection in the toilet mirror. The make-up artist had done a bloody good job of hiding how tired and stressed-out she looked. Her skin had a glow to it, and her cheeks were rosy, not angry. They couldn't hide her bloodshot eyes, though. And no amount of lipgloss could cover up how dry her lips were for long. She took out her lipgloss and topped it up.

How was Fayth so calm after everything she'd been through? How was she so goddamn stable, while Hollie fell apart at the tiniest thing?

Drugs. It had to be drugs.

Or alcohol.

Or better internal wiring.

Stupid brain.

When she emerged from the toilets, there were considerably more people in the lounge bar than when she'd gone inside. Her hands curled instinctively into fists. She wasn't on the verge of a panic attack, but crowds still made her uneasy. Not nearly as uneasy as Astin showing up, but she'd already decided he wouldn't be there. There was no way he'd agree to fancy dress with the attitude he'd had the last time she'd seen him. He'd barely put on a pair of jeans since moving into the hotel. His preferred option was tracksuit bottoms and a hoody: it was a far cry from the well-dressed man she'd met in New York.

And how would he manage the stairs up to the restaurant? There was no way he'd—

Shit.

She spotted him in the crowds, propped up on a set of elbow

crutches. His hair was longer and slicked back. His beard was still there, but more trim than it had been. Their eyes met.

Shit.

He began to walk towards her.

Shit shit.

There were people all around her. Her only means of escape was forwards, and closer to him. She looked around for someone to save her, but there was no one.

He reached her, resting his weight on his crutches.

His hair may have been cut and his beard trimmed, but it still didn't suit him. Neither did his navy suit with gold lapels and and camel waistcoat. There was no way he'd chosen that outfit himself. It had Liam written all over it.

'You look great,' he said.

'Thanks,' said Hollie, looking anywhere but at him. Her heart hammered in her chest. He needed to go away. She couldn't look at him. She couldn't register whatever emotion was in his eyes. Doing so risked every emotion she'd been suppressing erupting from her at the worst possible time.

Fayth and Liam were at the table where she'd left Fayth. Why had she left the safety of the stupid table? Being on her own left Astin with the perfect opening. Tate was one of his closest friends; how could she have expected him not to show up?

'Not that I'd expect anything less,' he added. He shifted his crutches slightly, and she had to stop herself from helping him. It wasn't her job any more.

Seeing him shattered any semblance of confidence she'd had. His presence no longer made her feel strong; it weakened her. It made her vulnerable. A fancy dress costume wasn't enough to protect her. She folded her arms.

'Excuse me,' came a voice she didn't recognise. She turned her head. Luke Andrews, boyfriend of Cameron and member of boyband HATT stood next to her, dressed as Rumpelstiltskin. His boyish face had a sympathetic smile on it. 'Hollie, have you got a minute?'

'Sure,' she said, happy to be led away, even if it was by someone she only knew by association.

'Thanks,' she said as they walked away from Astin.

'Cam said to look out for you,' said Luke.

'He did?'

'Yeah. He's worried about you. Not that he'll admit it to you.'

'Tell him he doesn't need to worry about me,' she said. 'Where is he, anyway?'

'We didn't think it'd be a good idea to go somewhere so public, since technically nobody knows.' The final part of his sentence – that he was gay – hung in the air. If it hadn't been for Cameron's past – or present – with Luke, Hollie wouldn't have known either. His record label had done a bloody good job of keeping it quiet. They couldn't afford for their female fans to find out the band's pretty boy was gay, let alone in a relationship with someone who looked more like he belonged in Fall Out Boy.

As they talked, she couldn't stop her gaze from flitting over to Astin. He'd moved on to a group of people she didn't recognise, but he wasn't as animated or talkative as she remembered him. He flashed forced smiles, only moving to speak to someone else or adjust his crutches. Each time she noticed him glance over, she averted his gaze. It was imperative not to make eye contact.

Tate stepped out on to a small stage beside the bar and stared out over the crowds. She grinned, waiting for everyone to stop speaking. It didn't take long. Tate turned heads wherever she went. 'Good evening everyone. I just wanted to thank you all for coming tonight. This is a cause that runs very deep into my heart. Not every child is fortunate enough to be adopted into a loving family, as I was.' Her gaze flitted to Jack, who stood beside Astin with his arms folded. He was open about how both his parents had died when he was a child, but the way he joked about it made Hollie wonder if he wasn't as over it as he claimed. 'When we're lucky, we must do things to help those that aren't so lucky. That's why I decided to organise this gala tonight. So please, be generous! And if you want children but can't have them, or just want to help someone, why not look into adoption? Not just of younger children, but of the older ones too. It's harder for teenagers to get adopted, but they need just as much love and guidance as the younger ones. It's so easy to get lost when we lose our family members and don't have anyone else, or our family can't look after us. There are so many definitions of family in the 21st century that there really is a home out there for everyone.'

Four

A barrier was removed from the bottom of the stairs and everyone was led up to the dining area. Astin and Jack were just a few feet away. Hollie held back, not wanting them to spot her. If Astin could manage stairs, he'd come a long way since she'd left. She always knew he would. He was determined like that. When he wanted to be.

He took the stairs slowly, clinging on to the railings with his left hand and Jack with his right. It should've been her he clung to.

She swallowed the thought and pushed her way through the crowds and up the stairs, overtaking them. No matter how vulnerable he was physically, it was no excuse for the way he'd acted.

The upstairs restaurant followed the same colour scheme as downstairs, with large tables laid out to seat six or eight. Hollie wandered around looking for her name. She'd forgot to ask Tate where their seats were.

A mop of blond curly hair appeared through the crowds. What was Lawrence doing there? Had Astin seen him? Probably not. If he had, someone would've had a black eye already.

Lawrence looked over. When he noticed her staring, he gave her a small smile. Bastard. Who did he think he was? She scowled in response. He looked away, no longer smiling. Good.

She found Tate stood at a table near the window, her brow wrinkled. She pointed to several name cards with her magic wand over and over.

'What's up?' said Hollie.

'These name cards aren't right. Astin shouldn't be on our table.'

'*Astin?*' echoed Hollie.

No. No no no.

To make matters worse, his name card was right beside hers. There were too many people sat at the other tables already for her to switch it with one of those. Switching the table arrangements would have to do instead. She switched Astin's name card with Tate's so that Tate was beside her, then Jack, then Astin. Sitting on the same table was one thing, but sitting together was just not happening.

She didn't pay attention to the other names on the table until Ariel approached with Sleeping Beauty. Was Trinity's Ariel costume the reason she'd dyed her hair red? She knew she could just get a wig, right?

Tate tightened her grip on her magic wand.

Trinity unhooked herself from Sleeping Beauty then air-kissed Tate. It was the most passive-aggressive thing Hollie had ever seen. 'Tate! Have you met my girlfriend, Kia?'

Tate raised her head in greeting. Kia gave a warm smile. She was petite, with a childlike face not dissimilar to Trinity's elfin one. Her Afro-Caribbean hair was chemically straightened and down to her waist.

'Hey,' said Fayth as she and Liam joined the table. When she noticed Trinity, her back stiffened like a threatened dog. Her left hand tightened around Liam's; her right curled into a fist. Liam's nostrils flared. Fayth leaned in to Hollie. 'What's *she* doing here?'

'Table mix-up,' said Hollie. 'She's not the only villain.'

Astin and Jack approached the table.

'You change something?' said Jack, tugging on the fake hair sticking out of his Mad Hatter hat. 'I thought we were over by the stairs, but the HATT kids are there.'

'No,' Tate growled, her eyes on Trinity.

Jack's eyes flitted to Trinity. He pursed his lips.

Both he and Tate thought Trinity had mixed up the name cards. But why? She was petty, sure, but what did she have to gain from it? Did she just want to see the world – or the people she'd once loved – burn?

'Why is everyone standing?' Trinity asked as she and Kia sat down.

'You tell me,' said Tate, crossing her arms.

Almost everyone else in the room had sat down. The time to change the seating arrangements was close to passing.

Trinity smiled, placing a hand in Kia's lap.

Her face tense, Tate sat down. Everyone else followed suit. Hollie had thought Astin sitting opposite her would be better, but it wasn't. She could feel his gaze on her already.

None of them spoke as they were served their glasses of

champagne. Hollie, Astin, Jack, and Kia were given orange juice instead. Apparently they could take note of who didn't drink, but not people changing the seating arrangements.

She picked up her orange juice with one of her shaking hands. She would *not* let Astin know he was getting to her. No one deserved to have that power over her, especially not after what he'd done. She'd stay strong. She had to.

'How's the outfit?' she asked Fayth.

'I've had so many comments! Everyone loves it!' said Fayth.

Hollie forced a smile.

'Loads of people have asked where I got it from. I wouldn't be surprised if you get some more orders in over the next few days,' said Fayth.

'Awesome,' said Hollie, but she lacked the enthusiasm such a comment would've given her a few months ago.

'I've had some comments too,' said Tate. 'Everyone's in love with the butterfly detail on the shoulders.'

Hollie forced another smile. Those appliquéd butterflies had taken *forever*. It was good to know they'd been worth it.

'Well my dress is custom Alexander McQueen,' said Trinity.

No one responded to her. Ha.

Trinity had gained weight since Hollie had last seen her, but it didn't make her any less attractive or plastic-looking. She'd gone from an eight to a twelve or fourteen, by sewing standards, not clothing-shop standards. Her boobs were almost bigger than her head, and she must've needed a serious amount of tape to keep them in place. There was no way boobs that big were staying put otherwise.

Hollie drew her gaze away; Trinity would notice and use it as an opening if she wasn't careful. She would tolerate her so long as they were sat together, but she'd never like her. She didn't know if Trinity knew about her breakup with Astin or not, but she had a feeling she did. Why else move his name card from another table? If it was her, of course.

'My jewellery is Harry Winston,' said Trinity.

'And it's beautiful, as are you,' said Kia, patting Trinity's arm.

Hollie forced back the bile in her throat. Obsequious, much?

'How's the new album coming along?' Tate asked Jack, placing her hand on his arm.

'Slowly,' he said, running his fingers over the brim of his purple hat. A piece of paper was stuck to the side and said 10/6.

'It's not easy creating something that makes people forget what a dick you were.' His eyes flitted to Astin. He didn't react.

'You'll get there,' said Tate, squeezing his arm.

'You could always get some guest vocals,' said Trinity, glaring at Tate.

'I will, once I've decided what kind of album I want it to be,' said Jack. 'I'm no singer.'

'Nonsense!' said Tate. 'I love your voice.'

'Nah, I hate singing.'

'So does Liam,' said Fayth, smirking.

He glared at her.

'I thought you said you couldn't sing?' said Hollie.

'Which is why he hates it,' said Fayth. 'Liam hates anything he can't do perfectly first time, like ice skating.' She gave him a teasing smile.

He huffed. 'Why am I with you again?'

'I keep you grounded,' she answered sagely.

Hollie was glad they'd seen sense and got together. It was about time Fayth was with someone who treated her right, not someone who took her for granted like Patrick had. Or like Astin had taken her for granted. Ugh. She glanced up at him. As expected, he was staring at her. She looked away. No matter how many times she met his azure-blue eyes, they'd always hypnotise her. They were like magnets, and the longer she stared into them, the more intense the lure became. His eyes had a darkness to them they hadn't had when she'd first met him, but the intensity they'd had, and the deep affection for her, remained.

'Say Astin, why aren't you and Hollie sat together?' asked Trinity. Bitch.

'Leave them alone, Trinity,' said Tate.

'I wasn't talking to you, I was talking to Astin.'

'Leave it, would you?' said Liam.

'Or what? You'll dump me for some woman nobody cares about?' growled Trinity.

Liam pointed to her. 'Shut the fuck up.'

A wry smiled played across Trinity's orange lips. 'What are you going to do if I don't?'

Kia sat silently. Some help she was.

'Stop it Trinity, for fuck sake,' said Jack.

'Or what? I only asked why Hollie and Astin aren't sitting together,' said Trinity. She was like a kid winding up a series of jack-in-the-boxes. She wouldn't stop until everyone's anger popped out.

'Because we're not together!' snapped Astin. 'We broke up, all right? Are you happy now?'

Hollie's heart fell. He'd played right into her hands. She wanted to reach out to him, to hug him and tell him it'd all be all right. But she couldn't.

'Oh, that's a shame,' said Trinity, her voice conveying anything but sorrow.

Hollie remained silent, staring into her orange juice. Where were the starters? She could've at least thrown some soup over Trinity. She'd risk splashing Liam and Kia, but it was worth it.

'You're such a bitch, Trinity,' said Fayth. 'Just because nobody likes you that doesn't mean you have to cause trouble in other people's lives.'

'When did you become so forthcoming?' said Trinity.

'When one of your crazy fans nearly killed Liam and me.' Fayth's voice was so cool and collected it was creepy.

The table fell silent. Nobody had seen that rejoinder coming.

'Are you just going to sit there and let her attack your best friend like that?' snarled Astin, staring straight at her. Everyone else's eyes were on her, too. Shit.

'Would you like some tea, Alice?' asked Jack. He picked up the water jug from the centre of the table and held it above her water glass.

Hollie relaxed. Typical Jack. 'No thanks, Hatter. I may pour it over someone's head.'

Jack gave her a knowing nod. He returned the water jug to the table.

'I'm sensing some real negative chi right now,' said Kia. 'Why don't we—'

'Why don't you shut the fuck up and stay out of this?' snapped Astin.

Kia's mouth hung open, but she didn't retaliate.

Surprisingly, Trinity didn't defend her either.

'Hey! She's done nothing to you!' said Hollie.

'What, you'll defend a stranger but not your best friend?' said Astin. Everything around Hollie fell away. She saw and heard nothing but Astin. The Texan notes in his voice had grown deeper. His eyes were narrow and filled with rage. They'd lost their earlier affection.

'Fayth can fight her own battles, I think she's proven that,' said Hollie.

Fayth put her hand on Hollie's arm and gave her a downturned smile. 'I'd prefer it if you didn't argue about me.'

'I don't think this is about you,' mumbled Liam.

'Can we all just stop, please?' begged Tate. 'This isn't the time.'

'Why isn't it?' said Trinity, a malevolent smile on her face.

'You know, I've heard worse ideas than the chi thing,' said Jack, fiddling with the edge of his shirt.

Tate glared at him.

'What? It might help us to—'

She continued to glare.

He sighed. 'I tried.'

'So tell me Astin, why did you two break up?' said Trinity.

Bitch. Utter bitch.

'Are you fucking kidding me?' growled Liam. 'Don't answer that, man.'

Would Hollie ever be anything more than a prop to Trinity? She longed to fight back, but the words just wouldn't form. They lodged themselves in the back of her throat so that when she tried to speak, only a feeble squeak or silence came out.

'I really think we should all take a moment to calm down,' said Tate.

'Stay out of this!' shouted Astin.

People from nearby tables turned to see what was going on. Waiters began to serve food to other tables, conveniently ignoring the one where everyone was arguing.

Astin was unrecognisable as the man she'd fallen in love with. He was bitter and angry. He'd lost respect for his loved ones, and his loved ones were on the verge of losing their respect for him. Hollie's heart was breaking all over again. Especially with Trinity stirring the fucking pot.

Tate wrinkled her nose. 'Don't speak to me like that.' Her voice was deep and stern. It was like being told off by the nicest teacher in school.

'Then stay out of this!' he repeated. 'This is nobody's business but mine and Hollie's.'

'No,' said Hollie, her voice hard. 'We have no business, no friendship, nothing. I will eat this meal and tolerate your company, but once I leave this room I never want to see or hear from you ever again.'

Silence fell over the table. Waiters began to dish out some sort of white soup, but nobody touched it. Everyone sat awkwardly, staring into their lap and occasionally trading glances with those they hadn't fallen out with.

Hollie picked up her soup spoon with her shaking hands. Could things get any worse?

Fayth put her hand on Hollie's. The small gesture was enough for Hollie to almost – almost – start crying there and then. 'I'm going to powder my nose.' She pushed herself away from the table and headed for the toilets, hoping Fayth would remember their code. It was one they'd come up with in New York, just in case one of them ever needed to get away. She didn't want to give in and leave the table after a conversation like that, but there was no way she was going to let Astin or Trinity see her cry.

Fayth took the hint and followed her. Once they were in the safety of the empty toilets, the floodgates opened. Fayth embraced her, squeezing Hollie so tightly she almost couldn't breathe.

'Do you really think it was Trinity that messed with the place settings?' asked Hollie, keeping her head slightly away from Fayth so that she didn't get make-up on to her outfit.

'I wouldn't put it past her,' said Fayth. 'I don't care who it was. When I get my hands on them they're getting a frying pan to the head.'

Fayth using a frying pan as a weapon. Now there was an image that made her smile.

'See? That's better,' said Fayth. She took some toilet paper and handed it to Hollie. To her surprise, her make-up hadn't budged. Whatever the professional make-up artist had used, it was bloody good stuff.

'I hate him. I fucking hate him,' said Hollie.

'I know you do,' said Fayth, 'but you can't let him get to you. That gives him power. It gives *Trinity* power.'

Hollie flinched. That was the last thing she wanted to do. Trinity had enough power already. She dabbed at her eyes some more, then reapplied her lipgloss and rolled her shoulders a few times. 'Say, are you and Liam OK? It can't be easy to be sitting with her after what you found out about whatsherface.'

'Why'd you think I flipped? But then, it's not really her fault, is it? How was she supposed to know she had a fan who was so in love with her she wanted to kill us?'

'I suppose,' said Hollie.

Fayth massaged Hollie's shoulders. 'Ready for round two?'

'Let's hope it's quieter than the first,' said Hollie. As they approached the door, her phone rang. Everyone knew that she was there. They wouldn't ring unless it was urgent. She removed her phone from her Dinah bag. *Mum.*

In no hurry to go back to the gala, she answered. 'Hey, what's up?' She tried her best to hide the wobble in her voice that would hint that she'd been crying.

Her mum inhaled. 'I don't want you to panic—' not a great way to start a phone call '—but your nan's had a stroke.'

'What? Wha—'

Fayth stepped closer to Hollie, leaning in towards the phone. Hollie tilted it so that she could hear.

'She's fine now. They think it was a minor one. They're going to run some more tests. She said not to worry.'

'Of course I'm going to worry! How can I not worry? I'm on my way.'

'No, you should stay and enjoy your party. She'd hate to think you cut it short because of her.'

Hollie scoffed. 'Believe me, I'm not missing anything.'

'We have to go,' said Fayth as they returned to the table. She sat back down and picked up her basket bag from the floor.

'Why? What's wrong?' said Liam.

Six pairs of eyes were on them.

'Nan's had a stroke,' said Hollie. Her voice was devoid of emotion. She stood behind her seat, her bowl of soup untouched. Most people on their table had barely touched their food. Trinity and Kia were the only exceptions, having devoured both their bowls of soup and what looked like half the bread basket.

'Oh my god,' said Tate. She put her hand over her mouth.

Liam stood up and hugged Hollie. Jack gave her a sympathetic smile. Trinity's face was emotionless. Bitch.

'I hope she's OK,' said Kia.

Hollie flashed Kia a forced smile. It wasn't her fault she was too spineless to stand up to her sociopathic girlfriend.

'Is she OK?' said Astin. He almost looked concerned. Almost.

Fayth stood up.

'What are you doing?' said Hollie.

'Coming with you,' said Fayth.

'You don't need to do that,' said Hollie.

'Yes, I do,' said Fayth, her voice stern. She kissed Liam.

'Go,' said Liam.

Fayth nodded.

'Don't worry about your things. Maddy and I will sort it,' said Tate.

'Thanks,' said Hollie. She was still angry at Tate for not intervening further, but she couldn't hate her. She was too good a friend. But that was Tate's problem – she was too busy trying to be everyone's friend.

'Let me know if there's anything I can do,' said Astin.

'There is,' she said through gritted teeth. 'Stay the fuck away from me.'

Five

Astin grabbed his crutches and hopped after Hollie. 'Wait,' he begged. He caught up with her at the top of the stairs. The people on the table nearby looked up and watched. He ignored them.

Hollie slowly turned to look at him, her jaw tense and eyes manic. 'I have given you so, *so* many chances. And every time, you've thrown it back in my face. I don't have time for you and your sadomasochistic attention-seeking any more. I have more important things to worry about.' She carried on down the stairs.

'Hollie, I—'

'Can't you take a fucking hint? She doesn't want to talk to you!' snapped Fayth. She put her arm around Hollie and the two of them hurried down the stairs. Astin and his crutches couldn't keep up. He banged a crutch against the marble floor.

Why couldn't they see that he was trying to apologise? That he was worried about her nan and he wanted to help? What was wrong with them?

'Everything all right?' said a voice.

Astin tensed. Lawrence fucking Roskowski was on the nearest table.

'Fuck you,' Astin spat. He tightened his grip on his crutches. How dare Lawrence ask if everything was all right? Everything was his fault! If it wasn't for him, he and Hollie would still be together. They wouldn't have moved in together so fast or got into an argument that ended with their break up. He'd still be able to work as a stunt performer and the life he'd planned with Hollie, their two imaginary dogs, and their future careers, would be right on track. He started to raise one of his crutches. Lawrence needed to pay in more than money for what he'd done.

'Come on, let's take you somewhere to cool off,' said Liam, appearing out of nowhere. He lowered Astin's crutch then put his hand on his arm and guided him away. Astin went, but under duress. One day, Lawrence would pay. He was sure of that.

Liam led him downstairs and into the hallway. Hollie and Fayth had already gone. Liam flashed the receptionist his most charming smile, and she agreed to give them a few moments alone. Astin collapsed on to one of the chairs and threw his crutches across the room. They chipped the edge of the desk, collapsing in a heap beside it.

Tate entered, a small coffee in her hand. 'Thought this might help.' She handed it to him. A macchiato. Small comforts.

'Thanks.'

'I left Jack to keep on eye on Trinity. Who knows what else she's got planned?'

'Oh I think Trinity's done exactly what she planned,' said Liam from beside the door.

Tate tucked her skirt underneath her and sat beside Astin, placing a comforting hand on his shoulder. Before he could stop it, he began to cry. Tate pulled him close, telling him he could cry as much, and for as long as, he liked. He'd ruined her fucking charity gala, and she was there comforting him. What the fuck kind of monster was he?

'Is everything all right?'

The hairs on the back of Astin's neck stood up. Hadn't Lawrence Roskowski done enough damage?

Astin stood. Liam put himself between them. Tate pushed in front, putting her hand on Lawrence's chest. 'Leave. Now,' she ordered.

'I just wanted to see if—'

'Haven't you done enough damage already?' snapped Astin, shaking with rage. Coffee spilled from the small cup in his hand and on to the floor.

'What are you talking about?' said Lawrence.

'Like you don't know,' spat Astin.

Lawrence looked to Tate.

'I don't know what you're doing here, but please either return to your meal or go. We don't need you down here,' said Tate.

'But—'

'Go!' shouted Tate.

His head bowed, Lawrence returned upstairs.

'What the fuck is he doing here, Tate?' growled Astin, still shaking.

'I don't know,' said Tate. 'But that's the last time I work with these event organisers. I'll do it all myself next time.'

Astin collapsed back into the chair. His body was so weak he could barely stand. 'I've ruined it. I've ruined everything.'

'That's a bit melodramatic,' said Liam. 'We're still here.'

'I don't know what happened. It was like I was possessed,' said Astin, his eyes filling with tears again. He didn't bother trying to stop them; he didn't have any energy left to.

'We should've chosen Dr Jekyll and Mr Hyde for your costume,' said Liam.

'Ha ha,' said Astin. 'I was sat there raging about nothing while her nan was—' He cut himself off, sobbing harder.

'You weren't to know that,' said Tate.

Liam stood on the other side of Astin. 'Doesn't matter now. The question is, do you want to fix it?'

Astin raised his head, his eyes sore. 'I can't. You heard her. I've ruined everything.'

Tate rubbed Astin's shoulders. 'You'd be surprised how much we'll put up with from the people we love.'

'And if anyone's going to know—'

Tate turned her head to Liam, her eyes daring him to continue. He was on to something – she'd put up with more from Jack than anyone else – but she didn't need the reminder. Liam didn't continue.

'How am I supposed to fix it?' said Astin. He put the macchiato beside him on the floor. The smell nauseated him.

Tate twitched her nose in a very Samantha Stevens-like way. She was hatching a plan.

'What?' said Astin.

She moved her lips around, then chewed on the inside of her cheek. 'You know you've been a tad…*difficult* lately, right honey?'

It was only when Cooper, his baby brother, gave up on him that he'd realised it. But then it'd been too late. Once he'd decided to go to the gala, he'd planned to at least apologise to Hollie, even if she wouldn't take him back. So much for that plan. 'How bad was I?'

Tate shifted in her seat, avoiding eye contact.

'On a scale of 1-10? 11,' said Liam.

Tate shoved him.

'What? Someone's got to be honest with him. Tiptoeing about is what got us here,' said Liam.

'Hollie didn't tiptoe. I ignored her. She even dumped me and I still ignored her.'

Tate patted his shoulder. It didn't offer much comfort.

'Well now you know,' said Liam.

'We can fix this,' said Tate.

Astin scoffed.

'You can. But you have to let her come to you,' said Tate.

'You heard what she said! She's never going to so much as look at me ever again.'

Tate pursed her lips. 'I wouldn't be so sure about that.'

'Do you know something I don't?' said Astin.

'Yes. I know more about love and forgiveness than the both of you put together. I forgave Jack because he was lost. He hurt himself because he didn't know how to handle what he was going through, and in turn, that hurt me. He didn't realise what he was doing until it was too late.'

'That sounds familiar,' said Liam, looking at Astin.

'Your point?' said Astin.

'Apologise. Let her know you're thinking about her. Then wait,' said Tate.

'"*Wait?*"'

He couldn't think of anything worse.

'Yes. Wait,' said Tate. 'She may never come back to you. But if she really loves you, and if you relationship is meant to be, she will.'

Astin stood up and kicked the desk. His foot throbbed, but he enjoyed the pain. He deserved it.

'Don't do that. I've already got to pay for the chip on the corner,' said Tate.

'I'll pay for it,' said Astin. 'It was my fault.'

'And it's that mentality that will get Hollie back,' said Tate. She stood up, running her hands over her dress.

He shook his head. 'Nothing will get her back.'

'You don't know until you try,' said Liam.

Astin took his phone from his pocket. Tate and Liam read over his shoulders as he typed: *I'm sorry. You didn't deserve that. You didn't deserve any of it. I'm a dick, but I'll always be here for you x*

'What do you think?'

Tate nodded in approval. Liam smiled. Astin hit send.

He never got a reply.

Six

Hollie sat in silence, staring out of the window as they drove to the hospital. She still had on her Alice costume because she hadn't wanted to waste time getting changed. The taxi had dropped Fayth off at Claridge's first, giving her just enough time to get changed before Hollie picked her up. There was no way she was driving all that way in an outfit like that. As comfy as it was, nothing was as comfy as jeans and a t-shirt. She also didn't want to risk damaging it – it was too pretty.

Hollie's expression was vacant as they drove down the M1. Fayth had a feeling her expression had been the same when she'd travelled to see her mum and sister. She hadn't known it at the time, but they wouldn't be alive when she arrived. Fayth desperately hoped that Hollie wouldn't have to go through what she had. Her nan was her best friend, and after everything else that had happened recently, she didn't know how much more Hollie could take. She had her business to focus on, but it was clear that Hollie was still kicking herself for the way Astin had treated her.

Fayth was kicking herself too. She'd thought Astin was good for her. Perhaps he was. Perhaps he still would've been if it hadn't been for the accident. She didn't blame Astin for being upset – he'd lost his career, his hobbies, and just about everything he'd spent his life working towards – but that didn't justify his taking it out on other people. Especially Hollie, when she'd done nothing but look after him and put her life on hold to do so. She was already a carer for her nan. But her nan had encouraged her to look after Astin, and Hollie had listened. Who could've known Astin would be so ungrateful?

Hollie dug into her Dinah bag and took out her phone. 'Oh my god.'

'What?'

'He texted me.'

Fayth assumed 'he' meant Astin. 'Saying what?'

'Apologising.'

'Wow.'

She shoved her phone back into her bag. 'After everything he said and did, he texts me apologising because Nan's in hospital? Twat. Absolute twat.' She unfastened the clips holding her wig in place and tore it from her head, tossing it into the back seat. Her hair had been fastened into a bun to disguise it, and she began to unravel that, dumping the grips and bobbles into the glove compartment. Fayth's hair was starting to hurt from the bun she had it in, too. She was pretty sure they'd used at least half a can of hairspray on each of them.

'Maybe it made him realise what a dick he's been lately,' suggested Fayth, tugging at her bun to try and loosen it. It didn't move. The damn thing was giving her a headache. As if she didn't have enough of those lately as it was.

'Who cares if it has? I don't want anything more to do with him.'

They sat in silence, the only noise the sound of other passing cars and the grumble of the one-litre engine. Fayth liked the buzzing of car engines. When they didn't sound like driving caused them pain, which Hollie's car did.

'Do you want the radio on?' said Fayth.

'Huh?' She jerked her head away from the window. Her eyes were filled with fear.

Fayth had volunteered to drive, worried that Hollie's anxiety would affect her driving skills. If the haunted expression in her face was anything to go by, Fayth had made the right call.

'Do you want the radio on? It might help,' said Fayth.

'Oh. No. Thanks.'

'Podcast? Audiobook?'

'I don't know,' said Hollie, twisting her fingers in her lap.

'I know it's easy for me to say, but letting your thoughts get the worst of you won't help any.'

'I know,' said Hollie. 'I just don't know what to think. Mum said they think it's a minor one. It doesn't seem to have done any major damage as far as they can tell.'

'That's good, isn't it?' said Fayth, flicking on the indicator so that she could overtake a lorry.

'Yeah, but it's still scary, you know?'

Oh Fayth knew. Fayth knew all too well. The only difference was that Hollie's nan's body was turning against her while her mum and sister had been in good health. There being no real reason beyond 'accident' was what haunted her the most, but that was the thing: there wasn't a reason or an explanation for everything, no matter how much we needed one. Some things were just random. Some things just happened, completely out of our control.

Like a stroke.

'She's a tough one, your nan,' said Fayth, hoping it would make Hollie feel a little better. Plus it was true. She'd already endured another stroke and a heart attack.

'I know she is,' said Hollie. 'But one day…'

Fayth reached over and touched Hollie's hands. 'It happens to us all one day. What matters is what we do before it does.'

They pulled up at the hospital just before midnight. Technically, visitors weren't allowed outside of visiting hours. However, there was every chance her nan was still in A&E. Fayth grabbed a parking ticket as Hollie called her mum to find out where they were.

'We're here,' said Hollie, crossing her legs.

'We're in the George Eliot Ward,' said her mum. They'd found a bed for her already. It had to be bad.

'I'll see you in a minute,' said Hollie, uncrossing her legs.

'See you in a minute.'

She hung up and got out of the car as Fayth returned and placed the ticket in the window.

'Know where we're going?' said Fayth. She locked the car and returned the keys to Hollie.

'Yeah.'

It was the same ward her nan had been in the last time she'd had a mini stroke. Memories of that time a few years ago came back to her as they walked down the empty hallway. It had been the Christmas holidays. Hollie had followed the ambulance to the hospital in her car. The very same car she and Fayth had just driven to the hospital in.

Her nan was taken straight through; they took blood and did other tests Hollie didn't understand. She'd sat quietly in the chair, holding her nan's hand as the colour returned to her cheeks and her face stopped drooping. That hadn't done any permanent damage either. Would they be wrong this time? Was another, more serious stroke on the horizon?

They reached the door of the ward and gelled their hands. The intense smell of alcohol filled Hollie's nostrils. God, that stuff was strong. She pushed the door open, Fayth close behind her. They found her nan in the far corner of the women's ward, sat up in bed and drinking a carton of orange juice. Hollie's mum sat in the chair beside her. Her fleece trousers and Me to You top looked a lot like pyjamas. They quite possibly were.

Seven other women slept – or attempted to sleep – in the other beds. Every so often, one of them let out a loud snore.

'What the 'ell are you wearing?' her nan asked when she saw her granddaughter.

Hollie ran over, wrapping her arms around her nan's neck. She'd almost forgot she was still in costume.

'Hey,' said Fayth.

'Thanks for driving her,' said Hollie's mum.

'Any time,' said Fayth.

'You're strangling me, gal. I'm still here, aren't I?' said her nan.

'Don't scare me like that!' Hollie squealed, loosening her grip so that she could see her nan's face.

'Well. You didn't need to cut your party short for me.'

Hollie scoffed, shooting Fayth a glance. Fayth gave her a downturned smile. She didn't want to tell her nan how badly things had gone at the gala. She didn't want to think about what had happened at the gala ever again. 'You're more important.'

Her nan fidgeted in the bed. 'Well. It's nice to know I'm still important after all these years.'

'Of course you are, Nan,' said Hollie.

'You can sit down, you know,' said her nan. She pointed to Fayth.

'Thanks, but I'm OK standing. All that driving has made my legs go numb.' She shook each of her legs out. 'Pins and needles.'

'Try sitting in this bed,' said Hollie's nan. 'I can't feel me arse.'

'Mother!' cried Hollie's mum.

'What? You know I'm right. These mattresses are 'orrible.'

No one argued with her on that one.

'So what's the latest?' Hollie asked, removing her grip from her nan and standing up. She stayed in close proximity, her hand over her nan's. It was cold, like it always was.

'They want to do some more tests, but they can't do any more until the morning,' said her mum. 'The consultant will be around to see her first thing.'

'You should get some sleep in the meantime,' instructed her

nan. 'And eat. I know what you're like.'

'I'm fine, Nan. I'm not hungry.'

'I am,' confessed Fayth. 'I'm starving.'

'There's some crisps in the cupboard if you want them,' said Hollie's mum.

'Thanks,' said Fayth.

Hollie's mum took out two packets of crisps. She handed one to Hollie and one to Fayth. Both opened them and devoured them. Hollie hadn't realised how hungry she was until food was put in front of her.

'If I give you a list, can you go home and get me some stuff please?' said her nan. 'I've not got anything with me.'

'OK,' said Hollie. She put the empty crisp packet in the bin, then took out her phone. The last thing she'd had open was Astin's text. She quickly closed it and opened a note. The hospital was not the place to get emotional about her ex. She jotted down the things her nan requested, then her mum chimed in with a couple more.

'Are you sure you'll be all right?' said Hollie as she returned her phone to her bag.

'I don't plan on having another stroke, if that's what you mean.'

'Reassuring,' said Hollie, her voice deadpan.

'Good. It should be.'

Hollie kissed her nan's cheek, gave her mum a hug, then she and Fayth left to go and pick up her nan's things.

'How you feeling?' Fayth asked as they walked back down the corridors.

'I don't know,' said Hollie. She put her arms around her friend's waist and leaned into her. She was in desperate need of a hug and someone to tell her everything would be all right. Her head was so full of emotions it was a miracle it hadn't exploded. She'd walked the halls of the local hospital hundreds of times, but no time scared her more than when her nan was in one of the wards. The woman who'd raised her, whom she'd grown up thinking was invincible, was reduced to some numbers and words like *diabetes* and *possible stroke* on a clipboard.

Fayth put her arm around Hollie and rested her head on her shoulder as they walked. 'Whatever you need, I'm here.'

'Thanks.' They continued walking through the maze of corridors back towards the car.

'I've been thinking about the text from Astin,' said Fayth.

'Mmm,' said Hollie, not really wanting to hear what she had to say.

They left the hospital and walked through the humid August air towards the car.

'He obviously still cares about you.'

'Shame he's an arsehole,' said Hollie, rifling in her handbag for the keys.

'Is he?'

Hollie stopped walking, utterly speechless. When had Fayth changed her tune?

'To apologise like he has takes gumption,' said Fayth.

'You know what he did, Fayth. I'm not putting up with that.'

'And I'm not saying you should. But we all make mistakes.'

Seven

Hollie lay in bed, curled up in the foetal position. Fayth was in her mum's room next door. They'd had some beans on toast before heading to bed, but Hollie didn't feel like sleeping. She knew she needed it, but that didn't make doing so any easier. Her mind flitted from her nan, to Astin, and back again. She knew what her nan would say about Astin: that he was an idiot. She'd already said it about him dozens of times. So had Fayth. But then Fayth had suddenly started defending him. What did that mean? What would her nan say? She longed to discuss the text with her nan, but all things considered, she couldn't.

If anyone could understand their body turning against them, it was her nan. The first mini stroke had come out of nowhere. It had humanised her seemingly invincible grandmother to her, and it made her more determined than ever to be there for the people she cared about because you never knew when you could lose them. Her nan's heart attack had cemented that decision. It had been at four o'clock in the morning, and thankfully on her mum's nights off. She'd needed to have a stent fitted, but it had been a minor surgery and the only noticeable side effect was that it had curbed her snoring.

Astin didn't snore. He slept soundly. He sometimes talked in his sleep, but it was mostly mumblings. He spoke more in his sleep since the accident. Had he slept better since she'd left? Worse? The same? Did he talk more? Less? She wished she could feel his warm breath on her neck, his arms wrapped around her. Despite everything he'd said and done, she still loved him, and no matter how hard she tried, she couldn't push those feelings away. They wouldn't go, damnit. Killing her feelings for Will had taken years, and what she felt for him was nothing compared to how she felt for Astin. Was he her true love? Had she bollocksed it up and not even realised it?

Stupid, stupid, stupid.

True love didn't exist. There wasn't one person for everyone.

Life was more complicated than that.

She sat up. Her nan had been married once. She'd got divorced after events she didn't talk about and that Hollie had never pressed her to discuss. Had he been her true love, or had he just been the father of her three children? Was he still alive? Would he care if he found out she was in hospital? How long would she have to stay there? The two weeks she'd had to stay in after her heart attack had been agony. Hollie couldn't take two weeks away from her nan, only speaking her during allotted hours. Not on top of everything else that was going on. It'd been hard enough when she was in London. She'd called her everyday – sometimes twice – to check up on her. But her being in hospital was different. She needed to be around her – to keep an eye on her – in case anything happened. In case the worst happened. She blinked back tears. She couldn't think like that. Her nan was tough. The toughest person she knew.

But she wasn't immortal.

Astin stared at the ceiling. Every part of him wanted to go to Hollie and be there for her, but he couldn't. She'd told him to stay away. Going against that wasn't romantic, it was stalking.

And he'd only get in the way if he went down there. What good would he be? He could hardly walk. What support could he give her that Fayth couldn't? So long as Hollie had Fayth and her mum there, she'd could handle it. That didn't make him want to go to her any less, though.

The foam of his collar scratched at his neck. The skin underneath was hot with sweat. He tore it off and flung it at the wall. It bounced off the wall and silently fell to the floor.

What had he done? How had he gone from wanting to apologise to Hollie to pushing her away further? When had he turned into Jekyll and Hyde?

He punched the empty pillow beside him. If he hadn't been so fucking stupid and pushed her away in the first place he could've been there for her when she really needed him, just like she'd been there for him. How had he been so fucking stupid? He punched the pillow over and over, picturing his own stupid, stupid face. He was such an idiot. Such a fucking idiot. Tears stung his eyes. He didn't care how much damage he did to the pillow, or to himself. He needed to get the rage out. He needed to fight the anger welling inside him. Everything had spiralled out of control and he had no idea how to fix things.

He fell into the pillow, cradling it as he cried.

He got out of bed and went into the bathroom. After going for a piss, he was forced to face his reflection in the mirror as he washed his hands. His beard was neater than than it had been, but it still looked horrible. It was a reminder of the monster he'd become. He scrambled for a razor in the cupboard and began to shave. He had to get that thing off his face. To see his real reflection again. He stole some of Jack's shaving foam then pressed hard as he dragged the razor over his skin.

What had he done? How had he managed to cut Hollie, Cooper, and even his grandparents out? His grandparents still called to check on him, but conversations with them felt more like they did it out of obligation. Cooper had barely spoken to him since he left, and Hollie hadn't spoken to him at all. Well, except for what had happened at Tate's gala. And that had gone *brilliantly*.

He pushed harder against his skin, desperate to remove any evidence of the beard he'd grown over the last few months. A beard. What was he thinking?

He needed to go home and apologise to Cooper and his grandparents. Find himself again. Work out if he could live without Hollie, and if not, find a way to get her back. And if that didn't work…

He pushed so hard against against his skin he drew blood. He didn't care. Thanks to his own stupidity, he'd spent his birthday alone with just a handful of people bothering to wish him many happy returns. It hadn't been a happy birthday. He'd spent it alone, playing games. He didn't even bother telling Jamal or Declan it was his birthday. For the first time in his life, he didn't want to acknowledge it. He didn't feel another year wiser, but he felt several decades older. His body still hated him. The doctors seemed to think some of it was caused by too much stress. They were probably right. He still refused to go for counselling when they offered it to him, though. What good would talking about his problems do? It wouldn't bring Hollie or Cooper back.

His chest heaving, he examined his reflection again. The person he'd once been still wasn't there. The beard was gone, but the haunted look in his eyes remained. His cheeks were still gaunt. It was even more obvious without the beard.

He sobbed.

What had he become? *Who* had he become?

Eight

Hollie never got to sleep. Her mum wandered in at some point, but she was gone before Hollie got out of bed. It was raining, so when Hollie got up to let George out, he refused to go because he hated getting his paws wet.

'Go, you big baby!' said Hollie.

He sat down by the conservatory door.

'Bloody dog,' she mumbled. 'Fine.' She slammed the door shut. George trotted back inside.

'Dogs, eh?' said Fayth.

Hollie jumped. 'Where'd you come from?'

'Upstairs, remember?'

'I didn't hear you,' said Hollie.

'Just call me Catwoman,' said Fayth, wearing a Catwoman t-shirt. 'Want breakfast?'

'Shouldn't I be offering you breakfast?'

'I've spent enough time here. It's practically my third home.'

'I'm not really hungry,' said Hollie.

'You should eat something,' said Fayth.

'I know, I know,' said Hollie. She went into the kitchen and opened the cupboard under the kettle. 'I'll have some Shreddies. You want anything?'

'Shreddies are good,' said Fayth. She sat down at the breakfast bar as Hollie made breakfast. 'How did you sleep in the end?'

'Great,' said Hollie sarcastically. She poured milk over their cereal then plonked the bowls and spoons on the breakfast bar. George lay at their feet. He had no interest in cereal. If they'd had biscuits it would've been a different story. 'If I wasn't thinking about Nan, it was him.'

'Astin?' said Fayth. The spoon hovered halfway to her mouth.

'Bastard,' said Hollie, stirring her cereal.

'But…'

'I don't know. I don't know,' said Hollie. She sighed. 'My head's all over the place right now. What am I supposed to do?'

'Right now you just have to see what happens and go from there.'

'Should I reply to his text? I mean, is it wrong of me not to? What kind of games is he playing to be such a twat in person then so nice by text? Is he waiting for me to reply?'

'Technically, the ball *is* in your court. However, one thing I do know about relationships is that the more you play games, the more likely the relationship is to fail. The strongest relationships are the ones where you're straight with each other.'

'When did you realise that?'

'When I realised what went wrong with my marriage, and what worked for my parents. If Mum thought Dad was being an idiot, she'd tell him. If it resulted in an argument, she didn't care. At least he knew where she stood. He was the same with her. They were together over thirty years, so they did something right.'

'Yeah,' said Hollie. Was it really that simple?

Hollie drove to the hospital looking but not really processing. The radio was on, but she had no idea what station was on. When she found her nan in the same ward she'd left her the night before, she was sat in the armchair, staring ahead. She turned at the sound of Hollie's wooden-heeled sandals against the lino. Hollie's mum sat in the armchair, dressed in scrubs.

When Hollie appeared in her nan's line of sight – just a few feet away – she said, 'There you are. I thought you weren't coming.'

'I wanted to make sure I had everything before I left,' said Hollie, heaving the bag on to the end of the bed. 'How did you sleep?'

'Crap.'

'Mum!' Hollie's mum took her glasses from the top of her head and placed them onto her nose. Her short, curly hair was dented from where they'd been. She stood up and began to sort through the bag.

'It's the truth. How people are supposed to heal in these places is beyond me,' said her nan.

Hollie took a plastic chair from the far end of the ward and placed it opposite her nan.

'So how was your fancy dress party?' asked her nan.

Hollie laughed, sitting down. 'It was a charity gala.'
'With fancy dress.'
'It was OK. We didn't miss much when we left.'
'You didn't have to leave.'
'We did. You would've done the same for me,' said Hollie.
'That's different.'
'How is it?'
'I'm your nan. It's my job to look after you.'
'No, it's my job to look after you,' said Hollie.
'We all look after each other,' said Hollie's mum. She put her hand on Hollie's shoulders. 'There's something she's not been telling us.'
'There is?'
Her mum flashed her nan a look. Her nan folded her arms, scowling.
'What?' said Hollie.
'She needs surgery to unblock an artery in her neck and she's refusing to go.'
'Nan!' cried Hollie.
'No. I'm too old.'
'You're not too old, Nan. You're never too old.'
'It's a routine operation that would take a couple of hours. She'd have to stay in until then, though,' said her mum.
'No. I'm not staying in here another night.'
'Nan—'
'No. No. No. No!'
'Mum—'
'No, Bernie. I'm not having surgery.'
'Mum, could you give us a minute please?' said Hollie.
'I'll go talk to the nurses,' said her mum. She patted Hollie's shoulder, then left the ward and went to talk to the nurses outside.

Hollie sat near the top of the bed and placed her hand on her nan's arm. She jerked it away. 'Nan, please. Don't be like this.'
'No. I'm 86. I'm too old for this.'
'No you're not. You're never too old. Please, Nan. I still need you. I'll always need you.'
Her nan turned her head back towards her. Hollie put on her best puppy-dog face. She couldn't give up. Not yet. Things were only just beginning.
'I don't want to go for more surgery.'

'I know you don't, Nan, but if it makes you better.'
'I'm too old.'
'Stop saying that! Don't you want to be around to see what happens with my fashion line? Or Fayth's photography? Or Liam's film career or Tate's next business venture? You're the one I go to when I need a shoulder to cry on, who doesn't judge, and doesn't try to fix me. You're just there, no questions asked. I can't live without you.' Hollie sniffled. She wiped a tear from the corner of her eye. At least if she did start crying, she didn't have any make-up on.

Her nan didn't say anything else. She pursed her lips and crossed her arms. The *I know you're right and I don't like it* look.

Hollie put her arms around her nan's neck and hugged her.
'You're a stubborn one,' grumbled her nan.
'Where do you think I get it from?' said Hollie.
'Not me.'
Hollie scoffed.
'What? You didn't!'
'You keep telling yourself that, Nan. You keep telling yourself that.'

Nine

A couple of days after her nan's stroke, a date was finally set for the sale of the Cock and Bull. Fayth returned home to help wrap things up before the sale was finalised. Hollie didn't mind – it gave her more time to spend with her nan before her surgery the following week. She spent every spare minute she had with her nan, only leaving when the Sister on duty kicked her out. They were stricter than the ones in London had been, despite her mum working there. Couldn't they see that she was worried about her nan and being around her reassured her?

She didn't get to see her nan on the day of the surgery. With her being diabetic, she was first in. She'd then have to stay in the theatre overnight so that they could keep an eye on her.

By nine o'clock that morning, when her nan was about to go in for surgery, Hollie had already walked George, cleaned the house and reorganised her desk drawers. Her bedroom had never been so tidy. When the house phone rang at half past nine, she dived for the phone expecting bad news.

'Hello?' said Hollie, her voice cracking.

Her mum watched her from the sofa, a Rosie Goodwin book in her hand. George raised his head from his spot by her nan's chair. He'd barely left it since she'd gone into hospital.

'Hollie, it's Maddy. I tried your mobile but you didn't pick up.'

'Maddy?' Her body relaxed. It wasn't about her nan. Realising this, her mum relaxed too and returned to her book.

'Sorry for calling. Tate told me what happened, but I thought you'd like some good news,' said Maddy.

'Good news?' repeated Hollie.

'CanItellhercanItellher?' came an excited Tate's voice. There was a few seconds' pause, then Tate came on the line: 'You've been invited to the new designer showcase in Barcelona!'

'I…what?'

Tate giggled. 'They saw your designs for the gala and my

video and want you to be one of their up-and-coming designers in their Autumn/Winter show next year!'

'I…'

She was too shocked to speak. Someone wanted to feature her clothes in their fashion show. *Her clothes in a fashion show.* Her legs went weak. She fell back into her nan's armchair.

'Hollie? You still there?' said Tate.

'I…'

'Don't worry about it now. I'll email you the details. Take care, and let me know how your nan is.'

She managed to say, 'will do,' before hanging up.

Hollie spent the rest of the day flitting between excitment and guilt. She went out for a meal to celebrate with her mum, but it didn't feel right with her nan missing. It wasn't a celebration. It was a pre-celebration. The real celebration would be when her nan was out of hospital, even if it was just something from the chippy.

They got a phone call later in the day to tell them the surgery had gone well. The hospital needed to keep a close eye on her for 24 hours, but she was awake and talking. Joking, even. Just like always. They could go and see her for half an hour later that evening. Hollie couldn't wait to tell her about the fashion show. It would give them all something to look forward to.

Hollie and her mum pulled up at the hospital car park around six o'clock that evening. She and her mum walked through the hospital in silence. Hollie had no idea what state her nan would be in when they got there. Her mum probably did, but she gave little away. A few people greeted them as they walked down the corridors, but Hollie barely acknowledged them.

She needed to see her breathing and blinking and her chest moving up and down. She needed physical proof that she'd survived.

They reached the theatre doors and one of her mum's friends guided them inside. She was so short she made Hollie feel tall. 'She's doing great,' she informed them. 'Keeps saying she can go home now.'

Typical Nan.

She was hooked up to more wires and monitors than Hollie had ever seen. They beeped and whirred, blocking her path to her nan, whom she desperately wanted to hug.

Her mum's friend stood a few feet away, studying a monitor and pursing her crimson lips.

'How are you feeling?' asked her mum. She stood at the foot of the bed, the sleeves of her jumper rolled up. Why she wore jumpers in August then complained she was warm Hollie would never understand.

'Been better,' her nan grumbled.

'How's your neck?' said Hollie.

'Numb. Doctor said I might never get any feeling back in it.'

'Really?' said Hollie. She couldn't imagine a part of her body being permanently numb.

'Small price to pay,' said her mum. 'We'd rather have you alive.'

'And I'm still going, aren't I?' said her nan.

'You'd better be,' said her mum.

'Can I hug her?' Hollie asked her mum's friend.

'Just be careful of the wires,' she warned.

Minding the wires, Hollie put her arms across her nan's chest. Her nan put her hands on her arms. 'I'm all right, gal.'

'I don't know what I would've done if you weren't,' said Hollie.

'Well now you'll have to wait a few more years to find out.'

'Good,' said Hollie. 'I couldn't imagine my life without you.'

'Of course you couldn't. Who else would give you my brilliant advice?'

Hollie glanced up at her mum. She was smiling.

'You mean where else would I get mass amounts of sarcasm from?' said Hollie.

'You mean *learn* sarcasm from?' corrected her nan.

'That too,' said Hollie. 'I like to learn from the best.'

'And there's no one better than your nan,' said her mum.

'Agreed,' said her mum's friend. She stood at the bottom of the bed, reading through a clipboard. 'When I mentioned to her I bought a dress from a vintage shop, she said, "Vintage? Is that what I am?" and didn't even crack a smile.'

'Oh Nan,' said Hollie, kissing her cheek.

Her nan kissed the top of her head. 'You don't need to worry so much. You can't rid of me that easily.'

SEPTEMBER

Fayth ran her fingers over the wooden bar for the final time. She inhaled the scent of real ale and stale alcohol. The creaky barstools; the rock-hard wooden chairs; the basement of nightmares; none of it was theirs any more. In just half an hour, Fayth, Brooke, and her dad would hand over the keys to the estate agent. They'd never pull another pint or serve another roast dinner. They'd never have to go down into that bloody basement ever again. Never have to think about it ever again. Not that she'd stopped thinking about it. She still dreamed about it most nights. The hard, metallic thump as the gun hit the back of her head. The bang as it fired.

As her dad and sister went to say goodbye to the picnic area, she kicked the door to the basement. Good fucking riddance.

While they were still outside, she snuck upstairs into the flat. The furniture was staying with it, leaving the relics of Fayth's failed marriage for the next inhabitant to decide its fate. She sunk on to the battered leather sofa, inhaling the smell of old leather. The only thing she'd miss was the bloody sofa. It was the only comfortable piece of furniture in the flat.

Fayth lay back on the sofa. She'd seen patterns in the artex ceiling so many times. Once, when she'd had the flu, she'd been convinced she could see her and Patrick with three kids and a border collie. Maybe, in an alternate universe, that could've happened. But not in hers.

She swung her legs around and sat up. Her future now lay in a path more different than she ever could've imagined. In just a few hours' time she'd be on her way to New York. She'd even move into Liam's apartment while she was over there. They'd get to act like a real couple. How would they cope with that? Living a sedate life at the pub was one thing, but New York was a city on steroids.

And she couldn't wait.

She hopped up off the sofa and opened the kitchen cupboards. They'd once been fully stocked with herbs, spices, tins and jars, but they lay empty, awaiting the new inhabitants' cooking ingredients. In the top left cupboard was a single jar of coffee. The last time it'd been opened was when Hollie had suggested they 'get away' nine months earlier. She laughed. That was before Astin's accident, before she'd even met him; before they'd even considered visiting New York.

She didn't miss her old life, though. She'd outgrown it like a child outgrows their school shoes each year.

'Fayth! You up there?' called her dad.

'Yeah. I'll be down in a minute!' she called back.

She threw the coffee jar in the air a few times then returned it to the cupboard. Nobody in her family drank it – it could be a gift for the new inhabitants.

She locked up the flat then ran downstairs, her footsteps echoing through the old building.

'Ready to go?' said her dad.

'Yep,' said Fayth.

'Mmm,' grumbled Brooke.

'You'll be fine,' said Fayth.

It wouldn't be long until her baby sister was off to university to train to be a counsellor. She'd realised that she couldn't face helping people get over their physical wounds, but after everything she'd been through herself, she could help people with their psychological ones. She was a great listener when she wasn't being a stroppy teenager. Fayth couldn't have been prouder. Whenever she tried to tell Brooke she got brushed off, but she kept telling her anyway. She'd learned the hard way the importance of telling your loved ones how you feel.

'Yeah. Well. I'm not the one going out with Liam York,' said Brooke.

'After everything that's happened, that's the part that you focus on?' said Fayth.

Brooke shrugged.

'I'm proud of you. Both of you,' said her dad. He pulled them into a hug, kissing Fayth's cheek, then Brooke's.

Brooke squirmed. '*Daaad.*'

'I get it. I embarrass you now. I'll never be the "cool dad".'

'No, you won't,' agreed Brooke.

'I'm fine with that,' said Fayth. 'Being cool is overrated.'

'Says the one who's—'

'Going out with Liam York. Yes. I get it.'

'Actually I was going to say "says the one who's going to photography school in New York",' corrected Brooke.

'Yeah. Well. One day it'll be time for your big adventure,' said Fayth.

Brooke snorted.

'It will. If you let it.'

'What's *that* supposed to mean?'

Fayth smiled. 'Life opens lots of doors for us. We choose which ones we walk through. Each door we don't pick is a missed opportunity. Maybe we'll find something better, maybe we won't. But we'll never get anywhere if we stay in the same room our whole lives.'

Brooke threw her head back. 'God, you're such a poet.'

'And you're such a teenager,' said Fayth. She gave her a playful shove. 'But I'll let you off. You never know – you might be as wise as Dad and me some day.'

He chuckled. 'She already is, she just doesn't want to be.'

'Typical teenager,' mumbled Fayth.

'Oi!'

Fayth smiled. The clock beside the bar said it was almost eleven. 'We should get going. I need to speak to Hollie before I head to the airport.'

'Why?' said Brooke. 'You two speak like, *all* the time.'

'She wants my opinion on some stuff for her fashion show I think.'

Brooke sighed. 'You two have all the fun.'

'No, we don't,' said Fayth. 'We just fight through the pain to get to the good stuff. Sometimes it's the only way.'

ACKNOWLEDGEMENTS

To everyone who enjoyed *What Happens in New York*, thank you for your patience as I wrote this story for you. I hope you enjoy it as much as – if not more so – than you did *What Happens in New York*, and that you continue to enjoy Hollie and Fayth's adventures over the coming years.

Thanks to Sunita and Lizzy for helping me figure out Astin's injuries, and to Silvia for making me realise I was forcing my characters into situations they weren't ready for.

To my lovely beta readers Jess, Sarah, Kate, Suzanne, Kerrie and Tori, thank you so much for your feedback. It helped me to make the book something I can really be proud of, and gave me the confidence to hit the 'publish' button. An extra thank you to Tori for answering lots of daft pub-related questions and suggesting deconstructed haggis with piped mashed potatoes and fresh seasonal vegetables as a special at the Cock and Bull. It gets me every time!

Thanks to Steph, my proofreader, for pointing out things I never would've noticed and teaching me new things about grammar.

A huge thank you to Mum, who got lots of stupid medical-related questions for this book. It's so much easier to be able to ask someone seemingly weird questions in the middle of the night than it is to look them up online. This book wouldn't have been possible without your help. This book also wouldn't have been possible without the support of Nan and Carl, the two sanest, strongest people I know. You always know what to say/do, and for that I'll be forever grateful.

ABOUT THE AUTHOR

Kristina Adams is a twenty-something author, poet, and blogger. She has a BA in Creative Writing from the University of Derby, and an MA in Creative Writing from Nottingham Trent University. When she's not writing, she's baking, sewing, or finding another way to avoid the real world. She lives in the UK with her partner.

To find more about the world of Hollie and Fayth, check out the What Happens Next? Facebook group at www.facebook.com/groups/whathappensinnewyork.

For an exclusive short story about Liam, visit www.writerscookbook.com/liam.

Printed in Great Britain
by Amazon